The Sleeping Bride
and
The Deadly Travellers

DOROTHY EDEN

The Sleeping Bride
AND
The Deadly Travellers

NELSON DOUBLEDAY, Inc.
Garden City, New York

Printed in the United States of America

The Sleeping Bride

1

It was quite late when the car, a sleek Jaguar, stopped at the café on the Portsmouth Road.

It was a makeshift café, merely a caravan with the side let down to expose the counter on which stood thick white cups, some of them still holding dregs of tea. Under a glass dome was a plate with a melancholy array of cakes.

The proprietor was elderly and a little short-sighted. He appeared from behind the counter where he had been reading a paper-backed Homer (he was something of a philosopher), and said, "What would you like?" Peering at his customer, he added a belated, "Sir."

"Two cups of tea, please. I want to take them to the car." The man smiled suddenly, with great charm. "My aunt is elderly and not very well."

"That's all right, sir. Milk and sugar?"

The customer had to go over to the car to ask. A clear-carrying voice answered.

"Milk and sugar for Aunt Blandina, thank you. No sugar for me."

The café proprietor was a little ashamed then that he did not provide such amenities as saucers. But these were not his usual customers. Lorry drivers, youths on bicycles, motor cyclists, stopped and leaned on the counter to drink their tea. But it was not often an expensive car, with this kind of customer, stopped.

As an unusual gesture of service he went over to the car presently to collect the cups. He saw the occupants, a good-looking dark girl and an old woman dressed in black with nicely waved white hair and several heavy rings on her fingers. She looked a well-cared-for old lady, plump and pink-cheeked. But it was her eyes which had a bewildered, lost look that he observed particularly.

So that was the trouble. It was not undue weakness in her legs but in her head that had made the polite nephew keep her in the car.

"I think she's feeling better now, Armand," he heard the girl saying as the man got back into the car. "Aren't you, Aunt Blandina?"

"Yes, dear. Much better, thank you." The thin, wavery voice caught the café proprietor's attention. "But I wish I knew where we were going. I don't know this road at all." She looked out of the car window as if she were seeing the dusk-dark landscape, the strips of cloud following a rising moon, the isolated lights shining in houses, and the long straight road, faintly gleaming, for the first time. And as if it were something seen in a half sleep, or a nightmare. "It's a strange road," said her anxious voice. "So strange. . . ."

It was two months after that evening that Aurora, the dark-haired girl, made ready to begin another journey. And this was not just a trip by car into the country. This was to be much longer, and quite final.

She had come to her decision with the greatest difficulty. Shock, suspicion, fear, and also, to be quite honest, a pleased appreciation of Philip Nash's admiration for her all came into it.

She had not meant to let the tall casual stranger, with that intense awareness beneath his air of languor, take her seriously. Nor had she dreamed that he would begin to do so. He was merely a wandering artist (as in medieval days he might have been a strolling player) who, back from the tropics, suddenly had a desire to paint the face of an English beauty, as a contrast to the dark natives his brush had been occupied with over the past few months. His direct approach to her in a coffee bar had been amusing and flattering. She would not have believed then that in a month she would have arranged to marry him.

But neither would she have believed some other things, much more startling and incredible. She would not let her mind dwell on those as she did her rather hasty packing.

It had been her plan, as soon as she had made her private decision to lead Philip to a proposal of marriage, to have that marriage performed as quickly as possible. When he became unexpectedly conventional about families and observing the usual courtesies she had had to get in touch with her alienated and more or less discarded family and suggest returning to the fold.

But that, too, eventually, began to seem a very good idea. It gave her a feeling of security and protection which at the moment she badly needed. It was a refuge. And also it made just so many more reasons why she couldn't change her mind, which she was so foolishly and dangerously tempted to do.

Besides, it would be nice to see Lydia, her young step-sister, again. So she gave her flat a sketchy tidying up, preparatory to hers and

Philip's return from their honeymoon some weeks hence, and completed her packing. She had done the wisest thing. Everything would work out very well. And safely. . . .

Having said her farewells at the office that morning she had meant to wait until Philip's return from Northumberland where he was visiting relatives. His train was due in the early afternoon.

But after listening to the footsteps on the stairs she couldn't bear to stay in the flat any longer. She had heard them so distinctly on the stone steps, the slow approach, the shuffling outside her door.

If it were that old woman again she couldn't bear it. She wouldn't open the door. She would stand not breathing in the tiny hall, listening to the long imperative ringing of the bell, then the rapping, and the scuffling in the letter-box. She had done this once before, and it had seemed that the old creature would never go away.

This time, however, the footsteps miraculously passed her door and went on laboriously up the next flight of stairs. Aurora sighed with relief. It had been someone else.

Nevertheless, now she couldn't linger. She was full of apprehension. Finally, tense and jittery, she rang to leave a message at Philip's rooms saying that she would look for him at Waterloo station at three o'clock, and if he were not there then he could follow her down on a later train. That meant that if he arrived back in London in time he could go straight to Waterloo.

He might think her odd, rushing off like this, but he didn't know how imperative it was.

There were no more footsteps, but the telephone rang just as she was closing the last suitcase. She jumped convulsively, then looked uncertainly and with apprehension at the inanimate instrument that emitted such a noise.

Should she answer it? Or should she just go? After all, had it not been for June Birch, her neighbor in the flat below, dropping in with final good wishes just after lunch she would have been gone by now, and the telephone would have been ringing in the empty flat.

She stood there, a slight, dark girl, hugging her arms round herself, her face expressing doubt and fearful eagerness.

The telephone went on ringing.

Why, it would be Philip, of course. How was it that he always came into her thoughts second? That was a fine omen for their marriage.

He probably wanted to tell her that he had got her note, and to arrange where to meet on Waterloo station.

She picked up the receiver with a flourish.

But it was not Philip after all.

"Oh, it's you!" Her face tightened. "I told you not to ring." Refusing to listen to the voice hidden persuasively within the receiver, she cried hysterically, "I told you it was no use. I told you!" And she banged the receiver down, cutting off the voice which had dilated her eyes and wrung her face colorless.

Then she was like a whirlwind, carrying her suitcases to the door, banging windows shut, throwing on her coat, and giving a last quick smoothing to her hair. Last of all she suddenly thrust her hand under the mattress of her bed, remembering something hidden there, and taking out a newspaper tore it into pieces and flung it into the wastepaper basket.

After that she was ready to leave. There was no porter to these unpretentious flats, so she had to carry her bags down the stairs herself. In the cold, draughty entrance hall, stone-floored, she met June Birch again, returning home with a laden shopping basket.

"Oh, Aurora, dear, you're just going! All by yourself?"

"Philip's going to meet me at Waterloo."

"Oh, well, then—you'll have a lovely wedding in the country. I hope the sun shines. But it never does, does it! I'll be looking forward to you coming back. Send me a postcard and I'll do some shopping for you. Get in the milk and bread."

"That's kind of you, June. Would you? I'll leave you my key. And I'll send you a note later. I've no idea, really, when we'll be back. Now I must fly."

She hoped the stupid little creature, all starry-eyed about a wedding, hadn't seen the tears on her cheeks. But if she had she would misinterpret them. Pre-wedding jitters. She, Aurora Hawkins, behaving like a jittery *jeune fille!*

She got a taxi almost immediately, and in it composed her face, renewing her lipstick and putting powder over the recent damp marks on her cheeks. When she reached Waterloo station and saw Philip's tall head above the crowd, she told herself, she would run towards him, flinging herself into the safety of his arms.

For now he was her safety, and everything was going to be all right. . . .

But Philip was not there. Either he was later than he had expected to be arriving in London, or he had not got her message. She waited ten minutes, watching the clock, filled with such a sensation of panic and urgency that she knew she must catch the next train. As she had not been able to linger in the flat, neither could she linger here.

She would have to go down alone. But first there was one thing she could do. Rush to the pub across the road and buy a bottle of gin. That would be necessary, if she were to face good-humouredly her mother's questions.

And also to drown this awful unreasonable remorse that was beginning to overwhelm her.

2

Millicent's letter reached Lydia in Paris. Lydia had just lost her job. Teaching English to two exceedingly spoilt and difficult French children was one thing, but having to fight off advances from their father was another. Even the thought of the summer in Paris and visits to all her cherished places did not make this worth while. Besides, the conceited father did not enjoy being rebuffed. He was astonished and angry, particularly that he should have been spurned by such a plain English Miss who should have been flattered and delighted by his attentions, and it was apparent her tenure in the Avenue Matignon house was going to be extremely brief.

So she acted on impulse, as always, and gave notice to the children's mother, the plump and stately Madame Bertrand, and in spite of shrill, indignant protests left the house that day.

She vaguely thought of looking for another job in Paris, but Millicent's letter, arriving just as she was saying her stiff farewells, changed her plans completely.

She could scarcely believe its contents.

Darling Lydia,

You must, when you get this letter, arrange to come home immediately, for what do you think has happened, Aurora has written to say she is being married, and wants to come home for her wedding. Needless to say, I am so delighted I can scarcely think coherently. Especially when a wedding, and an immediate one, is involved.

Aurora, the poor pet, says that it's all very well quarrelling with one's step-father and maintaining this hateful hostility when one is living an ordinary life, but when one plans to marry one needs one's family. So she has written asking to be forgiven for her behavior, which wasn't entirely her fault, as Geoffrey can be difficult, too.

You can imagine the whirl I am in. The date is to be the soonest possible. Aurora is leaving her job, whatever it was (she gives no information except the address of her flat which is 5 Radlett Lane, NW 8), and is coming home on Thursday. I've already seen the vicar and arranged about the church. Fortunately there are very few weddings this month, so we have the choice of several days, but Aurora says no guests except the family.

So, Lydia, dear, you must come home immediately. If your French family won't give you time off you must give up your job. You can get another one easily enough, and why does it have to be in Paris?

I'm turning out Aurora's room and making it fresh and pretty. Your father is in a state, there is no other way to describe it. Poor darling, he's had a guilt complex about not having been able to get on with Aurora. As if anyone could have. She does have those impossible moods, and she has always resented my marrying your father.

But now, as you can see, all is forgiven, and we're so happy. Come home at once, please. There is so much to do. But isn't it all heavenly!

Much love,
Millicent

PS. Aren't I absurd, I haven't told you who Aurora is marrying. She hasn't said much about him, but his name is Philip Nash, and he is just back in England after some long expedition somewhere. He paints pictures, also. So Aurora will have a life of immense variety, which I think should please her. Much love again, and do catch the next plane—or boat if you can't afford to fly, though I'm sure Geoffrey would send your fare if you are short.

M.

Millicent, her garrulous, kindly, and feather-brained step-mother, certainly had the gift of talking on paper, and her written sentences took almost as much interpretation as her vivacious, garbled spoken ones. She was a dear, but entirely exasperating, and it was not altogether surprising that Aurora, contained and uncommunicative, should have found her mother almost as difficult as her stiff and unbending step-father.

Lydia was extremely fond of them both. She understood her father, his rigidity of principle and his intense shyness, and although she had been only a baby when her own mother had died, and twelve years old when her father had decided to re-marry, she had had a sense of gratitude and pleasure at being gathered into Millicent's warm garrulity.

Aurora, her step-sister, three years her senior, Lydia had admired and longed to resemble. Aurora had treated her with occasional indulgence, but mostly with indifference. She had not understood Aurora's resentment at no longer being the whole of her mother's world, but had been increasingly aware of the hostility of her childhood and her growing up. Finally, when at the age of twenty-one Aurora had said she was leaving home to live in London, and would not be back except perhaps for a brief week-end visit now and then, it was impossible not to feel relief.

"She took after her own father," Millicent had said tearfully. "When he was angry he did these dramatic things. But she'll get over it. She is my daughter, after all, even if I don't understand her."

Aurora wrote occasionally, and several times telephoned. She gave no personal information about herself, and did not keep her promise to make week-end visits. Geoffrey, Lydia realized, was extremely grieved about the whole thing, but said the girl was of age and if she wanted to live her own life, entirely separated from them, they could do nothing about it.

Millicent had to agree, but her sentimental, effusive nature needed an outlet, and she turned to Lydia to express it. The two became devoted. Twisting Lydia's straight hair, Millicent used to say, "You haven't got Aurora's looks, but you're a dear child. And you'll improve. Anyway, beauty only brings trouble."

But no one knew whether or not it was a man to whom Aurora had gone.

Gradually Lydia, busy with her own pursuits, missed Aurora less. She realized that a storm-centre had been removed from the house, and her shock gave place to an intense curiosity as to what Aurora was doing. Some day she would find out.

Now it seemed that the mystery was to be cleared up. It was, as Millicent had said, intensely exciting. Lydia said a silent thank you to M'sieu Bertrand for his methods which had already organized her departure from the Bertrand household, and rushed off to the Gare du Nord to catch the first boat-train.

As Millicent had predicted, she could not afford the air fare, but with her packing done and her departure planned she would be home almost as quickly by channel steamer.

What, she wondered, having a similar afterthought to Millicent's, was this man Aurora intended to marry like?

Lydia arrived in London with some time to spare before catching her train home. She knew what she was going to do. She was going to the address Millicent had given her to see if Aurora were still at her flat. It would be fun to walk in on her and to renew their old relationship without Millicent hovering talkatively over them. What did Aurora look like now? Had she still that dark, exciting beauty? And what would she think of Lydia at twenty-two?

Not a great deal, Lydia reflected, with a complete lack of self-conceit. Even M'sieu Bertrand, with his ardent advances, had indicated that he did not consider her madly beautiful. But M'sieu Bertrand's tastes definitely leaned towards the voluptuous, and Lydia, with her high cheekbones and sparsely-fleshed body, must have represented a pitiable poverty of choice to him. It was really, in retrospect, rather amusing. She would tell Aurora about it when there was time.

If Aurora had not left London yet they could travel down to Lipham together, and catch up on each other's news.

The block of flats in St. John's Wood was not imposing. It looked respectable enough, but shabby. Lydia's eager feet took her up the stone stairs two at a time. What a good thing, she was thinking, that Aurora didn't have to live in these uninspiring surroundings all her life. But one hoped she was there for half an hour longer, at least.

It was too much to hope, apparently, for no one came in answer to Lydia's ring. She was absurdly disappointed.

It didn't matter. Aurora must already be home, and in two or three hours she would see her.

But it would have been such fun to have this private meeting first. In a vague attempt to make herself think the disappointment was not real, Lydia tried the door handle.

To her intense surprise the door opened. It had not been locked.

So Aurora must be here after all!

"Aurora! Can I come in? It's me! Lydia."

She stepped into a miniature hall and listened. There was no sound from within. The living-room was visible through an open doorway. She went in and noticed all the usual signs of the occupier of the flat being absent, the drawn curtains, the vague disorderliness which it hadn't been worthwhile to tidy after packing, an ashtray full of cigarette ends, a cup containing dregs of tea, a faint film of dust on the table. Also on the table was a newspaper which had been badly torn and which someone had been trying to piece together.

That was strange, Lydia thought, and glanced idly at its name. The *Daily Reporter,* dated the third of April, she noted, and tucked the information away in her mind to ask Aurora later what it had been she was trying to find.

"Aurora," she called again, uncertainly.

The bedroom also was empty. It was a slit of a room, prettily furnished, giving evidence of Aurora's femininity, but also of her absence, for the bed was made up without sheets, and the wardrobe empty of clothes.

In the kitchen it was the same story, neat cupboards, an empty refrigerator, attractive but inexpensive china, gay paint obviously applied by Aurora herself. The whole flat gave clear indication of its owner, a tidy-minded girl living alone and making the best of rather dreary surroundings.

There were only the two rather odd things to remember and comment on, the unlocked door and the torn newspaper on the table.

And a vague feeling of unhappiness.

The last was purely imagination. It came to Lydia only because of her own disappointment at arriving too late to find Aurora home. An empty flat was always strangely forlorn. She would go downstairs and ring the doorbell of the flat immediately below, and see what she could find out.

The woman who answered her ring was youngish, with primrose-coloured hair in curlers and dejected lines in her face. But she grew extremely animated when Lydia introduced herself—other people's lives were obviously of obsessive interest to her—and she probably saw in this reconciliation of Aurora with her family all the ingredients of a novelette.

"Fancy that! You're Aurora's sister! You're not a bit like her, are you?"

"No, I'm not."

"Oh, I don't say you're not nice looking, but Aurora's quite a beauty, isn't she? I always wondered why some man didn't snap her up long ago. I mean she's twenty-five, isn't she? I was married at nineteen, more fool me! And divorced at twenty-two."

"Look, Mrs.—"

"Birch. June Birch. Call me June."

"Look, June, I went up to see if Aurora were still there—"

"Oh, she's gone. You've missed her. She called good-bye about half an hour ago."

"Then why wasn't the door of her flat locked?"

"Wasn't it? Good gracious! She must have forgotten to lock it. Well, it's understandable, isn't it? Going off to her wedding. She was so excited."

But here, oddly enough, the talkative woman's words lacked conviction, and a brief puzzled look crossed her face. As if she had pondered on Aurora's lack of excitement.

"Well, anyway, dear, there's nothing to worry about. I have the key Aurora left with me. I'm going to do some shopping for her when she's due back from her honeymoon. I'll give it to you and you can tell your sister you locked up."

It was then that the utterly curious feeling came over Lydia that she didn't want to go up to the flat alone. This building was not wildly gay, but it was respectable, and without dark corners or shoddy stairways. It was filled with completely normal sounds, children's voices, a door slamming somewhere, a radio turned too high. Yet the feeling swept over her that this normality was deceptive. The emptiness of Aurora's flat was a lie. It had not been empty at all. Someone had been there watching her as she prowled about. The person who had unlocked the door and who, startled by her arrival, took cover. Where? Behind the bathroom door, perhaps, or behind the curtains in the living-room.

Oh, nonsense! she told herself. Was she becoming psychic?

But if June Birch would come up with her. . . .

"Since the door was unlocked," she said quickly, "I think we ought to make sure everything's all right. I don't know what should be there, but you do."

"Sure, I'll come up with you if you're worrying about burglars," June said good-naturedly. "But it would have to be a pretty slick burglar to find that door open and nip in all in the short time since Aurora left. Come on then, duck."

As they reached the first-floor landing Lydia could hear the telephone ringing in Aurora's flat.

That would startle the intruder, if there were one. She hastily approached the door, expecting every moment to hear the ring cut short as someone lifted the receiver. But the shrill sound continued, and when she turned the door knob, ready, with June Birch beside her, to burst in, the door was locked.

It couldn't be! Why, only ten minutes ago she had pulled it shut herself without having a key to turn in the lock. And now, as if she had suffered from an hallucination, it was firmly locked.

Even June, with her worldly air, was startled. "But you said it wasn't locked. Did you try it properly? You must have made a mistake."

"I didn't. I went in the flat. I told you. It's been locked since I was here. Just in the last few minutes." A tremor passed over her. "There must have been someone in there all the time."

June's heavily marked eyebrows rose. "Goodness! How queer! Must have been someone Aurora had given a key to. After all—well, I didn't pry, and she didn't talk much. A girl's entitled to privacy."

The telephone inside kept on ringing. Suddenly it was immensely important that it should be answered.

"Open the door," Lydia cried. "Hurry, I want to answer the telephone before it stops ringing."

The telephone was in the tiny hall. Lydia snatched up the receiver while June went past her, warily, into the living-room.

"Hullo!"

"Darling? Is that you? Thank goodness I caught you. I'm running awfully late, and—"

"Just a minute," said Lydia. "This isn't Aurora, if that's who you think you're speaking to."

"Oh! I'm sorry." The voice was deep and attractive. It seemed to vibrate through the receiver. Unconsciously Lydia hugged it closer to her ear. "Who is it, then?"

"It's me, Lydia. The beautiful younger sister."

"I'm pleased to meet you, Lydia. I didn't think that was going to be until this evening. This is Philip Nash speaking. I was trying to catch Aurora. Has she gone?"

"Yes, half an hour ago."

"Then I've missed her. I wanted to tell her I couldn't be at Waterloo at the time we planned. I've got held up all round. We were going to have tea before our train left. I'd better fly. I might catch her there now."

"Wait a moment," said Lydia. "I'm coming too. Where are you ringing from?"

"A call-box in Piccadilly."

"Then wait for me at Waterloo. I'll be about half an hour. If Aurora's there, tell her to wait. We can all go down together."

"Good idea. I'll see you then. And I am pleased to meet you, Lydia."

"I say!" Lydia cried. "Wouldn't it be a good idea to tell me what sort of person I'm to look for. I'm five feet six, and rather thin, and I'll be wearing a camel-hair coat. My hair is straight and inclined to be sandy, and I'm not, I'll repeat that, I'm not remarkably beautiful."

There was a faint, deep chuckle.

"That's fine, Lydia. Let's leave it. I'll find you."

She put the receiver down very slowly. She had forgotten for a moment that she was standing in Aurora's flat, and that there was a faint mystery about it. She suddenly knew that she was going to find this man, Philip Nash, with the deep, pleasant voice, standing beside Aurora possessively, on Waterloo station, and the thought filled her with the most unreasonable and inexplicable desolation.

"There's no one here," called June Birch from the bedroom. "The place is empty. And nothing's disturbed. As far as I can see, anyway. Whoever was here must have gone down the back stairway." Her voice came nearer. She stood at the door, hands on hips, her pale hair, when its cramping curlers were released, ready to frame a much younger and more hopeful face. "I guess we'd better not be too inquisitive. It's none of our business who might have a key. It could be someone who isn't particularly pleased about Aurora's getting married. So perhaps it's a good thing she missed him."

"But there certainly was someone," said Lydia thoughtfully. "Because that newspaper has gone."

"Newspaper?"

"Yes. There was one spread out on the table when I came in before. It had been torn, and then put together again. It's gone now. How very odd!"

3

Someone back from the Antarctic, or the headwaters of the Amazon, or the Sahara desert. Lydia looked for a heavy, broad-shouldered young man, sunburnt or wind burnt, with rugged features, and likely to possess the deep voice that had vibrated so pleasurably through the telephone.

A hand fell on her shoulder.

"Lydia? The beautiful younger sister?"

She turned and looked into the lean, pale face of an immaculately dressed young man, whose clothes proclaimed Savile Row and whose manners one of the older public schools.

"You can't be Philip!"

"Why not?" His eyes were very blue, and accented by heavy blond eyebrows. He looked deceptively frail, the skin crinkling over his thin cheeks as he smiled.

"But the crocodiles? The desert sunburn or whatever?"

"You mean the dried-up malarial look? I'm sorry. I always stay pink and white like the nicest English debs. Are you disappointed? If it comes to that, you aren't completely what you said yourself."

"How did you know me, then?"

"I don't know. How did I?" He frowned slightly. For a fleeting moment—even then she guessed that the casual merriment would not often be absent—his eyes seemed to go darker. And the tremor that his voice over the telephone had given her went through her again.

"Well, I was right, wasn't I?"

She nodded. She longed, suddenly for him to say that she was more attractive than she had led him to believe. But he made no comment on her appearance. He was very tall. He was looking down at her. She smoothed her hair, conscious of those very brilliant and perceptive eyes on it.

This was no M'sieu Bertrand with thick lips and fumbling advances. This, she reminded herself quickly, was Philip Nash, her sister's fiancé.

"Aurora's not here?" she asked politely.

"No, I must have missed her. We were to meet at platform 15, but if I couldn't be there in time I was to follow her down. I tried to make it, but everything held me up. I thought she might have got held up, too, and that was why I tried her flat."

"Tried it?"

"Telephoned," he said, eyeing her. "You answered. Don't you remember?"

"Yes, of course. It was just that—"

"What?"

"Oh, nothing." One couldn't tell him about the unlocked door, just supposing the visitor had been, as June Birch suggested, another lover. But was Aurora like that? One didn't know.

"Let's get the tickets and find our train," Philip suggested. "Then you can tell me."

She hoped he would forget the trivial subject. At first it seemed he had. They found an empty compartment, and settled down comfortably, facing one another. Lydia felt cosy and happy, and had forgotten the exhaustion of her journey from Paris. She hadn't yet the intimate talk with Aurora which was to encompass the lapse of time since they had last met, but Philip, at least, who had known Aurora long enough to want to marry her, could tell her some things.

"I'm staying at the Wheatsheaf," Philip explained. "We decided that would be best, while Aurora fusses with wedding things. I thought at first I was going to escape all that nonsense, but I'm told this is the big day in a girl's life, and she likes her family around."

"Yes," said Lydia uncertainly.

"Oh, you don't need to be cautious. I know all about the suspension of diplomatic relations. A poor show, I thought, and it's high time Aurora went home and had her bottom spanked."

"Then it's because of you that she's gone home?"

"No. It was entirely her own idea. But I was all for it. Odd, you know."

"How do you mean?"

His gaze was indolent, but sharp. The exasperating thing was that it gave nothing away. Did he think her very plain? Or was he noticing her appearance at all?

"That she should ignore her young sister, too."

"Oh, I don't suppose she forgot me," Lydia said uneasily. "It was just—well, the argument was with my parents. Daddy isn't the easiest person even as one's father, so as a step-father he's rather worse. And Aurora is pretty quick-tempered and temperamental. Unless she's changed, I expect you've found that out."

"Aurora," he murmured. "The sleeping princess. But she's far from sleeping. Far from it." And then he went back to the awkward subject.

"What was strange about her flat?"

"Strange?"

"You seemed to think I might have been there."

"No, I didn't at all. Actually the tenant downstairs, someone called June Birch, had a key and let me in. There was a torn newspaper on the table. I—I just wondered why Aurora had been trying to put it together."

"We'll ask her when we see her, shall we?" He adjusted the knot of his tie, and brushed a speck of dust from his lapel. "Intriguing," he murmured. "Well, Lydia, what's it going to be like suddenly having a—"

He had been going to say "a brother". She knew he had. But without changing his tone he finished smoothly, "Having your sister restored to you?"

Why had he changed his intended remark? Lydia's heart, to her intense annoyance, and for no good reason, was pounding.

"Is she just as beautiful still?"

He leaned back, his eyes narrowed. "Shall I tell you how I first saw her? Coming into a restaurant off the King's Road. I'd arrived in England that morning, after two years away, mostly in jungles surrounded with island beauties, and Aurora was—well, she was her name. I felt as if I'd burst through the thistles and brambles and there she was in front of me, like a goddess."

"Sorry to carp," Lydia said crisply. "But you said a princess a moment ago."

"Princess, goddess," he remained good-humoured. "It doesn't matter. It was raining, and her cheeks were wet and very bright, and she was alone. Gloriously alone. And, most remarkable and wonderful of all, she had no rings on her fingers."

"She'd been asleep for several years," Lydia pointed out, and refused to think of the ring that now sparkled on Aurora's finger.

"Yes. She must have been. That's the only explanation I can think of."

"But you woke her up."

"Yes. I did that, didn't I?" His voice was faintly questioning. Lydia momentarily forgot her sense of desolation and became curious.

"Aren't you sure about it?"

"Well, yes, of course. But a woman has to keep some sense of mystery, hasn't she? She's told me almost nothing about herself."

"Don't you even know where she was working?" Lydia asked, in surprise.

"Oh, yes, for some solicitor in the city. Armand somebody. Armand and his aunt, she used to talk about. He was a Frenchman, I imagine."

"French!" Lydia thought of M'sieu Bertrand, who had unfairly prejudiced her feelings about Frenchmen, and was not surprised that Aurora should have eagerly run to Philip's arms.

Philip was smiling. "You say that just like an English woman from the midlands."

"I've just come back from Paris," Lydia said defensively.

"Have you? What colour are your eyes, Lydia?"

"Can't you see?"

"No. They keep changing. Like water. Or jewels turned to different lights."

Lydia tilted her chin. "Save that for your sleeping princess."

"I can't. Black eyes are black all the time. Shall we see if we can find a drink on this train?"

"Are you getting nervous?"

"Lamentably. I've never met in-laws before."

But if he were nervous, Lydia reflected, looking at his fine, austere profile, it was not because of meeting Millicent and Geoffrey. But because of Aurora, and what her feelings were for him.

Or even what his were for her. . . .

4

A wedding in the country. The May trees were out, and the grass was green velvet. Two proud and stately swans were followed by cygnets on the pond adjoining the church and the moss-grown churchyard. Ring doves fluttered and cooed about the gables and chimneys of the Wheatsheaf. Cats slept on windowsills in the sun, and children skipped on the cobble-stones. The setting was idyllic.

Even Philip had had to admit that. Lydia, half irritated, half amused, had left him at the Wheatsheaf, fussing about the amenities. He said he would be up at the house in time for dinner. He positively must unpack, and have a bath and present himself in good order. If Lydia would meantime be the bearer of his respects to her parents and his love to Aurora. . . . When Lydia left him he was leaning his indolent length against the bar, chatting with the bar-keeper, and ordering another double whisky. As if he were indeed nervous. . . .

Millicent flung open the door as soon as she saw Lydia coming up the path.

"My love, here you are! I'm so glad you could come at once. Isn't it all quite wonderful! Aurora arrived an hour ago. She's been upstairs resting. She seemed very tired. You didn't happen to see Philip? He was to be on the first train he could catch."

Lydia disentangled herself from Millicent's embrace. "He came down with me. He's at the Wheatsheaf."

"At the Wheatsheaf! But why didn't you bring him here?"

"He wanted to tidy up," Lydia said, and realized how thin an excuse that sounded for a man in love, eager to see his bride's home and his in-laws.

"He's a very meticulous young man. He'll be here to dinner. Don't fuss, Millicent. It's enough that one person is going to fuss at this wedding."

"Who?"

"The bridegroom."

"Lydia, didn't you like him?" Millicent asked in alarm.

Like him? How had she felt about that elegant, irritating young man, seemingly occupied with trivialities, until one caught his brilliant, perspicacious glance?

"I don't know," she said slowly. "I suppose he could be Aurora's type. How does she look, Millicent?"

"Beautiful!" said Millicent ecstatically.

Lydia eyed her, too, with reserve. "I guessed that. I had to listen to Philip on the subject. But what is she really like? Is she happy, do you think?"

Millicent's face, carefully made up and surrounded by perfect, rigid grey curls so that she looked like a plump, pretty doll, was too open for dissembling. Apprehension showed already.

"She tells me nothing! She hasn't changed at all. If I don't ask her questions, that's fine. But if I do, there is that veiled look, instantly! Not exactly hostile. Just 'keep off the grass' sort of thing. With me! Her own mother! Oh, she was perfectly sweet, of course, and to Geoffrey as well. We had tea together. We talked about everything but personal things." Millicent began to tick off on her fingers. "We discussed flowers for the wedding, catering, guests, where she and Philip plan to live, her trousseau, even what we do with poor Mary's kittens nowadays. But as to what she has been doing in the last year, or how much she's in love, or why this rather sudden wedding—nothing! Silence! Utter and complete!"

Lydia laughed at the melodrama in Millicent's face. "You can't break the ice all in five minutes, darling."

"I don't think she even likes being home." This Millicent said in a low voice, looking round furtively as if she imagined Aurora might have come silently into the room.

"Oh, nonsense! You can't decide that immediately, either."

"I don't think she is happy, really. When she's not talking, a sort of brooding look comes over her."

"But she's still beautiful."

"Oh, yes. In that haggard, ravished kind of way. I can't think why she hasn't married sooner. Unless she has, of course, and said nothing. How is one to know? Something like that would explain her brooding look."

"Now you're romancing," Lydia chided. "You're aggravated that you don't know about those missing years, so you're making up a story to put in them."

"Perhaps I am. But why is she so mysterious?"

"It's probably an air she's cultivated." Even to the extent of making jigsaw puzzles out of an old page of the *Daily Reporter,* Lydia wondered privately. And to handing out keys of her flat indiscriminately? "When can I see her? Is she asleep now?"

"I don't know. Go up and see. She might talk to you when she won't to me."

Lydia impulsively kissed Millicent on the cheek. "Don't be so sentimental! Here's one daughter, anyway, who's pleased to see you."

"Lydia, darling, you're such a comfort. I adore you. Did you have a nice time in Paris? Was it awkward leaving so suddenly?"

"It would have been more awkward staying."

"Oh, dear! Those Frenchmen!"

"In the singular. And I haven't even Aurora's beauty."

"But you're very nice, dear. Fresh and young."

"A skinny pigeon," said Lydia. "That, more or less, was what he called me. I'm going up to see Aurora now, and if she's asleep I'll wake her up."

Aurora was not asleep. She was sitting at her dressing-table. She seemed to have been doing her nails, but as Lydia called softly, "Hi!" she made a quick furtive movement of her hand across her eyes before she turned.

It was almost as if she had been crying.

But her eyes were brilliant and dry as she sprang up and came towards Lydia. She was very slender, almost attenuated. Her dark dress clung round a ridiculously small waist. Her cheekbones were prominent, her lips full and pouting. She wore too much eye shadow and her eyebrows took soaring lines. She was absurdly unlike a daughter of Millicent's. Her elegance had a strangely un-English look. She was, Lydia realized, with a shock of disappointment, a stranger.

Her eager welcome died. She found herself holding out her hand formally and tilting her cheek forward for Aurora's kiss.

"Well, Lydia! You've grown up."

Lydia shrugged. "Did you think time would stop down here?"

Aurora gave a brief laugh. "Somehow I've always thought of you as a school-girl. Silly of me. You've changed enormously."

"Have I?" said Lydia absently, thinking that this was the face Philip had seen in the restaurant and immediately wanted to paint, this thin elegance, with high cheekbones and curiously forlorn eyes. No wonder it had remained engraved on his memory.

"It's nice of you to come home for my wedding."

"It's nice of *you* to come," Lydia said pointedly.

"Oh, that. I guess I've been waiting for an excuse to make up that quarrel with the parents. Incidentally, they haven't changed. I hope Millicent isn't going to fuss like this for three solid weeks."

"She will," Lydia promised.

"Oh, lord!" A spasm of irritation crossed Aurora's face. "I wonder if I can stand it. It's this business of waiting for a licence. Would you like a drink?"

"Now?"

"It's all right. I've got a bottle of gin here. I can't bear this cocktails-at-six rule. Can you drink it with water? Or neat?"

Lydia grimaced. "Both I detest. But I'll force down a watery one." She added with sudden shyness, "It *is* nice to have you home again, Aurora."

Aurora was pouring gin into a glass. She had her head bent. "I suppose I should say it's nice to be here, but frankly I feel like a fish out of water. I hadn't visualized all the fuss and excitement Millicent would generate, all this being a young and virginal bride sort of thing. After all, I'm not that young. I'm twenty-five, and as for the virginal part. . . ."

Lydia waited, but Aurora, handing her a drink, had veered from the subject and said irritably, "Mummy's so ridiculously old-fashioned. I should have remembered. But Philip seemed vaguely surprised about my lack of family, and—oh, one thing and another—"

It was the first time Philip's name had been mentioned. Lydia sipped her drink, winced at the taste, and said, "I came down in the train with Philip. So I've met him."

Aurora's eyes surveyed her over her glass. "Did you? And you spent the whole journey wondering why I was going to marry him. Or whether he wanted to marry me."

"He told me how he met you. He was enraptured from the first moment."

"Enraptured? Is that the word you'd use? Yes, I suppose it is."

One could see that Aurora had become an adept at making the indirect answer, of edging the subject into a less awkward channel. "He's very impulsive," she murmured. "He's probably already regretted that day."

"Why on earth should he?" Lydia demanded. But she was remembering Philip's tall, supple form leaning over the hotel bar, his hand reaching for a glass. He was drinking double whiskies, Aurora neat gin. Was all this especially significant, or just an indication of the way they usually lived?

When Aurora made no answer to her question, she went on, "Is Philip really an explorer?"

"Why not? He says so."

"He seems to me more like a dilettante. His conversation, his luxurious tastes."

"He's a little bit of everything, botanist, anthropologist, and he's sort of modern Gauguin—he's done some luscious paintings. He says I'm the first girl he's met since he's come back to England, so you see he's tumbled straight into my arms."

Lydia met Aurora's mocking eyes in some bewilderment. Was she very shy about showing her real feelings—or was she not in love?

"And you were ready—to tumble into his?" she murmured.

Aurora was laughing with amusement.

"Lydia, darling, how you've grown up! You're talking like a woman of the world. Millicent said you were in Paris. What happened to you there?"

Lydia shrugged. "The usual. Middle-aged wolf."

"You look as if you were able to cope."

"I ran away."

Aurora's eyes dropped. "Well, that's one way of coping. I'm all for it. Another drink?"

"No, *thank* you."

"I shall. I need it. I believe I'm going to be the jittery bride, just as Millicent hopes."

Lydia sat on the edge of the bed and said slowly, "By the way, I called at your flat this afternoon. I thought you might still be there and we could travel down together."

Aurora's head shot up. She was looking at Lydia with a strangely wary look.

"When?"

"Oh, apparently I'd missed you by about half an hour. Your neighbor, June Birch, told me."

"Oh, yes, June. She's rather a busybody, but she means well."

Lydia finished her drink, and as the anticipated warmth swam round her head she said levelly, "Who do you give the keys of your flat to, Aurora?"

Aurora didn't flush. Her face seemed to go thinner and paler.

She said, "June has one. Philip has one. At least, I think I gave him one. Why should I tell you, anyway? If it comes to that, why are you asking?"

"Because I found the door unlocked. I looked round and there didn't seem to be anyone there, so I went down to ask the nearest neighbor if you were about. That was June Birch, and she said you had gone. She said you must have forgotten to lock your door and she would do so with the key you'd given her." Lydia put her glass down and looked up into Aurora's intent face. "But when we went up again the door was already locked. So there must have been someone there who slipped out as soon as I went downstairs."

"Gracious!" said Aurora. "How odd of Philip to behave like that!"

"Philip!"

"It must have been him. He was going to pick me up if he could get to London in time and we were travelling down together. But he didn't make it, so I came on alone."

"It wasn't Philip. Actually, he was ringing up just as June and I went up to your flat again."

Aurora was leaning forward. Her eyes seemed suddenly enormous, the pupils dilated and black. "Did he say where he was ringing from?"

"Yes. Piccadilly."

"I think he was having you on, Lydia. He must have just slipped round the corner."

"Why on earth would he do a thing like that?"

"Goodness knows. Probably remembered he was back in England where it isn't always the thing to be found in a lady's flat."

"But one's fiancé!"

Aurora shrugged. "He wouldn't know who you were, would he? Why should you believe him, a stranger? Simple enough, isn't it? Anyway, I'll ask him when I see him."

"You're sure it would be Philip?" Lydia persisted.

"Darling, I don't give away keys indiscriminately. Would you like to see my trousseau? What there is of it? My wedding dress is here, too. And veil. I'm not crazy about all this fuss, but I knew Millicent would be wildly disappointed if I didn't do the conventional thing. By the way, you're being my bridesmaid, of course. We'll slip up to London and get a dress for you next week. Look, this is mine."

Aurora plunged into the wardrobe and brought out a simple, cream-coloured, satin dress which she draped over a chair. Then she was spreading out the veil, and delving into suitcases for various other items of clothing. All at once she was full of business and vivacity. Almost as if she were throwing up a smoke screen of activity to avoid another subject.

The subject of who else might still possess a key to her flat. . . .

"This is my going-away suit, though we haven't yet even decided where we're going. Probably Bournemouth! Philip says since he's only been in England six weeks nothing will drag him abroad until the end of the summer, at least. He says it's me and not a country or a fashionable holiday resort he's marrying. Look, do you like this nightdress? *Chi chi,* isn't it? And this négligée."

Scooping up the filmy garments from the suitcase something clattered to the floor. Aurora swooped to pick it up as if to conceal it. Lydia caught the glint of a gold chain.

"What's that?" she asked curiously. "A present from Philip?"

Aurora opened her hand slowly, then thrust out what it held with a sudden, almost aggressive, gesture.

"Not Philip's. My late—I should say my ex-employer gave it to me for a wedding present."

It was a heavy gold chain with an antique pendant of curiously and beautifully wrought gold set with precious stones.

"But, Aurora, that's lovely!"

"Well—not to everyone's taste. It's a bit heavy." She hung it against her slender throat.

"But it must be terribly valuable."

"I don't know. Probably not as much as you'd think. Anyway, he could afford it."

"It looks like an heirloom. Is he very wealthy?"

"I imagine so. I don't really know."

"Who is he?" Lydia persisted. "You remember, we don't know a thing that you've been doing since you left home."

"Nothing particularly exciting. Nothing secret or mysterious. I was a model until I couldn't stand it any longer, and then I got this job with Armand. He's a family solicitor, you know, the old-fashioned type. Lots of elderly respectable clients. He didn't make an enormous income—who does?—but he had several wealthy aunts. The job was interesting enough. He was sorry I was leaving. I'd been his personal secretary and we'd got along pretty well." She dangled the heavy ornament over her wrist. "I expect this belonged to one of his aunts. I'm not sure yet whether I'll keep it or sell it."

"I think it's beautiful."

Aurora smiled faintly. "Do you? How sweet you are!"

"Doesn't Philip?"

"I don't know. I haven't shown it to him."

For some reason Lydia was prompted to say, "Whoever was in your flat playing jigsaw puzzles with a piece of newspaper? Was it anything particularly significant that you had torn up?"

Aurora's eyes were suddenly quite still. They were remembering. They were, Lydia thought, re-reading what significant thing it was that had been printed on that torn sheet of paper.

"Are you—sure?"

"Perfectly sure. Because when I came back with June the paper had disappeared. I couldn't have imagined a goofy thing like that, could I?"

"No. I suppose you couldn't." Aurora spoke very slowly. "I suppose it was that bit about—I'd had some trouble about a driving licence. I'd had to go to court. Absurd, wasn't it?"

"Aurora! There was no one hurt!"

"No, I'd only scraped this wretched taxi's mudguard. But you know how it is when anyone reasonably young and good-looking goes to court. Though I must say—snooping!" She was thinking secretly again, her face closed. She picked up the gin bottle and pouring another drink swallowed it quickly, and with a disturbingly accustomed air. "Look, Lydia dear, don't mention that. You know how up in the air Millicent and Geoffrey would get. I'll have it out with Philip. Now what haven't I shown you? Oh, this cocktail dress. I love colors. Don't you think this is rather ravishing?"

"Whose car were you driving?" Lydia asked.

"Whose *car!* Oh, you mean that bother. Armand's of course. I was going to Waterloo to meet one of his aunts. Thank heaven she wasn't in the car when I had the contretemps with the taxi. We kept it from her."

"Who is we?"

"Why, Armand—Lydia, are you *cross-examining* me?"

"I just wondered what Armand was like," said Lydia blithely.

"Oh, he's got all those doting aunts who've completely ruined him. Honestly, I was glad to leave the office."

Now she was no longer talking slowly and carefully, almost cautiously. She was chattering on in the way one would have expected her to, as an excited bride. But it was too late to deceive Lydia.

She was pretty certain the story about the car accident and the lack of a driving licence was a complete fabrication. It had been some other fact that Aurora had been destroying in that sheet of newspaper. Probably, Lydia guessed, something much more personal. A divorce case, perhaps, involving herself, or some piece of scandal she preferred Philip not to know.

But in that case she should have been more careful about handing out keys to her flat and leaving incriminating evidence lying about. Evidence which had brought a pinched look of fear to her face. . . .

It was at this stage that Aurora suddenly decided she ought to ring Philip. She dashed downstairs to do so, and Lydia, fighting an ashamed desire to eavesdrop (was Aurora going to ask Philip if he had been the mysterious intruder in her flat, and, if so, what he had discovered in the resurrected newspaper?), went slowly to her own room and firmly shut the door.

From her window, looking across the village green, she could see the red-tiled roof of the Wheatsheaf, the spire of the church, and the pond where the swans, like ballet dancers, silently drifted. It was a golden, sleepy, fairy-tale afternoon. But something, the gin probably, had made Lydia depressed and uneasy.

She couldn't think of weddings and virginal blushing brides, as Millicent was probably doing. If it came to that, neither Millicent nor Geoffrey deserved a daughter like Aurora, who hid from them for months at a time, who had a guilty conscience about some newspaper report, who drank neat gin secretly in her room to give herself some necessary courage, and who was planning to marry a man whom she didn't love.

Now how had she come to think that last thing? Lydia was startled by her sudden unjustified intuition. Of course Aurora must love Philip. She was not, after all, the kind of a girl who had to desperately seize the first available offer.

Unless whatever had been in that newspaper had made it advisable to do so. . . .

But surely Philip was not the sort of man one could do that to. Except that he seemed extremely vulnerable to feminine beauty, and may, in a rash moment, have committed himself.

And Aurora was beautiful. She was the authentic fairy-tale princess, raven dark hair, huge, brilliant eyes, features and bones of extreme fineness. Millicent must have had an intuition that she would be a beauty when she had given her that romantic name.

Had she thought, too, about possible pricked fingers that would lead to doom?

Doom! What a word to think of! How even more absurd to think that Aurora, like the fairy-tale princess, had just woken from a long sleep and still had a nightmare lingering in her eyes. Or feared a nightmare about to begin. . . .

"Lydia!" called Millicent.

"Yes, Millicent."

"Your father has just come in from the garden. Come down and see him. And we've decided to dress for dinner. It will be nice, with Philip coming. Aurora has gone over to the Wheatsheaf. What are you doing in your room, darling?"

"Recovering from an alcoholic nightmare," Lydia wanted to say.

For now, all at once, everything was normal again. Her head had stopped spinning. Aurora's cream satin dress was spread on the chair in her room and the wedding would be like any other wedding, except that the bride and groom would be particularly memorable; such a perfect foil for one another, she so dark and fragile, he so tall and fair.

Millicent would have photographers from fashionable papers down. Everything would be too, too conventional.

And Lydia would never know what Aurora's private nightmare had been, if indeed she had ever had one.

5

Lydia welcomed her father affectionately. He was a silent, reserved man, difficult to know, possessed of rigid principles—with which Aurora clashed violently—but both fair and kind. Life with Millicent, garrulous and gregarious, had done much to make him unbend, but it was obvious that he was not altogether happy about this sudden invasion of Aurora and her intended husband. He wanted to be reassured.

"What do you think of it, Lydia?" he asked. "Millicent is prepared to accept it as the most natural thing in the world. Why shouldn't a girl want to come home to marry, she says? But I don't know. Of course, Aurora isn't my own daughter, and I frankly don't understand her. She seems quieter, I must say, and not so moody, but she's a much more devious person than her mother. Much more."

Lydia silently agreed with that remark. Indeed, Aurora was much more devious than ever Geoffrey realized. But unless someone sprang up in the church and declared an impediment to the marriage—the melodrama of which Millicent would adore, forgetting other issues—one could do nothing but accept the situation as normal.

There was no reason for her to feel as strangely unhappy and uneasy about it as she did.

"I shouldn't worry, Daddy," she said soothingly. "Aurora knows what she's doing. She always did. And it doesn't seem to have brought her to any harm. She's rather spectacular, isn't she?"

"Too much beauty can be a bad thing," Geoffrey said soberly. "I wish she'd tell us a little more about herself. Well, perhaps she will before the wedding. If her mother can't break her down, no one can."

Aurora arrived back from the Wheatsheaf just in time to dress for dinner. Ten minutes later the telephone rang.

"It's for you, Aurora," called Millicent.

Aurora appeared at the top of the stairs.

"Me!" Her face was flushed. She had obviously had more to drink at the Wheatsheaf. "It can't be Philip. He'll be seeing me in a few minutes." She giggled. "Isn't he getting passionate?"

She came down the stairs and shut herself into the small morning-room, not intending anyone to hear her response to Philip's passion.

But her caller was not Philip after all, because while she was still in there he arrived. Lydia took him into the drawing-room. She noticed that he looked surprisingly elegant in his dinner-jacket, his long, lean fingers taking on a rather impressive distinction. And there was no flush, engendered by alcohol or otherwise, in his cheeks. He looked cool and contained.

"Nervous as hell," he said unconvincingly. "Am I early or late?"

"Just about right. Will you have a drink? I'm afraid there's only sherry. Daddy has a thing about not spoiling one's palate. I could nip upstairs, though, and get you some of Aurora's gin."

"Why has she got gin upstairs?"

His voice was casual. It was probably only her too acute consciousness of him that made her think he was disapproving. She found his sudden intense blue gaze even more disturbing than her memory of it.

Damn him, why did he have to look so distinguished in evening dress!

"I suppose she's nervous, too."

"Aurora! Not of me, she isn't. I'll have sherry, thank you, Lydia. What a charming room. And you fit into it extraordinary well."

"Thank you," said Lydia absently. "Tell me, was it you in Aurora's flat this afternoon? And if it was, why didn't you say so?"

Philip took the glass of sherry she handed him, and set it down. "Do you mind telling me what you're talking about?"

"Didn't Aurora go over to the Wheatsheaf to ask you? She said she was going to. I'd better explain. I found the door of her flat unlocked and she said you were the person—or one of the persons—who had a key."

"Say that again!" said Philip. "I haven't a key to Aurora's flat."

"Then—oh, dear, I suppose I shouldn't have mentioned it—"

"I suppose you should," Philip began.

But at that moment Millicent, followed by Geoffrey, came in, and the awkward moment was over. Or postponed. Slightly distrait, Lydia performed introductions.

"How tall you are!" exclaimed Millicent, in her unexpected but disarming way. "Aurora says you've explored everywhere. Now please tell me about crocodiles. I've always been fascinated by them."

"Let me give you a sherry," Geoffrey said. "I can recommend this one. That's if you like something dry, but not too dry."

"I have one already, thank you, sir."

"Oh, splendid. Lydia's been looking after you. Where's Aurora, Millicent?"

"She's on the telephone. She thought it was Philip calling, and just couldn't get there quickly enough. Isn't it sweet, having two young people in love in the house. Your family comes from Northumberland, Philip, Aurora tells me. I suppose it was all those biting winds that sent you off to the jungle in the first place. Now do tell me about the crocodiles. Do they really have that awfully sinister saurian look?"

"Millicent, what a heavenly word. Saurian!" Lydia said.

"Yes, isn't it! I think it was in a detective story I read it first. I once had a friend who kept an alligator in a glass tank. She got quite fond of it. It was only a little one, of course. Do you know, I don't think Aurora's even dressed yet."

"Then we'll have time for another sherry," said Geoffrey calmly. "I hope you're going to be able to stand all this female fuss over a wedding, Philip."

"I rather take to it, you know," Philip lied obligingly.

Or perhaps it was not a lie, Lydia thought. Perhaps he couldn't wait for that delicious moment when Aurora, heart-breakingly lovely in her wedding dress and veil, came to stand demurely beside him at the altar.

After all, she didn't know him at all. He might be intensely conventional and sentimental.

"You've known Aurora for some time, I expect," Geoffrey went on.

"Four weeks tomorrow, to be exact." Philip's voice was blithe. "You see, I don't want to waste any time."

Sometimes, Lydia thought, her father possessed utterly no humor, for now he said, with some anxiety, "Goodness me, does your impulsiveness ever lead you astray?"

"Why, I think that's terribly romantic," Millicent broke in. "Just four weeks. But of course, if I were a man, I'd only have to set eyes on Aurora for one moment and I'd be lost."

"Exactly," murmured Philip. Lydia noticed that he had avoided answering Geoffrey's question. Anyway, could there be an answer, at present? He wouldn't know until he married Aurora, whether he regretted it. There must be so much he still had to find out about her—why, for instance, no other man had swooped her up. Or why she had resisted other men. . . .

There was no time to pursue the matter further, for just then Aurora came in. She had on a filmy, grey chiffon dress, and she moved very quickly and lightly. Her cheeks were still flushed, her eyes extraordinarily brilliant. She said, in a breathless husky voice, "Am I late? I'm terribly sorry," and crossed over to take Philip's hand and press it momentarily between hers. If it hadn't been for the traces of tears Lydia had seen earlier in the afternoon, and the rather desperate resort to the gin bottle, she would have given a very convincing act of someone deeply in love.

It may not have been an act, of course, Lydia told herself fairly. It may have been genuine. But one thing at least was certain, and that was that she had had too much to drink. She was obviously almost at the stage where she might begin to sing, or burst out with some wild indiscretion.

There was no time to wonder why she was doing this, drinking too much, and getting ready to singe herself in a flame or prick her finger disastrously, as had the princess in the fairy tale. Lydia, with some desperation herself, said, "Let's go in and eat. I'm absolutely starving," and Millicent came to her support with her ingenuous, "So am I. And Philip is much too thin. We must feed him up. Have you learnt to cook, Aurora, in that flat you had?"

"Oh, I'm an absolutely wonderful cook," Aurora said in her warm, breathy voice. "You ought to taste my *coq au vin,* and my *boeuf à la mode.*"

"Oh, dear, and we've just got lamb cutlets tonight. But I'm sure Philip will appreciate truly English food after what he must have been eating in the jungle. Tell me—you sit there, Philip, beside Aurora—is crocodile edible? Oh, I don't mean the ancient monsters, like old fallen logs, but nice young things. Or do they taste horribly of mud?"

Aurora began to giggle. She looked enchanting, with her flushed cheeks, her pale slender arms emerging from the filmy dress, her slightly mussed dark hair. At least a drink too many suited her, for it took away the taut, pinched look, the strange air of apprehension. If that was the way she usually looked when she was with Philip it was no wonder he had become infatuated. Aurora, the princess, rosy from sleep and too much nectar.

Philip, with a sideways glance at Aurora, began to talk of food he had eaten in different countries. Molly, the maid, brought in the lamb cutlets and the green peas, and the meal proceeded. It seemed to Lydia to go on for hours, for Aurora's irresponsible gaiety wore off with alarming quickness and it was impossible not to see that she merely picked at her food. Once, as Philip talked, she lifted her huge eyes and they seemed to be swimming with tears. But perhaps that was the effect of the candlelight. At any rate, she had grown quite silent. When they left the table and went in to sit round the fire, she sat in a corner, a little removed from everyone, like a dark-haired ghost.

When Millicent suddenly said, "Darling! Have you gone to sleep?" she started as if something much more alarming had roused her, and said quickly, "No, but almost. I'm going to get a little fresh air, when Philip goes, and then bed."

"Nothing like hastening my departure," said Philip good-humoredly. "Come along, then. You can walk me across the village green."

"Darling, put a wrap on!" Millicent cried. "It will be chilly out. And don't be late. You look dreadfully tired."

"Ten minutes, no more. Unless Philip buys me a nightcap."

"I'm not buying you any nightcaps," said Philip firmly. "You're coming to the green, and then turning round and going straight back."

Millicent wanted to wait for Aurora to come back.

"There's so much to discuss," she declared. "We haven't even talked about who we're inviting to the wedding, and it's only three weeks away! It isn't fair not to give people time. We must start making lists." She smiled happily. "I adore making lists. So satisfying. That crocodile man is rather sweet, isn't he? Though not quite—"

"Not quite what?" Lydia said sharply.

"Now, darling. I wasn't criticizing him. I was merely going to say not quite the type one would have imagined Aurora choosing."

"Why not?"

"I can't really say. It's difficult to put into words. I feel somehow they won't understand each other. Oh, well, perhaps I'm wrong. Or perhaps they like it that way."

"They must," Geoffrey said dryly. "They've been gone more than half an hour. It would take Aurora exactly five minutes to cross the green if she were not lingering. So I suggest we go to bed."

"To bed?"

"Your daughter's twenty-five, and Philip can't be much under thirty. Hardly the age one waits up for one's children."

"Oh, dear!" Millicent sighed. "And all those lovely lists I long to get at. Come along, then, Lydia. It's time you were in bed, at least."

"Even I'm an adult," Lydia reminded her good-humoredly.

But she went upstairs and firmly drew her curtains so that she would not be tempted to look across the green. Anyway, there was a slight ground mist, and Aurora, in her filmy grey dress, would melt into it, like a wraith. Philip would look as if he walked alone.

None of her business, she told herself, but as she undressed she looked at herself in the mirror with deliberately assessing eyes. If she were a man, she thought, what would she (or he, one should say) think of that form—long slender limbs, small breasts, slight hollows at the base of her neck, a face that looked elongated and anxious, eyes (what colour?), glass-green, perhaps, hair uncompromisingly straight, but thick and smooth and not too bad when well-shampooed and well-brushed. An eager, honest, quite ordinary face, she thought dispassionately, though the slight frosting of age that overlaid the mirror gave her a curious, waiting look, as if at the given moment she would burst into life.

"You'll never float down the stairs in grey chiffon," she told the waiting face, floating in its frosty haze, "but you might try dramatic colors, flame, emerald green. After all, the world doesn't hold only pawing M'sieu Bertrands. . . ."

Nor did it hold only strange, rather intriguing men with indolent watchful eyes, back from jungles and mountains. It was full of nice stockbrokers and solicitors and advertising executives and interior decorators and poets and peasants. One of them one day would find that of all things, he madly adored glass-green eyes and a long neck with delicate hollows at the base.

Climbing into bed, Lydia switched off the light, and lay smiling vaguely in the dark as she planned her dream home, and the people who would occupy it. She had almost forgotten the mists drifting over the village green, and Aurora in her smoky grey dress.

So it was not until the morning that they realized Aurora had not come home. At breakfast Millicent said benignly, "Let her sleep. After a good rest she'll be much more fit to help me with those lists. I couldn't get any sense out of her yesterday. She just said, 'Let us get married. That's all I want to do,' as if we were trying to stop her! But today will be different. I'll just tiptoe upstairs after ten o'clock to see if she's ready for some coffee, and then we can get down to business. Where are you going, Geoffrey?"

"Into the garden."

"Don't go too far. We'll probably need your help. And yours, too, Lydia. This is all too exciting for words."

But it was exciting in a completely different way when Millicent found Aurora's empty and unslept-in bed.

She gave a little shriek and then called Lydia in a hushed and conspiratorial voice, "Darling! Come here! S-sh! We must keep this from Molly. But look. Aurora hasn't come home."

Lydia stood at the door of Aurora's bedroom and looked at the bed, aggressively orderly amongst the disorderliness of open suitcases and strewn belongings. The wedding dress still lay over the chair, and the other things Aurora had been showing Lydia yesterday were spread about, the filmy négligée, the new shoes, the pile of underclothing, pristine fresh and dainty, the flame-colored cocktail dress.

The room was full of Aurora's dark, restless presence, but she was not there. The nightdress Molly had spread out for her remained untouched, the pillow smooth.

For a moment Lydia could say nothing. She had a clear memory of Philip fussing about hot water and a comfortable bed in his room at the Wheatsheaf, and although she had not seen the room they had given him she could now see, very clearly indeed, Aurora's dark hair spread on the pillow and her long pale arms lying outside the sheets.

But surely—in a small village—with their wedding so imminent—she thought incoherently. . . . Of course, they may not have stayed at the Wheatsheaf, they may have had enough sense to go farther away. Except that Aurora had no luggage and Philip had no car, and it had been too late last night to catch a bus.

"What do you think?" breathed Millicent, her eyes aghast.

"We can't ring Philip up. That's one thing we can't do."

"No, of course not. I understand. Most awkward. But really! He did say he wasn't even going to buy her a nightcap, didn't he? And I wanted to wait up, but your father wouldn't let me."

"What would you have done? Gone and dragged her out of his bed?"

"Lydia, darling! Oh, dear, this is all so premature! What are we to do?"

"Wait for them to turn up, if they have the face to. Aurora will want to collect her trousseau, anyway."

Millicent pressed her hands to her cheeks. "That beautiful virginal wedding dress! Lydia, darling, how many other things don't we know about Aurora?"

"I don't know," said Lydia slowly. "I don't know."

June Birch had intimated that she had had men friends, that it would not be strange for one of them to have a key to her flat. But Philip was to be her husband in so short a time. Surely, he at least would have behaved with discretion!

"We'll have to behave as if nothing has happened," Millicent said firmly. "And Lydia, dear, I think not even to tell your father. He's always been a little stern with Aurora, and I do so want her to have a beautiful wedding. Shall we just say nothing until they come? After all, they might have a perfectly good explanation."

This, however, was not so. For Philip arrived alone. He wandered in about eleven, gave Lydia his sudden smile, and said, "Where's Aurora? Isn't she up yet?"

Lydia gasped. "Don't tell me—"

"Don't tell you what?"

"That Aurora isn't with you."

"Why on earth should she be with me? Whether I like it or not, I have an austere single room at the Wheatsheaf."

"But Philip!" Lydia looked round swiftly. Geoffrey was still in the garden and Millicent, to work off her agitation, clattering dishes in the kitchen. "She isn't home! We don't think she's been home all night. We thought she was with you."

"What?"

"What else could we think? Her bed hasn't been slept in. Her things are scattered about her room just as she left them last night. Nothing's been taken, as far as I can see."

Philip gripped Lydia's arm. "But this is nonsense. She walked across the green with me as far as the pond, and then I made her go back. I watched her until I couldn't see her for mist. Her dress melted into it. But she'd only have another hundred yards to go then. You mean she hasn't come home at all?"

"She isn't here, I told you."

"I say—what is all this? She couldn't have been kidnapped in that last hundred yards. Anyway, she would have screamed. And there'd have to have been a car which we'd all have heard."

"Yes."

"Don't just say yes like that. Say what you think."

He looked at her accusingly, his eyes brilliant and direct. It was clear that he expected her to have more knowledge of Aurora's expected behavior than he had himself.

"What can I think?" she said helplessly. "If she really hasn't been with you she's gone somewhere else, hasn't she? I should think of her own free will."

"Of her own free will? What makes you say that, Lydia?"

"You must know yourself she isn't a person one can give orders to. I don't think I've ever known her to do something she didn't want to. So she isn't likely to have gone somewhere against her will."

"Unless she was overpowered."

"Between here and the village pond! And why? She hadn't even a handbag."

"She had other assets," Philip observed dryly. "Well, what are we to do? Sit and wait for her to turn up? Or ring the village constable?"

Millicent came in then and collapsed trembling into a chair when she heard the news. Geoffrey had to be called, and the story told again.

He said angrily, "Another prank of that girl's! I told you years ago, Millicent, that she'd bring you nothing but trouble. Now look at this, all of us a laughing stock. Particularly Philip. You'd better be thankful, my boy, that this has happened before and not after your wedding."

"But, Geoffrey, darling! She might have been kidnapped. Philip says so."

"Has to save his face, hasn't he? Not very amusing being jilted on the eve of one's wedding."

Lydia glanced nervously at Philip to see how Geoffrey's cruel words affected him. Was he in anguish? His lean face had a closed look, his eyelids drooped. He was not going to parade his feelings.

He said in a contained voice, "I think we ought to look at this from every angle. You might be quite right, sir, in suggesting Aurora has changed her mind, but actually if that were so I think she would have told me. She wasn't walking in fear of me, or anything like that. Actually, it wouldn't have surprised me if she had thought twice about marrying me. She hasn't known me for long, after all. But let's look at the practical side of it. She was dressed in a thin dress and thin shoes, and some sort of wool stole. Nothing more. Not even a handbag. A girl dressed like that isn't going to catch a train or take a bus. Unless she's desperate, of course. And I didn't notice any extreme signs of desperation. Did anyone else?"

Lydia remembered the way Aurora had swallowed those gins, hastily, as if she were drowning some pain. She would have to tell Philip that later—if Aurora didn't return. But surely at any moment she would walk in, her head held arrogantly high.

"She had that long telephone conversation before dinner last night," Millicent remembered suddenly. "She shut herself in the morning room. Now I come to think of it, she never told us who she was talking to."

"She didn't have to do that," Geoffrey said fairly. "But you answered the telephone, didn't you? Who asked for her? A man or a woman?"

"A man. I thought it was Philip."

"And when she came down to dinner she looked awfully excited," Lydia said. "Didn't anyone else notice?"

"Well, of course she would, Lydia dear. A girl is in a constant state of excitement before her wedding."

"This may not have been because of her wedding," Lydia murmured, and then could not bring herself to look at Philip to see whether or not he winced.

"She's made a rendezvous with this fellow," Geoffrey said. "That's what she's done. She left Philip last night to go and meet him. Don't you agree, Philip?"

"Could be," Philip answered, and still his calm voice did not betray his feelings. "Perhaps she had some unfinished business to settle."

"Oh, Philip darling!" Millicent cried. "I must say that's a most charitable way of putting it. But if that is so," she looked wildly round the room, "why didn't she come back hours ago? Before midnight, in fact?"

Philip straightened his long body decisively.

"I suggest the first thing we do is put a call through to her flat. I'll do that now, if I may."

But presently he came back to say that he could get no answer. If by any chance Aurora were there she was not answering her telephone. But it didn't seem particularly likely that she was there.

"I know," Lydia exclaimed. "I'll ring June Birch. Aurora's nosy neighbor. If she's been there, or anyone else has, June will know. She has eyes made for looking through keyholes."

So there was another wait while that call was put through, and presently June's strident voice shattered Lydia's ear. "Hullo! Hullo. Who is that?"

"You won't remember me, June, but I'm Lydia Deering. Aurora's sister."

"Of course I remember you! You were here yesterday. What's up? How are the wedding bells?"

"June—" Now it wasn't so easy, because one didn't really want to admit to this busybody that Aurora was missing—"has Aurora called at her flat this morning? Early this morning or late last night?"

"Not that I know of. And I usually hear everyone who goes to her door. What are you getting at, duck? Has she run away?"

Lydia winced at the rich relish in the strident voice.

"Of course she hasn't. But she said she'd forgotten some things and would be calling at the flat some time."

"If I hear her I'll give her a message, if that's what you want." June's voice was puzzled and full of curiosity. "But she hasn't been here. There's only been one caller and that's that daft old woman. And she hasn't got a key, I know that!"

"Meaning?"

"Well, between you and me, one or two others had, as I think you gathered yesterday. What do you want me to tell her?"

"Aurora? Oh, just that—that the vicar's coming to dinner, so not to be late. It's about the wedding date, and the church decorations and so on. We were afraid Aurora might stay late in town." (And June Birch isn't believing a word of this mild village social life, and her eyes are popping out with curiosity.)

"Of course, duck. Ring me any time. I'll be here."

And she would, Lydia reflected, putting down the receiver. She would stay there with one ear waiting for the telephone and the other for suspicious footsteps going up to Aurora's flat. There wouldn't be a thing she would miss.

"No luck," she said, going back into the drawing-room. "Now that rather horrid June Birch is going to talk madly."

"Everyone's going to talk!" Millicent lamented.

"I had to make up some story about the vicar coming to dinner. June didn't believe a word of it. But she swore no one had been to Aurora's flat except someone she called that daft old woman. I haven't a clue who that would be."

"But we don't know who any of Aurora's friends are," Geoffrey pointed out. "That's going to make the whole thing extremely difficult if we have to employ a detective."

"A detective," gasped Millicent.

"I'm afraid so, dear. With Philip's approval, I think we'd better get in touch with the police station. Not that I'm suggesting anything desperate has happened, but girls frequently have been picked up by strangers in cars, and 'coshed' I think is the word. Because of that possibility I don't think we should let too much time go by. What do you say, Philip?"

"I agree, sir. Especially considering the way Aurora was dressed."

It was then that Lydia got her first distinct feeling of fear. She stood at the open doors of the drawing-room and looked across the garden to the village green, innocent in the late morning sunlight. In the distance was the grey tower of the church, the tilted gravestones in the churchyard, the pond, a faint green shine where the swans floated.

Nothing could be more peaceful. But last night a ground mist had been drifting across the green: the houses, the church, and the tilted gravestones had been lost in the swirling vapor. Just as Aurora, in her grey dress, has been lost. As if in a fairy story she had been turned into a swan, or spirited away to be the sleeping princess, undiscovered for years. . . .

"Lydia what are *you* thinking?"

Philip had come to stand beside her. His voice was low and quiet, but it held a note of intense anxiety. "It wasn't me in Aurora's flat yesterday, you know. Who was it?"

"I don't know. I haven't the slightest idea."

"And this man she worked for. Armand whoever he was. Can he tell us anything?"

"I don't know. Except—oh, yes, wait a minute. I'll be back."

She was back very shortly with the heavy gold pendant in her hand.

"This is what Aurora told me Armand gave her for a wedding present. She hasn't taken it either. And I should think it's quite valuable."

Philip turned the glinting thing over in his hand. His face was puckered up in the sunlight. He looked pale and tired. "Aurora didn't strike me as the kind of girl who would forget something valuable."

"No. It means, of course, that she's coming back," Lydia said breathlessly.

"Or else that she's been given no choice but to forget it." Philip dropped the ornament back into Lydia's hand. She winced a little, suddenly not liking the feel of it, wondering where it had come from. "What are you really thinking, Lydia?"

"I don't know. But why should one's employer give one this sort of present? One might expect a week's salary, or something for the house, but not something so personal. . . ." Her voice died away. She saw the thin, hard bleakness of his face.

"But Aurora isn't like that, really," she added swiftly.

"How do you know? You haven't seen her for a long time."

"No. I suppose I don't know."

"And neither do I. I fell in love with the way she looked."

Lydia touched his hand. "It will be all right, Philip. I know it will."

"Bless you, Lydia. Of course it will."

6

The sergeant at the nearest police station was extremely regretful, but he feared they would find the lady had merely changed her mind.

"Women are liable to do that," he said with vast sadness. "Begging your pardon, Miss," he added, with scrupulous politeness, to Lydia.

He admitted that at midnight, in an evening dress, and out in the foggy dew, was a strange time to change one's mind. But that was another symptom of women's unpredictability and unreliability. However, he would make some inquiries at bus stations and railway stations, and find out if a woman corresponding to Aurora's description had been seen. She would have been conspicuous enough. In his opinion the telephone call had been the clue. The young lady had obviously made an assignment. Not very fair play towards one's prospective bridegroom, but there you were.

"Don't take our philosophic friend personally," Philip said to Lydia as they left the police station.

Lydia shrugged.

"How do you know I wouldn't be like that, too?" (Wandering about lonely roads at night in a chiffon dress, and high-heeled shoes. . . . Lying dead in a ditch. . . .) Suddenly she shivered.

"Philip, you must know! Would Aurora have done this to you?"

"Why must I know?" His voice was flat, giving nothing away.

"Surely you knew whether she loved you or not."

"I hope she loved me."

"But you weren't sure?"

His disconcertingly bright eyes were turned on Lydia.

"No. Frankly I wasn't. I felt I could very well have got her on the rebound."

"That she was fretting for someone else?"

"She was distrait at times, yes."

"This man who telephoned last night?"

"But we don't know who that was, do we?"

"This hypothetical character, then. If you must know, Aurora was drinking too much yesterday."

Philip grimaced. "Reminds me I'm thirsty myself. Let's have a drink somewhere."

"But shouldn't we go home? If Aurora has arrived—"

"If Aurora has arrived back from her stroll last night she can wait a little while for us. Can't she?"

"Oh, poor Philip!" Lydia exclaimed involuntarily, and then, because his look of angry cynicism was for someone else, and because she cried too easily anyway, tears suddenly filled her eyes and ran over to her cheeks.

"It looks more like poor Lydia," he said. "I should be shedding tears, not you."

"It's only that—supposing something has happened to her. We shouldn't only guess that she's run off with another man. I thought she seemed frightened, or upset anyway, when I told her about someone being in her flat."

"Nothing's happened to her," Philip said curtly. "She knows how to take care of herself. You'll see. Come along and have this drink."

But at the bar in the Wheatsheaf Lydia had the greatest trouble in controlling more tears. If Philip, to Aurora, had been a substitute for someone else, so was she now to Philip. And it was no fun at all. Because she realized with dismay what was happening to her, had indeed been happening since the moment of meeting on Waterloo station yesterday. She was falling in love. And nothing could be less propitious than to fall in love with a man whose mind held only Aurora's lovely face.

Into the disrupted house, with Millicent alternately hysterical and in a state of collapse, Geoffrey filled with his silent anger, and Aurora's room inhabited mutely by her discarded trousseau, Aurora's letter came as an anti-climax.

It arrived the next morning after the phlegmatic sergeant had telephoned to report that he had found no trace of any young woman in evening dress, nor had any unidentified victim of assault been picked up. It justified all he had predicted and all that Philip had bitterly guessed.

The letter was addressed to Lydia and postmarked London.

Lydia darling,

I'm too ashamed to write to Philip or to Millicent. I am a complete heel. But Philip knows I was never in love with him. There was someone else, and I thought it wouldn't work, but it is going to, after all. He came for me last night, and I just went, like that, because I hadn't the courage to come back and tell you. I don't expect Millicent and Geoffrey to forgive me, but I hope Philip will. And if ever this happens to you, Lydia, dear, as it is all too likely to happen to any girl, you will understand.

Be a darling, please, and send me that gold pendant. It's the only thing I want because I couldn't use the clothes intended for my marriage to Philip. Send it care of the G.P.O. Edinburgh.

And don't criticize me. Wish me luck instead.

Blessings, Aurora

There was a remorseful postscript.

I do know I'm a heel, but make everyone understand.

Was one to show this curiously callous letter to Philip? What else was there to do, since Aurora hadn't had the decency to write to him herself?

The writing was scrawled and shaky, as if she had had more than one neat gin before taking up her pen. There was a blot in one place that could almost have been a spilt tear, if one didn't get the undertone of suppressed malice and triumph all through the letter.

Lydia had an impulse to tear it angrily into bits and show it to nobody.

But her impulse instead brought back another memory—that of the torn newspaper in Aurora's flat.

Of course, it must have contained some information about Aurora's mysterious lover, or perhaps about both of them. It would have been this lover, retrieving the paper in Aurora's flat that day, curious to see what she had kept or destroyed. Which made one think that the evidence in it could be incriminating.

Now one had to get it and see for oneself. It was fortunate that she had noted the date.

If Aurora's family could not be told whom she was marrying, it was fair that they should find out by other means.

Because of her anger over Aurora's behavior Lydia forgot to feel relieved that Aurora had not been found dead in a ditch. The letter still in her hand—the postman had come before Millicent, exhausted after a sleepless night, had come down—Lydia impulsively sat down to write a reply.

Dear Aurora,

If you want your pendant you must come and get it. Write and arrange a place for us to meet, but I will not be your go-between by post. I feel very ashamed of you, and will only understand, as you have asked me to, when you have justified your behavior. If, indeed, you can.

Lydia.

She was not accustomed to being vindictive. She shed tears, afterwards. But that was when she went through the ordeal of breaking the news to Millicent and Geoffrey.

After that she walked across to the Wheatsheaf to see Philip, posting her letter on the way.

"Millicent says thank goodness Aurora isn't murdered, and Geoffrey says she deserves to be," she told Philip bluntly. "What do you say?"

Philip had read the letter. He put his hand over Lydia's.

"You don't have to apologize for your sister. Is this her handwriting, by the way?"

"I think so," said Lydia, startled. "But don't you know it?"

"No. We communicated by telephone. Seems I didn't know anything about Aurora except her face." His voice was wry.

"But if it weren't her handwriting, whose would it be?"

"Whose indeed? And why?"

"Philip, I'm afraid you'll have to believe it," Lydia said gently.

His eyes flew open to give her one of his long, thoughtful stares.

"That wasn't wishful thinking for my own benefit. Believe it or not, it's Aurora's health I was thinking of. One wonders who matters most, this secret lover or the pendant. Lydia, this is where we go to London. I've exhausted the possibilities of the Wheatsheaf, anyway. And I've an exhibition of paintings to organize. One's life doesn't stop—or so the book tells one."

This wry emotion was all he was going to show. Lydia said impulsively, "All girls don't behave like that, Philip."

"Strangely enough, I don't think even Aurora behaves like that. Let's go back to London and look up this old newspaper you talked about, and call on June Birch. We might have dinner somewhere later. Bring some luggage with you. Don't travel light as Aurora did."

"Philip, what are you getting at?"

At last his long intelligent face lost its cynical look, and became purely perplexed.

"I don't really know. I just can't quite believe this is true. It's too slick, somehow. And there's that mercenary element of the pendant which, knowing Aurora even a little, doesn't seem in character. I take it you're not sending it to Edinburgh?"

"No."

"Good girl. Bring it with you. It's time, anyway, that we made the acquaintance of Aurora's ex-employer. The mysterious Armand. And his aunts."

The page from the *Daily Reporter* of the third of April told them exactly nothing. They had called at the newspaper offices on their way from Waterloo, and anticipating finding the answer to a puzzle had eagerly studied that issue. But there was nothing in it remotely relating to Aurora Hawkins, unless she were using another name. Even then there was no event which could correspond with any of her possible behavior.

Lydia sighed over a long argument in the House of Commons, and Philip dismissed an attempted murder in Glasgow, a divorce case in which none of the participants was under the age of forty, and a brief paragraph about the unidentified body of an elderly woman discovered at the foot of a cliff.

"That torn newspaper can't have meant anything," Lydia said disappointedly.

"Unless they'd got hold of the wrong page."

"But there's nothing in any of this paper that could be associated with Aurora. Certainly nothing about a motor accident, but I never believed what she said about that."

"Why would she be lying?"

"Because she didn't want to tell me what really was in the paper, I suppose."

"We've just discovered there's nothing," Philip pointed out.

"So we have. Not even anything about this Armand she worked for. Did you read all the marriage notices?"

"I did. Supposing she had used a false name she could have been May Smith or Joan Brown or Hepzibah what's-her-name."

Lydia tucked her hand in his arm. "Don't let it hurt you."

He gave his faint ironic smile. "Let's skip the obvious, shall we? We're getting nowhere here, so what shall we do? Come to my rooms and I'll paint you."

She moved away from him, turning the newspaper neatly in its file. "I'd have thought you'd have learnt your lesson about picking up stray women to paint."

He could not be deceived. She knew by his sidelong look that he was aware of the unspoken words beneath her rebuke.

"You're eminently paintable," he said, in answer to her private grief. "I can see you against a dark red curtain. Simple, dramatic."

The clerk behind the desk was watching them, listening inquisitively.

Lydia tilted her chin. "Then come on, Annigoni. We're wasting our time."

"Gauguin, the critics say. We must listen to the critics. But you haven't seen my dusky belles. You must come to my studio. All right, I won't press you just at the moment."

They had to keep their conversation on this light plane, otherwise they would both see Aurora sitting, poised and beautiful, in Philip's studio, waiting.

And Lydia, to her shame, knew that she couldn't bear Aurora to be there. Even though it was essential to discover her whereabouts.

"Are you coming to Aurora's flat with me?" she asked.

"You're going there?"

"Of course. To see if anything has happened since yesterday. I found the key among the things Aurora left at home. We can talk to June Birch, if no one else. And besides there's something else. I've decided to stay in the flat until Aurora returns."

"Whatever for?" She had his full, slightly alarmed attention.

"Because surely it's a sensible thing to do. I'll know when Aurora comes back, and if she doesn't—I mean, if there's really anything wrong—I can perhaps find out who her friends are, who rings her up or who writes her letters."

"And who has a key to her door," Philip said sharply.

"Well, that, too. But I shouldn't think that's a thing to worry about because I expect it's the man she says she's marrying. So they'll both come back. And don't fuss about it, Philip, please. It's something I'm doing because Aurora is my step-sister and it's my duty. I used to be very fond of her. I suppose I still am, though I don't know her any more. But if she is married to someone else, it's no longer any of your business what happens to her. So don't make objections about what I'm going to do. Because I simply won't listen."

Philip took her arm.

"Shall we talk about this outside? And I intend to make strenuous objections. Not because of Aurora. Because of you."

They had stepped out into the sunlight. The traffic roared past. A flower-seller was holding out a bunch of yellow roses.

"You, Lydia," Philip repeated.

"I did hear you the first time." She doubted if he heard her small voice over the sound of passing cars. Of course he was thinking of her. He had lost one of the sisters. It wouldn't be sense to lose another, whether he loved her or not. "But I still mean to stay there," she added. "And why not? I have to get a job and I must live somewhere. Aurora won't mind. I'll explain when she comes back."

Philip took the bunch of roses from the flower-seller and paid for them. "Then we might as well have some flowers to brighten up the place."

Everything appeared to be exactly the same in Aurora's flat, except for the letters lying in the hall. Actually, there was only one letter. The other three envelopes were unsealed and contained circulars or bills.

The letter was addressed to Miss A. Hawkins. The writing was sprawling and shaky. It could have been written by someone aged, or, as Philip suggested, someone writing with his left hand.

"Why?" Lydia asked bluntly.

"To disguise the writing, of course. If you're looking for a mystery, we might as well think one up."

"We'll soon see," said Lydia with decision. "I'm going to open this."

The sheet of paper inside the envelope with the same shaky writing, was a letter, old-fashioned and formal.

Dear Miss Hawkins,

I apologize for writing to you again, and do beg you to forgive these incursions into your valuable time. The weather has been so charming that I ventured forth to call on you yesterday. But alas, without the good fortune of finding you at home. However, the outing benefited me. I walked all the way both ways, and although this is trying on shoe leather, it did save bus fares which, as you know, are not exactly negligible. The purpose of this letter, though, is to tell you that my sister has not yet returned and I am really growing most anxious about her. I called again at her hotel, only to be told that she had not come back nor had they heard from her.

My landlady is *not* a patient woman, and is growing very disagreeable. She says she will allow me to stay one more week, but only on condition that my sister sends my remittance as usual.

If she has forgotten to send it and I cannot discover where she is I am in a very distressing position, as I am sure you will see, my dear Miss Hawkins. I only trouble you with this long complaining letter in the hope that your kindness will persuade Mr. Villette to arrange something for me until my sister returns. You remember that you promised to do what you could.

Already in writing this I feel happier. As indeed I should be, with the weather so charming, and today, do you know, there were *two* letters for me. Such a surprise.

But soon I fear I shall not be able to buy more postage stamps. And then the postman will neglect me.

Dear Miss Hawkins, please write if you or Mr. Villette have any news of my sister.

Your troubled friend,
Clara Wilberforce

"She's nuts," said Philip.

"She's in trouble," said Lydia. "Aurora must have been helping her."

"Or this Villette fellow."

"Yes. That must be Armand. The mysterious Armand."

"Of course. Clever girl. He's a solicitor. This crazy creature must be one of his clients. Some solicitors have flocks of elderly female clients."

"Poor Aurora! If she was being pursued even out of the office like this, no wonder she ran away."

"She ran away from me," Philip pointed out.

"Not away from you. To someone else. There's a difference."

"It's so fine it eludes me. Well, what are we to do about the crazy Miss Clara?"

"What *can* we do? She doesn't even put an address on this letter. She must be the woman June Birch said had called yesterday. I should say she's Mr. Villette's affair. Let's look up the telephone book and see if there's an Armand Villette a solicitor."

"There is!" Philip exclaimed a few minutes later. "Armand Villette, solicitor, Pyne Street, WC1. That's Bloomsbury, isn't it? That must be our man. The famous Armand. Do you think Clara Wilberforce is one of his aunts?"

"Hardly. She doesn't address him as dear nephew. Yet she appeals to him for help, as if he would know about her missing sister. Oh, Philip!" Lydia pressed her fingers to her lips.

"What?"

"There *was* something in that newspaper. The only thing that could be associated with this. Don't you remember? The—" she winced at saying the words, "the body of an unidentified woman."

"I don't see why we should suppose—" Philip began slowly. "No, that's a very long chance."

"But Aurora had kept the paper for some reason."

"That may have been accidental. Perhaps Miss Wilberforce had brought it to show her."

"But it wouldn't be accidental that someone else was interested in it."

Lydia met his eyes reluctantly. Apprehension was stirring in her again. What was this they were stumbling into? A runaway bride? Or something more, something worse? Something from which Aurora had to be saved?

The sudden ringing of the doorbell made them both start violently. Then they both laughed and Philip went to open the door.

It was, as might have been expected, June Birch.

"I heard voices," she said heartily. "I must say I didn't think you'd be back so soon. Are you married already and skipping the honeymoon? Sensible, I call that. Saving all those hotel bills. Oh, it's not Aurora with you!"

"No, it's me," Lydia apologized.

"The beautiful younger sister," Philip said with a flourish, and suddenly it seemed years ago to Lydia that she had used that expression on the telephone.

"Can I come in? Where's Aurora? Jilted you?"

Her inquisitive eyes searched Philip's face, and then popped visibly at his nod.

"I'm afraid so, Mrs. Birch."

"Call me June," she said loudly, to cover her embarrassment. "Well, I'll be— But she was rather a flier, you know. I wondered if you'd find that out."

"The gentleman who had a key to her flat?" Philip suggested, with his elaborately impersonal air.

"Who was he?" Lydia asked eagerly. "We wouldn't ask if it weren't important now to know."

"Afraid I can't tell you." June tossed her pale yellow curls. "Oh, not that I wouldn't have found out if I could have, but Aurora was pretty cagey, you know."

"You mean you never saw him?"

"He came at—shall we say—discreet hours? I only saw his back once, going up the stairs. He was tall, well dressed. Wore a homburg. City type. That's all I can tell you, really."

"Young?" Lydia asked.

"Youngish. Rather like him, as a matter of fact." She indicated Philip with a nod. "Back view, anyway."

Philip laughed briefly. "Some people fall for similar types. Aurora probably did. It would have been more comfortable to know she didn't like them in the plural. Do you think, by the way, that he was the man she worked for?"

"I couldn't say. She never mentioned names. But putting two and two together, I'd say he probably was."

"Then why the devil," said Philip with contained fury, "didn't she marry him long ago?"

"That's what I wondered, too. But you never know, do you? I expect he had a wife already. Do you mean to say she's run off with him now? Wife or not?"

"We don't know what she's done," Lydia said. "But there are several things we'd like to know. First, the old woman called Miss Wilberforce. You've seen her, haven't you? You said an old woman called yesterday?"

"That one! Old goofy! Yes, she called all right. Aurora wouldn't fret about missing her."

"Why?"

"I can't tell you. I told you your sister was pretty cagey. But I do know she didn't always open her door to that old woman. If you ask me, she was nervous of her."

"Nervous?"

"Well, something. How do I know? It might have been the gentleman who made her act all trembly."

"Had this old woman called often?" Philip asked.

"No. Only in the last week or so. She wanted something, I think. Don't ask me what. I say, this is a do, isn't it?"

Lydia looked with acute distaste at June's eager, protuberant eyes and air of expectant relish. It was going to be difficult to endure this snooping kind of neighbor, but it must be done, even with friendliness. For June might conceivably be useful.

At least she would be someone to whom to turn if, by any chance, it was not the owner of Aurora's door key who was now in the process of marrying her.

If the smart city type with the homburg was still coming up the stairs, softly and at discreet hours.

"It isn't amusing," she said. "But actually it suits me in a queer way, because I want a flat in London for a while and I'll stay here until Aurora comes back."

"You won't be scared?"

"Scared?" said Lydia haughtily.

"What do you think?" June appealed to Philip. "With these goings on of your fiancée's—excuse me, she isn't that any longer, is she?"

"I couldn't be more opposed to Lydia staying here," Philip said flatly.

"Oh, Philip! Don't be absurd!"

June's eyes went from one to the other of them in knowing amusement.

"I'll leave you to fight it out between you. I'll be glad to be of help if you stay, duck, but I sleep like a log after midnight. So it's no use your screaming then."

When she had gone Lydia looked round the living-room, comfortable, tasteful, tidy, except for a faint film of dust on the polished furniture. She noticed things now that she hadn't done on her first brief visit. For instance, the room was furnished in a way that one would hardly have felt was within the scope of a typist who had no private allowance. The painting over the fireplace looked like an original. The lamp on the low table was surely alabaster. Lydia suddenly remembered an elaborate jewel-box on Aurora's dressing-table. And without knowing why she was thinking of the heavy gold pendant that was packed in her own bag at the moment.

That, Aurora had said quite frankly, Armand had given to her. Armand Villette, the solicitor in Bloomsbury who also was supposed to be helping the daft Miss Wilberforce. Were the other valuables in the flat from him? And in that case was it he who had run off with Aurora?

There seemed to be little doubt about it.

"I'd better unpack," she said absently.

Philip looked more closely at the picture over the fireplace, the only one in the room.

"I'm sure it is, you know. A Monet."

"No!"

"Much more valuable than that pendant she's fretting about. And yet she lets people wander about with spare keys."

"Well, if those people, or I should say that person, was the donor of the picture," Lydia said lucidly, "it would be all right, wouldn't it?"

"Of course. Logical. But the whole thing doesn't make a great deal of sense, does it. Lydia, I don't want you to stay here."

"Why ever not?"

"You're too young to be alone."

"Oh, nonsense!" she added shrewdly, "I won't be alone the way

Aurora was. Anyway, there's a chain on the door. I promise to use it at nights."

"It isn't necessary for you to stay here."

"Probably not. But I want to. I want to know who rings up, or calls. I—I'm not happy about any of this, Philip."

"I'm not madly enthusiastic myself."

"I think Aurora might need our help." She looked round, trying to suppress a shiver. "I don't know why, but this place—it's so pleasant and ordinary, and yet— Why hadn't you noticed before that that was a Monet?" she demanded.

"I had. But Aurora said it was only a copy. She'd bought it in Paris."

"And you didn't prove it?"

"No. To tell the truth, I wasn't thinking much about it at the time."

Lydia shivered again. Aurora was there, smiling her secret smile, enticingly lovely. No, she wasn't, the room was frighteningly empty. And Lydia didn't really want to stay. She longed to go to some impersonal hotel bedroom. Or perhaps to curl up happily on a hard couch in Philip's studio.

All she said was, "I didn't know Aurora had ever been to Paris. But I don't really know anything about her, as I said." She went to draw the curtains, and turned to see him watching her. "Now do stop worrying about my being here. I have a chain on the door and June Birch with her sharp ears sticking out downstairs, and the telephone. You can ring six times a day if you want to. But you don't have to. Actually, you don't really have to bother any more about any of this. Aurora has let you down, you're quite free to go back to your tropical islands if you want to. I can sort out Miss Wilberforce and the expensive presents, and what Armand is going to have to say about it all when I ring in the morning."

She raised her eyes to him. He looked very tired. His face was pale and had a far-off look. He was watching her without seeing her. He was seeing Aurora's head against that scarlet cushion on the couch. . . . Or that was how it seemed to be until suddenly he caught her arm so tightly that it was an effort not to wince with pain.

"I'd kiss you, Lydia, but not in this place. You absurd child! Come and let's find somewhere to eat. There's nothing like food to bring one back to sanity."

7

Contrary to her expectations, Lydia went fairly contentedly to bed in
Aurora's bed. She was very tired. The anxiety and excitement of the
day had been completed by dinner in a small restaurant in Maida
Vale, with Philip being attentive and charming only because presently
the dreaded lonely hours would be on him. That had been the biggest
strain of all, because she had longed so much to think that Philip was
perfectly contented in her company, when she knew very well that it
was impossible for him to be so. But his indolent gaze told nothing.
And finally the dim room, the black-coated waiters, the pink-shaded
lights, and the white tablecloths swam in a sleepy fog.

She left Philip at the door of Aurora's flat, nodding amiably but
drowsily to all his injunctions. Chain on door, telephone by bed,
don't get any crazy ideas and try to carry them out without telling
me, don't go out looking for this old woman, ring me immediately if
you're worried.

Finally he left without kissing her.

She listened to his steps dying away down the stairs. She knew he
had not particularly wanted to kiss her.

She lay in Aurora's bed wondering where Aurora was sleeping.
Hazily she imagined her shut away somewhere, lying on a magnificent bed, dust and cobwebs growing round her. . . .

Then she slept herself, and woke only to hear Aurora coming very
slowly up the stone stairs and fumbling at her door to get in.

When she found the door was locked—and apparently she hadn't
got a key—she began to rattle at the letter-box.

After a moment of that (and by this time Lydia was fully awake
and sitting up in bed, breathing suffocatingly), whoever was at the
door began to move away.

Lydia listened to the slow, deliberate footsteps pacing to the head
of the stairs, pausing, beginning to descend a few steps, pausing
again, returning. . . .

Was this the mysterious person who had the key to Aurora's flat?
If it were, he was behaving as if he were drunk, unable to find the
keyhole, unable even to decide whether or not he had a key.

Chiefly because she didn't want to be found helplessly in bed in a
nylon nightdress she got up and put on a housecoat. She was trembling as she tried to do up the buttons. It seemed to be bitterly cold.

She listened to the fumbling at the letter-box again, and with a tremendous effort of will made herself go and switch on all the lights, so that the innocent bright interior of the flat sprang to life.

Now she was all right. She had dismissed the nightmare. She was in Aurora's flat, and there was someone at the door who either had lost his way, or his key. That was all.

The time, she noticed with cool detachment, was just after midnight. The discreet time June Birch had talked about? And June sleeping heavily now, beyond waking with a scream?

The letter-box rattled again. Lydia, clinging to her self-control, went into the hall. Then she nearly did scream. For she could see the stubby fingers, curiously foreshorted, waving through the slit of the box.

There was something pathetic, helpless, and quite sinister about them.

She could do nothing but press her own fingers to her mouth, stifling the scream that was not going to bring her any help, even from June Birch.

She had to force herself to open the door. She knew that. She braced herself, and took hold of the knob.

Then it was that the voice, speaking in a loud whisper, came through the pushed-open letter-box.

"Miss Hawkins! I can see the light. I know you're there. Please open the door and let me in."

Lydia flung open the door and the elderly woman almost tumbled inside. She steadied herself and gave a small, pleased laugh.

"Oh, there you are, dear. I'm so thankful to find you home. I hope I'm not *too* late, but it was unavoidable."

It was anti-climax, after all. Lydia's legs abruptly felt very shaky, and she wanted to sit down. Also, somehow, she wanted to laugh. For her visitor was strange, a little wild-haired, pathetically shabby, unapologetic about her extraordinary behavior, but at once curiously endearing.

"I'm not Miss Hawkins," she said. "I'm her sister. But do come in and tell me what's wrong."

The woman started back, staring at Lydia's unfamiliar face.

"Of course you're not Miss Hawkins. I can see now. How stupid of me. I didn't know she had a sister. She didn't tell me. How odd."

"Why should it be odd that she didn't tell you?"

The faded, round blue eyes, with child-like candor, looked up into her face. "Because our conversation was always about sisters, you see. Always. I've lost mine, too."

"I'm sorry!"

"Oh, she's not dead. I haven't lost her that way. She's just missing. She left her hotel without letting me know, and she hasn't come back, or written to me. And I'm really in the greatest possible distress."

Here, the old woman swayed a little, and Lydia sprang to help her into the living-room and settle her on the couch.

"You're exhausted, Miss Wilberforce. You are Miss Wilberforce, aren't you? I'm going to make you some tea."

The woman settled back among the cushions, like a plump, elderly, stray cat, thankfully finding a welcome. Her bag, a large shabby black one, bulging noticeably, she placed carefully beside her.

"How delightful tea would be. And at such an unconventional hour. I do apologize for that. But circumstances dictated. Yes, I am Clara Wilberforce. How did you know?"

"I guessed. Actually, I read your letter to Aurora because—" She hesitated, the strange coincidence of two missing sisters striking her. Had that fact any significance? "I thought I should," she added. "You said my sister had been helping you."

"With moral courage, yes. She was *so* sweet and kind. She assured me Blandina would return. But she hasn't, you know. There hasn't been a word from her. Not a word."

Lydia looked thoughtfully at the small, round, anxious face. A crab-apple face, rosy and wrinkled, ready to sparkle with humor and gaiety, but now only lugubrious and very tired. Why, she wondered suddenly, had Aurora refused sometimes to open the door to her, as June Birch had said? One could not conceivably be afraid of a little creature like this. Although, of course, if the visits were made at such an unconventional hour as this it was understandable that Aurora might have grown annoyed and impatient.

"I'll make the tea," she said. "Then we'll talk. You can tell me everything."

But when she came back to the living-room with a tray she smiled with amusement, and something approaching tenderness. For her strange guest had fallen asleep. Settled into her nest of cushions, her head tipped sideways, her shabby black coat tucked round her, her plump little hand still clutching the handle of the bulging handbag, she slept like a child.

Lydia put down the tray and went to the bedroom to get a rug. This she laid gently over the little round form. Then she replaced the chain on the door, switched out the lights, and went quietly back to bed. Now she could sleep.

She was aroused, in full daylight, by an insistent prodding on her shoulder. Miss Wilberforce beamed down at her.

"The postman, dear! Your mail. Nothing for me, I'm sad to say."

Lydia sat up, taking the letter (which looked like an advertising circular) from her.

"But how could there be anything for you, Miss Wilberforce? You don't live here."

"No, of course, I realize that. It's only that whenever I move away from home I make arrangements for my mail to be sent on. I'm seldom neglected, you know. My bag is full of letters." She patted the shabby bag, explaining its rotundity. "I'm the greatest correspondent," she said with pride.

"I hope you slept well, Miss Wilberforce."

"Very well, thank you. It was so kind of you to let me stay. Otherwise it would have been a doorway for me. It really would, you know. Or perhaps a churchyard. My landlady turned me out. We had words, to be quite truthful. I was about to explain that to you last night when I so rudely fell asleep. But now it's morning, and I can say thank you from my heart."

Lydia pondered, and got nowhere.

"Let's have coffee," she said helplessly. "Or do you prefer tea? And then you must tell me the whole story."

It was a strange story, and Lydia's heart was beating uncomfortably fast when Miss Wilberforce had finished. For shortly she had to telephone Armand Villette. And she was overcome with stupid, unreasonable apprehension.

The telephone rang, and it was Millicent to ask if Lydia had any news, and to recount, at great length, the embarrassment and anticlimax she and Geoffrey were suffering from. Making explanations to the vicar, putting Aurora's trousseau out of sight, worrying. There had been no more letters and they were still completely in the dark.

Lydia said that she and Philip were also still in the dark, but made no mention of her guest. That would be too complicated to start relating to Millicent by telephone. Anyway—it might be better that Millicent and her father remained in the dark.

With Philip it was another matter. As soon as he telephoned, sounding pleased to hear her voice, the heavy feeling of apprehension lightened. She looked to see that Miss Wilberforce was pottering usefully in the kitchen, washing dishes and tidying, and began the story.

"Her sister Blandina has always made her an allowance, you see. She has absolutely no other means. Blandina was apparently very wealthy and refused to let Miss Wilberforce apply for a pension. She can do that now, of course, but it will take time, and anyway, who can live and pay rent on an old-age pension?"

"Stick to the point," Philip reminded her.

"Well, the point is that one day Blandina's money didn't arrive (she always sent it in cash because that was simpler for Miss Wilberforce), and when Miss Wilberforce called at her hotel in Bayswater—she can tell us exactly where it is—they told her that her sister had left several days ago, taking her luggage and saying she didn't know when she would be back, if ever."

"With not a word to this old girl?"

"Not a word. Although she said that wasn't surprising because they had never got on. Miss Wilberforce had always muddled along, doing foolish things, and Blandina, who had married well, despised her and was ashamed of her. The allowance was merely a cash transaction because of family duty. But it was understood that Miss Wilberforce should never intrude on Blandina's social life, whatever that was."

"And so?" Philip said.

"When the allowance didn't turn up for two weeks Miss Wilberforce remembered the name of Blandina's solicitor and went there."

"Armand Villette, of course."

"That's right. But she never got to see Mr. Villette himself. She only saw Aurora. Actually, this was only last week, and apparently Mr. Villette was away or unavailable or something. Aurora had promised to talk to him about Miss Wilberforce and see what could be done. They had handled Blandina's affairs once, but not at present. Anyway, that's where things stood last week. Then Aurora went away without doing anything about her, and she still hadn't been able to see Mr. Villette, so she was getting desperate. If she hadn't found me here she was going to the police."

"Where is she now?"

"In the kitchen. The door's shut. She won't hear. She lives in a world of her own, anyway."

"Ga-ga?"

"In the nicest way. Her ghastly landlady said she had to be out of her room by eight o'clock last night, so she walked here, all the way from Battersea. She was exhausted and just fell asleep on the couch. I can't think how Aurora could have gone away without saying a word about her."

"How do you know she didn't? She probably told this Villette fellow and he hasn't bothered. Penniless old women can be quite a trouble to a solicitor, especially if he really doesn't act any longer for Blandina."

"Philip!"

"Yes?"

"Do you think that bit in the paper about the unidentified—" She had her hand cupped round her mouth to stop any possibility of Miss Wilberforce overhearing. Then she couldn't go on with what she was saying, and finished instead, "That *was* the paper that Aurora had torn up."

"H'mm."

"That's not saying yes or no. All right. I suppose neither of us can say that. But I'm going to ring Mr. Villette as soon as his office opens."

"And what are you going to say when you speak to him?"

"I'm going to ask to come and see him on a matter of importance. I'll tell him I'm Aurora's sister. He'll see me," she added confidently.

"And supposing," said Philip slowly, "he is at this moment in Edinburgh with Aurora?"

"Yes, I know, I'd thought of that. I'll insist on getting in touch with him there. His secretary will know how to. Philip, come over as soon as you can."

Miss Wilberforce professed herself enchanted with Philip. She smoothed her unruly grey hair coquettishly, and said significantly, "Ah! I mustn't play gooseberry. You two don't want an old woman around."

Lydia was crossly aware that she was blushing. Philip gave his slow, maddening smile and said, "We're delighted to have you, Miss Wilberforce. We wanted to meet you."

"Did you really? How nice of you. Your Lydia is so sweet. Not a word of reproach about the time I arrived last night. I was horrified when I found it was past midnight. It had taken me much longer than I had anticipated in coming across the park. And I hadn't lurked."

"I'm going to put through this telephone call," Lydia said to Philip. "Talk to Miss Wilberforce for a few minutes."

But although the reassuring sound of friendly conversation went on in the living-room, she still found her hand shaking as she dialed the number. Why should she be so ridiculously nervous of a man she had never met?

A woman's crisp voice answered.

Lydia controlled the tremor in her own voice. "Can I speak to Mr. Villette, please?"

"Who is calling?"

"Miss Deering. He won't know who I am, but you might tell him I'm Aurora Hawkins's step-sister."

"Hold the line, please."

Philip's head stuck round the door. Lydia held up her crossed fingers. "He's there!" she whispered. He disappeared again, and the efficient voice in her ear said, "I'm sorry, Miss Deering, but Mr. Villette has a client with him at present. Can you leave a message, or can he call you back?"

Stalling? Lydia wondered. But why? At least he was not in Edinburgh with Aurora, or wherever she was. Was she relieved about that? She didn't know. She decided to make quite sure of his reactions.

"Actually, I'd like to see him if I could. I want to talk to him about my sister who I'm afraid may be in trouble, and also I have a sister of an old client of his here. Miss Clara Wilberforce. Her sister is Mrs. Blandina Paxton. Would you tell him both matters are urgent."

She waited again for what seemed an endless time. Then the voice came back. "Mr. Villette could see you this afternoon, Miss Deering. At two-thirty. Would that be convenient?"

The office was on the second floor of a tall, narrow, time-blackened house near to Bloomsbury Square. Lydia climbed the linoleum-covered stairs, and was out of breath at the top, not because of her physical condition but because of the way her heart was beating.

Was she building too much round Armand Villette's significance in the Aurora mystery?

Had she imagined that Aurora was hiding something more than affection for him? Was he the man who had the key to Aurora's flat? And where did Clara Wilberforce come into all this? She would soon know.

The time was two-thirty, and in a few moments she would meet Armand face to face.

There was no need to be nervous because Philip was strolling about, just out of sight round the corner. He had wanted to come with her, but she had said flatly no. Armand was much more likely to be frank if she were alone. And what, she asked, could happen to her in a respectable solicitor's office in mid-afternoon?

If he were respectable, Philip had retorted, and had added that if Lydia were not down within half an hour he was coming up to announce himself.

This was reassuring and it made her happy. Not that she was anything more than merely nervous. But it was wryly comforting that Philip was acting as her protector.

There was no one in the small reception office. Lydia stood at the counter, and looked across at the desk on which stood a typewriter shrouded in its plastic cover.

The owner of the efficient secretarial voice must be still away at lunch, though it was strange that she should cover her typewriter for the space of an hour.

Someone, however, had heard her come in, for one of the inner doors opened and a man appeared.

He came across to her holding out his hand.

"Miss Deering, I believe. Aurora's sister. This is a pleasure. Do come into my office."

He was middle-aged, of medium height, rather stout, grey-haired, ruddy-cheeked. He had large, round, pale-blue eyes and wore horn-rimmed spectacles. He was the facsimile of a million other business men. Quite unmemorable.

As always when she suffered from anti-climax, Lydia's legs became unsteady. She walked carefully round the counter and crossed over to the door which the man held open.

"You're Mr. Villette?" she asked, not quite able to keep the incredulity out of her voice.

"Armand Villette. Yes. Do sit down, Miss Deering, and tell me what the trouble is. My secretary gave me an incoherent story. A mystery about Aurora and something about some old woman. Shall we start with Aurora who, I might say, I was extremely sorry to lose. I understood she was getting married."

Lydia nodded. Completely ordinary. No, not completely when one looked at him more closely. He had a way of tucking his chin into his neck and looking over the top of his glasses, showing only the whites of his eyes. It gave him a scheming, slightly macabre look that did not fit in with his relaxed appearance, his hands clasped, his body still.

"Aurora was getting married," she said. "As far as we know, she is married. But it didn't take place at home, as we had expected. Nor to the man she was engaged to."

"Good gracious!" exclaimed Mr. Villette, his eyes growing rounder than ever. "How extraordinary! Who did she marry then?"

Lydia smoothed her gloves. "We don't know. She seems to have eloped." After a moment she added, "Actually, we hoped you might be able to help."

"I? Willingly, my dear Miss Deering. But in what way? Do you want me to get this extraordinary marriage annulled? You are, perhaps, on the side of the jilted suitor?"

Lydia didn't like the flash of his eye or the faint slyness of his smile—as if he took furtive pleasure in this kind of contretemps.

"We merely want to know the truth," she said shortly.

"Yes, of course. One understands that. Indeed, I should like to know it myself. An elopement, eh? Aurora was very attractive. She was a decoration to the office as well as being extremely efficient. But as to her private life, I knew nothing. Nothing, Miss Deering." His voice was involuntarily wistful. He sighed a little. Suddenly he looked more than middle-aged, a portly, rather dull solicitor sitting in his office surrounded by files and leather-bound law books.

So this was Aurora's Armand! Lydia still couldn't quite believe it.

"You gave her a beautiful present," she murmured. "That gold pendant."

"Oh, that!" Did he hesitate a little? "But for the wrong wedding, one perceives."

No particular reaction there. Yet it had been a surprisingly tasteful and original present for such a man to choose.

"If you're asking my advice, Miss Deering, there's nothing you can do except wait for Aurora to come back. She's of age. She's obviously gone of her own free will. And she's not a girl to tolerate recriminations. So you'd better tell the rejected fiancé to find himself another girl."

"You can really tell me nothing, Mr. Villette?"

He leaned forward across the desk intimately. "What did you think I could tell you, Miss Deering?"

Lydia was confused. "I—I don't really know. But you'd seen more of Aurora than we had over the past few years. I'm only her stepsister, you know. And she'd quarrelled with my parents. We'd rather lost touch."

"A love of the dramatic, eh? She should have been on the stage. Well, now, what's this about an old woman. What has it to do with Aurora?"

"A Miss Clara Wilberforce," said Lydia, watching him.

"Yes? Who is she?"

"You don't know? You haven't heard her name before?"

"Should I have?" His thick eyebrows rose. "Are you cross-examining me, Miss Deering?"

"Of course not. I just thought Aurora would have told you about her. She's in very distressed circumstances because her sister, too, strangely enough, seems to have disappeared, though it isn't an elopement in this case. Apart from being very upset about that, it seems the sister made her a weekly allowance and now that's stopped."

"Yes," said Mr. Villette. "Go on."

"That's all. She's been turned out of her room for not paying the rent and she's come to me—at least, to Aurora's flat. She means to go to the police if we can do nothing for her."

Mr. Villette tapped his finger tips together.

"This is all very strange and interesting, Miss Deering, but what exactly has it to do with me? In what way can I assist?"

"Didn't Aurora say anything to you? She promised Miss Wilberforce she would."

"Not a word. What was she to say?"

"Why, that Miss Wilberforce came here to see you because you used to act for her sister. She thought you might know something about her whereabouts. You were busy at the time, but Aurora apparently promised to tell you about it."

"Then I'm afraid your beautiful sister's mind has been on her own private affairs. This would perhaps be a little clearer, Miss Deering, if you can tell me the mysterious disappearing sister's name."

"It's a strange name. Blandina. Mrs. Blandina Paxton."

Mr. Villette sprang up so abruptly that Lydia was startled.

"But that's extraordinary! That's my Aunt Blandina!"

"Your aunt!"

"Yes, indeed. I took her down to my place in the country a little while ago. She hadn't been well. I at last persuaded her to leave that wretched hotel where she'd lived for years. Why, goodness me, I never knew she had a sister. Certainly not one dependent on her."

Lydia struggled with her perplexity. "Excuse me, Mr. Villette, but if Blandina—I mean Mrs. Paxton—is your aunt, isn't Miss Wilberforce also your aunt?"

"Not at all. Aunt Blandina is an aunt by marriage. She married my Uncle Paxton who died many years ago. My mother and she became close friends. We've always been very fond of her. But we never knew she had a sister, if you can believe anything so remarkable!"

"I think Miss Clara has been rather a black sheep."

"She must have been! How amusing! Well, well. One lives and learns about human nature. And I've acted for Aunt Blandina for years without her breathing a word. I must do something for this unfortunate creature. What's she like?"

"Very sweet, but a little frail in her wits."

"Then I know the very thing to do. She must come down to the country to be with Aunt Blandina."

He was almost benevolent. Had his eyes been still they would have been kind. But surely he was kind to instantly propose such a perfect solution to Miss Wilberforce's troubles.

"Why, that's a wonderful idea!"

"It's the obvious one. You must tell her. Or I'll come and see her. Is she staying with you?"

Lydia nodded. "She arrived late last night. She thought she was coming to Aurora. I can't understand—"

Mr. Villette interrupted soothingly. "Don't criticize your sister, my dear. Wait until you reach that happy day yourself."

Lydia winced inwardly at his ever so slightly false benevolence.

"If it *was* a happy day," she murmured.

"Yes, well, the minx deserves a good spanking, eh?" He laughed noisily, his face red and hearty, his large, pale-blue eyes rolling.

No, Aurora, so fastidious and exquisite, could not have thought twice about a man like this. He was just Armand-and-his-aunts, a dull little motley of elderly people.

And yet her voice, when she had spoken of him, had held a caress. . . . One had been so sure. . . .

"I'm afraid I have another appointment in a few minutes, Miss Deering. Now how would it be if I dropped in at your flat this evening and met Miss Wilberforce? Did you say her name was Clara— Aunt Clara, then. I am a man with many aunts, Miss Deering. They occupy almost all of my private life, I'm afraid, but what can one do? One can't leave them to die alone, or in destitution. Anyway, if Aunt Clara seems amenable, we'll take her down to Greenhill tomorrow or the next day. It's a large house. There's plenty of room. And I'm sure Aunt Blandina will be persuaded to forgive her sister for her black sheepmanship"—his noisy laugh burst out again—"and enjoy her company."

"Tonight?" said Lydia. "About eight?"

"That would be excellent. I shall look forward to it. Write down the address for me, will you. I never trust my memory nowadays. I'm so glad to have met you, Miss Deering. And I'll be more than interested when news of Aurora comes along. Can you—"

"Yes, I can see myself out."

"Good. Tonight at eight then. Tell Aunt Clara to put on her best bib and tucker for her long-lost nephew."

Strangely enough, the outer office was still empty as Lydia went out, the typewriter covered, the desk neat.

"My secretary has the afternoon off," called Armand Villette after her, as if he were uncannily divining her thoughts. "To go to a wedding. That might amuse you!"

His loud laughter followed her as she went down the stairs.

But when the man in the inner office was alone he quickly shut the door, then began to mop his forehead.

"You can come out now," he said, in an exhausted voice, and the door of the small washroom behind him slowly opened.

8

It was just after noon. The long, low car pulled up at a telephone box in the suburbs and a man got out. He went round the car and opened the opposite door for his companion.

"This will do. Make it snappy."

The girl crossed the pavement and pushed open the door of the telephone box. When the man made to follow her she tried to pull the door shut in front of him.

"There's only room for one."

"No, no plenty of room for two skinnies!" he said gaily. "Don't shut me out, darling. It's a cold wind."

"Cold! You're telling me!" she muttered. She asked for the number and waited to slide the coins into the slot.

She was conscious all the time of the man pressed against her back, watching and listening. Her excitement at his nearness was not excitement any longer. Or it was a different kind of excitement, devastating and dangerous.

Then Millicent's high inquiring voice answered, and she began to speak. "Mummy?" How long was it since she had called Millicent Mummy—not since she was eighteen—so why had she done so now?

"Aurora! It's not Aurora!"

"Yes, it is. Look, Mummy, I have only a minute—"

"But where are you ringing from, darling? Not Edinburgh?"

"No, not Edinburgh now."

"But are you married, darling?"

"Of course." Had she hesitated? She didn't think so. "Mummy, I'm catching a train. I truly have only a minute. Is Lydia there? I want to speak to her."

"She's not here. She's in London. She's staying in your flat, hoping you'd come back. Darling, you are going back, aren't you?"

"Not just yet. Later, of course." She felt the man prodding her elbow. "Mummy, would you give Lydia a message for me. An important message. I haven't time to put another call through now. Would you tell her that if she won't post that pendant on—you know, the one that was a wedding present, I wrote about it—would she take it to Mr. Armand Villette's office for safe keeping. Then I can pick it up when I get back to London. It's rather valuable. I don't want it lying around. Have you got that?"

"Mr. Armand Villette. What's his address?"

"34 Pyne Street, wc1. He's a solicitor. I used to work there. I've written him a letter explaining. Are you sure that's clear?"

"I think so, dear. But where are you now?"

"In a telephone box, and the train's just due to leave." The iron-hard hand was gripping her arm. "I have to fly."

"But, Aurora, who did you marry? You haven't told me—"

"Mummy, I'm not—" she began to say in a rush.

One hand went quick as a flash over her mouth. The other wrenched the receiver out of her grasp.

She looked up into his brilliant smile.

"Why did you have to do that? You beast! Oh, how I hate you!"

Tears of anger and pain filled her eyes. She moved sharply away from his intended caress. But the telephone box was narrow and she was jammed against the glass window.

"You don't really hate me, you know." His eyes were narrowed and tender, smiling, beguiling. "But we want to keep our secret a little longer, don't we? Don't we?"

She was hypnotized, as she had always been. And there seemed to be no other way anyway.

She nodded helplessly, and let him take her hand as they opened the door into the cold wind. The tears were still in her eyes.

9

"But I tell you, it's a splendid idea," Lydia insisted to Philip. "Miss Wilberforce going down to the country to be with her sister. We might have known there was a simple explanation to this silly mystery."

"You say this Villette fellow is middle-aged, not handsome."

"Far from handsome. He even looks aunt-ridden. He's the portly, unromantic middle-aged bachelor who conceals a heart of gold. How else could one explain him taking on another old woman so readily?"

"Sounds a little too ready."

"Philip! Why are you so suspicious?"

"So were you half an hour ago."

"I know, but I hadn't seen him then. I tell you, no one could be less of a Don Juan. Anyway, we don't even know he is a bachelor. He may have a wife."

"Darling, no one with all those aunts is likely to have a wife."

Lydia stopped involuntarily. They were walking on the edge of the park. The trees cast shadows like a French Impressionist painting, the grass was cucumber green.

"You called me darling," she said flatly.

"So I did. It suits you."

"Please don't again. It must be only a habit you have. You didn't ask whether I found out anything about Aurora. I didn't. Not a thing. Mr. Villette was—or seemed to be—as mystified as us. Although I don't think he thought it was an entirely unexpected thing for Aurora to do. He said she was very attractive. He asked me what I expected him to do, annul the marriage, or something?"

Philip took her arm. "You're talking too much, Lydia. Let's leave Aurora to her chosen husband, shall we? She's well able to look after herself, you know."

Lydia suddenly found his calmness infuriating and intolerable.

"How can you speak of her so objectively. You loved her, didn't you? Or if you didn't, why did you ask her to marry you?"

"She dazzled and bewitched me," Philip murmured. "I was going to have this lovely thing to paint forever. One shouldn't try to turn a dream into reality. Or should I say a ghost into a real woman?"

But his last words brought back that chilly vision of Aurora sleeping in a cobwebby bed.

Lydia began to talk vigorously. "How impractical you are! Would you really enjoy a ghost cooking for you? Ugh! Cobwebs and smoke. Let's hurry home and see what Miss Wilberforce is doing. She at least is someone real."

Miss Wilberforce had only one anxious query to make about her proposed visit to the country, "How far away was the nearest post office?"

"I'm a great letter-writer, as you know, I want access to letter-boxes and stamps. My friends would be so distressed if I stopped writing."

"Your friends?" Lydia queried, wondering where those particular people had been while Miss Wilberforce was in want.

"Look!" the old lady said proudly, tumbling the contents of her handbag on to the floor.

There lay scattered dozens of letters, surely the accumulation of months or years. But curiously enough almost all the envelopes, tattered and much handled, bore the same handwriting, the sprawling shaky hand of Miss Wilberforce herself.

"Well, isn't that splendid!" Lydia murmured.

"Yes, isn't it?" The old lady beamed with the greatest pleasure. "Do you know, I have discovered that if I post a letter early enough in the morning it reaches me the same day. Isn't that fascinating!"

"What do you write about?" Lydia asked, with interest.

"Oh, everything. The weather, the overseas news, the latest plays, the fashions. Oh, yes, my letters are very informative. Now do you suppose this place of my nephew is near to another village? It's the greatest fun to take a bus journey and post a letter away from home. It makes one feel one is on holiday."

"But you will be on holiday, Miss Wilberforce."

The old lady pouted a little. She didn't look particularly elated at the prospect. "With Blandina. Even as a child she was so bossy. I'm delighted she's safe, of course, but then one hardly expected anything really interesting to happen to Blandina. Well, we shall see. Perhaps I'll be able to sneak out and catch a bus now and then."

"I'll write to you myself," Lydia promised.

"Oh, my dear! Would you? But that would be tremendously exciting!"

Just before Armand Villette was due to arrive Millicent rang. Her voice was high and breathless.

"Lydia dear, I've been trying to get you. Were you out? Is everything all right? I've got the greatest news."

"What?" Lydia asked sharply.

"Aurora telephoned."

"Where from?"

"She didn't say. She hadn't time. She was catching a train. She didn't tell me anything, really, except that she wants you to take that pendant to Armand Villette's office. It's in—"

"I know all about Armand Villette," Lydia interrupted. "But is that all she told you? Just what to do with that wretched pendant?"

"Absolutely all. Isn't it maddening!"

"Well, I shouldn't worry any more about her, darling. She's just completely mercenary. I suppose this damn thing is valuable."

"Surely she can't be just thinking of its value! Unless it has a sentimental value."

"Not sentimental! I've seen Armand."

"Oh, dear! How very perplexing! Actually she did begin to say something else, but she was cut off. Never mind, Lydia dear, at least we know she's safe."

Lydia refrained from pointing out that there were varying degrees of safety. She didn't know why such a thought came in her head. If Aurora had rung Millicent, even in a tearing hurry, it must have been of her own free will. She was hardly a person to be forced into anything.

There was no time to ponder on this new development nor even to tell it to Philip (who surely must be hurt afresh that Aurora had not mentioned him), for the doorbell had rung and Armand Villette was there.

He stood, portly and exuding goodwill, on the doorstep. He had a large bunch of roses which he presented to Lydia with a small bow, saying they were in appreciation of her kindness to his Aunt Blandina's sister. Then he followed Lydia into the living-room and bowed again to Miss Wilberforce who had shrunk back into the couch in a way that seemed both nervous and hostile. Like a wary elderly cat, afraid of new surroundings, not used to being uprooted.

"So this is Aunt Clara," he said in his hearty voice. "I'm so pleased to meet you. Do forgive me for never having known of your existence!"

"That's not surprising," Miss Wilberforce said bluntly. "Blandina was always ashamed of me."

"And this is Philip Nash," Lydia said, indicating Philip who stood at the window. "Philip is—was—a friend of Aurora's."

"The jilted bridegroom," said Philip airily. "No doubt you guessed."

"Oh, dear, dear!" murmured Mr. Villette. "This rather brings that little contretemps home. I'm afraid I wasn't taking it very seriously when Miss Deering told me about it at the office. I mean, youth, impulsiveness, and so on."

"Aurora's twenty-five," Lydia said.

Philip's bland expression suggested that they were talking of someone he had known only casually, but she knew him better now. He did not indulge in a display of emotion.

"My poor dear fellow!" said Armand Villette unctuously.

"May the best man win." Philip was still airy. He held out cigarettes. "Do you smoke, Mr. Villette?"

"Thank you, no."

"Do sit down," Lydia said. "You'll want to talk to Miss Wilberforce."

Armand sat down heavily beside Miss Wilberforce, and the old lady, shrinking farther into the cushions, muttered, "Yes, she was always ashamed of me. I was a rather stupid and silly child, and of course her attitude made me much worse."

"Then we must make amends for all that now," Armand said soothingly. "Miss Deering has probably told you of my little plan. It will give me the greatest pleasure to have you at Greenhill, and I'm sure we can persuade Aunt Blandina to change her mind about you. Eh?"

Miss Wilberforce suddenly forgot her nervousness, or perhaps decided that this portly, kind man was not a person of whom to be afraid. She treated him to one of her round milky-blue stares.

"Why should you do this for me, a complete stranger?"

"Not a stranger, Aunt Clara! I won't have you calling me that." He was hearty, humorous. He almost wagged his plump forefinger. "I am a man who has had many aunts—seven, to be exact—and frankly I adored them all. Now I have only two left—Aunt Honoria, who lives in Brittany (she belongs to the French side of the family), and Aunt Blandina."

"What has happened to the others?" Miss Wilberforce inquired.

"Oh, passed away, I fear."

Miss Wilberforce's stare went milkier, and Armand said a little uncomfortably, "One grows old, you know. I'm fifty-one myself."

"I'm seventy-four," said Miss Wilberforce. "Blandina is seventy-six. Is she failing?"

"Naturally, a little. Her memory mostly."

"Then that's why she forgot my allowance."

"I'm afraid so. Otherwise she'd surely have told me when I decided to move her to Greenhill. She wasn't fit to stay on at that hotel alone. And if it comes to that, my dear Aunt Clara—"

"I'm perfectly fit!" Miss Wilberforce declared. "I am not yet to be one of your 'passed away' aunts."

"Not for a very long time," Armand assured her in tones of horror.

"Not living in the country in comfort," Lydia put in.

Armand flashed her what seemed to be, strangely enough, a look of gratitude. As if he had expected trouble and was glad of her cooperation.

Miss Wilberforce tossed her head peevishly. "I'm not at all sure that I want to go into the country with a complete stranger. I have no nephews, after all."

"But, Aunt Clara—"

"It's very late in the day, in my seventy-fifth year, to present yourself, nephew Armand!"

"But don't you understand, I didn't know about you. If I had known—"

"What would you have done? Buried me in your country house, away from post offices and other amenities."

Armand looked blank, and Lydia explained as tactfully as possible Miss Wilberforce's small eccentricity about writing and receiving letters.

"Oh, I see. That's simply arranged. The village post office is half a mile away, but we have our mail collected at the house. Nothing could be easier."

"But that's cheating!" Miss Wilberforce exclaimed indignantly. "One goes *out* to post a letter."

"My dear aunt—" Armand patted her hand. "That can be all arranged when you arrive. Now what do you say to tomorrow morning. I'll call for you in my car at eleven o'clock. It's only two hours' run. Very pleasant on a fine day."

Miss Wilberforce shook her head, suddenly stubborn.

"I find I don't care for the idea, after all. To stagnate in the country until I pass away. Blandina may not mind that idea, but I most definitely do."

"Aunt Clara—" Armand looked shocked, and was, for once, without words.

Lydia looked at Philip, who had been watching silently, then she sat beside the old lady and said, "Dear Miss Wilberforce, everyone has to die, but you're not going to for years. Mr. Villette is only trying to help you. He says you'll be very comfortable, and you will be with your own sister. After all, what can happen to you in London? Much as I'd like to, I can't keep you very long because this isn't even my own flat. It's Aurora's, and she won't be able to have you here when she comes back with a new husband." She noticed, out of the corner of her eye, Armand Villette's curious gaze going over the room and she knew, all at once, that he had never been in it before. His gaze stopped at the Monet over the mantelpiece, and became narrowed with speculation.

"I think you'll really have to go and give it a trial, you know," she went on. "If you hate it, perhaps you can persuade your sister to start your allowance again. But I really don't think you should go on living alone."

"Passed away, indeed!" snorted Miss Wilberforce.

"An unfortunate phrase," Armand murmured.

Miss Wilberforce suddenly gripped Lydia's hand. "I'll go if you'll come with me."

"Come with you!" She was aware, more than anything, of Armand's startled gaze. "He doesn't want me to come," she thought. "I wonder why?"

"Yes. Come and see if this woman is really my sister Blandina," Miss Wilberforce said eagerly. "I haven't seen her for so long, I may not even know her again."

"But Miss Deering has never seen her at all," Armand pointed out. "That really solves nothing, Aunt Clara."

Philip, watching, said nothing. Nor did his expression tell anything. He, Lydia thought, should have been playing Armand's part, if Armand really had something to conceal.

"Please come, Lydia dear," Miss Wilberforce pleaded. "I can't travel alone with a completely strange man. It would hardly be right."

"My *dear* Aunt Clara—"

Lydia, interrupting Armand, said clearly, as if she had abruptly changed her mind, "All right, I'll come. That will be all right, won't it, Mr. Villette? If it makes Miss Wilberforce happier. I can get her settled and catch a train back to London."

"Certainly, if you insist," Armand agreed stiffly. He could do nothing else. But his eyes were restless again. He looked at his hands, and then at Lydia. "It is quite unnecessary, you know. I don't want to take up your time, and I'm sure Aunt Clara wouldn't if she realized how unnecessary it was."

"Oh, I shall enjoy it," Lydia said blithely. "And I'd love to meet your Aunt Blandina. She seems, if you don't mind my saying so, something of a myth."

"No myth about her," Armand muttered, and suddenly Lydia knew something else—that his Aunt Blandina was not his favorite aunt. Then was he being a good nephew because of her money?

"I shall only stay if Lydia thinks it is all right," Miss Wilberforce declared, in her deep dramatic voice. "I trust her. Oh, don't think I'm slighting you, nephew Armand. But I don't know you, do I? I've never set eyes on you before."

When Armand had gone, making his deliberate pompous way

down the stairs, June Birch presented herself. She came in with her brash assurance and nodded to Philip.

"He's not the one, duck. He definitely wasn't her type."

"What do you mean?" Lydia demanded.

"I was just settling a small point," Philip explained coolly. "I asked June to keep an eye out for our expected visitor and see whether she recognized him."

"Oh, Armand hadn't been here before," Lydia said. "I knew that by the way he looked round this room. And that reminds me—never mind just now. Have a drink, June?"

"Love one, duck. I say, are you going to be stuck with—" She tilted her head significantly towards Miss Wilberforce, who had gone into one of her gentle blank stares.

"No, she's leaving tomorrow. We've got that sorted out. She's a connection by marriage with Armand Villette. You know, I can't think why Aurora didn't straighten that out. She can never have taken time to mention the poor old thing to Armand."

"Guess her own affairs were needing all her straightening powers," June said cynically. Philip handed her a drink and she added, "Here's the skin off your nose."

"I expect I ought to pack," observed Miss Wilberforce, who had no possessions at all except her bulging handbag, and the few toilet articles Lydia had given her. "I believe this *is* rather exciting after all. I haven't had a trip to the country for so long. The may will be out. And you will write to me, Lydia, dear."

"Miss Wilberforce adores getting letters," Lydia explained to June.

"Do you, duck. Bless you, then we'll all write to you." When June had gone and Miss Wilberforce had courteously excused herself to pack and to attend to "urgent correspondence" Philip said to Lydia, "And what were you reminded of a little while ago? I don't like half-finished sentences."

"Oh, that. I didn't particularly want June to hear. It's just that I can't understand Aurora's concern over that pendant which can't be a quarter as valuable as that picture, for instance. She goes away leaving her flat keys about almost indiscriminately, and yet fusses about a piece of jewelry."

"I expect the picture is well-insured and the pendant isn't. What about the pendant, anyway? Has something more come up?"

So then Lydia had to watch his face as she told him of Aurora's telephone call.

"Was that absolutely all she said?" he asked at last.

"Millicent says so. Aurora was catching a train and in a hurry."

"A convenient hurry?"

"Oh, I don't know, Philip."

His eyes narrowed. "She becomes a dream, the lovely Aurora. It's a pity she's still dependent on mundane things like trains. One imagines her spreading wings, like a moth. Or something less innocent and helpless, perhaps. A night-time bird. An owl. Or a bat."

Then his eyes flew open and shone with their sudden disconcerting intensity. "I apologize for that whimsicality. Even bats don't wear antique gold pendants. Are you going to deliver it to Armand Villette?"

"What do you think? If I had been going to I'd have given it to him tonight."

"Stubborn little sister, aren't you? Give it to me, will you?"

"Why?"

"Just a matter of curiosity. I'd like to take it to a jeweler and find out its value."

"What will that serve to explain?"

"Something, I should think. If it's worth five thousand pounds we know for certain Aurora is merely mercenary. But if it's worth only a fiver, which I strongly suspect is more its mark, we only have one other explanation. That it has deep sentimental value. Candidly, do you think it has?"

"As a present from the pompous Armand!" Lydia said incredulously.

"You see what I mean?"

Lydia shook her head slowly. "I'm sure of one thing only, and that's that he didn't want me to go down with him tomorrow."

"He isn't the only one with those sentiments."

"You!" Lydia exclaimed in surprise.

"Bless your kind heart, Lydia dear, but you've done enough for your stray old woman without getting involved with a shady solicitor."

"Do you think he's shady?"

"Didn't you decide yourself that he was a little too plausible? Everything fitting in, like a jigsaw puzzle. Everything, that is, except Aurora. And one couldn't even by the longest stretch of imagination, see them as lovers. Unless it were for gold pendants. . . ."

"Philip, don't be absurd! Aurora used to talk about Armand and his aunts. You said so yourself. None of this is really in the least unexpected. Anyway, what could he want with a penniless old creature like Miss Wilberforce? And he certainly wouldn't take me down tomorrow if there were no Blandina. Would he?"

Philip raised an eyebrow.

"All right. Have it your own way. Armand is a nice, plump, sentimental philanthropist, and Miss Wilberforce is being put into a comfortable pasture for her old age. After all, it's nothing to do with us, is it? We don't want to get as poky-nosed as June Birch. Damned boring. Now I'll go and look up train timetables."

"Why?" Lydia felt stupid and a step behind him all the time.

"To see what train you'll come back on tomorrow. And," he added sternly, "you be sure you're on it!"

10

Philip tapped at the receptionist's desk in the hotel. A middle-aged woman appeared from an office at the back.

"Good morning, sir. Can I help you?"

She looked overwhelmingly respectable. Indeed, the whole place did: drab, comfortable, genteel, infinitely depressing.

"I hope you can," he said. "I've just arrived in London from a long absence abroad and I'm looking for an elderly relative. This is the last address I have of hers. Could you possibly tell me anything about her? Mrs. Paxton. Mrs. Blandina Paxton."

"Oh, I am sorry, sir, you're just too late. She left here—let me see— a few weeks ago. I can give you the exact date if you like. She'd been here for years, too."

Philip made a suitable exclamation of disappointment.

"Now isn't that bad luck. Can you tell me where she went?"

"No, I can't, sir. I vaguely think it was Bournemouth. Her nephew took her away. At least, I guessed it was her nephew because he called her aunt. You'd know who I'd mean, perhaps."

Philip nodded.

"Then you can get in touch with him, can't you? We were sorry to lose Mrs. Paxton. She'd been here nearly twenty years, you know. The oldest inhabitant. But she was failing, poor old dear. Her memory was going. We were glad to see someone belonging to her turn up."

"You mean this nephew didn't usually visit her?"

"I can't really say, sir. I haven't been here long. And she always went out, you know, to tea or the cinema, the way old ladies do. He might have visited or she might have met him. But you can trace him, can't you?"

"Yes. Certainly."

"If it helps at all, he came in a Jaguar. Oh, and there was a girl. His wife, I expect."

The woman looked at him with a friendly smile, wondering if the conversation were completed.

"She moved all her things?" Philip asked.

"Mrs. Paxton? Oh, yes. Mr. Seagar's in her room now. But he won't last twenty years, I'm afraid. It's heart with him. Oh, by the way, there has been someone inquiring for Mrs. Paxton. A rather pathetic old creature who said she was her sister. She seemed upset not to find her. But Mrs. Paxton never mentioned a sister to anyone here. She never mentioned any relatives. We thought she was alone in the world until this nephew and his wife turned up."

"What did they look like?" Philip asked casually. "I just want to be sure which of my many cousins they would have been."

"Well, I didn't really see the girl. She stayed in the car. She had dark hair. The man wore dark glasses. He wasn't exactly good-looking, but he had such a way with him. He only had to smile. Even I noticed that!"

The woman colored slightly and remembered her dignity. "That's all I can tell you, sir."

"Thank you very much," said Philip. "You've been very kind."

From Bayswater Philip caught a bus to Bloomsbury. He found the office of Armand Villette without difficulty. He knew Armand was away for the day, dealing with yet another aunt. It was perfectly safe to go in without encountering him, and to get an impression of his office, and his secretary. To see the place where Aurora had worked, but to which she had never let him come. Perhaps to ask some pertinent questions. He was by no means satisfied about Armand Villette. The man was too plausible. And he had not yet seen him exhibit the charm that the receptionist at the Bayswater hotel talked about.

Yet what was there to put a finger on?

He obviously hadn't been Aurora's lover, and the old lady, Aunt Blandina, must be at his home in Sussex, otherwise he could not have risked Lydia going down.

If only one could find Aurora. . . .

But did he now want to find her? Wasn't he secretly relieved about the whole thing—except for her haunting beauty, which had first eluded him on canvas and now in reality.

Hadn't he begun to wake up from that bemused dream the moment he met Lydia on Waterloo station and thought, "Here's someone I can talk to."

If Lydia came back today and reported that all was well, that Blandina had welcomed her sister, and Miss Wilberforce had settled down happily, one would be tempted to dismiss the whole matter from one's mind, to plunge into work and forget this brief spring madness.

Yet here he was on his way to Armand Villette's office to take the opportunity of doing a little snooping. He wanted to talk with the secretary who probably had known Aurora. He hadn't met Aurora's friends. There hadn't been time. Wait until she had left work, she had said, and then, wait until they were married.

It seemed he wasn't to meet anyone today, either, for the door into Armand Villette's suite of offices was locked.

After he had tried the knob and knocked in vain, an elderly charwoman who had been cleaning the entrance hall called up the stairs, "There's no one there today. They're shut."

Philip came down the stairs. "I know Mr. Villette's away, but hasn't he a secretary?"

The woman came out of the shadowy part of the hall to look up at him. She gave a cackle of laughter. "She got the sack, that one!"

"Which one?"

"Why, the one that was here last week. Not the dark one who left to get married. She was all right. She'd been here a long time. No, the one that started last week. Didn't last long, did she?"

"Apparently not," Philip murmured.

"So that's why the office is locked up today. No one to look after it. I'd call again tomorrow, if I was you. Be back then, I should think."

The woman, fat and phlegmatic and not particularly interested, except in her brief maliciousness about the dismissed secretary, waddled off to her brooms and buckets.

Philip, too, had no alternative but to go. He had got nowhere, and did not know whether or not to place any significance in the secretary's dismissal. A week would have proved whether or not she was competent. It may genuinely have been a matter of incompetence.

Now he had only one matter left to attend to. He went into a jeweler's shop that showed a notice, "Secondhand jewelry bought", and produced the antique gold pendant.

The man behind the counter studied it closely through a magnifying glass. He looked up, with shrewd bargaining eyes.

"It's quite a nice piece, sir. Early Victorian, I would say. But there's no market for it. The diamonds aren't first quality and the ruby has a flaw. I couldn't offer more than twenty-five pounds for it."

"That's a genuine offer?"

"Certainly." The man was slightly offended. "You can take it somewhere else. You can have it valued a dozen times. But you'll find I'm not far out."

"Thank you," said Philip, pocketing the pendant, "I'll think about it."

He walked out of the shop into the cool spring sunlight. So it was sentiment and not greed that Aurora felt. Sentiment about Armand Villette, with his round, pale-blue eyes showing their whites above his spectacles?

Suddenly, for no apparent reason, he was wishing the day were over and Lydia back.

11

The house was, as Armand had said, about half a mile from the village. It was approached by a long drive bordered by thick shrubs, and came into view only when one virtually burst upon it at the last turn of the drive. It was a large, two-storey building of grey stone, well-kept, and attractive. Gardens, bright with tulips and apple blossom, stretched to both sides.

It was no run-down old women's home, but the estate of someone who enjoyed tasteful living. It looked as if Miss Wilberforce had fallen very firmly on her feet. This thought had apparently come to Miss Wilberforce, too, for she was smiling with pleasure and exclaiming,

"Isn't this grand! Do you really live here, nephew Armand? Does being a solicitor pay for all this?"

Armand gave his loose-lipped smile. His face had its usual genial look, but the whites of his eyes were showing over the top of his spectacles again, with that suggestion of hidden anxiety.

"I have a little money, you know, Aunt Clara. But Aunt Blandina will give you all my family history. Come along in. She's expecting you."

Lydia got out of the car and felt Miss Wilberforce grip her arm nervously.

"Oh dear! Is she annoyed with me for coming here? She'll feel I'm intruding, of course."

"Nonsense, Aunt Clara. Look at all these empty rooms." Armand
waved towards the row of windows. "I could keep a dozen guests
here very easily."

He led the way up the steps, through the white Queen Anne door,
into a spacious hall.

The carpets were soft, the curtains rich and tasteful, the few orna-
ments and pictures obviously of value. Even more in here than outside there was an air of unostentatious wealth. In spite of herself
Lydia was impressed. No one who lived like this could need to have
designs on an old woman.

Yet a niggling doubt remained in her mind. Armand Villette, genial, a little plump, just vaguely shambling, not particularly erudite,
as the desultory conversation during the two-hour journey had
proved, did not fit in here. It did not seem at all possible that the
mind responsible for the taste and graciousness of this house could
have been his.

The front door had been unlocked. No one came forward to meet
them. Armand, in his diffident way, suggested that before lunch Miss
Wilberforce should go upstairs and see her room and then have a few
words with her sister who was confined to her bed. He turned apologetically to Lydia and said, "Perhaps you wouldn't mind waiting
down here. Aunt Blandina is not at all well. The doctor says as few
visitors as possible. I think the meeting with her long-lost sister will
be all she can cope with just at present. There's a cloakroom through
this door. And then perhaps you would like to wait in the drawing-
room."

"But I'll get to see Aunt Blandina before I leave," Lydia told herself as she washed and renewed her makeup in the cloakroom. There
was no necessity to see the old woman, of course. Nothing could be
more highly respectable than this house, and in any case Miss Wilberforce, an acquaintance of forty-eight hours, should be no concern
of hers. Beyond the way a stray cat would be. Though actually she
felt rather strongly about all stray creatures, and it had become important to see that Miss Wilberforce, with her mild blue eyes and
crumpled cheeks, was happy.

Ten minutes later Armand came downstairs. He said, "Ah, now, a
little drink before luncheon. Aunt Clara will be down shortly. The
two old dears, bless them, are having a wonderful reunion. What will
you have, Miss Deering? Can I mix you a martini? I do them very
well." The whites of his eyes peered coyly over his glasses.

"Thank you," said Lydia politely. "What a lovely room this is."

"Yes, isn't it?" His voice was absent as he mixed drinks.

"And a lovely garden," said Lydia at the window, watching a tall young man mowing the lawn. "You're lucky to have a gardener."

"Eh? Oh, the gardener! That's Jules. Yes, I am lucky. He works hard."

What had he thought she had said? Lydia wondered. He had seemed startled.

"And he's young," she commented. "Usually gardeners nowadays are nursing their stiff joints."

"Jules is devoted to his work." Armand dismissed the gardener, and handing her a drink said, "Tell me if this is to your liking."

She sipped it with pleasure. She had needed it, and was at last beginning to relax. The journey was over. Miss Wilberforce had arrived. That strange episode, vaguely linked with the mystery of Aurora, was satisfactorily explained and ended. Aurora, also, would shortly turn up to explain her behavior. All was well. And Philip was meeting her train this evening. . . .

"Is it all right, Miss Deering?" came Armand's voice. He peered at her over his glasses, an anxious, slightly shambling middle-aged man, so kind as to become aunt-ridden, beautifully uncomplaining about a new claimant on his generosity. How could she have thought he was even vaguely sinister?

"It's very good indeed."

"Fine. There'll be time for another before Aunt Clara comes down. Well, this is an unexpectedly pleasant day." So Armand, too, was beginning to relax. But why had he needed to?

Lydia sipped her drink and watched the gardener moving slowly back and forth with the lawn-mower. He seemed to glance towards the windows occasionally as if in his turn he was watching her. But she couldn't be sure of that. The drink was making her fanciful.

"Did you ever bring Aurora down here?" she asked.

"Your sister? Yes. Actually she came the day I brought Aunt Blandina. History repeats itself, eh?"

He gave his thick-lipped smile, and his ingenuous glance, and Lydia said casually, "Was your Aunt Blandina the one Aurora mentioned? She said something about a car accident."

For a split second she saw his look of uncertainty, bafflement. Then he answered smoothly enough, "That was Aunt Honoria who was over for a visit just before Christmas. She lives in Brittany. Aurora was good enough to do things for her."

"You must miss Aurora," Lydia murmured.

"I certainly do, Miss Deering. I certainly do."

Lydia strolled round the room. "You have some wonderful pictures. Aurora has a Monet, you know."

"Only a copy, I'm afraid. She mentioned it when she bought it." But yesterday he had looked hard at that picture as if he had never seen it before, as if it being there on Aurora's wall had startled him. . . .

Lydia couldn't concentrate. The drink was making her extraordinarily limp and muddled. It must have been very strong. Deliberately strong? So she couldn't concentrate, wouldn't notice too much?

The tall gardener moved slowly back and forth in the sunlight, the colors in the garden blurred. . . .

"I'll just bring Aunt Clara down to luncheon," Armand said behind her. "Wait there."

Wait there! Why? Because he didn't want her to open any forbidden doors? The hall, the impersonal cloakroom, the lovely long drawing-room with its carefully chosen treasures, presently the dining-room. . . . That was all she was to be allowed to see.

But no! She was going to see Aunt Blandina. She had determined on that.

Armand came back, leading Miss Wilberforce. The old lady seemed to look bewildered and distressed. Or was that, too, her imperfect vision? Lydia shook her head impatiently, trying to clear it. Why had she weakly consented to drinking Armand's crafty martini when she could have had a simple sherry?

"I've been talking to Blandina," Miss Wilberforce was saying. "And Armand has given me a beautiful room. Such luxury. I don't know."

"What don't you know?" Armand asked genially. "Come this way. It's only a cold luncheon. I'm afraid Wednesday is cook's day off."

So no one was about. The table in the panelled dining-room was set with everything necessary—cold meats, salad, rolls, a piled dish of fruit.

"Was your sister as you remembered her?" Lydia asked.

"Not at all. At least, I can't be sure." Miss Wilberforce frowned, seeking an elusive memory. "It's so long, of course, and she's changed, just as she says I have. But she always had such a loud voice. She was so bossy. Now she's quite gentle. It's so strange. Somehow I don't know."

"People change," Lydia murmured from her fog.

"You must remember Aunt Blandina is ill," Armand said. "She's lost a great deal of her aggressiveness. Oh, yes, I too know how aggressive she used to be. But she's charmed to see you, Aunt Clara. I told you she would be."

"I was never good with strangers," Miss Wilberforce muttered.

"Don't be foolish, she isn't a stranger. She's your sister."

"After twenty years, she's a stranger," Miss Wilberforce insisted stubbornly. "Oh, yes, in spite of the allowance she used to send me, but that was impersonal, you understand, like receiving it from the Government, or something. Anyway, Lydia shall tell me what she thinks."

Armand, pouring wine into glasses, said, "Lydia has to catch a train after lunch, Aunt Clara. You know that. We can't take up her time indefinitely."

"Yes, of course, I know that. But not before she meets Blandina. You want to meet my sister, don't you, Lydia?"

"Indeed I do. And no wine, thank you, Mr. Villette. You must give me your special recipe for martinis. They would be a knock-out at a party."

He gave her his quick, secretive glance over the top of his spectacles.

"It wasn't a special recipe, Miss Deering. Merely the normal quantities. You probably need some food. And we must watch the time for your train."

In spite of everything being so pleasant, a luxurious house, a sunny garden, good food, he didn't want her to linger, he didn't want her to see anything except through a haze of alcohol. If she got to see Aunt Blandina, the old lady would be just another old lady in bed, cosseted, pampered, waiting to die.

It was Aunt Clara's stubbornness that brought about the meeting. She simply stated, after lunch, that now she was taking Lydia up to see Blandina, and when Armand looked fussily at his watch she said, with sudden authoritativeness, "Oh, put that away, Armand. If Lydia misses this train she catches the next. What are you worrying about? Come along, Lydia."

There was a grandfather clock in the passage outside Blandina's room. It had a deep, measured tick-tock that, to the sick old woman, must have seemed a deliberate counting away of her remaining days and hours.

But she was not a woman to be disturbed by time passing, Lydia saw at once. Although her nightgown showed her withered neck, and the scooped hollows of age at the base of her throat, and her grey hair straggled with exaggerated untidiness on the pillow, nothing could take away the vigorousness from her long nose and brilliant black eyes. One day her eyes would close and that arrogant aggressive light would go out of her face, but her long nose, poking heavenwards, would still defy mortality.

Yes. One could see the remnants of Aunt Blandina's bossy youth. And one felt there was a deliberate glossing over of that bossiness now. Miss Wilberforce had not noticed it because the voice Blandina used was deceptively gentle. But there it was, in the autocratic old face, angry at having to lie on a pillow, frantically jealous of and ready to hurl insults at those still able to walk about.

"Blandina, dear, this is Lydia. The nice girl I told you about. She has been so wonderfully kind to me."

"My dear, how good of you," came the weak, deceptively soft voice from the bed. "I've been so ill. Armand brought me here from that horrible hotel where I was all alone, and I just forgot all about poor Clara's money. I'm so ashamed."

"Now don't fret about that, Blandina," Miss Wilberforce said. "I've been all right, thanks to Lydia, and now to Armand. You always did very well for yourself, didn't you, Blandina? First a wealthy husband and then this amazingly kind nephew!"

"Yes. I've been fortunate. But you could have been, too, Clara, if you hadn't always been such a fool. We quarrelled, you know," she explained to Lydia, her sharp eyes seeming to burn into Lydia's face. "I'm not the forgiving kind, usually. I wasn't even very pleased when Armand told me Clara was coming. But when one knows one's days are numbered, well, then. . . ." The weak voice faltered.

Clara clutched at her bony hand. "Blandina, dear, you'll be all right. I'll be here now. I'll sit with you and read to you. I read quite well, you know. It's my training. Do you remember how when we were children you always wanted those soppy romances, and I wanted nothing but poetry?"

Blandina's eyes flickered open and shut.

"I haven't the faintest recollection of anything, Clara, except that you were always a perfectly detestable child, mooning, dramatizing yourself." She smiled faintly, but her eyes did not soften. They were set in their beady brilliance. "But that's all over long ago. Dear me, all those years in that dreary hotel in Bayswater. Tell me, is this child staying long?"

"No, she has to catch a train. Armand is fussing."

"Then we mustn't keep her, Clara." She held out a feeble hand. "Good-bye, my dear. Forgive my not getting up. But I'm very weak after this attack. Don't miss your train. And I hope my nephew has thanked you for your care of my sister."

"I don't want thanks," Lydia said stiffly. She already disliked the old woman in the bed. She found herself hoping, for Miss Wilberforce's sake, that she did not live long, that soon Miss Wilberforce would be the loved and cosseted surviving aunt.

But there it was. She couldn't interfere. And Miss Wilberforce's future was secured.

Afterwards she wasn't able to remember the details of the bedroom very well. The curtains had been drawn, she remembered, and the room dim. The light may have tired the old woman's eyes, but they had looked too bright and unquenchable and inquisitive for any light to be too strong for them. One was left only with the picture of her untidy grey hair on the pillow, her up-thrusting nose, and her busy, watchful eyes. Aunt Blandina had come to rest in a comfortable spot, and so, indeed, had the vague, charming, haphazard, forgetful Clara Wilberforce.

But one did wonder why a man would welcome two distinctly eccentric old women of uncertain memory to a home on which he had clearly lavished great care.

Blandina was wealthy, of course. But Clara was not. Blandina was ill, and Clara presumably in fairly good health. It looked, on the surface, as if Clara had the best of it all ways.

Lydia pushed the niggling doubts out of her mind and said good-bye.

"I'll write to you," she promised Miss Wilberforce. "And you be sure to write to me."

"Oh, I will," the old lady answered eagerly. "I shall be looking for your letters. Did you notice a post office in the village, by the way?"

"Yes, there is one," Armand put in. "But it's quite a walk. You only have to leave your letters in the hall, Aunt Clara, and they'll be posted."

"I enjoy a walk," murmured Miss Wilberforce, pouting a little. "It's much more fun. Even a little bus ride, now and then."

"We'll see," said Armand affably, patting her shoulder. "Jules is going to drive you to the station, Miss Deering, so I'll say good-bye. And thank you again for your help."

The Jaguar was drawn up outside the door. The tall gardener, dressed in pullover and corduroy trousers, stood waiting. He gave a quick glance at Lydia as she got into the car, then closed the door after her and slid into the driving seat.

The car moved off down the curving drive, and Lydia found herself studying the back of the driver's neck, reflecting that it was a good deal more attractive than Armand's. The neatly cut but luxuriant dark hair curled slightly at the ends, the ears were set flat, and the head held arrogantly. He may, she reflected, be a good gardener, but he was not a humble man, and as the thought passed through her head she caught his eyes in the driving mirror, strangely opaque blue eyes staring into her mirrored face unwaveringly.

For some strange reason she was embarrassed and disconcerted. It almost looked as if he were trying to tell her something. But he didn't speak, and it was left to her to open a stiff little conversation. "You're Mr. Villette's chauffeur as well as his gardener?"

"At times, madam."

She realized she had wanted to hear his voice, but the brief answer told her almost nothing. His tone was impersonal and correct. Had there been the slightest trace of a foreign accent?

"I expect he's a good employer. He's so kind to his elderly aunts."

"Yes, madam."

The grave, correct voice was completely at variance with that cold, blue, almost impertinent stare. Lydia was suddenly angry. She wasn't cross-examining him. She only wanted him to talk. But he obviously wasn't going to, and they were almost at the station, anyway.

In a few moments Jules had drawn the car up and leapt out. "You have seven minutes to wait for your train, madam."

"Thank you, Jules. I'll go on to the platform. Don't wait. Good-bye."

He stood very erect. His eyes were fixed on some spot beyond her head. He only looked at her direct in the mirror. He was not a person at all, but an image in a glass.

Even less than Miss Wilberforce and the frightening old woman in bed was he any concern of hers. She was glad to see the car move away.

If the train had not been ten minutes late she would not have got her crazy idea. But waiting restlessly on the sunny platform, smelling the country scents of trees in fresh leaf and fields of deep, thick grass, she had time to analyze her visit to Greenhill, and to reflect on how unsatisfactory it had been.

She had had Armand at her elbow for the entire time except for the brief interval in the cloakroom, and later when Miss Wilberforce took her up to see her sister. There had been no servant except the gardener in sight. In a house so well-cared-for there must be several servants. Certainly Armand had said it was the cook's day off, but the cook did not keep all those rooms swept and polished. Someone else surely could have waited on the table. It must have been that Armand wanted her to see as few people as possible. He had even tried to keep her from meeting his Aunt Blandina.

On the other hand he had not minded the gardener acting as chauffeur and taking her to the station. That could have been because he had other urgent business on hand, of course.

But if so, what would it be?

Really, she had achieved absolutely nothing, and she could not be in the least certain that it was right to leave Miss Wilberforce, an elderly and helpless woman, trusting and slightly feeble in her mind, in that completely strange house. Even with her own sister who was, after all, a sister who had showed hostility and a cold charity to her all her life.

Miss Wilberforce, who had landed, like a stray, elderly child, on her doorstep, was no concern of hers, she told herself firmly. Yet why had she not been allowed to see any more of the house? Why had no servants been visible? Why had Armand mixed that too strong drink? Why had the old lady in the bed stared at her like some hostile old bird?

A railway porter walked down the platform and, on an impulse, Lydia asked him the time of the next train.

"Seven-fifteen, miss."

"Thank you," said Lydia. She smiled and added, "That will suit me very well."

So she had three hours to walk back to Greenhill, to snoop about in the dusk, and then to come back to the station to catch the train. It would do very nicely indeed.

She had tea in the village. She found the post office and chatted to the postmistress, a garrulous spinster who promised to look out for Miss Wilberforce and see that her correspondence was attended to. She said it was nice that someone was living at Greenhill again as it was empty a good deal. She understood that Mr. Villette had a busy practice in London and had not much time to come down unless he had one of his aunts staying. Then, of course, he made the journey frequently. It was a pity the house hadn't a mistress, but in a way the elderly aunts provided that. The arrangement seemed to suit Mr. Villette very well.

"Does the gardener come from the village?" Lydia asked.

"Not that I know of, dear. Mr. Villette usually brings his staff with him when he comes, that is for a stay of any length. It would be some London person, I expect."

"Have many of Mr. Villette's aunts died down here?" Lydia asked casually.

"Died! Oh, no, dear! Whatever gave you that idea? I don't know of any that have died, and I've been here eleven years come Whitsun. Come to think of it, I don't think there's ever been a death at Greenhill. Not in Mr. Villette's time, anyway. Before that, of course, there was the previous owner who died and that's when Mr. Villette bought the property. Goodness, no, the old ladies stay, and then go back to their own homes, or that's what I've always thought."

"Unless they haven't homes of their own," Lydia pointed out. "Then they'd have to stay, wouldn't they? To die?"

"Well, I suppose so. But that's rather morbid, isn't it?"

By that time, with tea and the conversation with the postmistress over, it was early dusk. Lydia left the village and set off to walk briskly up the narrow country road to the house she had left some time before.

The big gates were still open. She started up the drive, keeping close to the edge of the shrubbery, ready to take cover, if necessary. This plan proved extremely prudent, for on the last curve there was suddenly the sound of a car, and Lydia had only time to throw herself into a rhododendron bush before the big Jaguar appeared. It nosed its way slowly down the narrow drive.

Because of its lighted interior Lydia was able to see quite clearly who was in it. Armand Villette at the wheel and Jules, the gardener, beside him. The two men were conversing earnestly. Armand's head was tilted a little towards Jules worriedly. Jules, Lydia noticed, was dressed as if for the city in a dark suit, and with his hair slicked down. He was talking to Armand as if he were relating something. The arrogance in the lift of his head which Lydia had noticed earlier was even more pronounced.

She found, when the car had disappeared, that she was trembling. It had come so suddenly and she had just escaped observation. But now luckily the way was clear. She could get as close as possible to the house without stumbling into Jules working in the garden, or Armand.

Although it was still not dark there were lights showing in the big house now, one in the drawing-room windows and two others upstairs in rooms situated a little distance from each other. One, Lydia imagined, was Miss Wilberforce's and the other Blandina's.

But no. She was wrong. For as, keeping close to the gloom of the bushes, she came nearer to the house she saw a woman's figure moving in the drawing-room. It was a tall figure, moving slowly but with authority. The cook, in that long dark-colored gown? One of the maids, previously unseen?

Lydia gave a suppressed gasp of surprise. It was Blandina. For as she stared the figure moved close to the window and looked out. There was no mistaking the long nose, the piercing black eyes. For a moment she stood quite still, her grey hair smoothly bound on the top of her head, her face brooding.

Then abruptly she lifted one of the strong bony hands that Lydia had last seen lying feebly on the coverlet of her bed and pulled the curtains across. The light was shut in. Blandina, no longer on her death bed, was enclosed with it.

Lydia was out in the dark.

12

Philip grabbed her arm as she came through the barrier.

"For heaven's sake, what happened? Why weren't you on the other train?"

"Philip, you haven't waited three hours!"

It was the first time she had seen him angry. It made his face brilliantly alive. Abruptly her tiredness and her vague anxiety and perplexity slipped away. Nothing at this moment existed but his hand gripping her arm painfully and his eyes, darkened with anger and strain, looking fiercely down at her.

This also was the first time that he had seemed to be fully alive since Aurora had left him. Her feeling of excited happiness made it difficult to be suitably apologetic for her impulsive and thoughtless behavior.

"I didn't *wait* three hours," he said impatiently. "I went away and came back. I did think you might have missed the earlier train, but I also imagined other things."

"What?" Lydia asked interestedly. "That Armand locked me up, or something? He wouldn't have dared to do that when he knew you would be waiting for me. Anyway, he didn't want to, I assure you. He wanted to get rid of me as quickly as possible."

"Why?"

"I don't know, except that Blandina isn't as ill as she pretended to be. She began to walk about the house as soon as Armand had gone. I'll tell you as we go. It is nice of you to meet me."

"You don't deserve it."

"I know. I'm growing as scatter-brained as Aurora."

"She isn't scatter-brained. She's quite the opposite. Deep and devious."

"If she's deep and devious," said Lydia slowly, "*and* mercenary, she'll come back for that Monet, as well as the gold pendant."

"She isn't that mercenary, because the pendant isn't particularly valuable."

"Oh! Did you find out?"

He nodded. "Of course there's the chance Aurora doesn't know its real value. But I'm more inclined to think it has some other significance. What, I don't know."

"Not sentimental?"

"With Armand Villette?" he said sceptically. "And besides, she hasn't got in touch with him, or he tells us so. Anyway, tell me what happened today."

When he had heard it all, Philip said that now their responsibility, if it had ever existed, had ended. Lydia had made the journey with Miss Wilberforce to see if Blandina really existed, and, as she had discovered, she did. Now Blandina had taken over the care of her sister, as was right, and whether she exaggerated her illness or not, it was no business of theirs.

"I suppose it isn't," Lydia agreed reluctantly. "Armand made that very plain. And after all, as you say, Miss Wilberforce is with her sister. But if she writes and says she isn't happy I am going to do something about it. I'll go back and demand to see her, whether you approve or not."

"Will you?" said Philip. "I believe you will, too. You seem to be as reckless as your sister." He glanced at her thoughtfully, then, as they had come into a comparatively dark street, he suddenly pulled her into his arms and kissed her.

It was a fierce kiss that seemed to be expressing his anger and hurt over Aurora more than desire for Lydia. After a startled and ecstatic moment Lydia pulled away.

"This is me," she reminded him a little resentfully.

"You don't have to tell me. The beautiful younger sister. I know very well."

Lydia shrugged disbelievingly. But his face was two inches from hers and she knew that all her life had been leading up to this moment. She hadn't known it would happen in a chilly spring twilight in a rather dingy street two blocks from Waterloo railway station, nor with a man who a very short time since had been about to marry her sister, and who was still closing his eyes and believing that it was

Aurora's lips he kissed. It should have been a long way from heaven, but actually heaven seemed very close indeed.

Philip lifted his head. "Are you hungry? Come back to my rooms. I'll light a fire and we'll have some wine. Let's get that taxi."

The cruising taxi stopped and Lydia climbed into its darkness. She found that she was trembling again. Dumb little fool! she apostrophized herself. You're only the younger sister. You happen to be the one who's here. But the trembling persisted, and when he put his arm round her shoulders she leaned against him, trying to grow calm, hoping he wouldn't notice her agitation.

How was it if one loved and the other didn't? Better, anyway, than the sorry affair of M'sieu Bertrand when there had been no love on either side. And the memory of the long, perplexing day was dying. There was only this cool darkness, and the solid form of the taxi-driver blocking the swinging lights in the streets from view, and the feel of Philip's hand over hers.

He had two rooms at the top of a tall house in Chelsea, one a bedroom and the other a large, rather bare studio. Lydia, in her haze of delight, found it wonderful and enchanting after the luxury of Greenhill. It occurred to her to wonder if Aurora had contrasted the two places, and decided that Philip's was the more likeable of the two.

But Aurora did not belong here tonight. Lydia walked about restlessly while Philip lit the fire. When he was in the tiny kitchen getting out a bottle of wine and glasses she looked at her face in the small circle of her compact mirror, and saw that her eyes were deeply green and shining. She combed her hair, smoothing it into glossiness. Would Philip care for this thin, pointed and eager face? Or would he close his eyes again and pretend that it was Aurora's, that the slim, taut body his remembering hands moved over was also Aurora's.

Or perhaps he would not touch her again. For he wouldn't know, unless her darkened eyes told him, that she longed to be touched.

"Is the fire burning?" he called.

"Yes. Beautifully."

"Why don't you sit down?"

"I don't want to."

"Then come out here and help me. Can you cook?"

Lydia stood in the minute kitchen watching him cut up a French loaf. "A little. Not *haute cuisine*."

"That's better than Aurora. Goodness knows what she lived on when she was alone. Cigarettes and China tea."

"Didn't you know her better than that?"

"No. Not in the simple ways. Such as how she brushed her hair or how she looked when she woke up in the mornings, or even how she felt when it was a fine sunny day."

"But you were going to find all those things out," Lydia murmured.

"Yes. Perhaps. Your eyes are green tonight."

"Are they?"

"Let's go by the fire. We can eat later."

"Philip, I'm not Aurora," she said again.

"No." His eyes were narrowed to a gleam. "But you're the girl who kept me waiting three hours. That's something, isn't it?"

"I won't be used like a drug to make you forget," she said angrily, waiting for him to come and kiss her.

"You're a drug all on your own, I assure you."

For a moment they faced each other.

"I mean it, Lydia," he said, in a roughened voice, but as at last he took her in his arms, at the precise moment when she almost believed in his urgency and sincerity, the telephone rang. The firelit silence was shattered. Lydia sprang away as if suddenly they were not alone.

"Damn!" Philip exclaimed, and picking up the receiver spoke curtly, "Hullo! Hullo!"

Then very slowly he said, "Aurora!" and stopped, as if he couldn't believe his ears.

Lydia wanted to weep. But her eyes were quite dry. This was not a pain to bring tears. It was too anguished for that.

Aurora! As if she had been watching them, waiting for the exact moment to break their dream. Or Lydia's dream, not Philip's. He had only been fooling himself, and almost successfully, too.

"Where are you? . . . Where do you want me to come? . . . I can't hear what you're saying. Yes! You're . . . What's that? . . . Oh! It's a bit late for that, isn't it . . . Yes, of course, I'm all right, if such a small matter interests you." His voice had become off-hand and haughty. "What? . . . Yes, my darling, of course I wish you well. You wouldn't like to tell me where you are or who you're with? . . . I'm not inquisitive, but your mother and sister— What's that? I can't hear! This is a bad line. Aurora! Are you there? Oh, for heaven's sake! We've been cut off."

He put the receiver down, and said without turning, "She's been cut off. There seemed to be a lot of interference. I haven't a clue where she was ringing from."

Lydia crushed down her private and very personal disappointment. "What did she say?"

"I couldn't hear her properly. First of all something about would I come and get her, things had gone wrong. And then she began to laugh and said she was fooling to see how I would react. Everything was splendid; but she was sorry she'd played such a dirty trick on me. She just wanted to tell me that. Then we were cut off."

"How did she sound?"

"Rather odd, actually. Almost as if she were a little drunk. Or half asleep."

Drunk! That would be possible, Lydia thought, remembering the secret bottle of gin. But the other state of strange drowsiness brought back that fantasy of Aurora on her forgotten bed, hidden behind the climbing nettles and cobwebs. The sleeping princess awaiting rescue. . . .

"Philip, are you sure it was her?"

Now he turned and she saw that his face was narrow and hard. "Quite sure."

"What can we do?"

"There is nothing to do, is there? She was only belatedly apologizing for her behavior."

"But those voices in the background."

"I told you it was a bad line. I think we'd got in on someone else's conversation. To tell the truth I'm not very interested in Aurora's tricks. Are you? Let's eat, shall we?"

He made a sudden apologetic movement, touching her hair briefly. His face was rueful. But Lydia knew that their moment had gone. Aurora was back. Her haunting beauty and the mystery that surrounded her was a far more devastating weapon than the momentary angry green fire in Lydia's eyes.

Over the meal which now neither of them wanted they waited for the telephone to ring again and for Aurora to finish her cut-off conversation. Philip had taken the gold pendant from his pocket and thrown it on the table. It lay between them, a barrier as effective as may have been the upthrusting nettles round Aurora's imaginary bed.

"You'd better ring Armand Villette in the morning and tell him we have this," he said. "Ask him if he's had any instructions from Aurora. He's sacked his new secretary, by the way."

"Do you think that's significant? She might have been a dead loss. New secretaries often are nowadays."

"Yes. And after Aurora, who at least was decorative if not efficient."

Lydia's honesty forced her to say what was worrying her. "Philip, do you think Aurora was perhaps really ringing for help?"

"To save her from the wrong man? I think she'll have to sort that out for herself." His voice was bitter and a little derisive, but even so Lydia sensed his uneasiness. Supposing Aurora were not just being provocative and changeable, crooking her finger with superb confidence when she wanted to win back a discarded lover, but really were in some strange kind of danger, and had not been allowed to say so.

"I think I'll go home," she said wearily. "It's been a long day."

"I'll take you."

"No, just get me a taxi, please."

"I'll take you," he repeated.

"But the telephone might ring."

"That can't be helped, can it? Put your coat on."

He didn't attempt to touch her now. He sounded tired and impatient, and she herself felt she no longer cared what happened. If he made love to her she would passively submit, if he didn't it didn't matter. Too much emotion and weariness had made everything neutral, dull, melancholy.

13

The girl lying in the big bed opened her heavy eyes to see who was rousing her.

"So you don't trust me, darling! You don't love me after all!"

She could see the brilliance of his eyes, his faintly smiling mouth, the lines and hollows of his adored face. Pleasure stirred in her tired body. Her mind was in a curious blurred state, and did not at once remember everything.

"I do love you," she insisted. "I do."

"Then why did you try to run back to your artist?"

"Oh! You were told!"

"Of course I was told. What did you expect?" His fingertips touched her forehead, her cheeks. She was so sleepy and warm, it was delicious.

"Did you think he could make you happier than I could?"

"No, not happier. No." Her mind struggled with the blurred images. Something awoke, a tension, a feeling of terror. "But safer," she added, and then shrank back from the scorn in his eyes. Although he still smiled.

"Who wants safety? Wouldn't you find it a little dull? Especially without me?"

She wanted him to scoop her up and hold her tightly in his arms. At the same time she shrank from his touch for some obscure reason she couldn't quite remember. The conflicting emotions left her deadly tired.

"Yes," she said obediently, "I expect I would. Very dull."

"Then be a good girl." He bent to kiss her lightly. "Don't do that again."

His voice was too light and affectionate to hold a threat. But the threat was there. She knew that now. Beneath everything, the pleasure, the love-making, the comfort in which she lived, there was the threat. Sometimes it didn't bother her too much, she thought the compensations were sufficient, but at other times the icy terror swept over her and she wanted to call to anybody, even a passing stranger, for help.

But that was only when she was alone and tense with wakefulness, and the least stir in the house, even the calling of owls in the garden, filled her with apprehension. When she was full of this heavy drowsiness, as at this moment, nothing mattered. She had forgotten what it was she was afraid of, and wanted only to sleep.

14

Lydia had to ring three times in the morning before she got a reply from Armand Villette's office. Then, in response to his familiar, deep, rather irritable voice, "Hullo? Who is it?" she said, "It's Lydia Deering, Mr. Villette. I wondered how your aunt was settling down. I got fond of her, you know. I'm really interested."

"Oh, she's fine." Subtly the brusque impatience of his voice changed to geniality. "She's written to you, I believe. She has this thing about letters, hasn't she? Wrote one to herself, too, and I had to post it in town. Well, it's a harmless eccentricity. I think you can decide she's in good hands now, Miss Deering. Her sister's delighted to have her down there. Bygones are bygones, and all that. So don't worry any more about it. I was about to ring you, as it happens. I've no secretary at the moment, and things are in rather a muddle."

"Why were you going to ring me?"

"Just to thank you for your very kind care of Aunt Clara, and to tell you you can put her out of your mind now. What are you going to do yourself, in the immediate future?"

"Oh, probably going back to Paris," Lydia, with some astonishment, heard herself saying. "I was working there when I had to come home for Aurora's wedding."

"That sounds most interesting. I wish you well." Did his voice sound relieved? She couldn't be sure. "By the way, I suppose you haven't heard from your sister again?"

She shut out of her mind that mocking, inopportune call to Philip last night, and said casually, "There was just her message about the pendant you gave her. I forgot to tell you yesterday. She asked me to return it to you for safe keeping. Did you know?"

"No. Certainly I didn't. In that case, perhaps you'd better drop it in to my office. I'll be here all day."

"Actually, I've decided to keep it myself until Aurora comes back for it herself," Lydia said. "I think she owes us—or Philip anyway—that, at least. She's been too casual altogether."

There was a very brief silence. "But if you're going to Paris, Miss Deering—"

"Oh, I'll arrange with my mother or Philip to keep it."

"You wish to take the responsibility?"

"Oh, heavens, yes. It isn't really valuable."

Afterwards she realized that the pendant had been Armand Villette's wedding gift to Aurora and that she had not been very flattering about it. There were two other things she realized—that Armand Villette was happy to think she was leaving London, and that he would very much have liked to get the pendant into his possession.

Well, she would thwart him in both of those objects.

But why did it matter?

Truthfully she wished she were going away. Less than a week ago she had rushed home so happily, and what had happened? Aurora had disappeared and left Philip haunted by her, and she, Lydia, in her turn, was fool enough to become haunted and obsessed by Philip.

It was not to be wondered at that she felt flat, tired and disillusioned. She began to think seriously of going back to Paris, not to the Bertrands but to some other, more pleasant, family. And if Philip decided he did care for her a little he could follow her.

Lydia sat in front of Aurora's mirror, her chin in her hands, gazing glumly at herself. The fleeting, green-eyed brilliance she had had last night had gone. Her eyes were no colour, her hair too straight, her cheeks vaguely hollowed. The glass that had so often held the exquisite oval of Aurora's face now held this white-cheeked urchin. Yet she had ambitiously hoped to impose this image, instead of Aurora's, in Philip's mind.

When the telephone rang she sprang up guiltily, afraid that the caller was Philip and that he would somehow be able to see as well as hear her melancholy.

It was Millicent, with her daily anxious inquiry as to whether there were any more news. Lydia listened gloomily to her high, expectant voice, and had to pull herself together to relate the news of Aurora's telephone call last evening.

Millicent listened in a silence punctuated by suppressed exclamations of disapproval.

Then she said, "I can't understand her, Lydia. She's being so tantalizing. Like a cat playing with a mouse." (Except that Philip was the mouse, as Aurora had yet to discover.)

"Do you think someone is making her do this?"

"Who?" Lydia asked sharply.

"Darling, how should I know? But it's so unlike Aurora. She may be flighty, but she isn't cruel."

"She wasn't very cruel last night. She was apologizing."

"That's all very well, but if she were truly sorry she would leave Philip alone. It must be just too galling for him. Don't you agree?"

"I expect so," Lydia said helplessly.

"Darling, what's the matter? You sound so glum. Why don't you come home? There's no point in staying in that horrid empty flat any longer."

"Yes, I know. I think I will come home."

She didn't want to stay even for another hour in the flat, yet something compelled her to. It couldn't have been the possibility of a telephone call from Philip, because she had nothing to say to him if he did ring. The flat was dreadfully empty and lonely. When June Birch asked her down to coffee she accepted almost eagerly.

But there wasn't much point to that either. June, with her molten-gold hair and inquisitive eyes, was a person one would normally want to avoid.

"You've been awfully quiet up there, duck. Nothing happening?"

"What's likely to happen now?"

"Oh, something will happen. We haven't heard the last of Aurora, not a dramatic person like that. She'll be back for her things, anyway, won't she? And to wind up her affairs." June laughed noisily. "That sounds a bit morbid, doesn't it? I mean to cancel the lease and so on."

"It's not Aurora you're expecting, is it?" Lydia said slowly. "It's the person with the key to her flat."

June nodded affably. "I don't mind telling you I'm breaking my neck to see that bird."

"He's the man she's married, of course."

"Maybe, but I don't believe a fly-by-night like that would get married. He'd be hard to catch. Well, of course, she might be just living with him, mightn't she? Take sugar in your coffee, duck? You're looking a bit peaky. What's wrong? Not sleeping?"

"I'm worried," Lydia confessed.

"Not falling for that good-looking artist, are you?"

"Of course I'm not!"

June looked at her shrewdly. "You're a nice kid, but no one forgets a person like Aurora overnight. Do they? Give him time." How much time, Lydia wondered, as she returned upstairs.

When the postman dropped a letter through the door she had a wild hope that it might be from Philip finishing what he had begun to say when Aurora's inopportune telephone call had come.

But it was only the one Armand had told her to expect from Miss Wilberforce. It was a short, stilted, bread-and-butter letter, and had in it none of the rambling charm Lydia would have expected.

My dear Lydia,

This is to thank you once again for your very great kindness to me, a stranger, and to tell you that I am extremely happy and contented here. My sister Blandina could not be more kind, though it is sad her health is so precarious. However, she is already a great deal better, and we are talking of a trip abroad quite soon. The weather is delightful, and my nephew Armand is full of thoughtfulness for my comfort. So please do not feel you have to think any more about me or my small, unimportant affairs. I am an old woman and a stranger who does not wish to intrude on your life. I wish you every happiness and good fortune in the future, and so good-bye, my dear Lydia.

Your grateful friend,
Clara Wilberforce

When Philip at last rang, Lydia's melancholy had given way to some ashamed tears. Even Miss Wilberforce did not need her any more, and was gently, gracefully, saying good-bye. Now she felt of use to nobody. She really would go back to Paris, perhaps even, in desperation, to the Bertrand family.

"What's the matter?" came his brisk voice.

"Nothing's the matter. Oh, well, yes, I'm rather sad because I've just had a letter from Miss Wilberforce. Saying good-bye."

"Really! That isn't like her, is it?"

"As a waif and stray, it isn't, but she's in the bosom of her family now. Even talking of trips abroad. It's a very nice letter. I think she feels she shouldn't worry me any more. After all, I was a complete stranger."

"But a very nice one," said Philip with maddening kindness. "Even I thought so." Was he saying good-bye, too? Her heart sank still lower. "Well, it goes to prove what I said last night, doesn't it? We can wash our hands of this business, and say farewell to the whole lot of them, Miss Wilberforce and all."

"I suppose so."

"After all, no one's dead, no one's hurt, and no one's in trouble."

"I know."

"Then what? Can I come round and see you?"

Not in that polite tone of voice, she thought.

"I'm just planning to catch a train home. Millicent wants me to come and there doesn't seem to be anything to do here. I've rung Armand and told him I'm keeping the pendant in the meantime, in case he gets any messages from Aurora. He seemed slightly disturbed about that, but I couldn't be sure. I'm beginning to read double meanings into everything. So I think a little while at home is a good idea. June can keep an eye on this flat. Or you can, if you like."

She realized she hadn't let him say anything for some time, and waited for him to speak.

"Would you like me to come down with you?"

"Good heavens, no! I imagine you never want to see that place again."

"I'll come if you want me to."

"No. I said no."

"Very definite, aren't you? Then what train are you catching? I'll see you off."

"There's no need even to do that," she said tightly.

"Lydia darling, you sound as if you hate me all at once. You think that I, like Aurora, was only fooling last night."

"Of course I do," she said lightly. "So was I. All right then, come to Waterloo if you insist. I'll catch the four forty-five."

But that was a mistake, too. Her taxi got into a traffic jam and she arrived with only a minute or two to spare. She hadn't even time to assess the look on his face, whether it was anxiety that she would miss her train or pain that she was going.

"Damn it, Lydia, now I haven't time to say a thing."

She laughed. "Good-bye, Philip. Take care of yourself. What are you going to do now?"

"Oh, carry on with that exhibition. It's supposed to open next week. Can I send you an invitation?"

"I'd love one, thank you. I hope it's a tremendous success."

"Lydia, don't do anything more about that old woman or anyone without letting me know."

"I don't intend to do anything more at all. It's over as far as I'm concerned. I must fly."

But he had bought a platform ticket and was following her. The train was about to move. A porter was slamming doors. Philip wrenched one open and helped Lydia in.

"Shall I come with you?"

She laughed again, although momentarily her heart had leaped. He had sounded eager.

"Don't be an idiot. You've got more important things to do."

"Lydia, I hurt you last night, didn't I? I didn't mean to. . . ." But now the train was moving, and when at last he had begun to say important things she could no longer hear them.

She could only stand and wave and smile until his tall form was indiscernible, and he himself would not be able to see the tears run down her cheeks.

Lipham was unbelievably the same as it had been a week ago. The swans still floated on the dark, weedy pond, the trees hung heavily over pools of shadow, even the flowers in the garden looked the same, as if no petals had fallen.

Millicent greeted Lydia warmly, but warned her not to talk about Aurora to Geoffrey as he was very touchy indeed about her. They were just behaving as if nothing had happened, as if Aurora were in London doing a job, and had never come home to be married.

Or as if she no longer existed, Lydia thought privately. As if she were dead.

It was when she went into Aurora's bedroom and saw in the wardrobe her belongings, the unworn wedding dress, and the honeymoon clothes, that it seemed as if Aurora really had died.

She shut the door hastily, and decided that her father after all was

the wisest for putting the matter out of his mind. She would try to do
the same.

There was only one small matter to wind up in connection with the
confused events of the week, and that was to answer Miss Wilberforce's letter. For, in spite of Miss Wilberforce's courteous but firm
good-bye, she remembered the old lady's passion for receiving letters.

She would like to have written, "Don't let Blandina put it across
you. She isn't as ill as she pretends to be." The firm hand drawing the
curtains that evening had not been that of a very sick woman. But
that was none of her business, and the main thing was Miss Wilberforce's contentment.

After all, what would they have done with her had nephew Armand not turned up?

Last of all, that night, Lydia thought of Philip and the sentence the
moving train had cut off. What had it been going to be? An apology?
A declaration of sincerity?

She didn't know. She wished she could put him out of her mind
also.

But none of them were really out of her mind, Philip, Aurora,
Miss Wilberforce, Blandina, Armand Villette, even the gardener with
his intent, stony gaze jostled in her dreams that night. She had, she
knew obscurely, finished with none of them.

Two days later, when Miss Wilberforce's answer to her letter arrived, she was appalled by her stupidity and complacency. How could
she have believed, in face of what she had seen, that all was well?
Blandina had not assumed her illness for her sister, but for Lydia, to
pull the wool over Lydia's eyes. As soon as Lydia had gone she had
risen, strong and well, to assume command of the household, to bully
her gentle, nervous sister, to keep out intruders. . . .

But all that Lydia had pushed out of her mind, because she had
been thinking of nothing but Philip and her unhappiness about him.
She had been selfish and cowardly and deliberately stupid. Now
something must be done.

In the same post as Miss Wilberforce's letter there was an invitation to Philip's exhibition. It had written across it, "Please do come."

It was an appropriate excuse to return to London. All at once she
did not know how she could have stayed away.

15

It was the second time that Miss Wilberforce had heard steps in the night. She cunningly lay very still, pretending to be asleep, while the steps came nearer, halting beside her bed. A shaft of light through the half-open door showed her the woman's form, the arm which reached out and deftly removed the glass of lemon and barley water from her bedside table, substituting another glass.

The woman was very thin and wore some dark garment. Both times she had come it had not been possible to see her face. She had been quick and silent, sliding away as softly as she had come. Miss Wilberforce had been too nervous and agitated to sit up and cry out.

The next time, she told herself, licking dry lips, she would do something. She would say, "Who is that? Is it Blandina?"

But she was certain it was not Blandina.

Besides, why would Blandina be prowling about in the night changing glasses of cordial? She wasn't well enough to do such things, and she wasn't so secretive. For what had been wrong with the cordial in the previous glass, or, more important, what was wrong with this one?

Yes, that was the point. The action of the nighttime prowler was highly suspicious, and Miss Wilberforce was not going to be tricked into drinking the new liquid. As soon as she thought it was safe, and indeed as soon as her trembling legs would obey her, she got out of bed and took the glass to the washbasin and emptied it.

That would foil them, she thought with satisfaction.

All the same, she still felt ill, as she had done for several days. She knew she would not sleep again, so leaving the light on she sat up in bed with her large black handbag propped up beside her and tried to absorb herself in the familiar pleasure of re-reading her correspondence. There were the letters that had come yesterday, the one from that charming girl, Lydia, who wrote so sweetly about keeping in touch, and letting her know if ever she were in trouble again, and the one she had written to herself which Armand had so kindly posted for her in London so that it really looked as if she had had an exciting trip to town.

That contained no real news, of course, but it was comforting to read it, because it made Greenhill seem such a pleasant place.

The birds sing and the May trees are in flower. The gardener keeps the gardens very nicely, though he does spend too much time near the house, and is inclined to neglect the lawns and beds farther away. I think he gets a little lonely, and likes to be within reach of voices. My nephew Armand does not come home every night as the journey is too arduous after a busy day. My sister Blandina, considering her poor health, and also that she has only been here a month, runs the house with admirable efficiency. I have been very poorly ever since the day after my arrival, and have had to keep to my room. But I am getting much better, with all this wonderful care. . . .

Miss Wilberforce smiled with gentle pleasure as she read this letter. She really did seem to be having a nice time in the country. The birds singing, the flowers blooming, the care she received when she was ill. This latter trouble she attributed to the unaccustomed rich food which was very different from the bread and cheese and boiled egg diet she had been living on in London.

She sat up in bed, her white hair mussed, her scrawny neck poking out of her silk nightgown (one of Blandina's, Blandina had always liked good things), her apple cheeks a little faded and blanched as if the country air, oddly enough, did not suit her, her fragile hands searching busily in the fat black bag.

What was this? Oh, yes, Lydia's letter from Lipham, full of kind concern. She would answer that presently, although Blandina had said that Lydia would not want to be bothered any more with a perfect stranger, and she must bring that friendship to an end.

But it was not true that Lydia did not want to be bothered any more, for this letter expressly asked her to write if she were in any trouble.

Was she in trouble, apart from feeling ill, and having that strange woman messing about with her drinking glass at nights, and apart from Blandina being rather more bossy than one remembered her, and also bewilderingly changed in appearance?

No, she wasn't in trouble exactly. But planning what she might write to Lydia was comforting, as also was re-reading her letters.

She scrabbled in the bag again, and brought out another folded sheet of paper. What was this letter? It looked rather new, as if she had not read it very often. The handwriting was strange. There was no address at the top, nor indeed any signature, and it contained only a couple of lines. But it was for her, undoubtedly. It read,

Dear Miss Wilberforce,

Don't stay here. They are all murderers. Go back to London and get a pension. You'll be far better off.

Miss Wilberforce gave a gasp, and dropped the paper as if it had been a beetle. Good gracious, how had *that* got into her bag? It hadn't come in the post, surely. She didn't remember having seen it before.

But she must have done, because here it was, removed from its envelope (and of course all letters were originally in envelopes with stamps), and put carefully in her bag.

How very odd! She just didn't remember having seen it before. And what a horrid letter it was. So vindictive!

As if Blandina and that kind middle-aged nephew of hers, Armand Villette, were murderers! Blandina had always been overbearing and unreasonable, it was true, and she was even more so in her old age, but she had never committed a murder, one was sure of that. And as for Armand, he was so fumbling, and rather shy and kind, he wouldn't hurt a soul.

Really, what a nasty, mischief-making letter for anyone to write. She would stuff it right to the bottom of her bag where she wouldn't come across it again for a long time. She would keep all the pleasant ones on top.

Murderers! How absurd!

Though one did have those uneasy feelings about Blandina looking so unlike herself. That was, if one remembered accurately how she had used to look. But surely one didn't remember that very long nose or the sharpness of her eyes. Age was to blame for those changes of feature, of course. Poor thing, she couldn't help it if her bossiness had come out, at last, in her nose. And she was very brave about not giving in to illness. She had determined to improve from the moment Miss Wilberforce arrived. And she talked at great length about things they had done as children, particularly their visits to the seaside at Bournemouth, and old Nanny, and one or two other people whom Miss Wilberforce had completely forgotten.

All the same, marriage to the long-deceased Mr. Paxton must have changed her a great deal. Sometimes she sounded like a complete stranger.

And there was this annoying way she had of telling Miss Wilberforce what she must write in her letters, especially to Lydia. One hadn't been able to tell Lydia any real news in that first letter. Blan-

dina had stood over her saying, "Your wits are a little feeble, Clara.
You can't write that rambling nonsense. Just say this. . . ."

And she had slowly and clearly dictated what must be written,
while Miss Wilberforce's shaky hand followed behind, unwillingly,
but helplessly.

"There," she had said, "that's a very satisfactory, courteous letter,
and now you mustn't bother that girl with your affairs any more. It
simply isn't done, Clara. It's the height of thoughtlessness and
selfishness."

But why not now, Miss Wilberforce thought excitedly, in the silence of this very early morning, write to Lydia exactly as she wanted
to. Then, as soon as it was daylight, she could dress and go for a delightful early morning stroll into the village to post the letter. That
way, Blandina need know nothing at all about it. She would be back
in her room for breakfast without anyone being aware that she had
gone out. She was sure she was strong enough, after all this resting in
her room, to take a walk. It would do her good.

Excitement brought a little color into her cheeks. Miss Wilberforce
pattered about the room getting out notepaper and pen and ink, and
climbing back into bed with them began happily to write.

She wouldn't tell about that silent figure changing the glass on her
bedside table in the night, for that might alarm Lydia into thinking
she was being poisoned, when of course she was much too shrewd for
that. Nor would she mention the strange letter that had somehow, by
mistake, got into her handbag. But she would express her doubts and
vague fear of her sister Blandina.

She has changed so remarkably, Lydia. Of course I know I
haven't seen her for very many years, and age does strange things to
one. Marriage, perhaps, too, to that Mr. Paxton whom she never
mentions, so probably he was not a good husband. And I know she
always despised me because she thought I was silly and empty-
headed. But I didn't think she would have grown old quite like this.
Neither of our parents had *quite* such a prominent nose. . . .

It was a wonderful relief to put all her strange doubts on paper. It
made them seem foolish, and she began to wonder if she had in-
vented them because, secretly, she was missing the busy, virile streets
of London which she had adored.

When the letter was finished at last, scrawled over four sheets of
paper, it was growing daylight, and the first birds were singing.

Now for the daring part of her plan, to get up and dress and slip out of the house to walk to the village. Was she strong enough? Would her stomach, which had been so unreliable lately, misbehave again, or would she have one of those nasty dizzy turns?

No, she decided with relief. She felt better this morning. A little light in the head, because she had eaten so little lately, but otherwise quite well. She was sure she could manage the walk successfully, and be back in time for breakfast at eight o'clock.

Before she was dressed, however, all the birds were singing, and there was a distant clattering of dishes downstairs. Then she began to get fussed. Time was slipping by, and her clothes wouldn't seem to go on properly. Her hands trembled and she dropped a shoe with a clatter. But at last she was ready.

Then she discovered that although she had addressed the envelope to Lydia she had not put a stamp on it. It would be too early for the post office to be open. She must find a stamp in her bag. She knew she had one, or even two, but where were they? She had to turn out every mortal thing to find those two elusive scraps of paper, and when at last she had run them to earth in a fold of the lining she was hot and trembling. Precious time had gone by. It was nearly seven o'clock. She would have to hurry.

It was possible to descend the stairs without being observed. But crossing the hall too hastily her foolish old feet tripped in a rug, and as she stumbled, Jules the gardener, suddenly appeared behind her.

She didn't know which room he had come from. She was surprised to see him in this part of the house at all. Her surprise took away what little composure she had left, and she looked at him guiltily.

"Good morning, Jules."

"Good morning, madam. You're not going out?"

He was a tall, slim, very straight person, with a peculiar arrogance, considering his position in life. He must have been very spoilt. Armand, no doubt, had been much too easy with him, and Blandina had always been foolish about good-looking men.

"Yes, I am," she managed to say in reply to his shocked question. "It's such a beautiful morning, and I was awake early. I thought I'd take a little stroll. I haven't been very well, you know."

"I'm sorry, madam. Then should you walk far?"

Did he need to speak so loud? In a moment those sharp ears of Blandina's would hear and she would come pouncing out of her room, like a great, long-nosed cat.

"You weren't planning to go all the way to the village with that letter, madam?"

His eyes were on the letter which, idiot old creature that she was, she had failed to conceal. But goodness me, why should a gardener, even a spoilt and arrogant one, interfere with her plans?

She gave her untidy white head a toss, refusing haughtily to make explanations.

"I am merely going for a stroll, Jules. Good morning."

But it was too late. Blandina had heard. She was at the head of the stairs calling in her loud, imperative voice, "Clara, whatever are you doing out of bed at this hour? Are you mad?"

Miss Wilberforce felt as if she were crumpling inside. Indeed, her legs literally were crumpling, and she had to grope for one of the tall-backed chairs and sit down.

"I was only going to post my letter," she said, with the sudden petulance of an old woman. "I don't see why I shouldn't be allowed to post it in the village if it gives me pleasure."

Jules, having caused the mischief, had discreetly disappeared, and Blandina was coming down the stairs. Clad in a dark red, wool dressing-gown, with her iron-grey hair scraped back from her bony forehead, and her black eyes glittering, she looked ridiculously frightening. Ridiculously so, considering she was one's own sister.

"My dear Clara, you shall go to the village as often as you wish at a reasonable time of day, and when you are better. But tell me honestly, do you feel fit at this minute to walk a mile?"

Miss Wilberforce reluctantly shook her head. She had felt fit when she had got up. But now, after all this distress, she knew she could not even have reached the end of the drive. It was doubtful if she could climb the stairs to her room.

"I'm sorry, Blandina. I suppose I was being foolish. But I so enjoy letters. You know I do. It isn't nearly so much fun if someone else posts them. Besides, you don't care for me to write to Lydia."

"So that's who you've been writing to. What have you said to her?"

Miss Wilberforce held the letter tightly, ready to tear it up if Blandina, in her overbearing way, demanded to see it.

"Nothing in particular. Just this and that. Lydia wrote to me as you know, and it is only polite to answer."

"Of course," Blandina agreed, with unexpected amiability. "You don't have to tell me what is good manners. But I've told you before I don't want that nice child worried. She has no responsibility for you, and you simply can't intrude on her like this, Clara."

"Worried!" repeated Miss Wilberforce in pained surprise.

"Haven't you told her you've been ill?"

"Oh, in passing, yes. I didn't dwell on it."

"I think it's better not to mention it at all. You must listen to me, Clara. Armand and I are responsible for you now, and we know what's best. Now supposing you destroy that long, foolish, rambling letter you've got there—oh, yes, I know that's exactly what it is—and we'll go upstairs and remember our manners and write a polite, graceful note, as we did before. Isn't that the best idea? Of course it is."

Blandina was being kind! The unexpectedness of this, when she had expected sharp words and disfavor, filled Miss Wilberforce with remorse. Was she behaving very ungratefully?

And of course Blandina was right. One couldn't go on worrying Lydia, tempting as it was to spread one's thoughts all over a sheet of paper. No, one must behave with thoughtfulness and discretion.

Slowly Miss Wilberforce tore the letter in her hand into small pieces. She had temporarily forgotten the creeping figure in the night, doing strange things with her glass of lemon and barley water, and the overbearing interfering way Blandina had. She was only conscious that now, for a little while at least, Blandina was being kind, and she was tremendously grateful. Besides she was beginning to feel ill and weak again. It would be nice to undress and get back into bed. No one made her get up if she didn't wish to. She could lie in the comfortable bed all day, watching the shadows move over the garden. The more ill she felt the less she longed to be back in London, holding her own with the jostling hurrying walkers down the hot pavements, window-shopping without resentment about her lack of money, listening to the virile cries of the paper boys, taking a sniff of the carnations on the corner stall, sharing a park bench with whoever else happened to be resting tired feet, buying her modest provisions for supper, and making her weary, cheerful way home. . . .

"Well, come then," Blandina was saying in her sharp way. "I'll help you upstairs. We'll write that letter after breakfast and Jules can take it to the post. Good gracious, you are shaky, aren't you? What will Doctor Neave say if he hears about this? You'd better spend the whole day in bed. Armand will be home tonight and you don't want him to see you looking so ill, do you?"

"I don't seem to recover as quickly as you did," Miss Wilberforce said meekly.

"Oh, mine was only one of my attacks. I told you that. They're only temporary. Different from your troubles, my poor Clara."

16

Lydia wandered about the gallery, vaguely unhappy that she could not at this moment concentrate on the pictures. They were full of color and life, and she was pleased to hear murmurs of appreciation from the small crowd which had come to the opening of Philip's exhibition. She was remorseful that she had not previously had the time or opportunity to see Philip's work. It had never been that she was not interested, but other matters had got in the way.

Since honesty was one of her less comfortable virtues, she had also to admit to herself that jealousy had come into it. It was as a painter that Philip had first been interested in Aurora, and to Lydia Aurora was now associated inextricably with his work. Even here, in these luxuriant tropical canvases, she seemed to see Aurora's radiance behind the brown-bodied native girls, as if even then she had been his exact dream, awaiting fulfillment.

"Lydia!" Philip had escaped from the small knot of people surrounding him, and was at her side. He had been going to say he was pleased she had come. That was clear enough because he had that polite look on his face. But as he looked down at her he said no more at all, merely gave her his disconcerting blue stare which told her nothing.

"Philip, I think your pictures are wonderful. I should have seen them before."

He raised an eyebrow. "We haven't had much time, have we? You were only in my studio once, and then—" He didn't mention Aurora's name, but went on quickly, "You didn't write to me. I suppose there's been no news?"

"Only a letter from Miss Wilberforce that seems rather alarming. I can't show it to you now. Later—"

There were people crowding round with congratulatory smiles. They were all strangers. They looked on Philip as a brilliant young artist, tremendously lucky to be holding a successful exhibition in London. They didn't know him as a jilted bridegroom burying his beautiful and unattainable dream.

Philip took Lydia's arm. "Hang around. I'll slip away at four o'clock. There's a coffee bar round the corner. I'll see you there."

An hour later, in this cosy gloom, redolent of coffee and expensive pastries, Lydia produced the letter which had given her an almost sleepless night, and watched Philip read it.

It wasn't fair to do this to him in the middle of his exhibition, but once more events seemed to be concerned with life and death.

Lydia knew the letter off by heart.

Dear Lydia,

   Thank you for your letter. It gave me great pleasure.

   But as I have already said, there is no need to worry about me, as I have my future very well taken care of. I cannot impose on your time and kindness any more. But I wish you happiness and good fortune wherever you may be.

Your friend,
Clara Wilberforce

That was fine. That was on the lines of the previous letter, a second reminder dictated obviously by another person that now she must keep out of Miss Wilberforce's life.

But the postscript had not been dictated by anybody. It had been scrawled across the bottom in large jerky writing:

I'm ill. I need help. Please come.

Philip looked up. "What do you think?"

"Why, that the postscript is the only part of the letter that's genuine."

"It's not the same handwriting."

"Don't you think so? Don't you think that could be the way Miss Wilberforce wrote when she was in a great hurry and very distressed? Or even drugged. Because of her illness, of course."

"Could be." Philip turned the envelope over. "This has been opened and sealed down again."

"I know. I noticed that at once."

"Hardly the work of a person who's dopey with drugs."

"No, but Miss Wilberforce isn't completely dumb. If Blandina has been too interfering she'd find a way of getting her own back. Blandina has said I'm not to come, and Clara wants me. That's how I see it. How ever she managed to send this message, she did send it." Lydia raised her eyes to his. "So I have to go."

"Of course you have to, Lydia dear. It's not your business and I'm pretty certain you're not going to be very welcome to either Blandina or her devious nephew Armand, whatever their game may be. But you can't resist a *cri de coeur*. Neither of us can. We'll have to go."

"We!"

His level eyes met hers.

"Did you think I'd let you go alone this time? Not on your life. I've wanted an excuse to see the respectable Armand's hideout, anyway. Now look. I can leave things here to my agent in another hour or so. I'll just make the public farewells. Have you any idea what time trains leave for this place?"

"Not very often. Let's ring up and ask."

"No, I've a better idea. I'll borrow or hire a car." He sprang up. "Let's say in an hour from outside here. What are you going to do now?"

"Drink coffee," said Lydia dreamily. "Think of what we're going to say to Blandina. Poor, sweet old Clara. We're too fond of her not to pay her a visit occasionally, aren't we? We were just passing through the village. . . ."

Philip drove up to the front door with a flourish. It was late dusk, but the curtains, Lydia noticed, were not drawn. She remembered Blandina's tall, sombre form from her last visit, appearing theatrically to sweep them across, and all at once her heart was beating uncomfortably.

"Come along," said Philip, opening the car door. He looked at her again. "You're not nervous, surely?"

"I am. Madly."

"Idiot. What can happen? This is a social call. Let's hope Armand is home. Besides, I'm here."

He grinned at her comfortably, and suddenly she was extraordinarily happy.

"Remember, we don't mention Clara's letter," she said. "We've just called to see how she is."

They could hear the distant ringing of the bell. It was some time before footsteps approached and the door was opened. There were no lights on, strangely enough, and it was framed against darkness that Lydia recognized Jules, the gardener.

He was dressed in an open shirt and corduroy trousers. If he were acting as butler his attire was very casual. But one would never produce servility in that arrogant head or cold blue gaze.

"Madam!" he exclaimed in surprise, recognizing Lydia.

"How do you do, Jules?" she said affably. "Is Miss Wilberforce in? We're giving her a surprise."

His eyes flickered from one to the other of them. He threw the door wide open, hospitably.

"Will you come in, please. Mr. Villette isn't home, but I'll let Mrs. Paxton know you're here."

They were taken into the spacious, well-furnished hall, and lights were switched on.

"I don't think she's very well, madam. But just wait, will you?"

Jules with his long, athletic stride, disappeared.

Lydia looked at Philip. "Cloakroom through that door," she said reminiscently. "I only saw this place clearly when I arrived the other day. After that I was plastered. Nice, isn't it?"

Philip looked round with interest. "One would hardly have expected such good taste from Armand. A scruffy little man like that."

"Yes, I know. Perhaps all those dead and gone aunts are responsible. One can imagine Aunt Blandina—"

Although her voice had been low, Lydia could not repress a guilty start when, from the stairway, Aunt Blandina's dramatic voice answered her.

"Miss Deering! What a surprise! But you should have let us know you were coming."

She was descending the stairs, leaning slightly on a stick. She wore a long, dark-colored gown, and looked immensely tall. Her hair, scraped back severely from her bony yellow forehead, made her face, with its strong jutting nose and intense eyes, look like a painting of some medieval martyr. There was no softness there. Even her polite smile was a facial contortion only. She was deep in her unhumorous, severe world. Though she leaned on her stick it was not possible that she needed it. Her body was full of tough, ancient strength.

Only the bedclothes and the soft pillows had hidden it and deceived Lydia when last she had seen her.

"How do you do, Mrs. Paxton?" Lydia said easily. If Blandina's apparent strength concealed weakness, so did her own calm voice conceal a suddenly racing heart. "This is a friend of mine, Philip Nash. We were passing this way on our way to the coast and thought —at least, it was my idea—that we'd like to call on Miss Wilberforce. I hope she's feeling better."

The brilliant black eyes of the old lady stabbed her. "You knew she was ill?"

"Jules has just told us. We're so sorry. Can we see her? She knows Philip. He met her at my flat."

"She's not at all well," Blandina said repressively. "In fact, I called the doctor again today. The trouble is partly nervous, as I guessed. Clara always had a weak stomach. I remember as children—but I won't go into those distressing details, ruined parties and so on." She stopped to measure them with her disturbing eyes. "It was very kind of you to call in. Will you take some sherry with me?"

Only sherry, thought Lydia. Blandina hadn't nephew Armand's dash. She did not go in for mixing quick-action martinis.

"Mrs. Paxton, we *do* want to see Miss Wilberforce. She isn't too ill, is she? I mean, if she is," she added ingenuously, "the doctor would have sent her to hospital, wouldn't he?"

"We'll stay five minutes, no more," Philip promised.

The sharp eyes darted from one to the other. The reluctance was obvious—but was it reluctance which genuinely protected her sister's well-being?

"Wait here," she said at last. "I'll go up and see if Clara feels she could see a visitor. She found the doctor's visit rather trying."

"Thank you, Mrs. Paxton," Lydia said. "That is good of you. You're quite recovered yourself?"

Now it seemed as if the old woman were angrily trying to read Lydia's clear eyes.

"I'm not at all well," she said huffily. "You saw the other day how I am in one of my attacks. They can come on me at any moment. Do please sit down. Jules will bring you some sherry. We have the greatest trouble in keeping servants, you know. The place is too isolated. They might have to exert themselves to get to a cinema, poor things. So Jules very kindly helps indoors as well."

"Oh," said Lydia politely. Armand, too, had made an explanation about servants and the village postmistress had said they came from London. It was very likely they wouldn't care about being in this quiet place.

There was no opportunity to talk with Philip, for as soon as Blandina had gone up the stairs in her slow, stately way Jules came with the sherry. He served them silently, his supercilious eyes looking at a point beyond their heads, yet observing, Lydia was sure, every slightest expression or movement they made.

The house was very quiet. She looked up the wide stairs and had a sudden crazy desire to run up them and along the passage at the top, throwing open all the closed doors. She imagined finding the ten bedrooms of which Armand had boasted, all occupied by old women, slowly mummifying. An army of ancient aunts, kept alive long after they should have died. And Armand himself, a strange nephew Bluebeard. . . .

Suddenly she shivered and didn't want to throw open any doors at all. She wondered for a moment why they had come, why they should think it was their duty to do something which Aurora had shirked doing about an old woman.

Then, as Jules went silently away, Blandina returned, descending the stairs as slowly as she had climbed them.

"You can go up for a little while. Just ten minutes. Clara wants to see you, of course, although she is very tired and shouldn't be getting excited. No, just you, Miss Deering," she added in her autocratic way, as both Philip and Lydia sprang up. "If you don't mind, Mr. Nash. One visitor is plenty, and my sister seems to have formed an attachment for Miss Deering." She spoke as if poor, silly Clara had always formed rash and impulsive friendships which had to be tactfully but firmly ended.

Lydia looked at Philip. He was ready to defy the rules of courtesy in someone else's house and come if she wished him to. But that was perhaps going too far. After all, her own eyes would tell her how it was with Miss Wilberforce.

"Then wait for me, Philip," she said lightly. "I won't stay long."

Miss Wilberforce was sitting up in bed, the fragile pink of excitement in her cheeks. Her hair was soft and wild round her sunken face. All her robust sprightliness had left her, and she looked very frail indeed. She had failed rather distressingly since Lydia had last seen her.

"My dear child, how sweet of you to come!" she cried with pleasure. "What a lovely surprise for me!"

Lydia bent to kiss her. "I'm so sorry you're not well, Miss Wilberforce."

"Yes, isn't it too aggravating! All this beautiful country air and I can't be outdoors. I can't even walk to the post office."

The door opened slightly wider and there was Blandina's tall silent form. Lydia didn't know Blandina had followed her up the stairs. She wished she had been allowed to talk to Miss Wilberforce alone, but one couldn't order one's hostess out of the room.

Miss Wilberforce was annoyed, too, for a quick, almost furtive expression crossed her face. She licked her lips, and with great presence of mind finished her sentence.

"Not that I need to walk to the post office, for Blandina sees that my letters are posted. How are you, Lydia dear? What have you been doing?"

"Just staying with my parents. Doing nothing, really."

"And that nice young man?"

"Philip? He's downstairs."

"Here! But he must come up."

Blandina interposed firmly. "I think not, Clara. You're getting over-excited already. You know the doctor prescribed complete rest."

Miss Wilberforce sank back in the bed. She looked small and withered.

"Yes. I've had this upset. I ate some mushrooms one day and they didn't agree with me. I can't seem to throw off this silly weakness. Blandina remembers I was always easily upset. She's been so kind. So patient."

The room was comfortable, even luxurious. Miss Wilberforce, in an expensive nightdress and woolly bedjacket, looked as if she were receiving all the petting and pampering Armand had promised. The doctor had been this afternoon. He obviously had not been unduly alarmed.

Yet she couldn't forget that scrawled line at the bottom of the letter, *"I need help. . . ."*

If only Blandina would leave her alone with Miss Wilberforce for five minutes! But it was clear she did not mean to do any such thing.

There was nothing for it but to say, "Then you're going to be all right, Miss Wilberforce? Can I help you in any way?"

"Help!" said Miss Wilberforce in surprise.

"Help!" repeated Blandina tartly. "Why, if I may ask, do you think my sister needs your help, Miss Deering?"

Lydia refused to be browbeaten.

"I know she doesn't seem to, but I hope she wouldn't hesitate to ask if she did. I imagine, if she doesn't soon improve, you'll send her to hospital or get her a good nurse."

Blandina's brilliant black eyes were narrowed and furious.

"After all, you haven't been well yourself, Mrs. Paxton," Lydia went on blandly. "And you say you can't get servants. You can't possibly do this kind of nursing yourself."

"Oh, but I'm going to be all right, Lydia," Miss Wilberforce said cheerfully. "It's sweet of you to worry, but really I will be all right."

"Of course you will be. But I'm going to keep in close touch all the same. So is Philip. We'll be popping in again, just any time."

"Oh, how nice, Lydia dear! What nice surprises you give me, bless you."

Lydia turned to go, her head in the air, defying the tall, possessive, angry old woman in the doorway. But suddenly she looked back.

"Have you any letters you'd like posted now, Miss Wilberforce? Philip and I can take them."

"My sister hasn't been well enough to write letters recently," Blandina put in in a tightly controlled voice.

Miss Wilberforce made an eager movement, instantly suppressed. She merely said tiredly, "No, I don't think I have, dear. Or did I write one this morning? My memory's getting so bad. Look in my bag. Over there, on the dresser."

Was it a signal? Was the old lady shrewd enough to give her a signal, or was she really too cloudy and vague in her mind? Lydia took a risk. She opened the bulging bag and with a clumsy movement spilled its contents on the floor.

"Oh, dear!" she exclaimed. "I'm so sorry. I'll pick all these up. They all seem to be addressed to you, Miss Wilberforce. Well, never mind, write to me as soon as you're well enough. I expect to hear how you are progressing, mind."

She was wearing a light loose coat with large pockets. It was easy enough, in her swift gathering up of the spilt letters, to thrust several of them into her pocket, especially the one that had borne strange handwriting that could, from the brief knowledge of it, be Aurora's. She hadn't expected her haphazard impulse to yield such a dividend.

Downstairs Philip was strolling about restlessly, and in the background Jules was busy with the tray of drinks.

"We must go now," Lydia said politely to Blandina. "We've a long way to drive. Are you ready, Philip? What a pity Mr. Villette isn't home. Do give him our regards, won't you?"

"Of course," said Blandina. She added, "Armand is not often home during the week. He finds it too far and prefers to stay at his club."

"How is Miss Wilberforce?" Philip asked Lydia.

"I thought she'd failed a great deal," Lydia met Blandina's hostile eyes. "Don't you think so, Mrs. Paxton?"

"She has scarcely eaten for a week. What can you expect? But she's a great deal better today. And kind as you are, Miss Deering, you mustn't think this is your responsibility."

"Oh, but we're so fond of her. Aren't we, Philip? We intend to call again in a day or two."

"Perhaps on our way back to London," Philip suggested.

"Yes, we'll certainly do that. If we're not a trouble, Mrs. Paxton." Lydia smiled sweetly. In the background Jules suddenly rattled glasses as he picked up the tray. Blandina made a movement forward, leaning heavily on her stick.

"By all means do that, Miss Deering. But as soon as Clara recovers we mean to take that delayed holiday abroad. I would be gone by now if it hadn't been for Clara arriving like this. However, I don't expect we'll be able to leave for a day or two yet. So we shall probably be here when next you're kind enough to call."

She didn't hold out her hand. She merely waited for them to go. But just as Lydia turned to the door, feeling obscurely that she had failed, that there should be some social law giving an outsider the right to interfere between two sisters in one of the sisters' homes, the doorbell rang.

The sound seemed to startle Blandina as much as it did Lydia. For a moment she stood rigid.

Then she said, "Jules!" and the tall man in the casual clothes crossed over to open the door.

Armand stood on the doorstep. The little, middle-aged, rather plump and shabby man, so out of place in this tasteful house, who did not come home during the week because of the distance, stood there silently disproving all his aunt had said.

He was as surprised to see them as they were him. He came forward with a quick, bustling movement, holding out his hand, exclaiming in a too loud voice, "Well, what a pleasant surprise! Miss Deering! Mr. Nash! I saw the car outside and thought it was the doctor's. Aunt Blandina, have you looked after these two young people? Have they been up to see poor Aunt Clara? She's not at all well, poor dear, but imagine if she were ill and still in that horrid bed-sitting room!"

"We're just leaving," said Lydia pleasantly. "We've been promising to call again."

"Of course, of course. How kind! And tell me, has there been any news of your sister? My eloping secretary," he turned to explain to Blandina. His large, round eyes were rolling behind their spectacles. They had their coy, jovial look. But his plump hands were clasped tightly together as if he were cold.

"Yes. We've heard from her," Philip answered briefly. "We know where she is, and hope to be having her back in London soon."

"Ah, indeed! With or without the dashing young husband, may I ask? But of course it will be with him. Inseparable, I imagine. You haven't decided to leave that gold pendant with me, as she asked, Miss Deering? Or do you still wish to take the responsibility?"

"Miss Deering is a young lady who enjoys responsibility," came Blandina's harsh voice. "Armand, we mustn't keep our guests standing here. They want to be on their way."

"Of course, of course. I've taken this unexpected trip down to see Aunt Clara. I've been worried about her. Then good-bye, Miss Deering, Mr. Nash. Do call again."

His affable voice followed them out into the night. It was a warm, early summer dusk, and perspiration glinted faintly on Armand's forehead. But he still gripped his hands together as if he were cold.

17

In the car, driving slowly towards the village, Lydia began to tick off points on her fingers.

"We were decidedly not welcome. In fact, we were very embarrassing callers. You were not encouraged to go up and see Clara, and I was not left alone with her. Why? Because she would tell me something I mustn't know? Blandina isn't, and never has been, I imagine, really ill. Then why did she pretend the other day, and how, in her present state of health and intelligence, could she have forgotten Clara's allowance after all these years? Armand wasn't pleased to see us either. He covered that up by talking too much, and practically pushing us out of the door. But the genial, generous nephew veneer was cracked quite a lot. He's not used to making a mid-week visit, but something brought him down tonight. What? Anyway, I've swiped a pile of Clara's letters and we'll study those presently."

"If you can stop talking long enough," Philip said pleasantly. He put his hand on hers and gave it a friendly squeeze. "It was quite an ordeal, wasn't it?"

Lydia sighed and leaned back. "I'm talking too much, just as Armand was. Only he behaved as if he were cold."

"He was scared to death," said Philip.

"Scared!"

"Couldn't you see?"

"But what of? Blandina? I admit that if I had an aunt like that living in an hotel I'd very happily leave her there. I don't believe she forgot Clara's allowance. She just decided that, having a place like this to come to, she'd wash her hands of her poor old sister."

"She acts as if she's lived at Greenhill for years," Philip observed.

"Oh, no, she's just that kind of woman. Takes over immediately she arrives. Tell me, what did you do while I was upstairs with Clara?"

"There wasn't much I could do. That fellow Jules never let me out of his sight."

"Really! Unwritten orders?"

"I should imagine so. I took a look in several rooms—I must have seemed an unmannerly snooper. He politely interpreted that what I was looking for was the cloakroom, and showed me in."

Lydia giggled. "Serves you right."

"I wanted to get upstairs, but it wasn't possible."

"Why? To look in all those empty bedrooms?" Lydia's voice was a little fearful. She was thinking again of her fantasy of the mummifying old women.

"Might have been interesting," Philip said thoughtfully. "Armand is no doubt a man of secrets. He looks to me like the kind of solicitor who should have been struck off the roll years ago."

"Aurora wouldn't have stayed with a man like that!" Lydia exclaimed.

"But we don't know Aurora very well either, do we? Well, perhaps I'm wrong. I suppose you hadn't a chance to find out how that cry for help got in Clara's letter."

"No. I could only hint at it, and Clara seemed quite bewildered. If she did write it she's forgotten. She's not dying, Philip. At least, I wouldn't think so. And now they think we're calling again they'll be pretty careful. But supposing. . . ."

She stopped, unwilling to put her thought into words.

"Yes?"

"Supposing they did want her to die. Why? She's a completely destitute old woman. They haven't a thing to gain."

"I know. It doesn't make sense. Nevertheless, we're going to make another call tonight. We're distant relatives of Clara's, and we're anxious about her. We want to be assured by her doctor that she's not seriously ill. What do you say? Doctor Neave, isn't it? Someone in the village will tell us where to find him."

"Yes," said Lydia eagerly. "That's exactly what we must do."

It was not to be expected that a doctor would divulge much information about his patient to what appeared to be a pair of complete strangers. But at least this visit gave them the opportunity to sum up the man whom Blandina and Armand had decided to call in, to see whether or not he appeared to be sensible and trustworthy.

Doctor Neave, in the small, dark, cluttered surgery into which they were shown, was an elderly, rather vague person with a kindly face.

He listened to their story, and said, "You understand, this isn't strictly etiquette. Your aunt—she is your aunt, I take it?"

"Distantly," said Philip.

"Ah, yes. Well—ah—I diagnosed the trouble as a small cerebral haemorrhage, in other words, a slight stroke, with symptoms such as nausea and confusion. At her age, of course—well—ah—none of us lives for ever, eh? But with care she'll be perfectly all right. Fortunately there's no paralysis. Normally I'd have put a case like that in hospital, but she seems to be getting such excellent care where she is, I feel one couldn't do better. I gather a holiday abroad is proposed when she is well enough to travel."

"Yes. So Aunt Clara mentioned," Philip said easily. "I suppose you've attended Mr. Villette—and his aunts—for some years, Doctor?"

"No, actually I haven't. Luckily for them—not, of course for me—" the labored joke brought a twinkle to the old man's faded eyes, "they haven't often needed a doctor. The last time was several years ago."

"Was that for one of the aunts?"

"Yes. It was. Let me see, what was her name. Honoria, Hortense, Hannah—that was it, Hannah. She had a long-standing heart ailment and died. But no, I haven't been called in often. Of course, as you know, the family doesn't live at Greenhill a great deal. They're rather cosmopolitan, I gather."

"Lucky things," Lydia sighed. "Money no object. Just as well for Armand, of course, since he's so aunt-ridden."

"Only one dead and gone aunt," Lydia said, when they were back in the car. "Then the others Armand mentioned must have died somewhere else."

"That's enough of that," Philip said firmly. "We can't clutter up things with ancient corpses."

"All the same, Armand must have kept very silent about Aunt Hannah's death, because the postmistress didn't know of it. What a honey that little doctor is. I'm sure he'll do all he can for Clara, won't he? And if it's a stroke, there's no one to blame, is there? She's not being poisoned, or anything melodramatic like that. What do we do now, Philip?"

"Have dinner in the first pub we come to, and read those letters you helped yourself to."

The waiter in the cosy roadside hotel looked curiously at them as he tried to set down their plates among the litter of crumpled letters spread over the table.

Most of the letters were in Miss Wilberforce's usual rambling style, and addressed to herself. Lydia put them on one side to study later.

She searched for the one in the strange handwriting, and when she opened it she gasped. For it was from Aurora.

It read,

Dear Miss Wilberforce,

I am enclosing five pounds which is all I can possibly send you. This will help you out until you have arranged something with the National Health people. Do go to them at once. (The last word was underlined.) Don't come here.

It was signed "Aurora Hawkins." The date was six weeks ago.

"Why did Aurora feel she had to send her money? What obligation was she under? How is she mixed up in all this, Philip? Just by being Armand's secretary?" The letter was just one more thing to baffle Lydia.

"Secretaries don't usually have to pay bribes to clients," Philip said. "Does one thing occur to you about this letter? It's dated about the time that Blandina moved from her hotel down to the country."

"Well, of course. That's when poor Clara's allowance stopped. But why should Aurora feel responsible? Really, this is too complicated."

"For me, too," Philip confessed. "I only have one idea. When we get back to London let's advertise in the personal columns for friends of Blandina's. Surely she must have had some friends."

"How can they help us?"

"Well, for one thing, they can tell us what she looked like."

"Philip! Are you suggesting that terrifying old woman might not be Blandina?"

"I'm not sure what I'm suggesting. But there's no harm in doing this, is there?" He began to write on the back of one of the tattered letters. " 'Paxton Blandina: Can anyone give an old friend any idea of her whereabouts. Have not been able to contact her since she left London some weeks ago.' How's that?"

"Splendid."

"She must have had some friends," Philip repeated. "I inquired about her at the hotel, but all they could tell me was about the nephew who took her out to tea sometimes."

"Armand, of course."

"The irrepressible Armand."

"He's after her money, Philip. Even though he seems to have plenty of his own. He doesn't want poor old Clara to get any."

"At the moment neither of them seems likely to get any. She looked as if she would live forever, didn't she?"

"But she must be Blandina, Philip. She's always talking to Clara about her childhood. And she's bossy, the way Clara said."

"Clara's memory is pretty bad. And it's easy enough to spin a story out of just a few correct details, especially to someone a little weak-witted like Clara."

"Philip!" Now the cold wind was blowing over Lydia again. The exciting tense evening had left her exhausted. She had no resources left with which to dispel this wave of fear. "You're thinking of that unidentified body again," she said, in a horrified whisper.

"I don't think such a long chance would interest the police at all," Philip said reflectively. "We must get one or two more facts straight. And we have a little time now. We're due to call in at Greenhill in two or three days, remember? To give them that nasty little surprise for which they'll have to be prepared. So they can't afford just yet to play any tricks. Cheer up, darling. Let's have a bottle of wine. The rest of the evening is ours."

"Ours!" echoed Lydia ironically. For how could it be, when Clara Wilberforce, shrunken, pathetic, and determinedly cheerful, sitting up trustingly in the comfortable bed in the comfortable room remained so firmly in her mind. And not only Clara, Aurora, too, with her mysterious part in this queer play. The servant Jules, suave, silent, and watchful. Armand, a little grotesquely coy, wringing his hands as if he were cold. And Blandina—or the two Blandinas—one the severe hostess, unwelcoming and hostile, long-nosed and autocratic, the other a ghost, unknown, bewildered, forgotten. . . .

It was after midnight when they got back to London. Lydia had dozed, and woke only when the car stopped.

"Here we are, my love. I'll come up with you."

"Will you," said Lydia sleepily. "I'd adore that."

"Well, that's better," he said, grinning down at her.

She became fully awake. "What did I say?"

"Just what you should have. I say, if you can't walk straight I'll have to carry you. We don't want our friend and neighbor sticking her nose out at this hour."

Lydia giggled. "Don't worry. This is her sleeping-like-a-log time. Of course you're not going to carry me," she added wistfully.

But she let him put his arm firmly round her waist, and with exaggerated caution they climbed the stone stairs.

Lydia was happy again. Her drowsiness and the space they had put between themselves and Greenhill had reduced the problem to something a great deal less pressing and personal. After all, as Philip had once pointed out, nothing tangible had happened. No one was hurt, or seemingly in desperate trouble, or dead. . . . Except the aged Hannah, legitimately, of a long-standing heart ailment.

Outside the door of her flat she groped in her bag, now as bulging and untidy as Miss Wilberforce's, with its clutter of correspondence.

But Philip's hand was suddenly on her arm. He was indicating the not-quite-closed door.

Someone was in there!

Aurora's mysterious friend?

"Oh! What do we do?" Lydia gasped.

Philip didn't answer. He gave the door a sharp push, at the same time groping inside for the light switch. The lights sprang on, but the door refused to open more than six inches. Something heavy lay against it.

Pushing slowly and carefully, Philip at last edged his way in. His voice, exaggeratedly calm, came out to Lydia.

"It's June Birch. She's hurt."

In a moment Lydia was inside bending over June, while Philip quickly switched on lights in the rest of the flat and checked to see that the intruder was no longer there.

June was just recovering consciousness. She was dressed in pyjamas and a cotton housecoat. She frowned at the light and moaned.

"O-oh! You've come at last. I thought—"

"Take it easy," said Philip. He had a glass of brandy in one hand, and raising June a little with his free arm he persuaded her to swallow some.

Lydia rushed to get cushions and a wet cloth. The bump on June's head was startlingly visible.

"Someone—knocked me out," she managed to say at last, grinning ruefully. "Gosh! That's some headache I've got."

"Did you see who it was?" Philip asked.

"No! Not a whisker of him! I thought I heard someone moving up here—oh, ever so softly, quite late—what's the time now?"

"Half past twelve."

"Then, my goodness, it was only ten minutes ago. You've just missed him."

"Oh, lord!" Philip exclaimed angrily.

Lydia had a rather fearful sense of relief. It was June who had suffered.

"I came up with my key to catch him red-handed. At least, to get a look at him. But as soon as I opened the door the lights went out, and wham! I got this on my head."

She slumped back. "Gosh! Only ten minutes ago! He's nipped down the back stairs, of course."

"Has anything been disturbed?" Lydia asked Philip.

"Of course it has. Everything's upside down. But whether he got what he wanted is another thing."

"What would he want?" Lydia asked fearfully.

"I don't know. I only make a guess. The pendant, of course."

"Aurora!" whispered Lydia.

"Come off it," June said feebly. "That was a man-sized wallop I got."

"She might have had a man with her," said Philip slowly. "Or it might have been just one man alone."

"Armand!"

"Perhaps. How do we know? Let's make June more comfortable. Do you think you can sit up? We'll move you on to the couch. Then I think—whatever you two may feel—it's a case for the police."

At that June sat up sharply. She clutched her head, but managed to say very definitely, "Don't be daft! The police will just treat this as an ordinary burglary, and we'll never find out who this guy is. It's not a burglary," she added soberly. "It's part of this crazy mystery about Aurora. And I might be wrong, but I've got a feeling if you call the police you'll never see Aurora again."

"What an extraordinary thing to say!" Lydia exclaimed.

June grinned wryly. "Maybe that bump on my head has sent me crazy. But that's what I think. And I want to meet up with this irresistible lover. Among other things, I've got a score to settle with him."

Philip said slowly, but with an excited gleam in his eye, "She may be right, Lydia. The police at this stage—hell, I don't know. Are they going to listen to a lot of fairy-tale nonsense about old women in the country and disappearing brides? They like facts. Stolen jewelry. Bodies. . . . I'd like to see what this advertisement about Blandina brings. And anyway we haven't lost the pendant. I've got it in my pocket."

June made a motion of clapping her hands. "Ha! The villain foiled!" she declared triumphantly.

18

"Aurora! Are you still sleeping?"

The familiar voice, close to her ear, stirred her reluctantly from deep slumber. She didn't want to wake. She didn't know why she wanted so much to cling to unconsciousness. She could hear birds singing, and the light against her eyes told her that it was morning and the sun was shining. Once she had loved to wake to a sunny morning.

"No! I'm awake," she murmured.

"Good girl. Look! It's a fine day and we're moving."

"Moving?"

"I told you last night."

"Did you? I don't remember. No, you didn't tell me."

She was coming slowly awake, sitting up in bed, seeing the now familiar room and his familiar head on the pillow.

The room with the locked door she was to leave behind, since he said so, but his face with the narrowed, amused eyes, the tilted eyebrows, the half smile that teased her, this face that she knew like a well-loved map, was coming with her. Every morning when she awoke she would find it on the pillow beside her. Blurred with sleep and languor, for a moment she was completely happy.

"Darling!" she murmured.

He smiled radiantly.

"That's right, my sweet. That's how I like to hear you talk."

She frowned a little. "Don't I always?"

"Not always. Not lately. Sometimes you've behaved as if you've hated the sight of me."

"Hated you! But if I had, I wouldn't have come away with you that night. Would I? Just as I was."

"Just as you were was sufficient, angel."

She smiled reminiscently. "You wouldn't even let me go back to pack a bag."

"I was afraid you might change your mind again."

"Oh, no. Not then. It was always you I loved. You knew that."

"So I did." He gathered her into his arms, pulling her down against his hard chest. "And I love you, too. When you're a good girl. Remember?"

It was strange the way she couldn't quite wake up. Her limbs were heavy and her head felt dull, as if she had had too much to drink, but was not quite drunk. Yet she didn't want to shake off this dullness because if she did there were vague frightening things that were no longer dreamlike. Things such as telephone calls, and voices shouting at her, and the key turning in the lock of her door. . . .

It was much better this way, being heavy and far-off, not even minding that the way he pressed her against him hurt her breasts, as if they were crushed inside the cage of his ribs.

"You said we were going somewhere?"

"Yes, I did. You've got to get up and pack."

"By train?"

"Perhaps."

"Oh, darling! We've caught so many trains. I'm really terribly tired."

"Do you want me to leave you behind?"

"Don't be silly! Of course I don't."

His smiling eyes caressed her. "Then wake up, Aurora darling. And be a good girl. No tricks."

"Tricks?"

Suddenly he pushed her from him.

"You know damn well what I mean. I think half the time you put on this being stupid act. Or didn't you take your pills last night?"

"Yes, I did. You watched me."

"They're good for your nerves. You know that, don't you. You've been quite ill, you know, and I don't want to have to put you in a hospital. I'm looking after you as well as I can. I'm looking after both of us." His brilliant gaze pierced into her. "Aren't I?" he asked significantly, and then gave his soft laugh.

"All right, angel. Don't worry about it. Kiss me."

Automatically she bent her head to obey. But as his arms tightened round her she began to shiver. It was not because of the pain of her crushed breasts, but because of that now familiar fear. His arms held this terribly frightening enchantment, and she could not escape. She was mesmerized, she would take the pills for her nerves, or anything else he told her to do. She knew that she was helpless against him, and so long as he wanted her she didn't care that he dominated her.

Yet when he had left the room, saying he was going to get coffee, and she got tiredly out of bed to sit at the dressing-table, the fear swept over her again.

For the face looking back at her from the mirror had changed so much. It was quite colorless, and rather puffy, with dark hollows round her eyes, and her eyes themselves dull and heavy-lidded. Her hair, too, was limp and flat against her head, all the life gone out of it.

He only loved her when she was beautiful. She knew that. Her beauty had been her weapon over him. So how could he love this white-faced travesty of herself?

And if he didn't love her, what was going to happen to her?

Footsteps outside the door telling her he was coming back made her seize the hairbrush and hurriedly try to brush some life into her hair.

But no one came in for a moment. There were voices instead. She could hear what was apparently the end of a conversation.

"But it's my wife, I told you last night. I have to go. I must go."

"It can wait a day or two."

"But if I don't go immediately she won't come back. I'll lose trace of her."

"My dear chap, if she's left you, you know the reason. It's a waste of time your pursuing her. And I can't spare you at present. You know that damned well."

"Then I shall go in any case."

"I don't think so. I really don't think you will, you know."

The voices stopped. The door opened. The girl at the mirror began to tremble.

19

The woman behind the reception desk in the Bayswater hotel bridled a little when Philip confidingly leaned across the desk to her.

"I was talking to you the other day, Miss—"

"Perkins. Miss Perkins. Yes, I remember you. You were asking about your aunt, Mrs. Paxton. Did you find her?"

"Actually, no. At least, I don't think so."

The woman looked mystified. "You mean you're not sure?"

"Not entirely. Can you describe exactly what she looked like?"

"Well—she was just an old woman, not especially conspicuous. Grey hair, of course. No identifying marks, as the police call them."

"Too bad," said Philip pleasantly. "Was she tall?"

"Yes, quite. Held herself well for an old lady."

Philip suddenly had an idea. He took a pencil from his pocket and began to sketch swiftly on the desk pad.

"Did she look like this?"

Miss Perkins studied the sketch and giggled nervously.

"O-oh! What a big nose. No, I don't think her nose was that big."

"But did she have a long nose?"

"Well, yes, I think you could say it was quite long. What are you getting at, if I may ask?"

"I'm just trying to satisfy myself about a point that's worrying me. Have you ever seen this before?"

Miss Perkins started back as he laid the gold pendant on the desk.

"Why, yes, I have. That's Mrs. Paxton's. I've often seen her wearing it. Well, if you've got that, you've found your aunt, haven't you? Or"—her eyes popped—"how else did you get it?"

"That's another story," Philip said. "Thank you very much, Miss Perkins. You've been quite a help."

"But what are you trying to do? Is it some plot? If it is," Miss Perkins was calling after him, her voice sharp with frustration, "why don't you get the police?"

"Can't tell you now. Watch the daily newspapers."

In the street Philip went into a telephone box and dialled the number of Aurora's flat.

"Hullo!" came Lydia's excited voice. "Is that you, Philip?"

"Yes. What's happened?"

"How do you know something has?"

"By your voice, stupid." He didn't add that already he knew every inflection of her voice, when she was happy, when she was tired, when she suffered from disappointment or remorse, or even when she coolly hid her feelings. All the little things he hadn't known about Aurora. . . .

"I've had a telephone call from someone who has seen our advertisement."

"Who was he? What does he say?"

Philip, fresh from his illuminating and disturbing interview with Miss Perkins at the Bayswater hotel, was almost as tense with excitement as Lydia.

"He says he has a café on the Portsmouth Road. He doesn't know Blandina, but about two months ago an old woman called by that name stopped for tea. At least, Blandina was a passenger in a car with two other people. He said he particularly remembered the name because it was unusual."

"Did you get his exact address?"

"Of course, what do you think!" came Lydia's cool voice. "When do we go down?"

"Now. I'll be round. How's June?"

"She's got two gorgeous black eyes. She says she's fine, otherwise, and is rather enjoying herself. I'm doing her shopping because she doesn't want people to think she's been beaten up. How long will you be?"

"Fifteen minutes. If you can stop talking. I've got a hunch we haven't much time to lose."

"Good. That will give me time to rush out for June's lunch," Lydia answered serenely. "Don't go without me."

"Don't go without me. . . ." The words echoed in Philip's head as he impatiently edged his way across London through the exasperatingly slow traffic. If she only knew, she had become, in these weeks, more than a habit with him. He had grown accustomed to her intensely alive face, her short, ruffled hair, her eager response, her impulsive and reckless kindness. She had kindled something in him that responded to a different kind of beauty from Aurora's exquisite perfection. But he made mistakes, choosing the wrong moment to tell her so, getting tied up with his sense of loyalty to Aurora whom, after all, he had been going to marry.

His thoughts had become incoherent by the time he reached the flat in St. John's Wood. He sat honking the horn until Lydia came flying out, hatless as usual, her cheeks pink.

"Just made it. June's staying out of sight, although I don't think she'd mind seeing you. She's more of a sport than I'd have thought at first. She's keeping her ears open again today for any suspicious sounds. But there won't be any, after last night. I should think the fellow would have the sense to keep away. He's probably been reading the papers to see if June's body was discovered." She gave him a quick rueful glance. "I'm talking too much again."

"Go ahead," said Philip mildly. "So long as you can stop to tell me where we're going."

"I'm sorry. If I don't talk this awful excitement, or whatever it is, just swells up inside me. We've got to look for a caravan café on the side of the road just before we get to Guildford. This man only rang half an hour ago."

"What did he sound like?"

"Rather slow and solemn. The philosopher type, I should think. Observing life from the side of a main highway. Did you find out anything this morning?"

Philip nodded and tossed his information over casually. "The pendant is Blandina's. Or was."

"Blandina's! Then—do you suppose Armand stole it? Or borrowed it? And that's why it's important to get it back."

"We might go on down to Greenhill and find out. What do you say? Tell him he doesn't need to go round hitting women on the head to get back his bit of jewelry."

"And demand to know what is in all those bedrooms?" Lydia said breathlessly.

"I don't know about the bedrooms. But we can try some bluff. I've a notion they're so deadly serious they won't be able to stand bluff."

"Armand will be in London."

"I've a feeling he won't. I rang his office just after I rang you and there was no answer. I think M'sieu Armand might be taking a day at home today. It's not surprising he sacked his secretary, you know. She might have been answering too many awkward questions."

Lydia let out her breath in a large sigh. "I don't think I can stand so much all at once."

"Don't worry," Philip reassured her. "We'll have a double whisky with the postmistress. It might even make her remember the deceased Aunt Hannah. When we've done with resurrecting aunts, we'll—"

"What?" Lydia asked fearfully.

"I don't know. But I think somehow, strange as it may seem, we'll have found Aurora."

The café proprietor was a lean, tall, lugubrious person who was absorbed in a book, and seemed loath to put it aside. He did so at last, carefully marking his place, and asked what they wanted.

"Tea," said Lydia blithely. "We'll talk while we have it."

The man was very perceptive. "You're the people who've been asking about the old lady!"

"That's right," Philip answered. "Can you tell us anything?"

"Nothing except the name. That, being unusual, stuck in my mind. And the fact that she seemed lost, sort of. I worried about her a bit. I live here by myself and I notice my customers. Anything different strikes me. I got this old woman on my mind for a bit, and then when I read your ad this morning I thought to myself, I bet it's that old woman they're wanting. It's the unusual name, see. Blandina. I haven't come across it before, even in a book, and I'm a great reader. Milk and sugar, madam?"

"Thank you," said Lydia. She admired the deft way he poured the tea, economical with his movements, no slopping in the saucer. The book he had been reading, she noticed, was the *Diary of a Country Parson*. In his own way he was as memorable as Blandina.

Philip produced the rough sketch he had made.

"Was this old woman anything like this?"

The man studied it, his head on one side thoughtfully.

"Sorry sir. You've had your trip for nothing, if that's the party you're inquiring about. It's not her."

"Are you sure?" Lydia exclaimed.

"Quite sure, madam. I know it was night time, but the light was on in the car and I saw her quite clearly. She wasn't like that. She was more crumpled, if you know what I mean. The way old people get when the flesh sinks back into their body. Consuming itself, you might say. This old lady was like that, and sort of scared and lost, as if she didn't know how she'd come to be in the back of that car."

"What make of car was it? Did you notice?"

"Certainly I did." The man drew himself up, his powers of observation challenged. "I don't often have Jaguars pulling up here. They're pub traffic, usually. They and the Bentleys and the Rolls."

"And who was this old lady with?" Philip asked softly.

"A man and a girl. The girl was pretty. She seemed to be comforting the old woman. I got the feeling they'd stopped for tea, unobtrusively, if you follow me, because the old lady needed some sort of stimulation. But they wanted it quick and without fuss, perhaps without being noticed too much. Yes, that's how I saw it. The man's name was Armand. I remember that. The girl said it. Both unusual names, in a way. But the Blandina one struck me."

"Thank you," said Philip. "That helps us a lot."

"You think that's the party you're looking for, sir?"

"I think so, without a doubt."

"I couldn't tell you where they were heading for. And I'm sure the old woman didn't know either. She was saying something about a strange road. I read too much, of course, being on my own all the time. But my fancy was she was being kidnapped. Well, you know. Taken somewhere she wouldn't like when she got there. One of those old women's homes she didn't want to go to, most likely. More tea, sir?"

"No, thank you. I'm afraid you do read too much, or your imagination is a bit vivid."

The man nodded eagerly. "I expect you're right. I watch all those cars whirling past, night and day, and I wonder where in hell they're all going, and if they know themselves. So then I get my nose in a book about the old days, nice slow jogging in carriages a few miles at a time. That would be the life for me. You'd know where you were going then. Not whirled away into the night like that poor old Blandina. More tea, madam?"

"No, thank you very much. It was very good. We have to go on. We're in a hurry, too. But we do know where we're going. At least—" Lydia hesitated. Nothing could be more ordinary than this caravan pulled in at the roadside, with its counter flaps down, than the cars speeding past, the clouds moving slowly over an early summer sky, the smell of hot sweet tea and petrol fumes, and smoke from a distant bonfire. Yet suddenly everything seemed completely unreal, as unreal as it must have been to a bewildered old woman, crumpled and nondescript, being hurried away in the night to some unknown destination.

Lydia began practising her friendly and casual smile some time before they reached Greenhill. As the miles slid away it became a little wobbly, and her heart was beating unevenly again. She rehearsed out loud.

"It's us again, would you believe it! How is Aunt Clara? And Aunt Blandina, you must have missed this piece of jewelry. Did you know dear nephew Armand had helped himself to it, and given it to someone else's bride?" She broke off. "But Philip! Who *is* Aurora's husband?"

"I should be surprised if she has one," Philip said, with a quiet grimness that effectively dispatched Lydia's frivolity.

"You mean, she's the decoy, or something?"

"She's in this, I'm sure. How, I don't know. But we'll find that out today, if I'm not mistaken."

Lydia hugged her arms round herself. She refused to start trembling again. It was so weak.

"If Aurora isn't married, if she's living in sin, that will be the end as far as Daddy is concerned. Even if it's been done at the point of a gun, I don't think he'd approve. Oh, gosh! We're almost there."

"If you're nervous, will you stay in the car?"

"Stay in the car! What *are* you talking about?"

Philip grinned, and made his familiar gesture of laying his hand over hers.

"Do you know something, Lydia? I didn't tell you before. It seemed disloyal. But Aurora asked me to marry her—well, before I'd got round to doing the asking myself."

Lydia looked at him in astonishment. "But surely, allowing for good manners and all that, surely a man doesn't have to accept a woman!"

"Of course not. I was crazy about her. I would have got round to it—it just happened a little sooner this way."

Lydia was sceptical. "I don't think that's true. I think she was afraid of losing you."

"No, not that. It's more likely she was trying to escape from something that frightened her. I offered as good a solution as any. And I really was crazy about her. A beautiful woman always knocks me silly. Beware of that in the future—give me a sharp kick when I start behaving oddly."

"My kick has quite a punch to it," Lydia murmured, mixing her metaphors happily.

In the future, he had said. After this nightmare visit, being made in brilliant sunshine in mid-afternoon, was over. . . .

The house looked very quiet, with all its windows shut. But that was not unusual. It had never betrayed signs of life. One rang the doorbell, and presently footsteps announced that someone was at home.

Lydia, standing very close to Philip on the doorstep, waited. The lawns needed cutting, she noticed. Jules must have been too busy in the house lately to attend to his gardening duties. It was strange that such a small part of the garden was cultivated. Beyond that the grass and weeds, pushing up among elderly rose bushes and shrubs, grew rank.

"No one's coming," she whispered.

He put his finger on the bell again, and held it there a moment. They could hear it ringing far off. But still it brought no footsteps. The door remained shut. The windows were closed and blank.

"They said there were going away as soon as Miss Wilberforce was well enough," Lydia said. "Do you think they've gone, whether she's well or not?"

"Cleared out before we called again? Surely they're not that scared of us!"

"Good heavens! Supposing they are. They must have awfully guilty consciences. Why? Philip, we've got to find out."

"I agree," he said tersely.

"Then why are we standing here? No one's going to open that door. Let's go round to the back. If there's no one home, you know—"

"I know. We break in."

"But we've got to find something unlocked. I expect the place is bolted like the Tower of London."

"If they've left in a hurry they might have slipped up on that. Let's see."

Ten minutes later they were inside the house. A loose bolt on a pantry window had given way to their joint pressure and enabled them to slip quietly inside.

But now Lydia was overcome with fear. Supposing, after all, the house was not empty, but that its occupants were deliberately not answering the door to callers. Supposing, at the next turn of the passage, they came abruptly on Blandina, silent and terrifying.

The large kitchen showed the remains of a hasty breakfast. Dishes were left untidily in the sink, there were broken egg-shells, and the remains of a glass of milk. Philip swiftly counted four cups. "Clara, Blandina, Armand, and Jules," he said. "Jules obviously eats with the family when they all eat in the kitchen."

"There's this glass of milk."

"They might have forced some of that down poor old Clara. She'd need building up for the journey. Come on. Let's look in the other rooms."

The hall, the dining-room, and the drawing-room, the only part of the ground floor that Lydia had seen on her previous visits, were the same as usual, except that the curtains were drawn in the dining-room, making it dim and gloomy. It was a chilly room. Lydia shivered, but had no time to linger for Philip was calling her. "I say, come and look in here."

He had opened a door farther along the hall, and was looking in at a library, cold, dark, and dusty.

"No one's been in here for years, by the look of it. It seems to me the main rooms have been used and kept tidy, and the rest of the house shut up. I shouldn't be surprised if there were no servants here at all except Jules."

"Because they couldn't get them or because they couldn't afford them?"

"Or because they preferred not to have any strangers about?"

"I was told it was the cook's day off," Lydia said.

Philip was sceptical.

"A long day, probably. My guess is that Armand doesn't come here very much and when he does strangers aren't encouraged. Let's go upstairs."

Lydia hesitated a moment, wondering how he could leap up the long flight of stairs so confidently. Then she resolutely followed him, telling herself that she had been longing, after all, to get a look into all those closed rooms.

One door led into Blandina's, and another into Miss Wilberforce's. The others. . . . Supposing the house were not empty after all. They hadn't really stopped to listen, to hear whether anyone stirred, or to see if anyone secretly watched them.

"Come on," called Philip. "You know whose these rooms were. The grandfather clock is still going, anyway."

Yes, that was the measured sound that accentuated the silence. The slow tick-tock that she had fancifully thought was ticking the sick Blandina's life away. But Blandina was not reduced yet to counting the seconds. She was superbly indifferent to them. It was poor Clara whose time was running out.

The first door Philip opened was that of Blandina's room.

Involuntarily Lydia hesitated on the threshold. She was so sure the wide bed would contain the old lady, her nose poking skywards, her sharp black eyes refusing stubbornly to close.

"What are you scared of?" said Philip. "There's no one here."

The bed was tidy, the heavy counterpane drawn up over any dishevelled bedclothes. The wardrobe, which Philip had opened, was empty of clothes. There were no brushes or cosmetics on the dressing-table. There was, indeed, little sign that the room had been so recently inhabited. A few hairpins and a grey hair or two in the old-fashioned hair tidy, a slightly dented cushion on a chair, and one of the floor rugs a little crooked. That was all.

Miss Wilberforce's room was much the same, except that there was a half-empty glass of lemon and barley water on the bedside table, and the bed had scarcely been tidied. She must have been got up at the last minute when the car was ready.

The famous black handbag had gone. Had she noticed it was a good deal lighter and slimmer?

"This is where I spilt the letters," Lydia said, because some normal conversation had to break the terrifying silence. "I wonder if I missed any. I couldn't look round very much with Blandina watching like a hawk."

She got down on her hands and knees to peer under the chest of drawers, then lifted the heavy valance of the bed.

"Oh, there's one!" she cried. "Oh, it's just one she's written to herself. No, it's not! No, it's not, Philip! There's something else stuck in the envelope. Look! It's in different handwriting. It—"

Her voice died away. The clumsily printed words, "Don't stay here! They're all murderers," seemed to quiver before her eyes.

"Philip! Who's written this?"

"Melodrama!" he murmured softly.

"It will be the person who added the postscript to that letter to me," Lydia exclaimed, answering her own question.

"Most likely. Keep that. And come on."

He was impatient to see what else was to be found, conscious of time growing more and more vital.

But the remainder of the rooms told little. There was one that seemed as if it had been recently occupied because of its lack of dust. The others were in a similar condition to the library downstairs, closed, chilly, slightly musty smelling, untouched for a long time.

Except one round the turn of the passage, and that was locked. Philip tried in vain to look through the keyhole. He rattled at the knob. All the doors in the house were solidly made of oak of the best workmanship. It was impossible to try to break in. Besides, what would be there, but more mustiness and dust?

"In the best fairy-tale traditions," Lydia said shakily. "The door that mustn't be opened. Oh, Philip, let's go."

"Scared?" he asked quizzically.

"Yes, I am. And I'm ashamed of it. I feel—ghoulish."

All at once there was a distant thud downstairs. She leapt into his arms.

"Steady!" he said. "Do you want to wait here?"

"No! I'm coming with you."

They hurried down the stairs.

"Is anyone home?" Philip called loudly.

In the kitchen a kitten miaoued. Philip laughed with relief. He found the tabby-striped offender and picked it up. It began to purr with a volume of sound completely out of proportion to its meagre body.

"It's followed us in through the window. Let's give it the rest of Clara's milk."

"And then let's go," Lydia begged. "There's nothing here. Frankly, I can't stand the place. I hope I never see it again."

Philip poured milk into a saucer and watched the kitten lapping.

"All right," he said at last. "But we'll have a word with the postmistress on the way."

The sun shone brightly over the strange, untended garden with its tidy centre—which was like the house with its dusted and polished pool of rooms flanked by the undusted airless ones. The rhododendrons were bursting into crimson bloom. A thrush was standing in a listening attitude on the lawn, and the kitten which had followed them out crouched with comical intensity, a miniature potential thunderbolt.

The brightness of the afternoon made the silent house with its untold story even more eerily mystifying. Looking up at the first-floor windows, it was possible to identify the one that belonged to the locked room. But it looked exactly the same as the others, blank and shut.

"But we haven't finished with this," Philip reminded her. "We're in it now, whether we like it or not."

Lydia shivered and begged again. "Let's go."

The postmistress offered them tea, and told them about the fast car that had gone through the village early that morning.

"I was just making my cup of tea," she said. "If my kitchen didn't face the street I wouldn't have seen it, it was gone that quick."

"Could you see who was in it?"

"No. It went by too fast. Well, now, what a disappointment, you coming all the way down to visit your friends and there being no one home. Are they close friends of yours?"

She peered at them with her faded, lavender-colored eyes.

"No. Not particularly."

The postmistress, who was a genial person, gave a snort of laughter and said, "Then I can say my piece about them folding their tents like the Arabs and silently stealing away. They do, you know. We know nothing about their comings and goings. They don't shop in the village, or even have a char from hereabouts. But there, you can't know everyone's family history, can you? Plenty of town people have country houses in these parts. They change hands from time to time, and you don't hear much about it. I understand these particular people were on the Continent a lot. I'm sorry I can't help you more."

Philip drove very fast out of the village. Lydia didn't ask him why he was hurrying so much. She was a little afraid to be told. But all at once she said intensely, "I know Aurora's in that locked room. I know."

"Sleeping for a hundred years?" Philip cocked an eyebrow at her. But he didn't laugh. Nor did he deny her fantastic statement. Instead, he slowed down the car.

"You know, there was a ledge along those top windows. I rather think I could work my way along and get in that room through the window."

"Could you? Could you really?"

He smiled at her eagerness. Now he stopped the car.

"I believe you're encouraging me to break my neck!"

"Don't be absurd! But supposing Aurora is there—I mean, it might be important to hurry."

"Let's go back," said Philip.

Lydia stood long enough in the garden to see Philip emerge from a window and work his careful way along the ledge to the safety of the next window.

"Nothing to it," he called down to her. "Easier than climbing a coconut palm."

Then he eased up the window and began to climb inside.

Lydia didn't wait any longer. Nervous as she was of the dim, eerie house, its only sound the ticking of the grandfather clock, like a ponderous heart, she raced up the stairs, arriving breathlessly at the other side of the locked door.

"Are you in there? Philip! Have you found anything? Open the door!"

Philip rattled the handle. After a moment he said, "Can't. There's no key. It's been locked from the outside and the key taken away. There's nothing here, by the way, except an empty bed."

Lydia sagged against the wall. "Then why is the door locked? To shut in a ghost?"

There were sounds from within as Philip opened drawers and cupboards. Then his voice came back, low and reflective.

"I believe you're right, Lydia. There is a ghost. Now I'm going back the way I came, so run along downstairs." His voice rose a little, tautly. "Get out of this damned place!"

She obeyed without speaking. She ran down the stairs as if the great clock, the only alive thing in the house, were swinging ponderous after her, its pendulum thrust out like a long grasping arm. She literally tumbled out into the cool garden, and looked up to see Philip completing his precarious climb.

Presently he joined her. She didn't immediately ask him what he had found. She clung to his arm with gratitude and relief.

"Were you scared?" he asked.

"Petrified."

"There's nothing to be frightened of now. There's no one there. All that's in that room is the dress Aurora was wearing the night she ran off. You remember? It was grey, thin stuff, like cobwebs. And her shoes. High-heeled bits of nonsense. Quite impractical for ordinary wear."

"Ordinary?" Lydia said faintly.

"One imagines she's decently equipped for other journeys."

"But why lock the door if that's all there is to hide?"

"I hardly know. Unless it's from habit. Come. We've got to get back to London before five o'clock." He added in explanation, "If that fellow Villette isn't in his office this time we go to the police."

"He won't be there," Lydia said fatalistically.

"If he has any business at all apart from—" Philip suddenly cleared his throat and finished mildly, "He can't completely neglect his business. He must leave instructions with someone."

On the steep, linoleum-covered stairway leading up to Armand's office they encountered the postman.

"Office is closed up there," he said. "I've been trying to get an answer for two days now. You don't happen to know if they're away on holiday, do you? There's no notice up."

There were also three bottles of milk lined up forlornly outside the door.

"If they were on holiday, one imagines they would notify the milkman," Philip said. "Afraid I can't help you. We were looking for Mr. Villette ourselves."

"Doesn't even have a girl in his office these days," the postman complained. "If you ask me, he's short of money and he's trying to get off with the trust funds!"

The man laughed loudly and clattered off down the stairs.

Lydia looked at the milk bottles and thought of a kitten lapping milk in an empty house in the country.

Philip seemed deep in thought. Suddenly he took her arm.

"Come on. Let's go to the nearest police station. It's better to have the law on our side before breaking down doors."

20

It took two hours and copious notes before they could convince the sergeant that there was real cause for their suspicions. He reprimanded them for not reporting the attempted burglary and assault on June Birch, but for the rest he kept muttering with the greatest scepticism, "Disappearing brides, kidnapped old women!"

He didn't care for it at all. If he let himself be taken in by it he would be laughed at by his superiors. But when Philip mentioned the torn newspaper and the paragraph about the unidentified body found beneath the cliffs along the Dorset coast, he grudgingly showed interest and said he would check to see whether identification had ever been established.

He had to go away to do this and when he came back he suggested that they might go and take a look at Armand Villette's offices. It seemed as if his activities, and particularly his files, might bear looking into.

"Don't suppose you noticed the number of that Jag?" he asked. "No? Well, let's go."

Lydia was asked to remain in the car while they went up the stairs to the office again. She seemed to wait a very long time. It was growing dark and the streets were emptying. Every sound was forlorn, the shriek of a car's brakes, the slow, dragging footsteps of an old woman passing, the rise and fall of a newsboy's call on the corner, somewhere a street fiddler playing a sentimental song. . . .

She wondered what she would tell Millicent when she had promised to ring that evening. One either said nothing had happened, everything was fine, or one began to prepare her for—what? This silly obsession that somewhere in another locked room there was not merely Aurora's cobwebby dress and high-heeled shoes, but Aurora herself. . . .

When at last Philip returned, he was alone. He said tersely, "I'm taking you home, darling. You can spend the evening with June, can't you?"

Lydia saw his grim face. "Why? What's the matter?"

"We found Armand Villette."

"What! Locked in, too? How did he explain that?"

"He didn't explain it. He was in no condition to do so—today or any other day."

"He's dead!" Lydia gasped.

Philip nodded. "The sergeant's sent for a doctor. But it's too late, I'm afraid. There's a fireplace full of burnt paper, and most of the files seem to have disappeared. He—or someone—had been having quite a clean-up."

"You mean he's been murdered?"

"No, it's obviously suicide. Sleeping tablets, I think."

"But why? This makes nonsense of everything."

"Yes, it does."

"He was frightened of something last night," Lydia said, remembering the man's sudden unexpected arrival, his uneasy eyes, and the way he had pressed his hands together. "Supposing he isn't the villain after all."

Philip frowned thoughtfully. Then he got into the car and started the engine.

"I'm taking you home. Stay with June in the meantime. I'll ring if there's anything to report. Get yourself a good meal. You look like a starving child."

But what did it matter how she looked? Lydia thought wildly. Where, anyway, did beauty get one, if one could take Aurora as an example?

It was the next day before the police traced the Jaguar to a garage in Brighton. It had been left there by a tall, good-looking man who said he was acting under instructions from the owner who would be out of England for an indefinite period. This person was obviously Jules, the gardener. He had been alone at the time.

After that the trail vanished.

A broadcast appeal had been made for relatives of Armand Villette, but no one seemed to be in the least interested in the stocky, grey-haired man, minus spectacles, eyelids firmly covering the round, rolling eyes, who lay waiting for someone to shed tears over him.

It was not possible to decide for whom the scrawled note found on his desk, written in a state of incoherent emotion, had been intended. *"Forgive me. I can't stand any more of this. It's too much. I'm caught in it too far."* And again. *"Forgive me."*

A hasty preliminary inquiry into Armand Villette's life and practice as a solicitor was being made, but the most urgent thing was not to reconstruct Armand's life, but to trace the two old women, Blandina Paxton and Clara Wilberforce, seemingly spirited away in charge of the gardener Jules. And, of course, Aurora Hawkins, who, if she was not actively involved in this abduction, could at least give the police a great deal of information. They would also try to trace the secretary who had followed Aurora, and who had had such a suspiciously brief stay in the office.

"They'll have gone to Aunt Honoria in Brittany," Lydia said, with certainty.

"But who would be taking them now Armand is dead?"

"Blandina, of course. She told me they would be going abroad."

"We're not even sure that woman is Blandina," Philip pointed out.

"Whoever she is, she knew her way around. I wouldn't be surprised if she mesmerized Armand into taking those sleeping tablets, especially when he had blundered."

"How had he blundered?"

"Why, in taking me down that first day, of course. I should never have been allowed to go there. Looking back, it does seem quite incredibly stupid, doesn't it? I wonder they didn't move there and then."

"Except that Clara was ill and couldn't be shifted. Her illness was genuine, I should think, as Doctor Neave told us."

"Then why that S O S in her letter?"

"Whoever sent that probably didn't believe her illness was genuine. Probably had reason to be suspicious." Philip rubbed his face tiredly. "You know, Lydia, that must have been Aurora."

"You mean she's been in that house all the time?"

"I don't know. It sounds crazy. But I wouldn't be surprised."

"Neither would I," Lydia admitted, for things were coming clear now. "She's been bribed or blackmailed into this. Those times she rang—she probably wanted help. Do you remember she began to say 'Come and get me.' She was probably interrupted by—well, by Blandina, I expect, who'd be enough to scare the wits out of anyone! And when she rang about the pendant, she was probably made to do that, too. I wonder why that pendant is so important."

"Of course it's important," Philip said harshly. "It's been identified as Blandina Paxton's. And supposing that old woman at the bottom of the cliffs is the real Blandina—"

"Then why on earth was Armand fool enough to let Aurora have the pendant?"

"He might not have known she had it. The old lady might have given it to her. She was in the car that night, you remember. The café man said so. Armand might only have discovered she had it when it was too late—I mean, after he had kidnapped her from her wedding."

"Kidnapped!"

"You don't suppose she would have gone with him willingly! He must have persuaded her, by some threat, to meet him just outside the village that night, and she went more or less innocently. After all, she had no luggage. She hadn't meant to run off that night."

"Then why didn't he make sure she had the pendant with her then?" Lydia demanded.

"At that stage he might not have known about it. But when she told him she had left incriminating evidence behind, as no doubt she did, in an effort to get away, he had to organize some means of getting it back."

"Why didn't he tell someone all this before he died? It's so useless to die this way." It was Lydia's turn to press her hands wearily against her face. "But where," she said, "is Aurora now? Armand is no longer holding threats over her. Why doesn't she come home?"

Philip turned away. "Perhaps she's afraid to."

Two elderly women, one very feeble, and an extremely good-looking girl, supposing Aurora were with them, would not be an inconspicuous trio.

The search intensified when it was established beyond doubt, after visits to the Bayswater hotel and to her doctor and dentist, that the body of an old woman who had met her death at the foot of a steep and lonely cliff, having obviously been driven there in a car, was that of Blandina Paxton.

It seemed evident that at the time she had died her solicitor, who was significantly in possession of a Power of Attorney from her, had thought she was completely alone in the world. She had not seen fit to divulge to him the existence of a feckless and shaming younger sister who later, deprived of her weekly remittance of five pounds in cash, began to make very awkward inquiries.

Whether that younger sister still existed was beginning to be a matter of grave doubt.

"But now Armand is dead, nothing can happen to her!" Lydia protested.

"Not if Armand was alone in the plot. I begin to think he was only the catspaw for that super dragon."

Lydia laughed shakily.

"You're mixing your metaphors. And June's still pining for the return of the man with the key to Aurora's flat. After all, we know now that wasn't Armand. I feel that all this has the simplest explanation if only we could think of it."

"We'll have to think quickly," Philip said grimly.

"You mean Clara's in danger?"

"Not Clara, no. I don't think they'll do anything to Clara now. It would be madness."

"Then you must mean Aurora," Lydia said slowly. "Because she knows too much?"

"She's always known too much."

"But if she's in it willingly—"

"Do you think she is? Armand, being a man, might have protected her, but now there's only that she-wolf, and I don't imagine she'll care any more for a young and beautiful woman than she did for the old and senile."

"There's the handsome chauffeur," Lydia said uneasily. "If he *is* the chauffeur I imagine he will have made himself scarce by now. If he isn't—"

Philip looked at her. "Are you thinking what I'm thinking? What we both should have thought long ago. That the handsome Jules may be the man with that door-key in his possession?"

Only one fact emerged in the next few hours, but that was a significant one. Blandina Paxton, a wealthy old woman living almost parsimoniously in a quiet hotel, had, in the past five years, used up the astonishing sum of nearly forty thousand pounds.

Securities had been sold, amounts had been withdrawn from her various banking accounts, all, apparently, for the purpose of re-investment in other better, but as it appeared, non-existent properties or shares.

It was as neat a piece of daylight robbery as he had come across, Sergeant Peters said.

No wonder Armand Villette had ducked out of trouble via an overdose of sleeping pills. He must have thought he was sitting pretty, a trusting, senile old woman like that, alone in the world, who had been pathetically easy to hoodwink. Although, at the end, she must have been troublesome, since it had been necessary to end her life. No doubt also she had had several predecessors. But the predecessors apparently hadn't had younger sisters, appearing so inconveniently out of the blue that a story had had to be spontaneously fabricated to prevent the police being brought in.

"They probably intended to tip Clara over a cliff, too," Sergeant Peters said. "But seeing she had this slight stroke they may have decided to be patient and wait until she had another. All nicely legitimate, as no doubt Hannah with the heart trouble was. But you two, with your poking and prying, forced their hands. And now what have we got? A suicide, and two run-away women, plus this rather anonymous bird, the chauffeur. Now that," he said thoughtfully, "is a man I'd like a word with."

Little as Philip liked Lydia staying in Aurora's flat, someone had to be there, for it was possible Aurora would try to make another telephone call.

Lydia was certain now that everything Aurora had done had been against her will. As witness the locked bedroom door, the smuggled messages in Clara's letters, the crumpled chiffon dress pushed into the back of the wardrobe in the locked room.

What was she wearing now, Lydia wondered. One of Blandina's (the false Blandina) cut-down, severe black dresses, so that no one would notice she was young and beautiful?

She insisted on staying in the flat, and then hated being alone and had to beg for June Birch's talkative company. So that there were two of them to jump when the telephone rang, or footsteps seemed to hesitate outside the door.

Usually the telephone caller was Millicent who had had to be told what was happening, and who was in a constant state of nervous panic.

Then at last Sergeant Peters rang to say laconically, "We've picked her up."

"Who?" Lydia cried. "Aurora?"

"No, the old lady. Clara Wilberforce."

21

She was having a nice strong cup of tea in the cafeteria at Victoria station. She had been there for two hours enjoying the freedom, realizing how much, during those days in the country, she had missed the bustle and noise and passing faces. She loved faces. They were like leaves turning in the wind, some bright and young and shining, some crinkled and dry, some showing their undersides, their seamy, private sides that were intensely interesting to the onlooker, but careless of them, poor dears. Because one didn't show one's more distressed and uglier thoughts, Miss Wilberforce mused as she sat on the hard chair, elbows resting on the plastic-topped table.

One determinedly made the best of any situation, even of the one in which she was placed. Though that had been a great deal more pleasant since she and Blandina had been alone at the seaside.

Jules had driven them to the station early the other morning and they had taken a train to Brighton. So exciting. Though there Blandina, in spite of her wealth, had turned mean and taken only one room in a rather seedy-looking boarding-house. The beds had been uncomfortable, and she had had to lie all night listening to Blandina turning and twisting and occasionally snoring when she lay with her long nose pointing to the ceiling.

Nor had Blandina let her out of her sight during the day, although Miss Wilberforce would dearly have loved to potter down the esplanade alone and perhaps post a letter on the pier. No, it had been the old, familiar, bossy attitude.

"You know you always managed to lose yourself at the seaside as a child!" Or, "You're not strong enough to walk that far. You've had a serious illness." Or, "Didn't the doctor say no letter writing."

On the other hand it had been rather nice to have someone genu-

inely concerned with one's welfare, and when Blandina was not flinging out sharp orders she was very quiet. She had a plotting, planning
look, and Miss Wilberforce was happy not to interrupt her in this private state of mind. It was exciting to breathe the crisp sea air and to
see life going on, and to be away, if one dared admit it, from the silent midnight intruder in her room, from the noise of Jules's mower
over grass that didn't need cutting, and above all from nephew Armand's generous but vaguely embarrassing attentions.

But this had lasted only for two nights and a day. Then Blandina
had had an urgent telephone call. She had come back to say curtly
that they were going to catch a train.

"Oh, I liked it here!" Miss Wilberforce said regretfully. "I was enjoying the sea air. It was doing me a great deal of good."

Something had upset Blandina, for her cheeks were sallow and
sunken, her eyes fiercely black and gleaming.

"Where you're going next will do you more good. Oh, *mon Dieu,*
can't you even keep pins in your hair to have a little neatness? No,
you must look always like a scarecrow."

She had never spoken like a Frenchwoman before. But all at once
she looked foreign, a sallow and old and bitter foreign woman.

Miss Wilberforce was frightened. She put her hand apologetically
to her soft, untidy hair and explained vaguely that since her illness
her hands shook so much.

Blandina quickly and roughly pulled the straying hair straight and
pinned it, and said, "Put your hat and coat on. Hurry! We have to
catch this train. It's very important."

"Where are we going now?" Miss Wilberforce asked timidly.

"Never you mind. But you ought to be happy. You'll be able to
write as many letters as you like. Yes, I promise you that. A dozen a
day if you want to."

"Goodness me, I don't know a dozen people!" Miss Wilberforce
murmured, overwhelmed. "But that's very kind of you, Blandina."

The old eyes snapped at her between their wrinkled bird's lids.
"Don't thank me. Thank your so dear nephew Armand, the fool!"

She said that as if she hated Armand. One had thought they were
so devoted. The problem was too much for Miss Wilberforce. It had
been difficult to concentrate since her illness. She really just enjoyed
sitting watching people, and this she was able to do in the train for
the next hour or so, and then in the cafeteria where Blandina had
taken her.

"We'll have some tea," Blandina had said, and had found an unoccupied table in the corner.

But after ordering the tea she had sprung up suddenly, saying she would be back in a few minutes. Clara was to wait there for her.

Miss Wilberforce wondered if she were feeling ill, she had left so abruptly. But even a few minutes' respite from her overpowering presence was a pleasure, and she hadn't been too alarmed.

Fifteen minutes, then half an hour had gone by. This was too much. At last Miss Wilberforce had had to go and make inquiries at the cloakroom.

But the attendant there couldn't be sure a very tall old woman in black ("with a rather long nose," Miss Wilberforce had specified, in curious apology—she had always been troubled by the length of Blandina's nose) had come in.

"I couldn't be sure, could I, duck? You can see how many people are in and out. Regular main highway, this. But she's not here now. If she's your sister you'd better go on home and let her find you there."

"Yes. Thank you," Miss Wilberforce murmured, with her infallible politeness, and went back to the cafeteria for another cup of tea. She enjoyed sitting there in this strange freedom, and some more tea might help her to think clearly.

For it did begin to look a little as if Blandina had left her behind, like a piece of unwanted or forgotten luggage.

At last the waitress, looking kind but bewildered, said, "You can't spend the day here, dear. Which train are you waiting for?"

"I'm not waiting for a train. I'm waiting for my sister. She said she'd be back, but she hasn't come."

"How long ago, dear?"

"Oh, let me see, about two hours."

"Well, I never! Hadn't you better give up and go home?"

"But I can't do that, actually. I haven't got a home except the one Blandina is taking me to."

"Blandina! Did you say Blandina?" The girl seemed very excited.

"Yes, I did. Do you know her?"

"Not personally, dear. But all the newspapers do. A name like that. Look, love, wait there a minute. Promise not to move."

"Of course I won't move if you ask me not to," Miss Wilberforce said with dignity, and thought the girl's face had been like a broad oak leaf, turning red in a frosty sun.

It was later that day that Lydia and Philip visited Miss Wilberforce in the hospital where she had been taken for observation and care. But she wasn't able to tell them any more than she had already told the police.

Her illness had been genuine, according to the doctor's report, she had been domineered and bullied by Blandina, but otherwise had been well cared for. She had exchanged no more than a few words with Jules, the gardener and chauffeur, although she said he had always seemed to be lurking near or in the house, and she had never seen Aurora unless she were the thin woman who had come and interfered with her drinking glass in the night.

The morning Blandina had taken her away she had thought she had heard someone crying, but Blandina had said she was imagining things.

The only thing that had seriously distressed her had been that when she had come to open her handbag in the train she had found that a great many of her letters had disappeared.

But no one was to worry, she said, smiling her gentle illumined smile. Blandina had promised she could write as many as she wished in the future.

"Did you ever think Blandina wasn't your sister?" Philip asked.

"That's what the nice policeman asked me, too. Yes, I did at first. It was that long nose. There's never been another like it in our family. But then when she was so bossy I knew it must be Blandina. I expect she's gone off again because she's ashamed of me. Not being able to keep my hair tidy and remember things. But isn't it nice that at last she's allowing me to write my own letters. I didn't like being treated like a child and told what to say."

So they were back where they had started, Philip said, with only a missing bride, and he was pretty certain she hadn't a wedding ring on her finger yet.

Looking at his haggard face, Lydia miserably twisted her own ringless finger. Aurora's absence, she decided, was even more effective than her presence. For this way, she haunted them completely.

22

The first thing Aurora saw when she opened her eyes was the photograph of the girl on the bedside table. The face was young, round, not particularly pretty, completely strange to her, and the girl wore an evening dress with sequined shoulder straps that had an old-fashioned look.

So the photograph was probably some years old. But whose was it, and why was it by her bedside?

She raised herself on her elbow and instantly the room swung darkly and dizzily. She felt terrible. She had missed taking tablets when they were travelling, but last night she had been forced to take them again. Jules had sat over her and there had been no escape.

So now her senses were completely blurred and she couldn't remember how she had got here, or indeed whose room in what house she was in.

A door banging downstairs made her start, and then she heard Aunt Blandina's voice declare loudly and bitterly, "It's madness, I tell you! Madness!"

Jules gave his familiar derisive laugh.

"On the contrary, it couldn't be more sane. There's food in the refrigerator, by the way. George won't mind us using it." Again he laughed. "You might get us a meal. Aurora should be awake by now. She'll be hungry."

Then his footsteps came up the stairs.

Aurora was lying tense when he appeared at the door.

"Well, darling. Awake? How do you feel?"

"Terrible! It's those pills." Her voice had developed a whine. "I don't want to take any more."

"Neither you shall in a day or two."

"Why can't I stop now?"

"Now?" He regarded her thoughtfully. "I think not, angel. I'm not quite sure—"

"Sure?"

"That I can trust you." He came to sit on the bed. "Isn't it ridiculous that I don't quite trust you?"

She evaded his smiling gaze. Her eyes went again to the photograph of the strange girl.

"Who is that?"

"Someone called Susie. Not particularly attractive, is she?"

"Then why is her photograph here?"

"Because this is—or was—her room."

Aurora started up.

"Isn't she coming back?"

"No. She's in Paris. She won't come back. Though if she does—"

"What?" Aurora asked in a whisper, because suddenly his eyes had that blank stony look again.

"If she does, it will be a pity because I will have to kill her," he said briskly. He saw her expression. "Now, don't look so outraged, I was only being funny."

"Funny!" she exclaimed. "Funny! Oh, God!" And she buried her face in the comforting pillow.

"By the way, I'll tell you something," she heard him saying. "You don't have to worry about that pendant any more. That little problem has solved itself. So long," he added inexplicably, "as Armand stays dead until I get out of the country."

I, he said. The first person singular.

The fact slowly penetrated Aurora's dulled mind. At the same time he had hold of her arms and was pulling her upright.

"But there is something I want you to do for me. Come along. Pull yourself together!"

She felt sick and dizzy as she sat upright. She couldn't remember when she had last eaten. He hadn't let her go in the restaurant car on the train. But that had been today? Or yesterday? Or last week?

"Come along, darling. Downstairs. I want you to ring the milk-man."

"The milkman!"

"Yes. We have far too much milk. Come and see."

He helped her down the stairs and along a narrow passage to the kitchen. Aunt Blandina, tall and sombre, was beating eggs in a bowl. There were five pint bottles of milk on the table, also several uno-pened newspapers.

"You see?" said Jules. "We've plenty of milk for as long as we're here. And we don't want any inquisitive milkman round in the morning."

Aunt Blandina raised her bleak face. "I've told you, it's madness to stay here at all."

"Nonsense!" Jules gave his charming smile. "It's as safe as houses. We've got to eat and we've got to sleep, and also to acquire one or two necessary articles. Where else better? George won't be back."

Aurora lifted her heavy eyelids, propping them up with her fingers. "Is George Susie's husband?"

"Yes, darling."

"Has he gone to Paris, too? Does he know we're using his house?"

"Of course, darling. We're very old friends. Now, this is the milk-man's number. I'll dial it for you—do buck up, for goodness' sake—then you just simply say you're Mr. Browne's secretary ringing from London, and as he's away he doesn't want any milk until further no-tice."

But now Aurora's head shot up with a semblance of her old alertness.

"Is this Mr. *Browne's* house?"

"Yes. I thought you knew."

"Then where is he?"

"I've told you. He's gone to Paris after his wife who, I'm sorry to say, has run off with someone else, as she's been threatening to do for years. George, as you can see, went off in such a hurry that he didn't bother about last-minute instructions to tradesmen. So we're doing him a service. Now are you going to do as I tell you?"

His eyes were stony, colorless, full of their hypnotic power. She nodded helplessly. "Tell me again—what I have to say."

It was not difficult after all. The chatty voice of the milkman at the other end of the wire told her he had been a little bothered about what to do since the Brownes didn't seem to be taking the milk in.

"Nearly got the police round," he said heartily.

Jules took the receiver from her and gently laid it down.

"That's fine, darling. You did that very well. Now let's see if we can find George's passport. He must have one somewhere."

"But you said"—her eyes met his and her voice trailed away—"he'd gone to Paris," she finished lamely.

He didn't answer. He didn't intend to answer, just as he never did when her questions were awkward or unanswerable. He began making an unhurried and systematic search in drawers until suddenly he gave a satisfied exclamation.

"Here it is. Good old George. Knew he wouldn't let me down. Now that photograph—fairly simple to substitute—"

"It's too risky," came Aunt Blandina's harsh voice at the door.

"Who's complaining of risks at this stage? This is what I came here for."

"Darling," said Aurora, with a tremendous effort, "won't we want Susie's passport, too?"

"But Susie *is* in Paris, I'm afraid. She's run off. I told you."

"Then—"

"I told you not to worry about it," came his voice, suddenly edgy, showing for the first time his extreme tenseness.

Aurora stared at him unbelievingly. She still felt terrible, her head was aching and her mouth tasted dry and queer. But all at once shock had cleared her mind. She was able to think. In Jules's smiling, watchful face she saw the truth. This was where, driven into a dangerous corner, he was deserting her. The terrible old aunt, sombre and unafraid, he may be taking, or leaving to her own capable devices. But Aurora was to be sacrificed.

It was not the girl in the photograph, the absent Susie, who was to be killed. It was she.

In that panic-stricken moment of knowledge she acted intuitively. She turned and made a dash down the passage for the front door.

But she was clumsy from weakness. She stumbled. Anyway, he had caught her almost before she had started.

He gripped her arm in his iron-hard fingers and took her back to the kitchen.

"None of that, angel. We can't have that. Aunt Blandina is making an omelet. She's very good at omelets. She'll be deeply hurt if you don't stay to share it. Look, anyway, you're as weak as a mouse. You'll fall if I let you go. See!"

Aurora swayed dizzily against the wall. Aunt Blandina's eyes dropped to the work in hand. She began to turn the egg-beater again, the rasping noise filling the small room. Beyond the window it was growing dark. The house, situated on the edge of a field, was isolated and lonely. If anyone saw a light in the window they would only think it was George Browne because he had not mentioned that he was going to be away.

And if by any chance his wife Susie, regretting her rash behavior, decided to return home and came walking innocently up the garden path, Jules, with his never-failing presence of mind, would ask her to share their omelet, before putting his iron fingers round her soft neck, or driving her to the edge of a cliff. . . .

Aurora wondered dully how long it would take him to make the necessary adjustment to George's passport, when the moment of good-bye would come for her. . . . She guessed that she probably had, like a condemned criminal, until morning.

They had their meal, eating Aunt Blandina's omelet, sitting at the kitchen table. Jules and the old woman, Aurora noticed incredulously, ate with good appetite. She, because they were watching her all the time, and because it was wise to eat (even though the rest of one's life was to be so short), forced herself to swallow a few mouthfuls. The food did her a great deal of good, which made her wonder how long it was since she had eaten. She was able to ask quite calmly, "Where is Miss Wilberforce? What have you done with her?"

"She's perfectly safe," Jules said, and the bitterness in his voice made her believe him. He had apparently failed with Miss Wilberforce, and this was serious. "This is all your fault, you know. If you'd told me at the beginning the old woman had a sister we would have managed a great deal better. But no, you had to let that young man of yours and his girl-friend meddle. You see now why I don't trust you?"

"Stop it now, Jules," said Aunt Blandina in her curt, angry voice. "We've got to get out of here before we start recriminations. Get on the telephone and make those air bookings."

"Yes, aunt dear. At once. Keep an eye on Aurora for me. She's not to be trusted."

Of course this old woman was not Aunt Blandina, Aurora reflected. She had been called that all the time, for old Miss Wilberforce's benefit, but one knew she was someone else altogether. Because the real Blandina, that vague, lost old woman who hadn't liked the long drive, and whom one had felt so sorry for, was dead. One knew that. It was the nightmare that had been with one for weeks. So this old woman must be the real aunt. . . .

She heard Jules's voice, crisp and businesslike, "Yes, a single ticket. The name? George Browne." Presently he hung up and dialling another number made the same request for a seat on an earlier flight. "For Miss Honoria Chabrier," he said.

Aurora saw the briefest look of satisfaction and relief pass over the old woman's face.

"We will travel by different air lines," she said calmly.

Honoria Chabrier. So this, at last, was the famous Aunt Honoria. It was, ironically, a relief to know that one aunt did exist!

Jules came back into the room.

"You'll have to be at the airport at 7 A.M.," he told her. "Air France flight leaving at seven forty-five. They'll have your ticket ready. There's a train about six. I'm afraid you'll have to walk to catch it. Pity George didn't have a car."

"And you?" the old woman asked tensely.

"I follow in an hour." His gaze flickered to Aurora. "Time enough," he said, and his face was deeply lined, brooding, queerly angry.

If she had still been under his spell, in that moment Aurora would have been sorry for him. Because he didn't really want to kill her. Old women who were soon to die were one thing, but this was another. The act was being forced on him, and it made him frustratedly angry, even more so that there was the night to spend first.

Or should he wait all night? Those were the thoughts behind his graven face, and now that she was no longer mesmerized by him she could understand him. It was her own fault entirely that she had shut her eyes to his cold ruthlessness for so long.

"We've got to get away from here," the old woman was muttering uneasily. "I still say we were mad to come here, in spite of getting that passport."

"Oh, shut up! Wash the dishes, and then let's get a bit of sleep. I've told you, we're safe as—"

His words were cut off by the telephone ringing.

It was like a rude intruder into their isolation, a vociferous Peeping Tom.

Jules froze. "Let it ring!" he snapped.

"But who is it? Supposing it's one of the neighbors!" The old woman's face had gone yellowish.

"Let me answer it! Let me answer it!" Aurora sobbed. Jules's hand caught her wrist. He was taking no chances. The shrill bell went on for another quarter minute. Then, with a hopeless ping, it stopped.

Aunt Honoria dropped the cup she had been holding, as if her hand had become nerveless. It smashed on the tiled floor, but its clatter brought her back to life. "We can't stay here now. I've told you all along—"

"Then go!" shouted Jules, his taut nerves snapping also. "Go and shiver all night on the railway station, and have fifty people asking questions. But Aurora and I stay here. We're safe. I've told you. Do you go rushing over to the house of every person you ring without getting an answer? Of course you don't. You say they're out, and forget about it. For heaven's sake, Aunt Honoria, I counted on you keeping your senses."

"It's been—a long day," the old woman muttered. "Very well. If you stay, I stay."

Jules patted her arm. "That's better. Now I suggest we put the lights out, and sit in the front room. If anyone should come we'll see them first, and we can either lie low or slip out the back way. But no one will come. Who is there to come?"

Who? Aurora wondered desperately. Not even Susie, ashamedly back from her jaunt to Paris. . . .

23

When the telephone rang and the woman's voice spoke Lydia thought it was Aurora.

She said, "Hullo!" breathlessly, and the speaker, under the same misapprehension as Lydia, went on rapidly.

"Is that you, Aurora? You remember me? I'm Joyce Walker. I took your job at Mr. Villette's office. I say, isn't it *awful* about his death? I've been in Spain for a holiday—I went after he sacked me— and I've just got back and read about it. What on *earth* happened?"

"He took sleeping pills," Lydia said automatically. "I'm not Aur—"

She was interrupted by the excited and shocked voice.

"Sleeping pills! Is that what it was? But he didn't seem the sort, did he? I mean, so good-looking and *virile*. Though I thought he was getting a bit odd. He just told me one lunchtime not to come back, he wouldn't be wanting me any more, and paid me a whole month's salary. So I went on this holiday. How is old George taking it?"

"Old George?"

"George Browne. I always called him old George. He's so middle-aged, isn't he? I've been trying to ring him, but I can't get any answer."

"*Who* is George Browne?" Lydia asked tensely.

"Why, Armand's partner. I say, this *is* Aurora, isn't it?"

"Actually it isn't," Lydia confessed. "I'm her sister. I've been trying to tell you. But I'd love to know about this George Browne. Do you know where he lives?"

"Down in Surrey, just outside a village called Moston. And he doesn't get on with his wife. He used to look awfully miserable. I say, why are you so worried about him? I thought it was the handsome Armand who had taken the sleeping pills."

"So it was," said Lydia breathlessly. "At least, until five minutes ago. Look, I think I'll have to ask you to ring off. I've an awfully urgent call to make."

The constable who answered her call to the station, however, did not share her excitement.

"Sergeant Peters has gone down to the country, miss."

"When will he be back?"

"In the morning, miss. It's nearly midnight, you know."

"Yes, so it is. I'm sorry. But something important has come up in the Villette case."

"Villette? The suicide chap? Oh, yes, what information have you got?"

"Mr. Villette's secretary has just rung me. She's back from a holiday abroad and read about Armand Villette's death. She says he had a partner."

"Did you take her name and address, miss?" came the maddening prosaic voice.

"Oh, not her address. I'm sorry. But she told me about this partner, George Browne. She says he lives near Moston in Surrey."

"Moston in Surrey. George Browne. Yes, I've got that. I'll tell the sergeant in the morning. You really ought to have got that young lady's address."

"Is the morning soon enough?" Lydia cried, obsessed with her feeling of urgency.

"Houses don't run away. We can take a look at this place tomorrow if the sergeant thinks it's important, and have a word with Mr. Browne."

But they couldn't have a word with Mr. Browne, Lydia thought fatalistically. Because now she was almost sure of the truth. But it would be useless to try to make that prosaic constable who lived by facts believe her fantastic intuition.

There was only one person who would do that.

She dialed his number feverishly.

Presently a sleepy voice grunted into the receiver.

"Philip! Are you awake? This is terribly important."

He came awake at once. She could almost see it happening.

"Aurora!" he shouted.

"I don't know. It might be. Can you get a car?"

"Even if I have to steal one! What is it? No, tell me when I get there."

His response was more than satisfactory. She had to crush down the jealous pain that he was flying so fast because of Aurora. This was no time to be thinking of herself.

He was there in an incredibly short time, and clattered up the stairs, careless of the noise he made.

"Moston in Surrey. No, I don't know where it is, but we'll find it. Who's there?"

"Armand's partner, George Browne, should be. But if not him, at least his wife."

"Is she going to mind us calling in the wee small hours? Well, who cares? Coming?"

"I say, what are you two up to?" demanded June Birch, sticking her be-curlered head out of her door. "Eloping?"

"Not today. Tomorrow," said Philip over his shoulder. "Sorry, June. See you when we come back."

Lydia was beside him in the car. He started the engine and they shot off with a roar.

"Now," he said, "tell me. How did you find out about George Browne, and where is he?"

"I think," said Lydia, very slowly, "I think at this moment he is waiting to be the principal figure at his own inquest."

Finally, however, they got lost. They were in the heart of the country, and everything was asleep. The last person they had asked directions of was a night porter at a railway station. After that, all the houses were in darkness, all the roads empty.

"It's three o'clock," said Philip, stopping the car. "I think at this stage we'd better wait for daylight. Are you tired?"

"Practically dead."

"Put your head on my shoulder."

Lydia obeyed, closing her heavy eyes.

"Probably that constable was right after all," she murmured. "Can you sleep, Philip?"

"I'll just have a cigarette."

"I hope we're not too far away from Mr.—I mean, Mrs. George Browne. But supposing her husband hasn't been home lately, why hasn't she been alarmed?"

"At the crack of dawn we'll find out. Go to sleep now."

And she would too, she thought, with remarkable contentment. For this may be the only time ever that her head would rest just there.

It seemed a very short time later that Philip was announcing, "Crack of dawn. There'll be someone about. Let's get moving."

He was restless, and in a hurry to move on. The brief enchantment of the darkness was over. Lydia tried to smooth her tumbled hair, and was conscious of her heart, like a stone, low in her breast.

"Where are we?"

"We'll ask at the first house. Must be approximately there. That railway porter said it was only a few miles."

The first house was a farmhouse. A burly, elderly man was clanking milk pails on the concrete strip at the back of the house.

He was the local milkman, he said, and certainly he knew the George Brownes. But it wasn't any use their calling because there was no one home. There hadn't been anyone home for a couple of days. He wouldn't have left the milk, but no one had asked him to stop it until last night.

"Who asked you then?" demanded Philip tensely.

"A young lady, sir. Said she was his secretary speaking from London. Go on over there if you like, but you won't find anyone home."

Philip got back into the car.

"A couple of miles," he said to Lydia. "There isn't anyone home, but we'll take a look all the same. It could be that whoever is there just doesn't like milk."

The house, a two-storey period cottage, was set in a garden behind a high privet hedge. It was in a rather isolated position, with fields running behind it down to a stream, and beyond that the railway line. Mr. George Browne apparently liked a quiet country life, with no immediate neighbors. In this, in a more modest way, he resembled his employer, Armand Villette.

The similarity between the two men's homes and habits did not stop there, for this house, like Greenhill, had a silent, deserted look. Certainly it was very early morning, and it was not likely that windows would be thrown open and people stirring. But the curtains were drawn in all the downstairs rooms, and before they walked up to the front door Lydia knew with certainty that no one would answer their knock.

"It's an awfully strange hour to call if there is anyone home," she murmured.

"It's a custom in the States to invite people to breakfast," Philip said inconsequentially, and put his finger on the bell. They could hear the sound shrilling through the house, but when it ceased there was nothing but silence.

They stood on the doorstep breathing in the exquisite early morning air full of the country fragrance of fresh grass, lime trees and the wisteria blossoms on the strong, ancient creeper climbing up the front wall. It was an enchanted landscape, just as it had been in the village where Aurora's wedding had been planned. It seemed quite fantastic that there could be any undercurrent of mystery and violence.

"There isn't even a clock ticking this time," Lydia murmured. "Knock, Philip."

He pounded on the door in an unmannerly fashion, but again there was no sound from within.

"Let's go round to the back," he suggested, and they picked their way across the dew-soaked grass to the back door, which also stood firmly shut and secret.

"Wherever George Browne is, he's not here," Philip said at last. "We've had our trip for nothing."

"But, no!" Lydia gripped his arm. "Didn't that milkman say he had been leaving milk. Then where is it? Who has taken it in?"

"He said a woman had rung him from London," Philip said slowly. "But if the milk's gone, she's been here to move it, hasn't she?"

"She rang from here!" Lydia declared, and now she was whispering, for it seemed that after all the silent house must have ears. Listening ears, hidden furtively just inside that closed door, or behind the curtain-drawn window.

"Was she here alone?" she whispered.

Again Philip gripped her arm. His face was tense and excited.

"This is where I do my coconut palm trick again. The curtains weren't drawn across the upstairs windows. I'm going to climb up the wisteria and take a look inside."

"Oh, yes, do!"

"We can't wait all day for Sergeant Peters who goes gallivanting in the country." At the foot of the wisteria he spared time to give Lydia a quizzical glance. "You're all for this breaking and entering, aren't you?"

"I'm absolutely terrified. Can I come up, too?"

"You stay right where you are."

In no time he had reached the low top-floor windows, and was looking in.

There was one moment when his lean body seemed frozen. Then he shouted abruptly.

"Throw me up a stone. Anything. I want to smash this window."

Lydia, acting instantly, threw up her shoe. Then there was the sharp splintering of glass, and Philip's arm was inside the window undoing the catch. In a moment he had wriggled through the narrow space into the room.

But it seemed an eternity before the front door opened, and he stood there, grim and haggard, saying, "Come upstairs! Quickly!"

She lay there on the bed in the small, low-ceilinged room. Her dark hair was spread on the pillow, and her dark lashes rested on her white cheeks. She looked beautiful and completely remote, an ice maiden, a sleeping beauty wrapped in her centuries-long sleep.

But she was still breathing.

Philip straightened from feeling her pulse. The limp hand dropped from his.

"Where's the telephone? It's too late to try coffee, but you might make some. Don't worry about the back door. It's open. He's gone."

"Gone!" Lydia repeated stupidly. "Who?"

"Whoever was here when we were knocking. He's making for the railway, I should think. I'd like to get him, but we've got to try to save Aurora."

"Can you wake her?"

"You try. Sleeping pills, I should think. I guess that's what he's been doing to her all the time."

The little telephone was in the little sitting-room downstairs. Philip picked it up and began to dial.

"I shouldn't worry about that," said a voice behind him. "We've already picked up Armand Jules Villette. The real Armand Villette. Interesting, eh? I've been paying a visit to his country house and discovering quite a lot. Now, where's the body?"

It was Sergeant Peters. He stood there, smiling faintly.

"Been trailing you," he added. "Nice work. You flushed out the rat."

"Aurora's upstairs," said Philip tautly. "But get a doctor first. It's urgent."

She was not dead. With youth and luck on her side, the sleeping princess would open her eyes to see her kingdom again. And not, after all, a greatly changed kingdom.

Philip was still there, the old woman, Clara Wilberforce, garrulous and cheerful, was still there, also Lydia, Millicent, waiting impatiently and anxiously at home, and June Birch, as golden-haired and blasé as ever.

George Browne, Armand Villette's chief clerk, kept in the background because he had been struck off the rolls as a practicing solicitor some years ago, but duly grateful to Armand for giving him a job, and unable to refuse any strange and guilty task asked of him because he was well-paid for these, and if he lost his income he might also lose his restless, extravagant, dissatisfied wife Susie, was off the scene permanently.

It was George Browne who lay quietly waiting for his own inquest. Having at last lost his adored but faithless wife, and knowing the depths of his implication in his employer's affairs, he had given up.

The man Sergeant Peters had arrested as he attempted to catch an early-morning train at Moston, his shoes wet from the long, dew-drenched grass, and a false passport in his pocket, was Armand Jules Villette. His elderly aunt, Honoria Chabrier, tough, callous, and, when caught, as venomous as a snake, was picked up at London Airport.

They were charged with the murder of Blandina Paxton, who, before she had fallen seemingly accidentally over that steep cliff on the Dorset coast, had been systematically robbed of all her wealth. There would be several similar cases in the process of investigation.

It looked as if Aurora Hawkins had been an accessory, but, with the evidence of constant drugging, in addition to the assets of her youth and beauty, she was likely to get off lightly.

The story was over. Or was it just back to where it had begun, with a wedding being arranged in an idyllically lovely English village?

Several hours later Aurora had recovered sufficiently to see Lydia.

She lay flat in the narrow hospital bed, and opening huge black eyes said faintly, "Darling, you look like something the cat brought home. Honestly!"

Lydia smoothed her tousled hair. She said apologetically, "I've had no sleep."

"Not like me. I seem to have slept for years. Literally. Armand made me take those relaxing pills, or whatever they were. Otherwise I was not to be trusted, he said." She sighed deeply. "It doesn't matter now. I've told the police everything."

"Aurora darling, are you well enough to talk? It was a—a near thing, wasn't it?"

"So I gather. Yes, I want to talk. I told you, I've been sleeping for years. But Armand made me."

"You keep saying Armand. Didn't you call him Jules?"

"Yes, sometimes. It was the name his family used. His aunts." Her voice was full of weary disillusionment. "I was madly infatuated with him. I had been ever since I started work in his office, and if he'd told me to go to the moon, I'd have had a shot at it."

"You mean, he persuaded you to help with the old lady, Blandina Paxton."

"Yes. But only to come with him when he took her to the country. I thought she really was his aunt. He'd had several—like that." Aurora's face was pinched and full of misery. "It was only after I read about the unidentified body found on the coast and added up one or two things that I guessed the truth. But I couldn't go to the police about it. I loved him too much. I just got so shocked and frightened that I decided to marry Philip, whom I'd just met, and get away. I'd make myself forget Armand."

She shivered a little.

"But I couldn't, you see. He wouldn't let me. He pursued me. I thought at first it was because he loved me. He'd given me expensive presents in the past, and he'd always said we'd get married one day. When he rang me at Millicent's that night he said we'd go to Edinburgh and be married. So after I left Philip at the other side of the village green I went and met Armand, like a fool. He was waiting in his Jaguar just round the corner. I only meant to talk to him, but he more or less kidnapped me, there and then. He said he couldn't let me go about talking, in case I said too much. It was better to be married because a wife didn't have to give evidence against her husband, supposing anything went wrong. I was mesmerized by him again, if you can understand that. And I really think things would have been all right if I hadn't told him, carelessly, that the old lady Blandina Paxton had given me that pendant, because she was grateful to me for being kind. Kind! And I'd left it behind. And also I hadn't told him about the sister turning up because I was so afraid he would get her, too. So everything began to go wrong. We never did have time to get married, and after that he didn't want to. He was too busy. You had started interfering, and old Clara Wilberforce had appeared on the scene again. Armand made poor George Browne impersonate him when you came into the office that first time. George had no idea where all this was going to lead him, poor devil." Aurora sighed again, with immense weariness. "After that it was too late to do anything except try to warn Clara, and try to stop them poisoning her."

"Were they?" Lydia asked, horrified.

"I don't know. They say they weren't. She was ill, anyway. But I was scared. I used to change her glass of water at night. That was when I wasn't too sleepy and stupid. Half the time I hadn't the faintest idea of what was going on. Armand made me take those pills. You don't know what he's like when he's charming and irresistible. He used to stand over me while I made those telephone calls." She stopped. A tear rolled down her cheek. She looked white and forlorn, with the face of a prematurely old child.

"Then?" Lydia prompted.

"Then he heard about George's suicide—and it was all rather awful. He knew he had to get out of England, and he could only do it on a false passport. Because if Armand Villette lay dead, Armand Villette couldn't be catching a plane. Could he? So he took a frightful risk and went to George's cottage. And that was the end. I knew he meant to kill me, and after a while, like poor old George, I decided it would be just as easy to be dead. So I let him give me the pills. He didn't even have to force me. He was—just a little sorry."

Lydia took her hand. "Forget about it now. You're going to be all right. Philip's waiting—"

Aurora opened her eyes. "Philip!"

"He saved you, you know."

"You did, too." Again she smiled, her heart-breaking attempt at casual raillery. "My God, darling, you do look rather a mess. Do go and put on some make-up. By the way, that nice sergeant thinks I might be able to go home when I get out of here. Do you think Millicent—"

"But she'll adore it!" Lydia cried. "She's waiting. She's on the telephone every ten minutes."

Aurora closed her eyes.

"I'll start again," she whispered. "Truly."

When she got back to the flat, Lydia, as she had promised, immediately rang Philip.

"She's going to be all right, Philip. She's dreadfully miserable, but she'll be all right. You'll be able to see her by tomorrow."

"Good," said Philip briefly.

The silence became awkward. Lydia had never before been bereft of words with him.

"She wants to go home. Millicent is delighted. She'll pamper her, and Geoffrey will sulk, and everything will be the same as it always was." She thought of the sleepy, tree-shadowed village, with the languid swans, and the church bells, and added, irrelevantly, "Even the chestnut blossom won't be over."

"Fine," said Philip. "May I come over?"

"Here? Why?"

"I want to see you."

"Oh! I look rather ghastly. Aurora said so, too. If you don't mind."

"I don't mind," he said, and hung up.

Lydia sat in front of Aurora's mirror, and put rouge on her cheeks, then rubbed it off because it looked so startlingly red. She was too tired to do it properly. Anyway, it didn't matter. In a few days Aurora would have her brilliant beauty back, and she, Lydia, would be just the younger sister, not particularly noticeable, not even particularly witty or amusing to compensate for her lack of beauty.

She shouldn't mind. She had always been perfectly happy that way.

But even as far back as a month ago, she had not been in love. . . .

The door was opening behind her. "Sorry," said Philip. "Did I startle you? You're getting just like your sister, not closing your front door properly."

Lydia put her hands to her cheeks.

"No, I'm not like Aurora," she said automatically. Then she tried to pull herself together. "She didn't ask for you because I expect she doesn't want you to see the way she looks just now. But she's going to be all right. She's awake again, anyway."

"So am I," said Philip.

"But you always have been!"

"Not quite, Lydia dear. Not enough to know how much more I prefer a face like this—come here, let me look at it—yes, it isn't quite at its best, is it?" He traced the shadows beneath her eyes, her creased forehead, the tense line of her mouth. "It is rather the worse for wear." Sharply his voice trembled. "But it's the kind of face I like."

And at last he had her in his arms, so tightly that for a moment she thought she had lost consciousness.

Then she heard his voice indignantly. "Lydia! My God, why are you crying? Now!"

The Deadly
Travellers

1

The house was on the outskirts of Rome, in a rather mean street which turned off the via Appia. There was a group of dusty cypresses on the corner, and then the row of shabby houses with their peeling paint and faded colors. Some children were playing in the dust. A woman flung open a shutter and leaned out to call something shrilly to them, and they scattered like disturbed sparrows.

In the other direction, towards the via Appia, the Street of the Dead, with its crumbling tombs and catacombs, there was a stream of traffic, fast cars, buses laden with sightseers, and noisy, impatient motor-scooters. It was no longer a way of peace for the sleepers in the tombs on the roadside, but then it never had been. Long ago it had rung to the marching feet of legions, or the shouts of the persecutors, and the weak cries of the crucified. In comparison, the screech of klaxons and the ear-splitting roar of the motor-scooters seemed harmless and innocent.

Perhaps the taxicab that was drawn up outside the house in this shabby street was also going about perfectly innocent business. The man watching in the shade of the cypresses would not have paid any especial attention to it if it had not seemed an unusual thing for a taxi to come to this kind of street. And to that particular house. So instead of strolling past casually he had drawn back to the slight cover of the cypresses and, with his hat pulled well down over his eyes, watched.

It was only a few minutes before the door of the house opened and a young woman came out. Tall, slim and attractive, she was the most unexpected sight of all, so far. For what would a fashionable young woman whose camel-hair coat might have been bought in one of the better Paris or London stores, and whose dark hair had a casual, expensive cut, be doing in this locality?

She was talking to someone out of sight. Presently a rather stout little girl dressed in a white frock, with a large blue bow in her hair, appeared and climbed into the waiting taxi. Behind her darted a thin, dark woman with a suitcase. The suitcase was placed in the taxi, the girl held out her hand to shake hands with the thin, dark woman who, dressed in a faded cotton dress and scuffed-looking slippers, was the only person in this small scene who appeared to be in character, the only one who could have been expected to emerge from the shabby house in the rather furtive little street.

Then the tall girl climbed into the taxi, too, and the door banged. The watcher made an involuntary step forward, but he was too far off to hear the instructions given to the driver. He swore under his breath, then strolled studiously and casually in the other direction as the taxi whirled around and proceeded towards the city. As it passed him he caught only a glimpse of its two occupants, the fluttering butterfly bow in the child's hair, and the girl's dark head turned towards her young companion. But he heard the child's voice, shrill with excitement, *"Arrivederci,* Gianetta!"

So there was no more time to investigate the shabby house. Now perhaps there was no need to. Fingering the worn covers of the notebook in his pocket, remembering the scribbled address of this house in this street, and the cryptic added note *"might be using a child,"* he hurried to the busy highway and impatiently waited for a taxi.

It was impossible to be certain where the previous taxi had gone, but by the child's luggage, and the girl's air of haste, one assumption could be made.

When at last he was able to secure a car, he gave the driver his destination, *"La stazione, pronto!"*

The driver nodded his head, grinning with wicked pleasure at being given a free hand to mow down as much of the traffic as possible. At his destination the man cursed again, this time at Mussolini and his grandiose schemes for building such a superb railway station that made one cross acres of floor-space before reaching the train.

As he had expected, it was the Milan train just due to depart. Indeed, it was at that moment pulling out. He had to elbow people out of his way, and run for his life to get on the last carriage.

"Bravo! Bravo!" called a porter, white teeth gleaming, dark eyes ashine.

But the man was not amused. Did the Italians consider all contests with speed and danger, so long as they themselves remained onlookers, a pleasant diversion? Did that explain a great deal of their mentality?

Perhaps it did. Perhaps that was why he was here.

A good-looking young woman, probably English, and a

child. . . . And that other face that it was not possible to forget, for a drowned face, even had it been that of a stranger, was not an easily forgettable sight. And this had not been a stranger's face. . . .

2

That morning two days ago in London, Kate did not see Miss Squires, as usual. The girl at the desk of the little employment office with its provocative title "Job-a-Day," and in smaller letters "Also Objets d'Art procured," said in a slightly awed voice that Mrs. Dix herself had asked for Kate when she came in. Would Kate wait while she found out whether she could go up now?

It had been William who had first suggested Kate going to Mrs. Dix. William, who was as practical as Kate was impractical, said that if Kate planned going on living in London (as she certainly did) she would have to supplement her very precarious employment as a commercial artist. So why not do the odd jobs, such as taking out old ladies, or poodles, meeting trains at melancholy stations like Liverpool Street, doing Christmas shopping for the bedridden, or even baby-sitting, providing the brat wasn't too spoilt and loathsome.

This suggestion of William's had turned out excellently. It provided Kate with three or four days' employment a week, which, added to the earnings she made from her drawings, enabled her to keep the basement flat in West Kensington. She was attached to this flat chiefly because of her landlady, Mrs. Peebles, who was as endearing as a poised tomahawk and just as stimulating. With Mrs. Peebles lurking about the house, life was as full of surprises as Kate liked it to be. In addition to the satisfaction of earning extra money, she found the work with Mrs. Dix interesting and enjoyably unpredictable. Also, she had got several excellent sketches of strange old-lady faces, Rembrandt style, and had some rather enchanting drawings of dogs skipping about Kensington Gardens, among the blowing autumn leaves and the chrysanthemums. These she hoped to sell.

Apart from the money angle, she found it made life pleasantly interesting, not knowing, each time she visited Miss Squires, solid and placid in her little dark office under the stairs which led up to the so far unseen apartments of Mrs. Dix, what strange task awaited her, whether it were catching a train to Southampton to meet an elderly

American couple, or to go to the Portobello Road market to search for a specified piece of junk required by a client.

Mrs. Dix, until this morning, had remained a mystery. Miss Squires hinted at a Tragedy. Fifteen years ago Mrs. Dix's husband had been missing on a secret mission, some hush-hush task that could only be mentioned in the sacred precincts of M.I.5, and the poor lady still refused to believe that he was dead. She got up every morning with the renewed optimistic conviction that this would be the day he returned home. She kept his bed aired, a plentiful supply of food and drink, and contrived, Miss Squires said pityingly, to infuse into her cluttered rooms an air of excited expectancy. It was very sad, because after fifteen years there was really no hope. There had been that body washed up on the coast of Portugal that had never been positively identified, but there was little doubt that it had been that of Major Dix. If it hadn't, then there was the Iron Curtain, and no one was likely to survive fifteen years of that. Anyway, there had been not a word, not even a rumor of an unidentified Englishman in some Siberian prison. Not even a question in the House. So it seemed that Mrs. Dix, poor soul, would go on living in her fool's paradise.

But until this day, Mrs. Dix, who had infused her special brand of eagerness and eccentricity that was almost genius into her business, had remained as invisible as her husband. At least, to Kate, one of her minor employees. No doubt she gave audience to the important people, the ones entrusted with special jobs such as shopping for the Prime Minister's wife, or the ones who requested, not a warming-pan to be turned into some kind of barbecue business, or an umbrella stand that would adequately hold flower arrangements, but the Faberge chess set last heard of in Alexandria, or the late duchess' diamond and ruby tiara which one had heard was being sold. . . .

Admittedly, these last were rare requests. Miss Squires, who liked Kate, sometimes became a little less reserved and imparted a breathless rush of information, about acquiring skeletons for medical students, and other macabre objects. It was tragic that although Mrs. Dix could acquire white camels from Arabia, or pearls from the Great Barrier Reef, she could not find her missing husband. But she still refused to admit that he lay in an unnamed grave somewhere along the banks of the River Tagus.

Reflecting on all this, Kate was a little nervous about at last meeting the fabulous lady. Passing Miss Squires' room on her way to the narrow stairway, she heard Miss Squires call, "Is that you, Kate? Special mission for you today. It'll be a nice jaunt."

Kate stuck her head around the door of the dark little office. "Where am I to go?"

"None of my business, dear. But you'll enjoy it. Lucky girl."

The room in which Mrs. Dix sat was a quite ordinary living-room, a little over-furnished and with an extravagant number of bowls of flowers. It did not in any way resemble an office. Mrs. Dix sat on a faded, green velvet couch.

She was a very plump lady with prematurely white or bleached hair, in, perhaps, her early fifties, though her extreme plumpness and her white hair may have added an unnecessary ten years to her age.

She wore brown velvet, with a little ruching of lace at the throat. She was, Kate thought, like a chocolate meringue.

Her smile was winning. She waved a dimpled hand towards a chair. "Sit down, my dear. Forgive my not getting up. My heart, you know. The doctor forbids any exertion. You're Kate Tempest, aren't you?"

"Yes, Mrs. Dix." Kate obediently sat down and refused the proffered box of chocolates.

"Oh, not just a little one, dear?" Mrs. Dix cried, disappointed. "Try this knobbly one. It'll have a nut. Not so bad for the figure. Though really, I do assure you, you nave *no* need to worry. You're a sylph, positively. Now me, I'm past redemption. But I do so adore chocolates."

She beamed at Kate. Her cheeks were delicately pink, her eyes a faded blue, benign, a little far-off, as if her visitor were not quite real to her, but that instead she was looking beyond, to the door, which might open at any moment to the one she wanted to see above all.

"Now, you're wondering why I've sent for you, of course. Miss Squires has told me about you. She says you're reliable, sensible, sophisticated, not likely to lose your head in a crisis."

"Thank you," Kate murmured bewilderedly. William had always said exasperatedly that reliability was her least obvious quality, but neither Mrs. Dix nor Miss Squires knew her as William did, and it was her business to see that they never completely achieved this knowledge.

"Most important, those qualities," Mrs. Dix emphasized. "Now tell me a little more about yourself. You live alone?"

"Yes." Though one could hardly call it living alone, with Mrs. Peebles' watchful eye and attentive ear, overhead.

"Family?"

"Only a stepmother who lives in the country."

"How do you get on with her?"

"She's perfectly sweet, but I only acquired her when I was eighteen, so naturally she's not deeply interested in me. Since my father died she has taken up growing flowers for the market. Even when I visit her she forgets I'm there. She's cutting roses, or transplanting polyanthus, or something."

"Marriage plans?" Mrs. Dix asked in her friendly, inoffensive voice.

Kate thought of William and said definitely, "Not at present. None at all."

"Well, that all seems very satisfactory. It leaves you completely free to do these things for me. I like to know my employees are without urgent family ties, when I send them on jobs abroad. Shall I tell you what I have in mind for you? It's a very important mission, but actually very simple, and only requires travel sense and, of course, responsibility. You've been on holidays abroad, Miss Squires tells me."

"Yes, several times." On a shoe string, of course, staying at pensions or youth hostels, walking blisters on to one's heels, living on rolls and spaghetti.

"Splendid. Have you been to Rome?"

"Once only, for two days."

"You don't speak Italian?"

"Almost none at all."

"Well, that won't matter greatly."

"But what am I to do, Mrs. Dix?"

"Oh, a very simple little mission indeed. You won't have a chocolate? I shall, I'm afraid. My husband is to blame, you know. He indulged this passion of mine. I shall tell him, when he comes home, how he is to pay for it, with all these pounds of flesh." Mrs. Dix chuckled, squeezing at her plump waist. "My dear, you have beautiful blue eyes. With that black hair. Quite arresting."

Kate sighed. "Yes, but my nose is wrong." William's healthy outspokenness never allowed her to become conceited.

"Not seriously wrong. I'm wondering if Miss Squires is right, after all. Are you the right person to send? But if you're used to travelling, and you promise to behave with discretion—" Mrs. Dix's pale blue eyes suddenly flew up, looking directly at Kate instead of at the distant door. "Rather a pity, isn't it? Well, never mind. It's a very simple thing we want you to do. Merely to bring a child, a little girl, to London. You are to be her courier, in fact, or her nannie, if you prefer to look at it that way." Mrs. Dix's plump fingers dipped into the box of chocolates again. She leaned back on the couch smiling benignly. "Well, my dear, how do you like the idea of that?"

Kate privately liked it very well indeed. Her one brief trip to Rome

had filled her with a passion for that ancient and fabulous city, and
the chance to go back, with all travelling expenses paid, seemed too
good to be true. Instinctively, she began to look for the flaw in the
plan.

"May I ask you some questions, Mrs. Dix?"

"Indeed. Go ahead."

"Who is this child? An Italian?"

"Yes; of divorced parents, unfortunately."

"Does she speak English?"

"A little. Very little, I believe."

"How old is she?"

"She's seven, only a baby, poor pet, and her name is Francesca. I
can visualize her, can't you, dark-haired, shy, unhappy."

"Why unhappy?"

"Because her parents are fighting over her. That's the story, you
see. The court granted the mother, who now lives in London, cus-
tody, but the father wasn't having any of that, so what does he do but
nip over to London and kidnap the child. Quite illegally, of course.
So there has been more action about that, and now he has agreed to
give her up. But someone has to come and get her and travel back to
England with her. Naturally, a child of seven can't travel alone."

"Why doesn't the mother go?"

"She's just recovering from an illness, brought on by all this worry.
She won't completely recover until she has her child again. So see
what a good deed you will be doing, besides seeing your beloved
Eternal City again."

Kate hadn't said that it was her beloved Eternal City, but refrained
from pointing this out. Indeed, she was beginning to feel pleasantly
excited and stimulated. Perhaps she could arrange with Mrs. Dix to
go a day earlier than planned, and have one free day in Rome, to
wander about sketching the wild flowers growing tenaciously in the
centuries-weathered walls of the Colosseum, the gargoyles, with their
noses rubbed flat, on old cathedrals, and the hurrying people along
the pavements, silhouetted against the ancient splendor.

"Well?" said Mrs. Dix, with her comfortable smile.

"I'd love to go," Kate said enthusiastically. "But—"

"You're wondering about your fee? I think you will be quite happy
about that. Francesca's mother is prepared to be generous. Considering the exertion and responsibility, we thought twenty guineas, and
expenses paid. You'll travel first-class both ways, and there'll be a
night in Rome when, of course, you must be comfortable. Comfort's

such a necessity, isn't it?" Mrs. Dix's fingers hovered over the chocolate box.

"But, Mrs. Dix—"

"Aren't you happy about the fee, my dear?"

"Yes, indeed. I think it's very generous. It makes me feel Francesca must be a very important child." Or a very difficult one, she
thought to herself.

"A bone between two dogs, a poor little creature. Then I take it
you agree to go?"

"I'd absolutely love to. But can I see Francesca's mother first?"

"Rosita? Whatever for?"

"I'd like to talk to her. If the child can't speak English we may
have trouble about the sort of food she likes, and so on." She refrained from adding that she wanted dearly to see Francesca's background, to get a complete picture of the situation. Was her mother really ill—or just lazy?

Mrs. Dix hesitated. She said doubtfully, "I shall have to see. I shall
have to ring Rosita. But yes, of course, I think it is a very good idea.
She would like to see you, too. After all, it is her child whom all this
fuss is about. Yes, I think that can be arranged. I'll let you know."

But was it Kate's imagination that now, all at once, Mrs. Dix's pale
blue eyes did not quite meet hers?

Kate didn't know why she had this curiosity to see Rosita. Was it
because the child, Francesca, the unknown little Italian, a bone between two dogs, as Mrs. Dix had called her, wouldn't seem real until
she had talked to her mother? Or was it because she imagined Rosita
to be a spoilt, olive-skinned beauty with hypochondriac tendencies,
and wanted to see for herself who most needed sympathy, the bereft
mother, or the father, obviously emotional and affectionate, who had
come to England to swoop up his daughter and fly with her.

It was probably foolish of her to risk getting emotionally involved
in the problems of two strangers, but all her life she had never found
it possible to stand aside as a spectator of other people's happiness or
unhappiness. She had always plunged in, to share or sympathize. It
had not always been rewarding, and William constantly warned her
that her quixotic tendencies would finally lead her into some inex-
tricable and insoluble problem. Kate didn't worry much about that. It
made life exciting and unpredictable, and one owed it to people to be
interested in them.

As she went down the stairs from Mrs. Dix's room, Miss Squires
poked her head out from her small dark office.

She was a little rotund person with shortsighted brown eyes and an anxious forehead. She had taken a fancy to Kate, and twice had invited her to her prim little cottage on the Sussex downs, where she lived alone, except for a large black and white cat called, unimaginatively, Tom.

"Are you going to do it?" she whispered, as if, all at once, she was nervous of the plump, chocolate meringue woman in the room upstairs.

"Oh, yes. It's wonderful. Perfectly wonderful."

The corrugations in Miss Squires' forehead deepened. "I thought you'd think that. Actually, it was I who suggested giving you the job. You're reliable, and I thought the poor kid would like someone young and gay."

"How nice you are!" Kate said sincerely.

Miss Squires, middle-aged and plain, and obviously unused to compliments, flushed.

"I said nothing but the truth. But I hope it will be all right. This trip," she added.

"Why shouldn't it be? Oh, you mean Francesca might be unmanageable?"

"That, and her father. We don't know about him, you see."

"But if he's promised to let the child go."

"Yes, of course."

"And I'm going to see the mother this afternoon."

"Oh, well, then—"

As Miss Squires hesitated, Kate laughed. "I do believe you're one of those old-fashioned people who don't trust foreigners!"

Miss Squires flushed again and said gruffly, "Not always without reason. Well, take care of yourself. Come down to the cottage for a weekend when you get back."

Rosita lay on a couch in a high-ceilinged, luxurious room in a house in Egerton Gardens. She was small and dark-haired, with a pointed, sallow face, and eyes that made Kate think fleetingly of Raphael's "Portrait of a Woman." It was not so much that they were full of secrets, as that they would like to seem so. No doubt this pose was quite successful with men.

She did not look particularly ill, Kate thought. Her languid handshake seemed to be a pose, too.

It was true that she was merely spoilt, probably disliking the thought of the long journey to Rome, or not wanting to risk another encounter with her ex-husband.

There seemed little doubt that he would not be the only man in her life.

Kate looked around the room, noting the couch with its pale green brocade covering, the curtains of rich crimson Italian damask, the gilt-framed mirrors, the cushions and small tables. Was this a good environment for a child of seven—a tense, unhappy and probably maladjusted child? With a hypochondriacal mother lying on a couch extending a languid hand to callers?

She spoke in English that had only the slightest accent.

"Miss Tempest, it is so good of you to come to see me. Mrs. Dix told me how thorough you are. That you want to find out about Francesca before the journey."

"It's a long journey," Kate said.

"You are so right. That's why I can't possibly go myself, much as I would like to. But I really can't stand it. All this upset has made me ill. Antonio behaving like this—"

Her face puckered as if she were going to cry. She hastily controlled herself. If she were not ill, she was extremely nervous, Kate thought, and wondered why. Although the reason seemed obvious enough. A kidnapped daughter, and all the entailed fuss.

"You'll find Francesca a very good child, Miss Tempest. Even a little—how do you say it—solemn? She won't give you any trouble. She doesn't speak much English, but enough to get by. She's well-grown for her age. Oh, and don't forget her doll. She must always have her doll or there are fireworks at bedtime. Miss Tempest, you will take good care of her, won't you?"

"Of course I will."

"Mrs. Dix said you could be trusted. I wish I could go myself. I might have flown, but Francesca's crazy, but crazy, about trains and boats, the Channel ferry—ugh!—and the Eiffel Tower."

"The Eiffel Tower?"

"Yes, she adores going up it. To the very top. I hope you have a head for heights. I haven't."

Rosita shuddered, and Kate suddenly wanted to laugh. This was going to be a light-hearted odyssey after all, with a child who adored continental trains, and Paris from the top of the Eiffel Tower. Now she had become a person, and a person of definite character. Suddenly Kate was looking forward to meeting her.

"Why are you smiling?" Rosita asked suspiciously.

"I like the Eiffel Tower, too."

"Good heavens! How very extraordinary! Then the two of you should get on very well."

"Indeed we will," Kate said cheerfully.

She got up to go. The limp hand came out again. But this time, to her surprise, it clung to hers with surprising strength. It was cold and a little damp. It was, strangely enough, like the hand of a person who was afraid. . . .

Mrs. Peebles had to be told, of course. Apart from her grudging but fairly accurate delivery of telephone messages, she liked to know what Kate was up to. Since all Kate's visitors had to come through the front door and negotiate the stairs to the basement they had to endure the sharp surveillance of Mrs. Peebles, and this was another source of interest for that lady who was frank and uninhibited in her comments.

"That young man last night, Miss Tempest. Bit of a weed, wasn't he? You can do better than that," or, "She'd be a flighty piece, that Miss Edwards. Pity the man who gets her."

Of William, surprisingly enough, she approved, which was rather boring. Kate felt that a few waspish comments from Mrs. Peebles would have made her fly hotly to William's defense, and perhaps have made her fall in love with him. As it was, they disagreed about almost everything, from the latest play to the color of William's tie. William was slow in his movements, and untidy and forgetful, and appallingly frank about either Kate's work, her appearance, or her behavior. He treated her, she complained bitterly, as if they had been married for years. But somehow they stuck together. Or rubbed along. And the odd, weedy or more flamboyant types of whom Mrs. Peebles disapproved did not take her out a second time. Perhaps it was this quality of outspokenness that drew Mrs. Peebles and William together. Whatever it was, Kate suddenly felt enormously relieved at the thought of escaping, for a brief time, from both of them.

Mrs. Peebles was sharp, small and spry. At the sound of the front door closing she appeared, like a mouse from the wainscoting, ready to dart back into her hole the moment she had seen all that was necessary.

"Oh, it's you, Miss Tempest. Only one message. From Mr. Howard. He said to tell you to keep tomorrow night free because he had tickets for the Old Vic."

"He'll have to take someone else," Kate said pleasantly. "I'll be halfway to Rome."

"Rome! Whatever do you want to go there for?"

"Just a job. I'll be away about three days, so if anyone rings—"

"Oh, yes, scribbling away at that telephone when I should be doing my work. Then you'd better ring Mr. Howard."

"Later," said Kate, going towards the stairs.

"He'll be around."

"Not if I know it. I have to pack and have an early night."

"Rome!" muttered Mrs. Peebles. "What are they sending you there for? Turning you into a spy?"

"Something like that," Kate said cheerfully. "Just my cup of tea, don't you agree?"

The early night was not possible, for, as predicted by Mrs. Peebles, William did come around. He was a tall young man and heavily built. Kate's one armchair sagged perilously beneath his weight, and although she had a reasonable amount of floor space, his comfortably sprawled legs formed a constant hurdle as she tried to do her packing and cope with her barrage of questions.

"It's fishy," he said.

"Don't be absurd. What's fishy about bringing a seven-year-old child to England?"

"Why don't they let you fly?"

"I've told you. Because Francesca loves trains and wants to go up the Eiffel Tower. It's a special treat."

"She sounds like a spoilt brat."

"She probably is, but for twenty guineas pin-money I'd travel third-class to Greece and back. And they're giving me time in Rome to rest. I'll be dashing madly about, of course. I want to get a good face for my new illustration."

"For the hero? An Italian?" William said sceptically. William edited a small, highly literary, topical magazine himself, and was often irritatingly facetious about Kate's endeavors in the romantic field.

"No, for the villain. Someone madly wicked and irresistible. I'll probably fall in love with him."

"Don't do that," said William mildly, tapping out his pipe and scattering ash indiscriminately.

"Why not?"

"You wouldn't be happy."

"I suppose you think I'm more likely to be happy with someone like you, cluttering up my flat, criticizing me, wearing foul ties, needing a haircut—my God, you do need a haircut!"

"I'll go out and get some beer," said William.

"You won't come back here with it. Honestly, I haven't time. Please go so that I can concentrate on what I'm doing."

"All right. I can see when I'm not wanted. Want me to come to Victoria in the morning?"

"For heaven's sake, no!"

"Then I'll meet you when you come back. Send me a postcard or something."

"I'll have the child then, and goodness knows what."

"If the 'what' is an Italian count, I can always punch him in the jaw."

"Don't be absurd! Only three days and travelling all the time. And with my face—"

"Even with your face. Snub nose, crooked mouth. You're an ugly, adorable little devil."

He didn't take her in his arms in a civilized way, he swooped over her like a great tree whose branches suddenly engulfed her. Tweedy, redolent of stale pipe smoke, strong. . . .

Kate struggled impatiently and ineffectually, then submitted. Really, it was too boring. Why did William have to be so masterly?

3

Francesca. The name conjured up the picture of some dark, thin, flashing-eyed temperamental child, full of charm and animation.

Kate was frankly taken aback when she met the real Francesca. Just as she had been taken aback at the sight of the street and the house where she had been instructed to pick up the child.

Her mind flashed back to Francesca's mother, lying languidly on a couch in a luxurious room, and to the excellent arrangements made for her own trip to Rome, the good hotel at which she had spent the night, and the ample money she had been allowed.

Francesca, obviously, was a valued and much-desired child, and her parents not lacking in means. Why, therefore, was she living in such a squalid house? Even temporarily.

And why was she in the charge of such a dirty, down-at-the-heel woman as the one who came to the door in response to Kate's knock?

It was late autumn, but still hot in Rome. Kate had undone her travelling coat, and her hair was ruffled from her nervous gesture of pushing it back when she was agitated. She thought the taxi-driver had brought her to the wrong street. She looked at the row of shabby, paint-peeling houses in astonishment, and hesitated to get out and knock on the door of Number 16.

When the woman, whose quick smile seemed to hide uneasiness, opened the door, she was even more sure she had made a mistake. Yesterday, exhausted by her long journey, and yet determined to make the most of this brief visit to one of her favorite cities, she had rushed from the Colosseum to Hadrian's Arch, and then to the Borghese Gardens, and late in the evening had done a tour of the fountains. Tiredness and excitement had given her a queer feeling of being transported to the past, to the days of hungry lions turned on living human flesh, the crack of the slave-driver's whip, and the cries of a rabble demanding a victim. This morning, when her journey to get Francesca had taken her so near to the Appian Way, the mood had persisted, and she was temporarily haunted by a heavy sense of decay beneath the splendor, and of death.

But the woman in the shabby little house, strangely enough, was expecting her. Apparently she had come to the right place.

She called in a shrill high voice, "Frances-s-ca!" and took Kate inside, although she said in halting English that the child was ready, and had been for the last hour.

The dark little room in which Kate stood smelt strongly of garlic. She wondered hazily, with yesterday's tiredness still hanging over her, whether this woman was now married to Francesca's father—but surely the elegant and expensive Rosita had never come from surroundings like this.

The woman was explaining something in a gabble of Italian when the little girl came slowly in.

Kate had another surprise, for this stout, heavy child, with the heavy-lidded sullen eyes, was utterly unlike the Francesca she had imagined. It seemed, however, that within the fat little chest of the sulky and silent child there must dwell the phantom of Kate's imagined Francesca, for she had chosen to wear, of all things, a white organdie dress, elaborately starched and ironed, and in her straight dark hair was a huge stiff bow.

She was a little girl going to a party where, despite all her parents' attempts to make her decorative and appealing, she would remain clumsy, silent and hurt.

She was pathetic.

Kate realized it at once, and went quickly towards her.

"Francesca! Hullo!" Her voice was warm and gay. "My name is Kate, and I'm taking you to your mother. But first, of course, we apparently it was her much cherished one, for Kate remembered now that Rosita had said she would never go to bed without her doll.

Nevertheless, such was her stolidity, that when the woman thrust it into her arms, she held it almost indifferently, and indeed for two pins would have dropped it on the doorstep. However, she was still holding it as she climbed into the taxi, and it was there, too, that she found her tongue, and called in almost as penetrating a voice as the woman's, "*Arrivederci, Gianetta.*"

In the train the two of them faced each other warily across the narrow space of their first-class compartment.

"Is this your first trip to England, Francesca?"

Since her sudden boisterous goodbye, Francesca had remained stubbornly silent in the taxi, behaving, when Kate spoke to her, as if she were stone deaf.

But now she suddenly broke her silence and said flatly, "No spik *Inglese.*"

Oh, dear! thought Kate. Was that true? Or were those heavy-lidded eyes that made the child look like a junior Mona Lisa hiding secrets? Surely, with Gianetta, her nurse, speaking English fairly fluently, and her mother speaking it very well indeed, she would have learnt at least a few words. Kate decided this was more than probable, and before the journey was over she would have caught her out. In the meantime, she would chat pleasantly, whenever necessary, and pretend that it was of no importance whether or not she were answered.

"We'll be having lunch shortly. Do you like eating on a train? I still think it's one of the most exciting things to do. Next to sleeping on one, of course. When you wake up tomorrow morning you'll be practically in Paris, practically at the foot of the Eiffel Tower."

Francesca's eyes suddenly flew wide open and a gleam of excitement showed momentarily in them. This was no proof that she had understood anything except the last two words, but it did show that she set great store on her visit to the Eiffel Tower. She began to spread her dress carefully about her so that it would remain fresh and uncrushed for so important an occasion. No doubt it was for that purpose that she had insisted to the disapproving Gianetta that she would wear her party dress.

Going up the Eiffel Tower represented a party to her. Probably it was the only real thing that emerged out of the confusion of her separated parents and her loss of security. Encouraged by this success, Kate persevered with the conversation.

"What's your doll's name?"

have the train journey, and a visit to the Eiffel Tower, and lots c
good things to eat."

The child surveyed her stolidly and mutely. The woman shook he.
head. "She does not understand. She speaks very little English. Anc
you, signorina?"

"No Italian," said Kate, laughing. "Never mind, we'll get along. Is
she ready? Does she have to say goodbye to anyone?"

"No, no. That is all done. Her papa yesterday when he brought
her here. I was her nurse, you understand? He did not wish the last
farewells."

She made the motion of wiping her eyes, and Kate had a moment
of sympathy for the absent emotional father who perhaps was the
more deserving parent. For it was a little difficult to imagine this
child fitting into the London drawing-room of her attractive mother.

She felt uneasy and a little sad, and had to remind herself that
none of this was her business before she could take the child's soft
broad hand and say, "Then we're all ready, Francesca. Your bags?"

"Just this small one," said the woman, handing Kate a rather battered and cheap-looking suitcase. Then she swooped over the child to
give her a hug. The child stiffened, and backed away. The woman
hugged her, nevertheless, then had to straighten the preposterous blue
bow and the unsuitable dress.

She shrugged her shoulders. "She would wear that dress, signorina.
I know it is foolish, but when Francesca insist. . . ." She shrugged
her shoulders again.

Looking at the stubborn, unmoved face, Kate could very well understand what she meant. There might, she feared, be more than one
silent battle before the two of them reached London. This probably
explained the generous fee she was to receive. Well, never mind, she
would earn it. . . .

"The taxi's waiting," she said. "We'd better go. Thank you, si
gnora. . . ."

The child walked quite placidly beside her. She hadn't spoken
word.

They were stepping out into the brilliant sunlight when sudden
the woman gave a shrill cry and called to them to wait. She dart
away, saying something that sounded like "bambino," but when :
appeared a moment later she had only a quite small doll in
hands. It was not a particularly attractive one. Its blonde hair had
come stringy, and its silk dress was slightly grubby. It didn't <
look as if it had been an expensive doll, the kind one would l
imagined parents like Francesca's would have lavished on her.

The Mona Lisa look came back. Kate picked up the doll lying rather forlornly on the seat, and pointed to it.

"Who?"

"Pepita," said Francesca sulkily, then suddenly snatched the doll from Kate and clasped it possessively.

"That's a Spanish name."

"*Si.*"

It didn't seem to matter. The doll, with its ragged blonde locks, was obviously the only other object of Francesca's affections. The Eiffel Tower and a shabby doll, and a white organdie party dress and a festive blue bow in her hair. All at once, strangely, Kate wanted to cry.

The train rocketed on through the dry autumn countryside towards Milan. Kate tried out her few Italian words on the waiters in the restaurant car. Her charge remained silent except when at one stage she made a long excited speech to one of the waiters.

The man grinned. Kate asked, "What was all that?"

"She says she like ravioli, signorina."

"And there's no ravioli?"

"Only spaghetti, signorina."

The waiter shook his head regretfully, and Francesca stolidly but expertly wound enormous quantities of spaghetti into her mouth. She was a philosophical child. She made the best of what she could get. No doubt her short life had already taught her that necessary lesson.

No one came to share their compartment. Towns, in an afternoon haze of tawny roofs and old, sun-faded walls, went by. There was more arid countryside and shabby villages, with splashes of paint, orange and violent blue. Francesca had dozed after lunch, her doll clasped firmly on her spaghetti-filled stomach. Now she was wide awake.

"We change trains here to cross the frontier," Kate explained at Milan. "Then we change again at Basle, and there you'll have a bed for the rest of the night."

She didn't know whether the child understood, but she came docilely to climb off the train and follow Kate through the jostling, excited, noisy mob that was Milan railway station. She was a plump incongruous little figure in her now crushed white organdie and nodding blue bow. At least, Kate thought, those foolish clothes made her too conspicuous to get lost.

But with her lumbering docility, that was like that of an elderly and faithful dog, it did not seem probable that such an emergency would arise.

The man with his hat still pulled too low over his eyes changed trains at Milan, also. While Kate fussed about finding their compartment and getting Francesca safely on board he, however, had time to make a telephone call.

Although, since it was a trunk call, it seemed at the last minute that it wouldn't come through in time, and he was tensing and untensing his long, nervous fingers in impatience and anxiety when at last the clerk called to him.

"Your Swiss call, signor."

Then it took some time to make himself understood. After all, it wasn't an ordinary call inviting himself to stay overnight because he happened to be passing through Basle. It was something very different.

But at last he thought all was well.

He paid for the call and walked away slowly, reflecting on the split-second timing required, the crazy improbability of the whole thing.

Then a thought came into his head and his eyes narrowed and grew grim. This had to succeed.

Once more he had to run for the train. It very nearly left without him. Cursing the way Continental trains deliberately sneaked out of stations as if trying to leave passengers stranded, he sprinted after it and just hauled himself on board.

Kate left Francesca for a few minutes to go and wash and try to revive herself. Her enthusiasm and expended energy had caught up on her, and now she was very tired. She hoped Francesca would sleep when she finally got her bedded down in the Paris train, because she herself was going to sleep like a log.

Her face, pale with fatigue, looked back at her from the blurred mirror. Only a trickle of water came from the tap into the not-particularly-inviting basin. She would have to make do with a little coolness on her temples and a freshing of her lipstick. After all, did it matter, with only Francesca's hooded eyes to look at her?

Certainly she would have dinner in the restaurant car at Basle. But even then, all alone, with Francesca safely tucked in bed, travel stains could not matter less.

Francesca was sitting bolt upright when she returned to the compartment.

"Man," she said succinctly.

"A man?" Kate looked at the other unoccupied seats. They had been lucky so far, having a compartment to themselves. Not many people seemed to be travelling first-class on this train.

"That's all right," she said. "Other people can sit in here if they wish to."

The child's eyes looked burningly at her, and she spoke in her rapid, incomprehensible Italian.

"Did he talk to you?" Kate said. The child did not seem frightened, only wide awake and interested. Someone apparently had had a conversation with her in her own language, and it had cheered her up. Perhaps this stranger would come back and talk in English, too. In the meantime the barrier of their different languages was between them again. Francesca, rocking her doll in her arms, had found someone she had liked. Perhaps, taking after her mother, she responded more to men than to women. At least it had made her find her tongue for she said something else, ending with "Londre."

"London?" said Kate sharply. "Did he ask if you were going to London?"

"Londre," said Francesca again, and held up two fingers.

"Two," said Kate, puzzled. "Twice?"

But did she mean the stranger had been to London twice, or that Francesca herself had?

Surely this rather comic-opera journey with the doll, the organdie dress and the Eiffel Tower looming ahead, as a lure, had not happened previously!

At Basle there was slight pandemonium, for a party of schoolgirls from the ages of seven to twelve boarded the train, and there seemed to be confusion about their seats. There was a great deal of arguing and chattering going on, and the two mistresses in charge of them, after talking emphatically to an ever-growing group of railway officials, at last shrugged their shoulders fatalistically and herded the children on board.

Kate, with her passports, baggage and her small travelling companion safely passed by the Customs, found their two-berth sleeping compartment and went into it thankfully. Francesca by this time was more than three parts asleep. Kate produced the bread and the cheese she had bought at Milan, anticipating the child's inability to stay awake for late dinner in the restaurant car, but even these Francesca was too tired to cope with. She gnawed at the bread for a while, then yawned widely and clambered into her bunk.

"Oh, not in your dress!" exclaimed Kate. "If you sleep in that it will be quite ruined."

But her endeavors to make the sleep-drunk child sit up and be divested of the now sadly crushed organdie were useless. She did not intend to have her dress removed. Either she was genuinely asleep or she was foxing, and Kate was even less able to cope with her stubbornness than the absent Gianetta had been.

Actually, she didn't think Francesca was foxing, for her doll, Pepita, lay forgotten beside her, and she had the gnawed piece of bread still clutched in her hand. She was just worn out, poor little thing. After all, although she hadn't responded to any friendliness, neither had she complained. There had been no tears or whimpering, which represented rather astonishing self-control for a seven-year-old. One had to remember that.

But that dress was going to be a travesty by morning. Kate opened the shabby little suitcase to see what Gianetta would have considered Francesca's requirements on the journey. To her relief she found a blouse and skirt and a light tweed coat. Somehow the blouse and skirt would have to be forced on to the child in the morning, or, as a last resort, the coat could cover the crumpled dress.

So all would be well. The worst part of the journey was over. By morning they would be in Paris and by evening in London. Kate pulled the blanket high around Francesca's sleeping face, and switched off the light over her bunk. Now she would relax with some food and a glass of wine in the restaurant car, and then get some much-needed sleep herself.

It was quite a journey to reach the restaurant car, and she was thankful the train had not yet left the station. For she had to step over little clumps of schoolgirls who, apparently just as weary as Francesca, had bedded down in the corridors, anxiously supervised by the two harassed mistresses.

One of the mistresses, a young girl with a round, freckled, hot face, said indignantly to Kate, "There's been a mistake over our reservations, so we have no seats at all. Can you imagine? And we've been travelling all day. The children are worn out."

"They look it," said Kate sympathetically. "Can't you find any empty seats?"

"Oh, we've parked a few of them here and there. There are thirty of them, and only two of us to look after them." She pushed the damp hair off her forehead and sighed. "Oh, well, as long as no one falls over them. Kids sleep anywhere. But I do think these Continental trains are the end!"

Kate thought of the turmoil in the morning when everyone wanted to get into the toilet at once. She picked her way down the narrow corridors, over the children, over stacked luggage, past standing passengers, and the bitterly harassed official with the list of couchettes, past crowded compartments packed with weary tourists already trying to find welcoming spots for their heads, even if it were their neighbor's reluctant shoulder. Twenty guineas, she was beginning to think, was not such a generous fee after all. Someone struggling on to the train dug the corner of a suitcase into her shin, and behind her the sorely tired official said in tones of the greatest entreaty to an importuning woman, *"S'il vous plaît, madame . . ."*

Then a man, leaning against the window, suddenly smiled at Kate. His eyes were dark and intense. "Some scrimmage," he said.

She assented wearily. Then suddenly she laughed back at him. It was funny, after all, and they were both English being amused at the ways of foreigners.

The fragmentary encounter cheered her up. Also a savory smell indicated the nearness of the restaurant car. She came into its comparative emptiness and quiet, and, shown to a seat by a courteous waiter, she sat down and relaxed with pleasure.

She had only glimpsed the man's face. But she was quick at faces. Almost now she could have sketched it. It had been dark and narrow and, for he did not seem old, surprisingly deeply lined. In repose, she guessed, it would be aloof and withdrawn, but his smile brought it to life.

If the sitter for Titian's "Head of a Man" in the Louvre had suddenly smiled, he would have looked like that, she thought.

She fumbled in her bag for her pencil, and began sketching on the menu the waiter had given her.

Soup was brought, and when she looked up the young man was sitting opposite her.

He smiled. "Do you mind?"

"Not at all."

The train was moving now. Suddenly she was aware of the strain the day had been, and the deep relief she felt now that the journey was so far accomplished. The lights swayed a little to the rocking of the train, and it seemed to her that the face of the man sitting opposite her swayed a little, too, blurring and becoming clear again. She was very tired indeed.

"You're travelling to England?"

"Yes. By ferry tomorrow."

"So am I. We may see one another again."

Was he going to be the "romantic interest" of her trip? But it was a little too late in the journey to have this happen, and there was all

day tomorrow to be occupied with shepherding the silent Francesca
about Paris. Besides, it was a pity she was so tired.

"You've been on holiday?" went on his pleasant, polite voice.

"No, on a job. Well, a sort of job. It gave me an excuse to get to
Rome again."

"Tell me your favorite part of Rome."

"The Colosseum, I think. On a sunny, windy day, when the wild
flowers are blooming in the cracks of the walls."

"And you don't hear the lions roaring any more."

She nodded. "Just silence and peace."

"Everything's the same in a thousand years. It doesn't really matter much if you missed your chariot in A.D. 80 or your train in this
year of grace."

His eyes were dark and sparkling, but his mouth had a definite
line, and there was a certain grimness to the deeply-scored lines in
his cheeks. He could be anything, anybody, a philosopher or a buc-
caneer.

"That's a rather dangerous philosophy," Kate said.

"Is it? Would you care to share a bottle of wine with me?"

"Thank you. I'll probably go to sleep, but I suppose that will all be
the same in a thousand years, too."

"Even Helen fell asleep." His eyes on her were frankly admiring.
More wide awake, she might have felt a little embarrassed. Now it
was mildly pleasant to toss the conversational ball to such an enter-
taining stranger.

"My name's Lucian Cray," he said.

"I'm Kate Tempest. Not so romantic."

"Romantic?"

"Yours is a little, isn't it. Actually it sounds like a stage name. You
don't mind my saying so?"

"Not in the least. After all, Shakespeare could have known you and
called you Miranda."

She laughed. "Don't be absurd. Not with my nose!"

The waiter had come with the wine list. They both discovered they
preferred vin rouge, and somehow this seemed another bond between
them. Another one? Kate puckered her brows. What was the other
bond? That somehow she knew intuitively Rome affected him in the
same way as it did her. The settled dust of long ago pandemonium,
and the peace of old stones. . . .

She realized that he had taken the menu from her and was studying
her sketch.

"Do I look such a haggard individual?"

"That wasn't intended for you to see."

"Clever. If this is a habit of yours, you could become a menace."

"I know. But faces fascinate me. If I don't put them on paper they seem to stay graven on my mind."

"So that's what you've been doing in Rome, looking for faces of gladiators."

"And the ones Michelangelo and Leonardo da Vinci used to discover. They're still there, you know. If you sit in the via Vittorio Veneto, they all pass by, the beggars and the misers, the corrupt and the crafty. If you changed their clothes you'd find the Pharisees in the Temple and the Caesars and the Judas's, the hungry and the lonely and the good."

He poured wine into her glass.

"I've travelled for nearly three days," she said. "I'm beginning to talk nonsense."

"On the contrary. I wish you'd go on."

"No, my job is drawing, not talking. Have you been on holiday?"

"I had to see some people in Rome," he said, with what seemed to her deliberate vagueness. "Ah, well, Paris tomorrow, then London. Perhaps I'll see you in London?"

"Aren't we getting on a little fast?"

He smiled, with that sudden, disconcerting look of rakishness. His eyes were brilliant and bent only on her, but there was a certain coldness, almost a calculated look to them.

"Yesterday the Roman gladiators were only just around the corner, today the twenty-first century looms over us. Too fast? My dear Kate!"

She began to laugh. The wine and her tiredness and the movement of the train made her feel as if she were on a merry-go-round, a very gay, fast one whirling her towards some inevitable destiny. He began to laugh too, touching her hand, and suddenly she was lightheartedly, unquestioningly happy.

She did not think of William at all.

She left him at last. She had to get some sleep in order to cope with Francesca the next day. But she knew she would see him again, perhaps at breakfast, perhaps on the Channel boat, perhaps in London. . . . He still hadn't told her anything more about himself except that slightly unlikely name. But that didn't matter. She would find out. There was plenty of time.

People and luggage still cluttered the corridors of the train. Kate made her way back to her compartment, carefully picking her way among the piled bags, the weary passengers, and, in her own carriage, two knots of sleeping schoolchildren.

The jolting of the train bumped her against a man standing near the door to her compartment. He turned to say "Pardon!" He was smoking a large cigar. He looked at her with bold, dark eyes. She frowned a little, knowing she would have to pass him again, with her sponge bag, on her way to wash—if one could pick one's way over sleeping bodies to the toilet. There would be the squeezing past again, the murmured apology.

But she was wrong. When she came out again he had gone. She had to stand in the rocking corridor in a dispirited little queue for fifteen minutes, and was thankful all the time that Francesca was fast asleep. She had not stirred when Kate had entered the compartment. There was the unmoving plump hump of her beneath the bedclothes in the shadow. She'd probably wake frightfully early, and, sleep-dazed and out of temper, Kate would have to cope with her objections to wearing anything but the crumpled white organdie.

Well, no use in anticipating trouble. Live in the moment—in this particular moment of watching the miserly trickle of water coming from the faucets, and seeing in the swaying speckled mirror not her own face but that of her dinner companion, dark-eyed, somber Lucian Cray. It was not a name one would forget. Or a face. . . .

In spite of her extreme tiredness, she did not sleep well. She dozed, and woke with a start every time the train jolted to a stop. Somewhere behind these drawn blinds and this stuffy little room a world existed. One heard it in the shouted names of the stations, ringing through the abruptly still night, like battle honors. Then the more mundane chattering of late travellers, the slamming of doors, the sliding forward and the increasing rhythm of the wheels again, lulling her to uneasy sleep until the next jolt came, and the voices from another world shouted. Once there was scuffling outside her door, and one of the schoolgirls whimpering. The soothing voice of the mistress calmed her. Thank goodness her own charge was much too stolid and placid for upsets. She slept like a log. Once Kate leaned over from her bunk to see the tuft of hair unmoving on the pillow. If only she could sleep as soundly herself.

But the night passed in this uneasy, half-conscious dozing, and when the first light crept through the edges of the drawn blinds her head was still tight with exhaustion and her eyes felt full of grit. She sat up to reach for her hair brush, and at that moment the pandemonium started outside her door.

It was those wretched schoolchildren again. There were their concerted voices, all speaking at once, and above them that of one of the mistresses who was obviously begging for quiet.

"Now, if you'll all just stop talking for a moment and listen to me. Mary, you say Annabelle was beside you when you went to sleep."

"I thought she was, Miss Rickerby, but Helen says she saw her go to look out of the windows at the other end of the corridor."

"But she came back, Miss Rickerby, because I saw her fixing her coat to put her head on."

The mistress was obviously getting a little panicky.

"Didn't I tell you all to stay here and not move."

"But sometimes we had to go—"

"Oh, I understand that. Annabelle isn't there now, is she?"

"No, we told you. There's a man in there shaving. He's taking simply ages."

"Never mind him. We must find Annabelle. Miss Jones has Laura and Jennifer and Caroline, and there are four in the compartment at the end of the corridor where some kind people let them sleep on the floor. How many of you here?"

"Eleven."

"So Annabelle is missing. Then she must be in one of the compartments. I'm afraid we'll have to knock politely at doors and ask people."

At this stage, Kate climbed out of her bunk, and pulling on her sweater and skirt, opened the door.

"Are you in trouble? Can I help?"

The young mistress, whose round, freckled face was hot and flushed again—had it remained so all night, or was it permanently so? —looked up quickly.

"One of my charges seems to be missing, but she can't be far away. It's all right, really."

"You poor thing," said Kate sympathetically. "I have only one to look after, and that's responsibility enough. You with all these."

"It would have been all right if our reservations hadn't been muddled. Still, we're through the night, aren't we, children? When we find Annabelle and we've all had some breakfast we'll be as right as rain."

"What does Annabelle look like?"

"She has red hair—"

"And freckles," echoed the children.

Kate smiled. "She should be conspicuous enough. I'm sorry I haven't got her under my bunk. Shall I help you look?"

"Oh, no, thank you. We can manage very well. She wouldn't possibly have left this carriage. Actually she's rather a timid child. I thought she was dead asleep when I saw her last. She must be in one of the compartments. I'll just take a quick look. I'll give you a shout when I've found her, if you like."

"Yes, do."

Temporarily giving up ideas of a wash, Kate went back into her compartment and shut the door. Francesca would wake any minute, but one might as well let her sleep as long as possible. It was only six o'clock. She would leave the blinds drawn and rest a little longer herself. The poor girl with all those children to look after. No wonder one of them had gone astray.

But she couldn't be far away. Children didn't disappear off trains unless someone deliberately pushed them off.

And now it was tomorrow, and there was Francesca, and the Eiffel Tower, and later the ferry to Folkestone, and perhaps a glimpse of Lucian Cray somewhere in the crowd, perhaps that flashing smile of his across a multitude of heads.

Kate dreamed pleasantly as the light grew, and through the chink of the blind she could see the stubble and the faded tawny look of the gentle French fields. Gray clusters of houses, leaf-stripped trees, white horses browsing on the autumn grass, and occasional fairy-tale turrets, or the glimpse of a white chateau among groves of beeches.

But a little later her reverie was broken by an apologetic tap on her door.

"Who is it?"

The young mistress, even hotter of face, slid the door back and put her head in.

"I'm so sorry, but there absolutely isn't a sign of Annabelle. Do you mind awfully if I look in here? I'm sure she wouldn't hide herself away uninvited, but just in case—"

"Of course. Look where you like. But there's only Francesca here. She's still asleep. You can see."

"Oh, I'm sorry—honestly I'm at my wit's end—"

"It's time Francesca woke up anyway," said Kate, and pulled the blinds up with a clatter. "There, now you can see for yourself that I've no redhead—"

But her words died on her lips. For the sound and the light had woken the child in the bunk, and she turned sleepily, lifting her tawny head, opening pale green eyes, and showing clearly her face with its comic mask of sandy freckles!

The child was not Francesca at all. She was the missing Annabelle, who, recognizing her hot-and-bothered schoolteacher, began to smile, revealing two missing front teeth. Smiling an idiot's grin, Kate thought frantically, as she began to realize the dreadful implication.

It was not the tow-haired Annabelle who was missing. It was Francesca!

4

The girl *was* an idiot, Kate thought furiously. For she seemed to have no idea how she had come to sleep the night comfortably in a first-class compartment while her schoolmates huddled miserably in the corridor. She said she had gone to sleep beside Mary and just woken up here. That was all.

"What was your little girl like?" the schoolmistress asked sympathetically.

The past tense, thought Kate, with renewed anger. As if Francesca were dead!

"She's dressed in a white organdie dress, and she has a large blue bow in her hair. She's Italian and speaks almost no English."

She was aware of the young mistress, smug now that she had the full count of her pupils, eying her with the faintest scepticism. Perhaps it did sound an unlikely description of a child on a long journey, but that wasn't her fault. Anyway, she had Francesca's modest suitcase, with the more conventional clothes in it, to prove that everyone wasn't quite mad.

She dived under the bunk to produce it. But it wasn't there. At least, not where she had put it. It must be in the rack—or somewhere. In her exhaustion last night she had moved it, and forgotten.

"What are you looking for?" asked the other girl.

"Francesca's suitcase. I thought I put it under the bunk. It must be here somewhere."

In a panic she was dragging the blankets off the bed, lifting the mattress.

But there was nowhere in a small railway compartment that a suitcase could be completely concealed. The fact was too obvious to deny. Both Francesca and her belongings were gone. They had simply vanished into thin air.

"How very odd!" murmured the young mistress, the scepticism in her eyes. In the narrow doorway she was now surrounded by curious, peeping children. Frantically, Kate searched their faces, round ones, long ones, heavy ones, grubby ones. But there was no small Mona Lisa, no hooded, secretive eyes that told nothing.

"She *must* be on the train somewhere," Kate said.

"Well, she shouldn't be hard to find in those clothes. But she's not in this carriage, because I'd have noticed her when I looked for Annabelle. Would you like me to help you?"

"Oh, if you would!"

"Of course I will. The children will help."

"Her name's Francesca, and I'm taking her to London to her mother. She doesn't even belong to me, you see. That makes it more awful. I left her in the bunk fast asleep when I went to have dinner last night, and when I came back she hadn't moved. At least—" That must have been when the strange thing had happened, when the sandy-haired Annabelle had got into Francesca's bunk and Francesca had gone off—or been taken off. Because she could swear no one had come into the compartment during the rest of the night.

"It's a pity Annabelle doesn't remember anything," the other girl said. "But she always was a sleepyhead. I'll get Miss Jones to help, too. Surely with all of us we'll soon find her."

The children thought it was a game. They surged through the train like a small tornado, shouting, "Francesca!" and bursting unceremoniously into compartments, squalid in the growing light, with tossed bedding, luggage, and half-awake, unshaven, tousle-headed travellers.

Kate, following in their wake, asked politely but urgently if anyone had seen the little girl in the white organdie dress. Everywhere she was met with blank faces. No, no one had seen such a child. A white organdie dress! But that one would remember. What had happened? Had the child been kidnapped? But that would be impossible on a train. She must be somewhere.

Yes, Kate agreed feverishly. She must be somewhere. But where? And why had she disappeared?

An irate guard, trying to stop the avalanche of children, demanded to know what was happening, and Kate explained what the trouble was, first in English and then, seeing he was only half understanding, in her careful French.

"You say the child was in the bed when you woke this morning?"

"But not the same child, I'm trying to tell you."

His eyes popped slightly. He was short and rotund, and looked quite stupid.

"M'selle, children do not change overnight."

"You don't believe me! But it's true! Someone must have changed them over. One of the schoolchildren, a completely strange child, was in the bunk."

"Ah-ha! A joke, m'selle. You have a friend on this train who likes to play jokes?"

"I don't have any friends on this train," Kate snapped impatiently. "And it isn't a joke. Or if it is, it's a monstrous one."

"You have the little girl's bags, perhaps?"

"No, they're gone, too."

The little round, popping eyes surveyed her with what was now becoming familiar scepticism.

"M'selle, you are sure you began the journey with a child? You did not just imagine a little girl in a white dress with a blue ribbon in her hair?" A creature from a fairy tale, a figment of the imagination. . . . That was what he was saying to her.

"Or perhaps she flew out of the window!" he suggested, with heavy jocularity.

There was a hand on Kate's shoulder.

"Kate! Is there some trouble?"

It was Lucian. Kate almost flung herself into his arms.

"Yes, there is. I've lost Francesca."

His forehead creased with concern. But even his concern, she could see at once, was not serious. Or was she getting into the state where she suspected everyone?

"You didn't tell me anything about a Francesca last night. Who is she? Your poodle?"

"No, she's not a poodle. She's a child. Seven years old, and dressed in white organdie, with a large blue bow in her hair." She went over the familiar description wearily, and waited for the inevitable reaction.

But she was grateful to see that he didn't think the description so improbable. He said quite seriously, "A child of seven wouldn't get off the train by herself, unless she fell off, and that's even more unlikely. Have you looked right through the train?"

"Almost."

"Then let me help you with the rest. Which way?"

"This. It's awfully good of you. I *must* find her before we get to Paris because there, in the crowds, it wouldn't be so difficult for someone to whisk her away."

He turned in the swaying corridor to look at her.

"Why should anyone do that?"

"She's the child of divorced parents, and they're fighting over her. I was bringing her to England."

"Ah! Spies!"

"Lucian, don't joke! It's serious."

"I'm not joking." He put his hand back to take hers. She found the pressure of his cool, strong fingers immensely reassuring. In that moment, in the muddle and worry and exhaustion, she fell very briefly in love with him.

Suddenly she was remembering the man whom she had bumped into in the corridor the previous night, standing near her compartment and turning to give her that long, insolent look.

Perhaps he was the person who had substituted Annabelle for Francesca, and then, with enormous confidence, lingered to see whether she would notice the change-over when she went to bed.

But *why* would he do it? And if he had done, he must have Francesca on the train somewhere. Unless he had left at one of the stops during the night, when the phantom voices had called, and everything had seemed to be happening in a dream.

The children came bursting back to say that there was absolutely no sign of any little girl in a white dress on the train. They had looked *everywhere,* even in the toilets, and the guards' van.

One of the mistresses followed, nodding her confirmation. "I'm awfully sorry. But it does all seem so strange, doesn't it?"

She meant that none of it was real. And neither did it seem real, in the cool, growing dawn, with fatigue-marked passengers making their way to the restaurant car for coffee and rolls, and others snapping suitcases shut, and preparing for their arrival in Paris.

Kate pressed her hands to her forehead. Was she awake or in a nightmare?

"Kate—you did have this child with you?"

The schoolmistress had looked sceptical, the little French guard, stout and stupid, had looked sceptical, the passengers with their dull, sleepy eyes had shaken their heads with a polite lack of belief. Now, as the last straw, Lucian, who might at least have been the one to help her, looked disbelieving also.

"Do you think I was drunk and imagining things? Of course I had her with me."

He was not smiling now. His face had its somber, rather gaunt look.

"You didn't mention her at dinner last night. I thought you were travelling alone."

"I'd put her to bed. She was fast asleep. I didn't tell you everything last night. Should I have?" Her brows were raised haughtily. She was no longer in love with him. She hated him. He must know she was frantically worried, and yet he chose to think she was inventing a fantastic story about travelling with a child and losing it.

"You have her luggage, perhaps, her passport?" he said gently.

"No, I haven't. That's disappeared, too. Believe it or not!"

Curious passengers were listening now. She seemed to have eyes staring at her from all directions. She thought she would lose her difficult self-control and begin to scream.

"Find her for me!" she begged in a whisper. "Ask me questions afterwards."

No little girl in a white frock! No little girl in a white frock! The answer seemed to come automatically from all around.

Suddenly Kate saw the man whom she had bumped into the previous night. He was still looking at her with his sly, dark gaze, but when she burst out accusingly, "Have you seen a little girl in a white dress?" he shook his head and said in bewilderment, in a broad Bradford voice, "Ee, have you lost one?"

No one with a voice like that should look so sinister. It was so unexpected that it was wildly funny. Kate thought she must be going mad. Then the train seemed to spin dizzily, and she had to grip the window ledge.

Lucian's hand was on her elbow.

"Are you all right, Kate? You'd better come and have some coffee."

"I can't. Not without Francesca. She needs coffee, too."

"We'll be at the Gare du Nord in half an hour. Ten minutes for coffee isn't going to affect Francesca one way or the other, but it is going to stop you from fainting."

"Lucian, what am I to do?" she implored.

"Have coffee and we'll talk."

It was useless to talk, of course. She could only repeat how she had put Francesca safely to bed in the lower bunk the night before and then had had that moment of utter horror and disbelief on seeing the strange child's face in the morning.

"Freckles! Missing teeth! And she hasn't a word of explanation."

"She wouldn't have climbed in that bunk if it hadn't been empty."

"You mean she deliberately got in herself?"

"I should think so. Half asleep. Looking for somewhere to be comfortable. Naturally she isn't going to admit she remembers."

"But, Lucian—" She gave him a long look over her coffee cup.

"You still don't believe me, do you? You think it's I who have been dreaming up things."

"Have you Francesca's railway ticket?"

"She wanted to keep it herself with her passport. She's an experienced traveller. Everything was in her suitcase." Kate pushed away her coffee cup and stood up. "What on earth am I going to tell her mother and Mrs. Dix?"

"We're coming into the outskirts of Paris," Lucian said. "Look."

Kate took an anguished look at the slate-gray roofs, the amber chestnut trees, the slowly awaking streets. Clasping her doll, determined and silent, Francesca was to have made her promised ascent of the Eiffel Tower. . . .

How *could* she have disappeared into thin air? She couldn't. That was nonsense.

Kate stood up decisively.

"The moment we arrive, I'm getting the police."

It was impossible, in the fuss and bustle of arrival, to see whether anyone anywhere was trying to smuggle a fat complacent child off the train. Although she hung out of the window to get a good view of the moving people, the shouting porters, the babble of several languages made her feel only baffled and confused. The two schoolmistresses, with their clutch of children anxiously shepherded, passed by. One of them looked up.

"We're terribly sorry we can't stay to help. But we can't risk losing any of our own."

"That's all right," Kate called.

"So sorry about all that mess up. . . ." They were pushed out of sight. The man from Bradford, hurrying past with brief-case and raincoat, paused to give her a wink and his sidelong glance. But the business man in him was already uppermost, and he had forgotten her trouble. The train was almost empty now. It seemed useless to search the empty compartments littered only with orange skin and cigarette butts.

If Francesca were there she would be making her presence known —if she could still speak. . . .

Suddenly, in a flash of illumination, Kate was remembering the child's efforts last night to tell her that a strange man had talked to her. Someone interested in her, someone who had excited her, and told her something that pleased her. Her eyes had been shining.

Had he been making an irresistible bribe to her? Had he asked her to get off the train when he came for her?

Because now Kate was convinced the change-over of the children had been made while she was having dinner with Lucian.

Francesca must have been taken off the train at the last minute before it left Basle, but her abductor naturally would not want Kate to discover her absence until morning. So the sleep-drunk Annabelle, luckily to his hand, had been substituted. . . .

"Kate," came Lucian's voice, "there's no use in waiting here."

Kate turned slowly. "What am I to do?" she asked again.

"Call the police if you like. But I doubt if you'll convince them a child existed. I suggest you should first put a call through to London and get your instructions from there."

"Yes. I'd better telephone Mrs. Dix. But however am I to tell her. . . ." She felt dazed now, with worry and exhaustion. She was temporarily content to have him lead her.

"Put your coat on. Where are your bags?"

"There's only one. Francesca's—" Her voice trembled. She made herself say carefully, "You're very good to me, although you don't really believe there is a Francesca. I've got some gloves somewhere— oh, look!" Her cry was chiefly one of surprise, as if she, too, had been becoming convinced that Francesca did not exist. "Here's Francesca's doll. It's got pushed behind the mattress. There you are! That proves she was here!"

Triumphantly she held up the slightly shabby doll, pathetic and somehow without personality now that it lacked an owner.

"You have to believe me now," she said.

"Any child can have a doll," he murmured. "But, Kate dear, I've never disbelieved you. Come along, let's get off this ghastly train."

Francesca lured somewhere on a false bribe, without her promised trip to the Eiffel Tower, without her precious doll. A little girl determinedly dressed for a party that seemed to be fast becoming a tragedy. . . . Kate resolutely swallowed the lump in her throat and followed Lucian.

They had to wait for the London call to come through. Lucian had arranged it. He had somehow got several talkative and gesticulating railway officials persuaded of the urgency of it, and had also the tired and irritable guard, who had first heard Kate's report of the child's disappearance, to bear witness. They all stood and watched as Kate at last got through and heard Mrs. Dix's voice which seemed to come from infinitely far away. Yet even in that wispy sound she could hear the breathless eagerness of the "Yes! Yes! Who is it, please?" and she realized the forlorn and fantastic hope that was running through Mrs. Dix's mind. Even after fifteen years of silence, any telephone call from abroad revived her tenacious optimism. This, perhaps this, was the one to tell her that her husband had come back from the dead. . . .

It was cruel to shatter that expectancy, and even in this emergency Kate hesitated.

"It's Kate here, Mrs. Dix."

"Kate? Kate?" The disembodied voice had lost its liveliness. It sounded groping and lost, as if the transition from hope to reality was too much for its owner.

"Kate Tempest, Mrs. Dix. I went to Rome to get Francesca."

"Oh, yes, I remember. The Italian child. What about it? Where are you speaking from? Has something gone wrong?"

"Terribly wrong, I'm afraid. Francesca's missing. Lost. She disappeared off the train. And no one has seen her."

They were all watching her in the dreary brown room, Lucian, the telephone operator, and the officials who had argued and protested that the whole thing was imaginary, unnecessary. Relatives had picked up the child at Basle—if there had been a child. . . . Pouf, anyone could leave a shabby toy on a train. . . .

"Missing! Oh, goodness me!" The flurried voice told Kate that Mrs. Dix was groping in a convenient chocolate box for sustenance.

The disappointment that the call from abroad was not from her long-lost husband after all, and now this news that Kate's mission had gone so badly astray, would throw her off balance.

"Shall I call the police in? That's what I must know."

"Those foreign police—so excitable—just to find a child who's run away. Can't you look for her?"

"You don't understand, Mrs. Dix. She's been missing all night. We think she was taken from the train at Basle."

"We?"

"The gentlemen here," Kate said, looking placatingly at the avidly listening gentlemen. "The railway officials, and an Englishman who has been very kind."

There were sundry strange noises coming through the receiver that may have been Mrs. Dix clucking in alarm, or merely munching a chocolate. But when she spoke again her voice was surprisingly decisive.

"Not the police yet, dear. Must get in touch with Rome, with her father. Oh, dear! What a bore! And we thought you so reliable. Miss Squires said—dear! dear! Not those dreadful foreign police, making an international incident out of it. Wait there till I call you back. What's your number?"

"Can I get a call here?" Kate whispered frantically.

This was the signal for a great deal more arguing to go on, but finally it was agreed that if it came in a reasonable time it would be permitted. It was the best that could be done. Sitting in the stuffy office waiting for the telephone to ring, catching the hostile glances of French officials who thought her infinitely careless, to say the least, to lose a child on a journey—if there had been a child—Kate realized what the note beneath Mrs. Dix's breathlessness and alarm had been. Not disappointment. Fear.

Or had she imagined that, too? Had she imagined everything, even the small shabby doll, Pepita, packed now in her capacious handbag?

But the second call, when it came, was complete anti-climax. Mrs. Dix's voice bubbled over with reassurance.

"Kate dear, not to worry. Everything's all right. Francesca's home."

"In Rome?" Kate gasped.

"Yes, with her father. He's very bad and quite unscrupulous. When she had gone he suddenly decided he couldn't bear it, or perhaps it was spite against Rosita, of course, but he telephoned some friends in Basle and had Francesca taken off the train. At a moment when you were not observing, of course."

"But how extraordinary!" Kate gasped.

"Isn't it?" Mrs. Dix's voice was full of cheerfulness. "He's nothing better than a brigand. Giving you all this worry, poor Kate. Rosita is broken-hearted, naturally. She wants you to stay in Paris for a day just in case we have any further instructions for you. Go to the Hotel Imperial in the Rue St. Honoré. And get a rest. You must be worn out. We'll call you there if we need you. And fly home in the morning. Miss Squires will arrange for your air ticket to be sent to the hotel."

"Mrs. Dix, are you sure Francesca's all right?"

"I can only tell you what that rogue has told me. And *quite* unashamedly. He thinks he's very clever, in fact. But in case he should repent, which is unlikely, Rosita thinks you should stay until tomorrow."

"I've messed it up so badly."

"My dear, no one could have anticipated this. You said there was an Englishman?" Mrs. Dix's voice lilted naughtily. "And you're in Paris. Go and have fun."

Kate put the telephone down slowly. She gathered that everyone listening had got the gist of the conversation, for there were wreathed smiles and shrugging shoulders.

"What did I tell you?" said the now affable guard. "She flew out of the window, pouf!"

"It has been a storm in a soup plate, no?"

It was only Lucian who was not smiling. He was looking at her with a long, curious, thoughtful look, neither surprised nor relieved at the solution to the small drama, but rather as if when he had persuaded her to ring London he had known exactly what the result would be. And almost as if it amused him a little.

But why should it be amusing? She herself felt remarkably far from mirth. For apart from the pathos of it—Francesca, lonely and bewildered, snatched away from her promised party, deprived of her favorite doll, and bundled back to Rome like so much merchandise, probably to the rather grim Gianetta and the squalid little house off the via Appia—there had been that strange note of fear in Mrs. Dix's voice.

Even during her second call, when she had bubbled over with cheerfulness, Kate had calmly and uneasily sensed the apprehension. What, in the foolish and abortive episode, would make her afraid?

5

The gentle click of the door opening aroused Kate late in the afternoon.

"Who is it?" she asked sleepily, not fully aware of where she was, or why she had been asleep when afternoon sunshine was still filtering through the windows.

There was no answer.

She sat up, blinking and looking at the closed door. But she was sure it had opened. That was what had woken her. Had someone come to the wrong room?

Or had someone been walking about softly in here, and left hastily when she stirred?

Fully awake, Kate sprang out of bed and hurried to the door. The corridor was empty. Somewhere she could hear voices speaking in rapid French, and on the ground floor she heard the lift gates shut. These were normal enough sounds in an hotel and nothing to get perturbed about.

Funny. She had been sure something had aroused her. Perhaps it had been the door of the next room opening and closing. Anyway, here was the day almost gone, and she had not yet had more than the glimpse of Paris that she had got on the brief taxi journey from the Gare du Nord to the hotel. Lucian had brought her here. He had told her to get some rest, and, if his business permitted, he would telephone her before eight o'clock that evening. He had been very kind. He had seen her through that nightmare hour when she had been searching uselessly for Francesca. But there was no reason why he should go on being responsible for her. She had realized that in the slightly withdrawn quality of his voice when he said goodbye to her. As if an unexpected duty had been safely discharged.

Well, he had thought the whole thing a hoax, anyway. He still did not seem entirely to believe that there had ever been a child, in spite of her conversation with Mrs. Dix, and in spite of the doll, which could have belonged to one of the schoolchildren.

Kate shrugged as philosophically as possible. After all, it could be Lucian who had been the ghost. He was even more transitory than Francesca. The only record she had of him was the sketch she had done on the menu card, and that was not particularly good. She took it out of her handbag to look at it again. His remarks about it were right, she thought, as she looked at the incomplete lines. He did look haggard and grim, like someone engaged in a losing battle or a lost cause. She would tear this up and forget it. And him.

But this she could not quite bring herself to do. She left it lying on the dressing-table, and picked up the telephone to ask for a bath. Her exhaustion still clung to her, and it made her feel strangely sad and gloomy. She had made such a mess of her mission to Rome, and the thought of Francesca, an innocent seven-year-old, caught up in quarrels that were not hers, depressed her. The child should be having the normal fun and security one associated with childhood.

However, a bath and fresh clothes, and then a quick excursion around Paris would take away her morbid feelings. The hotel was old-fashioned, and she was escorted, with ceremony, by an elderly porter with a towel draped over his arm, to the top floor where the bath was filled almost to overflowing with very hot water.

In this she lingered longer than she had meant to. When she returned to her room she wondered if Lucian had been trying to get her on the telephone. But it was foolish to stay in on the chance of a call from a virtual stranger who by now was probably too busy with his own affairs to worry about her. She would go out for a brief sightseeing tour while the daylight lasted.

But it was a pity. . . . His face remained persistently in her mind.

That sketch—where was it? She thought she had left it on her dress-ing-table. She was positive she had. But it was not there.

Neither did it seem to be anywhere else, not even in the wastepa-per basket. Someone must have come in to tidy up the room.

But nothing else had been touched. The bed was left rumpled from her long sleep. Her things were flung carelessly about. With a small stirring of uneasiness she remembered the real or fancied opening of her door as she awoke from sleep. Had someone wanted to come in then, but finding her there, gone away? It would be difficult to know whether or not anyone had searched her suitcase, for its contents were already untidy enough. Her handbag she had prudently taken up to the bathroom with her, so her money and passport were safe. Only the menu card, quite valueless, was missing. . . .

In the Luxembourg Gardens a little girl was trying to catch a kit-ten, but it had escaped and somehow climbed the statue of the Cy-clops hanging over the Fountain of the Medicis. The dark, still water, sprinkled with amber leaves and flashing with the amber shine of darting goldfish, separated the child from the kitten. Her face had a lost, longing look. She instantly made Kate think of Francesca, and the look that would be on her face now that she had lost her doll and her party. Surely something could be done, even by an outsider, to make that child happy. She must talk with Mrs. Dix when she re-turned to London.

Meantime . . . the lovely slender queens with their flowing stone draperies stood in their calm circle round the plots of red geraniums, the grouped nannies and babies, the autumn-leaved chestnuts and the fountains. Some of the little girls playing on the grass wore starched white frocks. Kate found herself walking closer to them to look into their faces. How foolish she was not to be able to get it out of her mind that somewhere, somehow, Francesca really was in Paris. Per-haps having her promised ascent of the Eiffel Tower. . . .

Of course. That's where she should go before the light faded. She took a taxi, and was whisked across the city at an alarming speed. In spite of it being late afternoon there was still a crowd of tourists lin-gering about the preposterous erection, and the lifts creaking up and down were packed.

But as soon as she had arrived Kate realized what a forlorn and useless thing she was doing. Francesca was not here. Even if she were mysteriously in Paris whoever had seized her would not be the kind of person who would indulge her desire to ascend the Eiffel Tower.

A lift had just opened to disgorge its occupants. An official was saying beguilingly to Kate, "Ticket, m'selle. The view is marvellous. Such a clear afternoon."

Still in her dreamy and slightly haunted daze Kate went to the ticket office and bought a ticket. After all, the man was right. One might as well see the view. She filed into the lift with the waiting queue of people, and the doors shut. Slowly the creaking mechanism worked, and the city began to fall away. Kate edged to the side to look down. Suddenly she saw a flash of white in the crowd below.

"Kate! Kate!"

The lift creaked louder and around her people chattered excitedly in various languages. Kate wanted to shout frantically, "Be quiet! Be quiet! Someone's calling me!" She was gripping the side of the lift which dragged her inexorably away from the glimpse she had caught of a white frock.

Oh, if only they would stop it! *Had* someone called her? Now, as the crowds on the ground grew smaller it was impossible to know. Certainly a child had called. But had the name been Kate? Or was that her own wishful thinking? And thousands of little girls in Paris wore white dresses.

"Crazy structure," said a friendly American voice beside her.

Kate smiled vaguely at him, and began to push her way towards the doors.

"You had enough already?" his voice followed her.

The lift shuddered to a stop at the first floor. Kate pushed her way out. "Excuse me. I have to hurry. Excuse me." They would think she was ill, or had no head for heights. It didn't matter. Now she could run down the steps and be on the ground in a few minutes.

But would that be soon enough to know whether, indeed, a little girl had called excitedly to her?

She hurried out into the leisurely gaping and chattering crowd. She called "Francesca!" in a voice as high and shrill as any Italian's. But apart from people looking curiously at her, and another American, a woman, saying sympathetically, "Have you lost someone, dear?" nothing happened. The cry to her had been an illusion.

Or if it had not, Francesca had been taken swiftly away. . . .

Now, all at once, Paris was beautiful and hostile, and for the first time she had to fight against tears. She felt as if she were in the middle of some strange, fascinating, lovely but treacherous nightmare. The Seine, dark and smooth beneath its high banks and bending trees, the gladioli glowing in the street-sellers' stall, the wandering tourists, priests, soldiers, and thin girls with long hair and secret faces were all part of it. She must get back to her hotel with its shabby, warm, red carpets and glowing brass, where Lucian might be waiting for her, and she could disperse the nightmare.

It was not Lucian who was waiting for her. A completely strange man stood up as she came into the foyer. He eyed her tentatively until the clerk at the counter nodded to him. Then he went over to her.

"Miss Tempest?"

"Yes." Kate was surprised. Why should this stranger approach her? He was certainly English. Apart from his voice, everything about him from his tweed jacket to his clipped moustache, rather plump ruddy face, and air of confidence, proclaimed the fact.

"I'm Johnnie Lambert," he said. "I got into Paris this afternoon, and Mrs. Dix suggested I look you up. She said something about a spot of bother."

"I don't follow—"

"Of course you don't." He took her arm in a friendly way. His voice was slightly hearty. But he looked pleasant enough, and he was not part of the nightmare. That was the important thing. "Come and have a drink and I'll explain."

He took her into the bar, and asked her what she would drink, then before she could answer said, "We're in Paris, so let's have something typically French, eh? How about a Chambery?"

He was undoubtedly the masterful type. But kind. And she needed someone like that just now to dispatch the nightmare.

"I'm beginning to follow," she said, as he sat down with the drinks. "You work for Mrs. Dix, too."

"That's right. I've just had a spell of tutoring two young Arab princes. Glubb Pasha stuff in an academic way. But I'll be glad to get back to London, I'm telling you!"

"In the Arabian desert?" Kate asked, thinking that of course this was exactly his sort of thing. Schoolmastering with a difference, the tweedy-sporty type, full of good humor, fond of a dash of adventure, not quite middle-aged, and never allowing himself to admit the approach of that time.

"No, Beirut. Fair enough, but it palls. I just got in this afternoon, and when I rang Mrs. Dix to report she told me about you. We're flying home on the same plane in the morning, so she thought I might cheer you up. Said you were worried. Something went wrong with your trip. What was it? A disappearing child or something?"

"Sounds like a magician's trick," Kate said ruefully. "I don't see how I could have prevented it, even if I'd held her hand all the time.

If her father insisted on her going back to Rome, who was I to refuse to let her go?"

"Quite. Quite. Matrimonial squabbles are the devil. But it was hardly fair on you, playing a trick like that. Is the father an Italian opera singer or something? Sounds like a love of melodrama. Did the child just disappear without leaving any trace?"

"She left her doll, which is another thing that worries me. She was very attached to it. I've been carrying it around in my bag."

"Her doll, eh? Well, that's proof, isn't it. Too bad. Poor little devil. Well, not to worry, Mrs. Dix says."

"Yes, I try not to, but I keep thinking of it from the child's point of view. So bewildering for her. And she wanted to go on the Eiffel Tower, too. A little while ago when I went to the Eiffel Tower I thought I heard her calling me. A voice just like, 'Kate! Kate!' I suppose I'm tired and I've let the thing haunt me. It couldn't have been Francesca, and yet I'm sure it was."

"You've had a tough time," said Johnnie Lambert sympathetically. "Have another drink."

"No, thank you very much."

"Then let's go out to dinner. I know we don't know each other, but we both belong to the same firm. We're both alone in Paris and we're both browned off with kids at the moment. Three good reasons. What do you say?"

"I'd like to, but I'm expecting a telephone call. I ought to wait in."

"When is this call likely to come?"

"Oh, any time."

"Give him until eight o'clock and if he hasn't phoned by then, come out with me. Fair enough?"

"Him?"

The blue, glinting eyes of Johnnie Lambert watched her humorously.

"Kate, you're much too attractive to be sitting in a Parisian hotel waiting for a girl-friend, or an elderly relative. We only have this evening, and I can show you a most intriguing little place on the Left Bank. Home by midnight. How's that?"

He was a little too hearty and masterful, but he meant to be kind. And it was quite true, an evening alone would be unendurable. How could she be sure Lucian would telephone? The answer clearly was that if he did not do so by eight o'clock he was tied up with other business or that he did not particularly want to see her again.

"All right," she said slowly.

"Fine." Johnnie's voice was full of enthusiasm. "I'll meet you here at eight, but if you absolutely can't make it, I'll see you on the plane in the morning."

The intriguing little place that Johnnie knew was startling enough to make her temporarily forget her strange worry about Francesca, and her illogically deep disappointment that after all Lucian had not telephoned.

Johnnie Lambert had not Lucian's distinction of feature or interesting somberness, but he was pleasant, kind, and a little overpoweringly jolly. It amused him to see her reactions to the night club which flourished in the remains of a medieval dungeon. It was entered by way of a steep, winding staircase, the worn stones of which had carried feet in less happy circumstances, and the age-blackened arched ceiling of the dungeon itself was low and a little claustrophobic. Once, Johnnie told her in his hearty, untroubled voice, people had been flung in here to die. Either starvation, sickness, or the rising water of the undrained cellar carried them off. No one but the persons who occasionally flung them food, or pushed in another victim, would have heard their cries. But if their ghosts lingered, it was in a very different atmosphere of dim lights, smoke, and the sound of a piano played by a middle-aged woman, with very blonde hair and very long teeth. Now and then a singer would appear to croon some low song. Once it was a man with a curious smooth face, like wax, untouched by the lines of age, yet with cold, disillusioned eyes, and later Madame herself, magnificent in black velvet, with even blacker hair, who came to roll her large, liquid eyes at her male customers.

"Do you like it?" Johnnie asked Kate.

"I'm not sure." She looked at the low ceiling, and the protruding hooks which once must have been grasped by desperate fingers. "I think of the past."

"Bless your kind heart. That's all over long ago. Water under the bridge. Dead men rise up never. That sort of thing. What shall we eat and drink? Shall I order?"

"Please do. And it is fun. But such an odd place."

Later the singers sang old French songs, "Sur le pont d'Avignon" and "Frère Jacques." Kate hummed the melody, relaxing at last, and Johnnie, who really was very kind, leaned towards her and said, "That's better. Now you look happy. Have you stopped worrying about that kid?"

"Yes, I think so. I expect she's all right. I'll send her back her doll when we get to London."

"Tell me exactly how all this happened."

Her glass, she noticed, had been filled again. The wine and the music and the smoke and the flickering colors of the dancers' skirts were all combining to make her pleasantly fuzzy in her head. But she still had an obscure longing to be sitting in her bedroom at the hotel waiting for the telephone to ring. At this very moment, she thought, Lucian was standing somewhere, impatiently dialing the number and waiting for her to answer.

She tried, with exactitude, to recount to Johnnie the events of the journey from Rome, but her story strayed a little, and he had to keep bringing her back to the point.

"You say no one believed you had a child with you. Not even this man who helped you?"

"Lucian? But he had never seen Francesca and I hadn't talked about her. One doesn't relate all one's affairs to a stranger over dinner."

Johnnie's hand, square and soft, rested momentarily on hers.

"I wish you'd break that rule, Kate."

She looked at his face which was now very close to hers. It was too large and too red, and all its expression seemed to be in its lips. She couldn't take her eyes off those waiting lips.

Suddenly she wondered overwhelmingly why she was here, in this fusty place, its atmosphere of doom only veneered with gaiety. Why had she come? Why had she not gone to the opera, or just had a respectable early night?

It had been because Johnnie was kind, and because he worked for Mrs. Dix, which somehow made them seem to be old friends.

She made herself smile and speak lightly. "Then tell me about yourself. You have a wife and children?"

"Not me. I'm a rover. I don't like shackles. Well—depending on how decorative the shackles are. Do you know, you're very attractive. How did Mrs. Dix come to let you travel alone? Normally she's much more cautious."

"I'm competent, usually."

"I'm sure you are."

"How long have you been working with Mrs. Dix?" Kate asked.

"Five, six years. I was a schoolmaster originally, but that got too dull. I've done these odd tutoring jobs. I took an American brat, pots of money, around the world. Once I was secretary to an oil magnate, but we didn't hit it off very well. Still, this way one gets around."

The man with the wax-like face was singing again, accompanied vigorously at the piano by the lady in the mauve dress. Kate pressed her hands to her eyes and longed for fresh air. It was only eleven o'clock. Would Johnnie be hurt if she suggested leaving so early? Later, one imagined, it would be impossible to breathe in here. More people were coming down the narrow stairs, and being seated in dusky corners. Madame, large and overpowering, in her sweeping black velvet, appeared to sing "Alouetta." She was rolling her large eyes at Johnnie and he was appreciatively applauding. Kate wished she hadn't drunk so much wine. How much? Not more than two glasses. How idiotic to get so fuzzy-headed on that. She waved away the waiter who would have refilled her glass, and leaned back in her chair. Madame's voice, rich and deep, seemed to fill her head. It made it swell, made her vision a little imperfect so that the lights seemed to flicker, and Johnnie's face, nodding in time to the music, seemed far away.

"Kate"—his voice was far away, too—"are you all right?"

"I'm rather tired," she said. "I wonder if you'd mind—"

But she never finished her plea to leave, for at that moment, without warning, all the lights went out.

There was instantly a storm of voices and cries. A girl began to giggle irrepressibly. People blundered about. Madame's voice, domineering and calm, sounded above everything.

"You will please sit still. A little accident in the fusebox—in one moment it will be fixed."

"Kate, are you all right?" came Johnnie's voice very close to her ear, and he felt for her hand.

Someone began striking matches, and faces appeared phantasmagorically and disappeared. They might have been the faces of the long-ago doomed, flung in here to rot slowly. Johnnie's hand, holding hers so firmly, might have been that of a despairing fellow-prisoner. Madame suddenly appeared carrying a branched candlestick with the candles alight, and her face, large and white, floating behind it, seemed bloated and full of evil amusement.

Kate couldn't breathe. She struggled to her feet.

"Sit down!" said Johnnie. "Lights in a minute." But already she was making her way to the door. She tripped over a stool, and heard the grate of the table as Johnnie hurriedly pushed it back to follow her.

"Kate, don't panic!"

"All is well, madame. The lights in one moment. . . ."

The twisting stairway, as black as a pit, was just ahead of her. Determinedly Kate groped towards it. Uncertainly she negotiated a step. Oh, for the stars, the clean night air.

"Kate, you little idiot. Wait."

Another step. . . . And then the light shone in her face, blinding her. She moved sharply backwards and lost her balance. The other voice calling "Kate!" seemed to come out of a dream. . . .

6

But it was not a dream that she was in a taxi with Lucian. She opened her eyes slowly, because for some reason her head was aching intolerably, and saw his head silhouetted against the window.

"Lucian!" she said cautiously.

He turned his head.

"Hullo," he said coolly.

"You didn't telephone."

"I couldn't earlier, and then when I did you'd gone out."

Kate tried to sit upright. Pain stabbed her head.

"How did you know where?"

"The hotel porter told me. He heard the address you gave the taxi."

"Did you follow us?"

"No."

There seemed no retort to that flat, unexplanatory answer. Kate let another street or two slide by before she said, without particular interest, "Where's Johnnie? Why am I with you?"

"Johnnie was decent enough to bow to my prior claim. Besides, he realized by then that you didn't like that particular place."

"In the dark it seemed haunted. I had to get out. I just had to." Her voice shook, as she remembered that claustrophobic horror, with the disembodied faces floating in the intermittent match-light.

"Did I behave very stupidly?" she asked, with shame.

"You gave your head a nasty bang on the stone steps. You seem to have a talent for getting into trouble."

"You frightened me, with that torch. It was you, wasn't it?"

"Coming to your rescue," he said in his detached way.

"But there wasn't really anything happening, was there? You didn't have to rescue me?"

"From a case of claustrophobia, yes. Your friend Johnnie's ideas for a gay evening didn't work out so well, did they?"

"Johnnie's all right," she said defensively. "It wasn't like going out with a stranger. He works for Mrs. Dix, too. She told him to look after me. And I really was feeling a little morbid. I kept thinking about Francesca. I thought I saw her this afternoon."

"That's absurd. Your airplane ticket has arrived, they told me at the desk. So catch that plane in the morning."

"I suppose so."

They had reached the hotel. Lucian paid the taxidriver and helped her out. The soft night air swept about her face, reviving her. She wished vaguely that Lucian were not so cool and detached. He had been interested enough to find out where she had gone that evening, but only as a self-imposed duty. His manner remained aloof and rather chilling. If she were a trouble to him she wished he would go.

"Good-night, Lucian. Thank you for bringing me home."

"Better now?"

She nodded. "It was only fresh air I needed."

"And stop worrying about that child."

"I will when I know definitely where she is. I still keep thinking—"

"She's all right," he said impatiently.

"But you couldn't know that, could you? You don't even believe she exists."

He looked at her in the calculating way that was becoming a little repellent.

"Lock your door tonight," he added obscurely. "And catch that plane in the morning."

He was already going. She thought, for a dizzy moment, that all this had been imaginary.

"Why must I lock my door?"

"Foreign hotels! Here's your handbag."

"Oh, I'd forgotten it. I left it in that place."

"Yes, we found it. You need looking after, you see. All right now?"

"Yes, thank you."

"Take some aspirins. They'll fix your head. I'll see you in London, perhaps. Goodbye. . . ."

When she reached her room the telephone was ringing. She picked it up dubiously.

"Kate? Is that you?" It was Johnnie's hearty voice, untouched by either resentment or worry.

"Yes, it's me. Where are you?"

"I'm still at this dump. The lights are working now. Sorry you seemed to get a scare. Why did you?"

"I don't know. I must be susceptible to atmosphere." She was, of course. She remembered her desolate feelings of the afternoon in the Luxembourg Gardens, the garden of queens, with their lonely stone faces, and then the strange shivery feeling that was almost fear which had swept over her when she had thought she heard Francesca calling to her at the Eiffel Tower. Then that dungeon-like room, where one still seemed to hear doomed voices. . . . No, she was no person to cover with a veneer of gaiety the irretrievably lost and forsaken.

"Well, too bad. Rather a flop, the whole thing, eh?"

"Lucian came," she said feebly.

"You're telling me. You fell and knocked your head on the stone steps, and this character just swept me aside, saying he had the prior claim. You were his girl. Are you his girl?"

Kate remembered Lucian's cool, detached manner, and thought of William waiting in London, and sighed.

"I'm not anybody's girl."

"If I'd known that I wouldn't have behaved so decently! Well, can't be helped now. I'll see you on the plane in the morning. Just wanted to know you got home safely. So long, my dear."

The airplane ticket was in an envelope on her dressing-table. Kate looked at it thoughtfully. Then she picked up her handbag to count the money she had. It was a large bag. Previously to this evening there had been plenty of room to stuff even Francesca's doll into it. But before going out she had tossed the doll into her suitcase so that the bag would not bulge quite so inelegantly. Her stepmother had given her this bag a year ago, when she had been making the move to London. She had said that at a pinch it would serve for an overnight bag. It was a beautiful quality antelope, lined with silk. Kate valued it very much. In consequence it distressed her now, when she opened it, to see that the lining had got torn. There was quite a large slit in it.

She was quite sure it had not been like that before she had gone out that evening. She remembered suddenly, and with a queer, distressed feeling, Lucian saying, "You forgot your bag. We found it."

But what, in the interval before finding it, had happened?

Forcing herself to remain calm and to think, Kate searched the contents. Her passport was there, also her wallet which seemed to contain the amount of money it should. Her cosmetics were untouched, and the keys to her flat were still there. Nothing seemed to have gone. Nothing at all. Yet the lining was carefully and unobtrusively slit, as if someone had been looking for something.

It must have happened during that frightening few minutes when the lights were out. Johnnie had been sitting beside her holding her hand. He could not have held her hand and searched her bag at the same time.

It could not have been Johnnie.

But there were sundry odd people in that place. Who knew whether the lights going out had been accidental? Perhaps it was a trick that happened regularly.

But nothing had gone from her bag. No one had stolen anything, even money, which would have been quite safe and untraceable.

There had been the very short period, of course, when she had panicked and knocked herself out in the dark on the stone steps. As Lucian's torch shone in her face. . . .

It was Lucian, apparently, who had got her into a taxi and gathered up her belongings. There would have been plenty of opportunity for him to search her bag. Plenty, indeed.

But why on earth should he? And why should he have told her to lock her door?

Abruptly the ache returned to her temples. Something was going on. Something very strange. Francesca's disappearance, the menu card that had vanished from her room while she was having her bath (because it had Lucian's face sketched on it, she realized, with sudden clarity), and now the queer happenings of this evening, that could have been caused by her own behavior. Or her behavior could have fitted in very nicely indeed with someone's schemes. . . .

In a daze, Kate walked to the door and turned the key in the lock. But it was with a perfectly clear purpose that she dialed the number of the airways office.

When the clerk answered she said, "Please cancel my ticket for flight 61 in the morning. Miss Kate Tempest. No, I won't be travelling by a later plane. I'm crossing by ferry. Thank you. Good-night."

After that she had to telephone for train and steamer departure times. She would have to be at the Gare du Nord at 9 A.M., the clerk told her. But that was easy. That was the train Lucian would probably be catching, and she would be able to ask him why her handbag had been so thoroughly searched, and what he had hoped to find. She could also look for Francesca.

Something told her that the steamer she caught at Calais tomorrow would also be the steamer on which Francesca travelled to England.

For now she no longer believed that the child had been taken back to Rome. It was not so simple as that. How could it be when these mysterious things were happening to her? If her head were not aching so acutely she might have been able to think of a reason for her foolish imaginings. But just now she couldn't.

In the morning, when she had slept, she would be able to cope.

7

When Mrs. Dix was worried she found that her passion for chocolates, even the richest and creamiest, was not satisfying in itself. But with a dash of brandy the recipe was perfect, and she could face anything.

After Miss Squires had left for her country cottage last evening she had been alone in her over-heated, over-decorated upstairs flat, and there was no one to whom she could talk. Not that she could talk to Miss Squires very much. It wasn't wise. But at least Miss Squires knew about that poor girl in Paris, bewildered and alone. Except for the strange Englishman she had mentioned, and who was he? That was the worrying question.

Miss Squires had had the utmost faith in the girl's discretion and level-headedness, in spite of her seeming a little too attractive and lively to be over-supplied with the more mundane qualities. But Miss Squires, least of anybody, had expected this particular contretemps.

Long after Miss Squires had gone home Mrs. Dix kept having small nips of brandy interspersed with chocolates. At midnight she got out the last gift her husband had given her, a rather heavy, antique gold pendant, and clasped it around her neck, and wept a little.

Then, still sitting in her chair, a rotund little figure looking strangely young and vulnerable, she fell asleep. She slept until the first light was coming through the windows, and spasmodic footsteps and cars starting up sounded without. Then she woke with a start. The lights were still burning and she didn't at first realize it was morning. She poured another brandy and drank it quickly. Then she lifted the telephone and asked for the Hotel Imperial in Paris.

In a short time the connection was made, and she could hear Kate Tempest's clear but slightly alarmed voice at the other end.

"It's just Mrs. Dix, dear," she said reassuringly. "Calling to see if you're all right. No more trouble, I hope."

"No, not really trouble. Just a slight mix-up."

"Mix-up?"

"Oh, with this Johnnie Lambert of yours, and the other man I met on the train, Lucian Cray. I got an awful crack on the head and Lucian took charge. But Johnnie was awfully sweet and understanding. It was nice of you to tell him to look after me."

"Me! Tell him to look after you." In spite of the warm, cushioning brandy, the fear was sweeping back, making her heart thump and the palms of her hands moist. "Who is he?"

"Johnnie Lambert. I told you. He's just back from Beirut. You remember, the tutor."

"The tutor," echoed Mrs. Dix foolishly.

"I guess you can't remember the names of all the people you get jobs for," came the girl's voice philosophically. "But he did say you had specially told him—I say, Mrs. Dix, didn't you tell him at all? Weren't you speaking to him on the phone? But in that case how did he know who I was?"

In the midst of her flurry and apprehension Mrs. Dix was sure of only one thing. Miss Squires had been wrong and she had been right. Kate Tempest had not been a suitable person to send on this job. She was too gay and ebullient, too quick to talk to strangers, and also, worst of all, too inquisitive.

"Just come home, Kate, dear," she begged. "We can talk about it then. You have your plane ticket, haven't you?"

"Yes, but I'm not using it. I'm travelling by ferry. I have a hunch, stupid, I expect, that Francesca might be on it."

"*Francesca!* What are you talking about?"

"The little girl. I don't think she's gone to Rome at all. I think someone has been playing a trick on me. I'll tell you all about it when I see you. Anyway, I enjoy a sea trip. *And* a spot of detective work. I can't face Rosita without Francesca, can I? And now I've got to rush to catch the train. Apologize to Johnnie for me if he gets home first. I'm looking forward to seeing that gentleman again."

The telephone clicked. The young, optimistic, ebullient voice vanished.

Mrs. Dix had one hand clutched to her bosom where she felt a sharp, strangulating pain. She wanted to reach for the brandy bottle to have another quick nip which would not only reassure her but dispatch the pain and breathlessness.

But suddenly she felt incapable of moving. What had she done wrong? Surely yesterday, in a moment of mental aberration, she hadn't told someone to call on Kate. But if she hadn't, *who* was Johnnie Lambert?

8

It was terribly disappointing. Kate had walked from end to end of the train, but there was no sign of Lucian, certainly no sign of Francesca. Her hunch about Francesca, in the broad light of day, seemed fantastic and completely unreasonable, but Lucian had told her he was travelling back to England by ferry steamer. So why was he not visible?

Feeling flat and out of temper, and with her head beginning to ache again, Kate found a seat and tried to relax. Had Mrs. Dix been annoyed with her for not using the plane ticket? She couldn't be sure, because that issue had been lost in Mrs. Dix's perplexity about Johnnie Lambert. She had sounded so uneasy and alarmed, and she said she had not spoken to any such person on the telephone. It was possible she may have had a lapse of memory—her voice had sounded fuzzy and wandering as if she were drugged or drunk. Living in her world of unreality, neither of these things would have been unexpected. But it may well have been that it was Miss Squires to whom Johnnie Lambert had spoken. It was much more likely that Miss Squires, brisk and down to earth, would suggest that Kate be looked after.

Anyway, that was unimportant. She would discover the truth when she returned to London. She was not particularly interested in Johnnie Lambert. It was Lucian whose dark, secret face both haunted and repelled her.

She should have sent a cable to William, too. He would be hurt at her neglect. But just at the moment William, too, seemed unimportant. There were only two people in her mind, the lost little girl Francesca who may badly need rescuing, and Lucian Cray who seemed to know more than he should. Otherwise why had he told her to lock her door last night?

The ferry was drearily crowded. There was the usual babble of voices, the blue-overalled French seamen begging and exhorting the pushing and struggling passengers, the dedicated rush for possession of deck-chairs, the luggage dumped where one tripped over it, the queue for the bar and the restaurant. A cold wind blew over a choppy gray sea. Even in harbor the ship was rocking noticeably, and passengers, determined to be ill, were wearing looks of stern martyrdom.

Already Kate was realizing the foolhardiness of her plan. On a crowded ferry, with its passengers constantly moving about, what chance had she of finding one small girl. Luck would need to be with her, and she didn't at the moment feel lucky. She was remembering she had had to skip breakfast to catch the train, and now, from hunger and an aching head, and the gentle rocking, she was beginning to feel a little queasy. She decided to join the queue for coffee and sandwiches, and it was then that suddenly she saw the man with the slanteyes and a slightly Chinese face. He was standing beside a pillar watching her. At least, his slanting eyes seemed to be fixed directly on her, because when she caught his glance it slid away. A small shock of uneasiness went through her. She didn't like being stared at so intently. And she remembered now having seen him on the Paris train when she had strolled through it looking for Lucian. He had seemed to be watching her then, too. Could it be that he was following her on this journey?

If she had caught the plane would he have been on that, too?

Nonsense, she told herself vigorously. One frequently encountered the same faces on a long journey. And it may be that this rather unsavory-looking person found her attractive to look at.

Nevertheless, Kate had lost her appetite. She left the stuffy saloon and made her way up on deck again. They had left harbor now and were moving into a steadily increasing sea. It was going to be impossible to walk about very much, even if one's legs felt steady. Which hers suddenly didn't.

How idiotic this was, to set out on a private investigation, and be overtaken by seasickness! It was a situation that would amuse only William.

Yet it would have been rather nice if his strong arm was around her now. She had to admit that. Lucian? No, she couldn't face him at this moment. . . .

"Kate! Kate!"

Kate started up wildly from her half doze. But among the people scattered about there was no little girl, no one had cried out. Only a seabird was circling overhead, and they were just coming into Dover harbor. The voyage was ended, and had accomplished exactly nothing but nearly two hours of misery.

Kate gritted her teeth and, gathering her possessions, forced herself into the queue so as to be one of the first ashore. From a good vantage point in the Customs shed she could make a belated watch.

Sheer determination made her succeed, and she had the satisfaction, as she stepped on to the gangway, of seeing the Chinese-looking man far down the queue. Then suddenly she saw Lucian, too. At least, it had looked like Lucian, but he was a long way back and, as Kate stared, he was lost to sight.

Kate looked helplessly at the wedged people. She hadn't a hope of pushing her way back to where she thought she had seen him. Even now she was being swept forward by impatient people behind her. Would she see him again?

Hopefully she achieved the Customs shed, and lingered near the door. The people surged in, faces of all descriptions, young, old, eager, tired, sick. Again, as if it were fated, she caught a glimpse of the sallow-faced, slant-eyed man, and immediately behind him, as if they were following him, came two men carrying a long wooden box.

That was when Kate's heart turned over in horror. It was a coffin. Surely it was a coffin. A child's. Francesca's.

A dizzy wave swept over her. She found herself blundering forward and pushing her way after the two men. They reached the desk with their burden. They put it down and waited for the Customs official. The sallow-faced man had disappeared.

Kate fought her way forward. The box had a padlock, she saw. It was really only a chest. But in horrified fascination she waited for it to be opened. The official questioned its owners. A key was produced. The lid was lifted.

It was not Francesca's composed and stolid features that lay within. It was the round, flat, white face of a grandfather clock.

The anti-climax was too much. Kate had to stifle her giggles.

"Oh, William!" she said to herself. He was the only one with whom to share this macabre joke.

But the diversion had been fatal to her plans. Now the huge room was packed with milling people, and her chance of seeing Lucian was again negligible.

She told herself disgustedly that she was about as successful as a rabbit at private investigation.

There was still, of course, the train to Victoria, and this a familiar English train in which she would not have any nightmare feeling that people were mocking her in strange languages.

She had no difficulty in getting her own baggage through Customs. Perhaps the official noticed her wan appearance and was sorry for her. He chalked her bag and handbag with scarcely a look at them, and at last she made her way to the train.

It seemed, because of her strained and over-tired state, that she had been living on trains for months. There were the familiar piles of luggage in corridors to be climbed over, the people who impatiently let her squeeze past, the suspicious and faintly hostile look of passengers in compartments as she peered in with a murmured apology. This time she didn't ask if anyone had seen a little girl in a white dress, because it was certain Francesca would no longer be wearing the white organdie dress. In her tweed coat she would now look like any other child.

But if Kate failed instantly to recognize her, she would recognize Kate and would cry out, as she had already done twice. Or had it been only once, at the Eiffel Tower? Or had it not been at all?

The train went smoothly and swiftly on its way, the countryside, English now, with the gentle Kentish hills and haystacks, and redbrick farmhouses, went past, the passengers chattered and dozed and consumed quantities of bread and jam and tea in the restaurant car; everyone was intent on his own business, and there was no sign of Francesca, or of Lucian, who at least should have been there.

Ironically enough, but not unexpectedly, the Chinese-looking man, with his slanted sideways glance, was the only person Kate recognized. He was not watching her now. He was standing in the corridor staring out at the passing landscape. He seemed deep in thought. He looked, Kate imagined, as if he were as disappointed as she.

Yet on the platform at Victoria Kate thought she saw Francesca. The square back of a dark-haired little girl clad in a tweed coat. Being dragged along, with apparent unwillingness, by someone Kate couldn't see in the crowd.

She began to elbow her way urgently through the jostling mob.

Strong arms swooped around her, holding her stationary. "Hey there! What's the hurry?" said William.

Kate could have slain him. "Let me go! You fool, let me go! Now I've lost her!"

"Lost who?" But William's grip had slackened and Kate had darted away.

As was to be expected, there was a queue at the barrier. When she tried to squeeze her way ahead she was glared at ferociously. She had to content herself with standing frantically on tiptoe and seeing nothing but the heads in front of her.

"Who are you looking for?" William asked mildly.

"Francesca, of course. I saw her a moment ago. At least, I think I did."

William took her arm quite gently. "Don't be a clot. She's back in Rome."

"You're saying that too!" Kate exclaimed furiously. "What do you know about it, anyway? No, don't tell me now. Thank heavens we're through the barrier at last. Wait for me at the bookstall. I've got to look for this child."

Had it been Francesca she had seen? It couldn't have been because she hadn't been on the train. At least, she hadn't seemed to be. And she wasn't now in the small, depressed-looking queue waiting for taxis. Either she was nowhere or else in Rome and Kate the victim of her own foolish obsession.

Irritably she made her way back to William.

"How did you know I would be on this train?"

"Because when you thoughtfully sent me no message of any kind, not even a postcard from the Eiffel Tower, I rang Mrs. Dix. She said you would be home alone. There had been some agonized reappraisals and the child had gone home to Poppa."

"But I don't think she has," said Kate intensely.

William took her arm. "My darling, you look remarkably like something the cat brought home. Come and have a cup of tea and tell me why you're turning this into a Hitchcock thriller."

In the café, where an overworked waitress blotted up spilt liquid from the glass-topped table, and wearily asked them what they wanted, William went on, "Mrs. Dix didn't like me phoning. She was very cagey indeed. She said you hadn't told her about me."

Kate opened her eyes which had temporarily closed. She was suddenly extraordinarily tired.

"That's true. Should I have?"

"She seemed to think so. Family background and so on."

"Oh, I told her about my stepmother. Don't be silly, you're not family." But Mrs. Dix had probed a little about friends, she remembered, and, thinking of William with whom she had just quarrelled at the time, she had dismissed the question.

"That's another thing," said William amiably. "Anyway, Mrs. Dix didn't seem overjoyed to chat with me. I wonder why?"

"I suppose you wanted to know too much. After all, she's been brought up on hush-hush stuff. Years ago her husband was in intelligence."

"Ah, that's the answer. Anyway, she did finally tell me your trip had come unstuck, and the child had been whisked back to Rome. You must have had quite a time."

Kate nodded drearily. "Seasick, too. Would you believe it? Just when I wanted to be particularly alert. And I never want to see another train in my life. Or a tourist."

The waitress had brought the tray of tea. She said, "There!" in a kind voice, as if temporarily forgetting her own troubles, whatever they were. Dirty dishes, slopped tea, sore feet. "I must look awful," thought Kate, "to take priority over those things."

She sipped the hot, strong tea and was suddenly glad William was there. Glad and grateful, but not excited. It was only William with his broad shoulders and untidy hair and penetrating gaze. Not Lucian's dark, exciting face.

"There was this Eastern-looking man all the time," she said. "I expect he was born in Bermondsey or somewhere, but he had a dash of Chinese or Malay that made him look sinister."

"When did you first see him?" William asked.

"This morning on the train. Probably he had been there all the time and I hadn't noticed him before. Though I don't see how he could have had anything to do with it, any more than Johnnie or Lucian."

"You'd better start at the beginning. And please be coherent."

Afterwards, William said the only possible thing that was sinister or suspicious was her room and her handbag having been searched. But that did not necessarily need to have any connection with Francesca at all. It looked as if she had been the victim of a confidence trick perpetrated by either Johnnie or Lucian, or both of them. It was lucky she had lost nothing.

"But why did I lose nothing?" she demanded. "Confidence trick men want money. I had quite a lot of francs in my bag."

"These must have been looking for something else. They may have picked the wrong woman, and discovered it too late. The lights going out at the joint certainly sounds like part of the plot. But I can't see that it's anything whatever to do with the child. And why you should think she's been brought to London is beyond me."

"I saw her! At least I thought I did."

"There have been scads of kids running about Victoria station."

"I heard her call me at the Eiffel Tower. I'm certain of that. Besides, who would take her back to Rome? No one there cared enough about her."

"I thought it was her father who couldn't bear to let her go."

"Him! He didn't even say goodbye to her."

"Kate! You're crying!"

Kate blinked angrily. "She was only a baby and she had on her party dress. She's been tricked and it's my fault for not looking after her properly." Kate blinked again, and the tears ran unashamedly down her cheeks. "I tell you, I won't be happy until I see her again and know she's all right."

"You're not going to Rome again?"

"I don't think I'll have to. I'm certain she's not there."

"Kate, darling, it isn't your business any longer."

"It is my business! And it isn't your business if I go straight back to Rome." Kate blew her nose, ran her fingers nervously through her hair and pushed back her chair. "Now you can take me to Mrs. Dix. She'll understand why I'm worried. On the journey it got to the stage where no one really believed there was a child at all. But Mrs. Dix knew there was. I have to talk to her."

Miss Squires was just getting ready to leave when Kate burst in. She looked up in a rather startled way, her eyes flickering behind her round, owl-like glasses.

"Why, Kate! What are you doing here at this time?"

"You know I lost Francesca, don't you? I want to see Mrs. Dix."

"Oh, dear! I don't think she'll want to be disturbed just now. We're closed, really. I'm just leaving."

"But, Miss Squires, this is urgent! It's about a lost child!"

"Not lost, Kate dear." Was there something evasive, a little uncertain, even frightened, about Miss Squires' manner? "She's been taken home."

"I'll believe that when I have proof," Kate said firmly. "Now take me up to Mrs. Dix."

"Very well. I'll see." Miss Squires was definitely flustered. Kate paced about the tiny office restlessly while she disappeared up the steep, dark stairway. Presently she came down again.

"Mrs. Dix will see you, but she's not at all pleased. She says you should have telephoned and come to see her in the morning."

"And in the meantime a child might be murdered!"

"Kate! How can you say such a thing?"

Miss Squires' eyes were suddenly enormous, her face full of uneasiness.

"I don't really mean that," Kate said quickly. "But I must be sure. Francesca wasn't exactly lovable, but she had a sort of private courage. Oh, well! I'll go up to Mrs. Dix."

Nothing had changed in the cosy, upstairs flat. Mrs. Dix wore the same brown velvet dress, and her face was pink and benign. She held out her small plump hand to Kate and then waved her to a chair. She gave no outward sign of the displeasure Miss Squires had mentioned, but she did look a little tired. Her eyes were heavy and a little glazed, and there was a strong, rather stale, smell of brandy in the room. Was brandy, as well as chocolates, one of her weaknesses?

Kate was offered the inevitable chocolate out of a particularly lush box (did a woman buy chocolates like this for herself, Kate wondered curiously), then Mrs. Dix said in her warm intimate voice, "Miss Squires tells me you're worried, my dear. But didn't I assure you none of this was your fault? If Francesca's father decided to play a trick like that—pure comic opera, I must say—none of us could help it. Rosita, although she's stricken, naturally, doesn't blame you at all. Poor Kate, you must have had a dreadful time."

"Mrs. Dix, I don't believe Francesca was taken back to Rome."

"Good gracious me! What do you believe, then?"

"That someone has brought her to London secretly for some purpose of their own. Perhaps it's to bribe her mother, or to hold her as a hostage. I don't know. But whatever it is, we've got to find that poor child."

Mrs. Dix's round soft mouth had dropped open. She was surveying Kate incredulously. "Whatever makes you say that?"

Patiently, Kate went through her reasons once more. Mrs. Dix seemed to be listening closely, but the lids had dropped slightly over her eyes, hiding their expression. And her nervous fiddling with a piece of tinfoil wrapping gave away her tension. Miss Squires had looked uneasy, too, Kate remembered.

When she had finished, however, Mrs. Dix leaned back with a relieved air.

"My dear girl, I thought you had something dreadfully sinister to tell me, but that all sounds *quite* explainable. The strange child in the bunk—such a shock for you! After that I'm sure you'd imagine you saw Francesca everywhere or heard her calling you. Someone in some book explains that kind of hallucination. It's quite common, especially after a death."

But that last word brought a sudden little silence into the room. Mrs. Dix's eyelids flew up, as if someone else had said it, and startled her, then dropped again, and she fumbled automatically for her source of comfort.

Kate watched her bite into a chocolate cream, and said rather coldly, "My things being searched was not an hallucination."

"But I told you to be careful, dear. You shouldn't trust strange men in a foreign city. Not even Johnnie Lambert who, by the way, has left a message for you. But I'm sure Johnnie would never have done a thing like that."

"You said you didn't know who he was," Kate pointed out.

"A slight mental lapse, dear." Mrs. Dix's eyes did not flicker. "I shouldn't have telephoned you so early this morning. I was only half awake, and I'd completely forgotten about talking to him the day before. He flew in this morning, very disappointed you weren't on the plane, but much more angry with me for sending him off immediately on another job. But I had an urgent mission that only he could do. He speaks Arabic, you see."

"What was the message he left?" Kate asked, much more interested in this than in the surprising information the rather simple, hearty Johnnie Lambert could speak Arabic.

"Oh, just to tell you not to forget him, you'd be seeing him again before long. He seems to have taken quite a fancy to you." Mrs. Dix wagged her forefinger coyly. "He was terribly distressed about that little contretemps last night. The lights going out must certainly have been a planned thing, he said. He questioned several people after you'd gone, but of course one gets nowhere with that sort. However, no damage was done, thank goodness. Now tell me, please, about this other man on the train."

"He was just someone who helped me," Kate said aloofly. "He had nothing to do with Francesca's disappearance, because he was with me at the time when it must have happened. We were having dinner. I shouldn't have gone to dinner. I shouldn't have left her."

"Now, my dear, don't fret! The child's perfectly all right. I spoke to her father, the scoundrel, yesterday. I told you."

"She left her doll. She isn't happy without it."

"Have you got it with you?"

"It's here, in my handbag." Kate opened her capacious bag and took out the crushed-looking, shabby doll.

Mrs. Dix put out her hand.

"Give it to me, dear. We'll send it on to Francesca."

But Kate shook her head. She returned the doll to her bag.

"I don't think so. I'll keep it until I'm quite sure where it's to go."

Mrs. Dix was annoyed. Kate knew, by the way she picked up a chocolate and squeezed it, smearing its liquid center over her fingers. She made a cross little noise and wiped her fingers fastidiously.

"Really, Kate dear, I know you're tired and overstrained, but aren't you being a little exasperating. If both Francesca's parents swear she is safely back in Rome—"

"Let me speak to her on the telephone," said Kate.

"To Rome! My dear, a trunk call—"

"I'll pay for it myself."

"But the child can't speak English! You know that."

"She'll recognize my voice and I'll know hers. Please, Mrs. Dix! Put the call through. Then I'll be satisfied and I won't worry you any more. You can post the doll on to her, and we'll forget all about it."

"This is absurd!" Mrs. Dix muttered. "No one asks you to be so conscientious. Do you really insist on my doing this? I haven't time and it's most inconvenient."

"Then give me the number and I'll do it."

"No, no, that won't do at all." Mrs. Dix petulantly picked up the telephone. "Very well, if this is the only thing that will satisfy you I will put the call through. Perhaps you will join me in a brandy while we wait."

William was waiting, too, but that couldn't be helped. If she could speak to Francesca and take that dreadful weight off her mind she would go down to William and be perfectly charming to him, and not let Lucian's face come into her mind once.

Mrs. Dix tossed off her brandy very quickly, so Kate did the same. A little of the tension went out of her, but on Mrs. Dix the brandy seemed to have the opposite effect. She grew very flushed and no longer concealed her nervous glances towards the telephone. When it did ring she jumped violently, then gave a little girlish giggle and said, "I always do that. Isn't it silly!"

It took a minute or so to make the connection, and Mrs. Dix kept saying in a high voice, "I want to speak to Signor Torlini, personally. No, personally, I insist. He is out? Oh, dear! Then be good enough to get his daughter to come to the telephone. His daughter! Francesca! What's that? I can't hear you! No, I don't want her nurse. Oh, you say she's in the park. The gardens? Yes, I see. They went on a little outing. Quite, quite. They won't be back for a little time yet? Oh, too bad. . . ."

Kate was leaning forward tensely, her hand out.

"Mrs. Dix, let me speak. Please!"

"No, no, it can't be helped." Mrs. Dix's high, firm voice swept on. "Thank you, thank you. No, it isn't important. Goodbye. *Arrivederci*."

She put the receiver down.

"Mrs. Dix, why didn't you let me speak to whoever that was?" Kate was almost in tears from rage and frustration.

"To Antonio's secretary. That silly conceited little man! But there was no point, was there? Francesca's out. Her nurse has taken her to the Borghese Gardens. A treat, I expect, to make up for her disappointment at missing the Eiffel Tower. So we've wasted the call. Isn't that annoying. But surely it proves to you that the child is safely home and well."

"It doesn't prove anything," said Kate slowly. "How do you know whoever spoke wasn't lying?" She hadn't been able to hear what the voice on the other end had been saying. It had been a shrill gabble, a tiny, distorted, ghostly sound that seemed to her to grow more and more reiterant. It surely couldn't be that the speaker was speaking in Italian.

"Antonio's secretary lying!" Mrs. Dix exclaimed.

"Whoever he was, doesn't he know public gardens close at dark." Kate glanced out of the window. "It has been dark for over an hour, in Rome as well as in London."

Mrs. Dix drew up her stout little body haughtily.

"Miss Tempest, you're exceeding your duty—"

"I'm worried!" Kate cried. "Aren't you worried? But then you didn't see Francesca in her absurd organdie dress. She was dressed for a party, and there was no party. We just didn't manage to give her one. If you'd seen her, you wouldn't just say casually, 'She's all right.' You'd want to see her or speak to her, just to know. And that's what I intend to do, even if I have to go back to Rome to do it."

"Kate!"

"Oh, it's all right. I'm not going back immediately. First I'm going to make sure, somehow, that she isn't in London."

William was sitting with his finger gently on the horn of his car. Kate could hear the dirge on one note as she came down the stairs. She hurried, tripped slightly on the narrow steps and began to laugh as she saved herself. William was infuriating and absurd, but he had a happy knack of reducing even a nightmare to everyday proportions. She laughed again as she came out on to the street and saw him with his head stuck out of the car, in earnest conversation with a policeman, but still not stopping the monotonous dirge.

Then he saw her and grinned, and lifted his finger from the horn.

"I'm sorry, officer. I agree with all you said. But if your girl kept you waiting, especially a girl like Kate, wouldn't you do the same? Meet Kate, officer."

The policeman, very young beneath his helmet, gave a half-nod, an embarrassed grin, and moved on.

William said to Kate, "Thought you'd slipped out the back way and caught a plane back to Rome."

"No, I didn't, but we've talked to them. At least, Mrs. Dix has."

"And?"

"And Francesca at this moment is playing in the Borghese Gardens in the dark. With, I suppose, Caesar's ghost. They couldn't even think up something better than that to tell me."

"Mrs. Dix believed it?"

"She'd believe anything. She's been at the brandy bottle, and anyway she doesn't care."

William sniffed. "I'd say you'd been at the bottle, too."

Kate shivered and moved close against him. "Br-r-r. It's cold. And I've got a nightmare."

William methodically switched off all the lights and took her in his arms. She was enveloped in tweed and the scent of tobacco smoke, and she was kissed with gentle and prolonged affection. She lay quietly, feeling his exploring lips on her closed eyelids, her cheekbones and then her own lips. The sensation was agreeable, but somehow shadowy, as if it were happening to someone else. Finally William delicately lifted one of her eyelids with his fingertip.

"I told you, I've got a nightmare."

"That's what lovers are for, catching burglars and dispersing nightmares."

Kate sat up. "You're not my lover."

"Soon will be, sweetie. I keep my fingers crossed."

She wouldn't let him come in to her flat. She was going straight to bed because tomorrow she wanted to be fit and alert for what she had to do.

"Such as?" William inquired.

"First I'm going to see Rosita, Francesca's mother. If nothing comes of that I'll get another inspiration."

"Don't stick your neck out too far." For the first time William's voice was anxious. "It's really none of your business, you know."

"The welfare of a child is everybody's business," said Kate heatedly. "How can you be so callous?"

Mrs. Peebles popped out swiftly as the front door opened.

"It's you," she said. "Back."

"Yes, I'm back. Any messages?"

"Not if you've seen Mr. Howard."

"You know very well I've seen him," Kate retorted. "You were looking out of the window just now."

"I wasn't looking at you and him, Miss Tempest. I was seeing if that prowler was still there."

"Prowler?"

"Someone's been strolling about rather more than necessary. I'd lock your windows tonight, if I was you."

Kate's heart missed a beat. "If he looks suspicious, why don't you call the police?"

"He doesn't look suspicious, exactly. I wouldn't have noticed him except that he had that Chinese look. That's why I remembered him the third time he passed. But he's gone now. Lor', Miss Tempest, you don't look like your holiday did you any good."

"It wasn't a holiday," Kate snapped.

"I can see that. Regular washed out, ain't you? I'd go straight to bed, if I was you. But call if you hear anyone scrabbling at the window."

"Don't be absurd, Mrs. Peebles. Who is going to scrabble? A burglar doesn't make a noise."

"Not if he's a good one. But he has to learn, doesn't he? Some of them amatoors must scrabble, by accident, anyway. Dear, oh dear, it's a sad thing my husband isn't alive. He'd have dealt with him, Chinese or not."

9

So the prowler, according to Mrs. Peebles, was already a burglar. Kate tried to dismiss the suggestion as absurd, but the coincidence was too strong. A Chinese-looking face, which meant he must be the man who was already her familiar, and the fact that last night in Paris her handbag had been searched. And her room, too, probably, when that sketch of Lucian had disappeared.

She had a panicky desire to ring the police and ask for protection. Or at least to summon William back. Then she told herself not to be absurd. Mrs. Peebles, a widow living alone except for the lodger in her basement, had taken exceptional care to make the house burglar-proof. All the windows had bars, and the doors double locks. No one could get in. It was perfectly safe. And, anyway, why should anyone get in? The person who had ransacked her room in Paris must have discovered that she had no valuables.

But if the man with the yellow and slant-eyed face were the same, how had he found where she lived? He had not followed her here because he had been here first.

It was more than strange. It was rather frightening. Kate put out the light and drew aside the curtain to look up on the street. There was no one about. It was a quiet street. A cold wind and a smell of soot drifted in. She was back in London. She was safe—surely. . . .

But as she drew her head back slow footsteps went past. She could see dark trousers, and a small, neat foot. Without leaning out and drawing attention to herself, she could not see more. As she waited, breathless, the small feet and the trousers disappeared. The footsteps died away. They did not come back.

The streets were public. Anyone was entitled to stroll down them. Kate told herself not to be foolish. If she were going to listen to every step that went past she was not going to get much sleep, and she needed sleep.

But it was odd about that prowler.

Mrs. Peebles' tap at the door made her start violently.

"I forgot these. They arrived this afternoon." She thrust a bunch of carnations into Kate's arms. Her narrow face was alive with curiosity. She knew very well that William did not send Kate carnations.

The note with them was from Johnnie Lambert.

"In case Mrs. D. forgets to give you my message. I'm devastatingly sorry about being pushed off on another trip straight away, but I'll be seeing you—maybe sooner than you think. Love and kisses, Johnnie."

Kate said aloofly, "Thank you, Mrs. Peebles," and wondered why, for that wild moment, she had thought they might be from Lucian Cray. He did not even know her address. He had not asked for it. She wouldn't be seeing him again—ever. She hadn't even a sketch of him. She just carried his face in her mind.

It was nice of Johnnie to send her carnations. Life was always this way, William meeting her, Johnnie sending her flowers—the one with the dark, exciting face that she couldn't get out of her mind, silent.

The only face that should be in her mind was that of Francesca.

There was one more thing she could do tomorrow, if her visit to Rosita proved as unsatisfactory as had been her visit to Mrs. Dix. When Mrs. Dix had asked for the telephone number in Rome she had surreptitiously written it down. The feeling had grown on her since that Mrs. Dix and the person at the other end had been talking at cross-purposes. While someone had chattered bewilderedly in Italian, Mrs. Dix had improvised a conversation suitable for Kate's ears.

But tomorrow, if necessary, she would ring that number herself.

Now she was too tired, mentally and physically, to do anything but sleep.

It was some hours later that she was aroused by the scrabbling at the window.

No, oh, no, a burglar wouldn't make a noise like that. He would be stealthy and silent.

Kate sat up, breathing with difficulty. The windows were locked. There were bars across. She was perfectly safe.

But who was out there?

It was useless sitting here shivering. That got her nowhere. She would have to go to the window and look out. Quickly, before the would-be intruder knew he was being observed.

With resolute speed she sprang out of bed, crossed to the window and pulled back the curtain.

She found herself looking into the face of a large, black-and-white cat. It stood on the sill opening its mouth in a soundless miaou. Kate collapsed weakly.

This was all of a piece with the whole affair. The freckle-faced Annabelle sitting up in the bunk in the train, the grandfather clock with its bland white face in what she had thought had been a coffin, and now this stupid cat, pretending to be a burglar, or worse.

Perhaps everyone was right and she was turning into a nightmare something that was perfectly simple and explainable. Francesca was in Rome with her father, Lucian Cray was home from an innocent business trip; Johnnie Lambert, bored and fretful, was halfway to Arabia; Mrs. Dix was deep in a brandy-induced sleep, dreaming not of a lost child but of her lost husband; Madame and her confederates in their ghoulish nightclub in the Latin quarter were looking for another prey with a well-filled purse; the man with the Oriental face was merely looking for lodgings, or a friend's house.

And she, startled by a wandering cat, was very definitely going back to bed to sleep.

It was as well for her peace of mind that she did not notice the shadow, as long and thin as a tree, that fell across the wall, and that moved stealthily when her curtain was drawn across the window once more. Her sleep, after that, was too deep to be disturbed by the second furtive but useless testing of the very efficient bars of the window.

The sun shone the next morning. Kate got up feeling well and cheerful. When Mrs. Peebles called her to the telephone she sprang up the stairs full of excited but unreasonable anticipation. Things were going to happen today. She would make them happen.

The caller was Miss Squires. "Good morning, Kate. Could you come in as soon as possible."

Was it news of Francesca? "Why?" Kate asked eagerly.

"Just a little errand. Mrs. Dix suggested you do it."

"Of course. In an hour?"

"Is that as soon as you can make it?"

"Afraid so," said Kate, keeping silent about her intended call on Rosita on the way. She was learning to be circumspect.

"Good morning, Mrs. Peebles," she called cheerfully. "I did have the scrabbler in the night. A cat."

Mrs. Peebles gasped.

"Oh, dear! Didn't you scream?"

"Almost."

"Ever so brave, aren't you?"

"Oh, I can face a cat. I'm a craven coward in real danger."

"Better keep out of it, then," said Mrs. Peebles sensibly.

It was a nice enough day to wear her gray suit. She was meeting William for lunch. She might as well look pleasant for him, as for whatever elderly client she had to meet off a train or take shopping. And also for Rosita.

She had the doll Pepita in her bag. It was Rosita who had first mentioned the doll. She would probably shed tears over it, and perhaps talk more than she would otherwise have done. In this way perhaps Kate would discover whether Francesca's mother were satisfied or happy about her child's whereabouts.

It seemed more than four days since Kate had first gone to the house in Egerton Gardens. So much had happened since she had walked up those steps to the elegant oak door with its shining brass knocker.

A woman who had been cleaning the hall opened the door. Kate thanked her and said she wanted to see Mrs. Torlini.

The woman looked puzzled.

"No one of that name lives here, Miss."

"Yes, there does. In that room at the top of the stairs. I called the other day."

"That door, Miss? That's Mrs. Thompson's room."

"Mrs. Torlini was there the other day," Kate said pleasantly. "Let me go up and see."

"You can do that, but you'll see it's Mrs. Thompson. We don't have no foreigners here."

The thin, dark, suspicious face of the cleaning woman watched her as she went up the stairs. Can she see my heart beating? Kate wondered. Can she see the nightmare coming on again? Because of course Rosita is in that room. I *know* she is!

A completely strange, elderly woman with straggly, gray hair opened the door. She peered irritably at Kate and said, "Yes? What is it? What do you want?"

"I want Mrs. Torlini. This is her room, isn't it?"

"You've made a mistake, dear. I've been here fifteen years. You must be in the wrong house."

"But I'm not," Kate insisted earnestly. "This *is* the house. I remember the carpet on the stairs, and that picture. Why, I was here only four days ago, and I saw Mrs. Torlini. In this room, lying on the couch."

"Well, she's not here now," said the old woman tartly. "I've never heard of her in my life. Have a look, if you don't believe me."

Fascinated, Kate edged into the room and stared.

It was the same room. She could swear to that. There were the long windows, the dark-red damask curtains, the numerous chairs and couches, the fireplace where she remembered it. It was the same, yet different. For it had a musty fuggy air, as if years had passed, and dust and cobwebs and an accumulation of junk had been strewn over it. A Rip Van Winkle of a room belonging to an old woman who didn't open the windows, and who kept two elderly Pekingese which came snuffling towards Kate, as bleary-eyed and suspicious as their mistress.

"But I was here," Kate protested.

"You can't have been, Miss, unless it was before 1942."

"We talked about Francesca, Mrs. Torlini's little girl. I was going to Rome to get her. Rosita was lying on that couch—no, not that one, perhaps. It looked different."

Of course it had looked different, it hadn't been covered with a shabby rug sprinkled with dog's hairs, it hadn't even been in that position facing the fireplace. Or had it?

Was she dreaming?

"You see, you are in the wrong house, dear," the old woman said. "It's easy enough to make a mistake. All these big rooms look alike. I certainly never saw you before, and neither did Mrs. Lusk. Did you, Mrs. Lusk?"

"Did I what?" called the thin, dark woman from the bottom of the stairs.

"See this young lady before?"

"Never seen her in my life."

"Rosita let me in herself that day," Kate said weakly.

"Not in here, she didn't." The old woman chuckled maliciously. "Timmy and Tommy might look harmless, but they nip the ankles of intruders. Yes, they do, don't they?" She scooped one of the over-fat, snuffling animals into her arms.

The fuggy atmosphere hit Kate afresh and her head began to swim. She must have made a mistake. It was the child in the train situation all over again, the strange, freckled face staring at her. In the same way this old woman with the straggling gray hair was not Rosita. Inexplicably, the normal bright morning had once more turned into darkness and nightmare.

But the house *was* the same one. Numbers did not change overnight, and she had this one written clearly in her diary. Besides, everything was the same about the architecture. Only that fusty room and the grotesque pair of elderly Pekes and the woman with the straggling witch-locks had been overlaid with a film of age.

Perhaps when she found Francesca she would discover that over her, too, the years had passed, and she would be a grown young woman, self-assured and independent.

Kate arrived breathlessly at the office. She swept through the outer office into Miss Squires' small, dark sanctuary.

"Miss Squires, what is Rosita's address?"

"Rosita!" Miss Squires blinked her owlish eyes. "Who is Rosita?"

"Francesca's mother, of course. Surely you know."

Did a shade come down over her eyes? Levelly she answered, "I'm afraid I don't. I never knew much about that particular mission. It was Mrs. Dix's pigeon."

But the small plump pigeon who spoke only in her own language was lost. Or stolen. . . .

"But listen, Miss Squires. I've just called on Rosita, exactly where I interviewed her the other day, and she isn't there."

"Gone away, I expect," said Miss Squires laconically.

"Perhaps. Nothing would surprise me now. But the old woman says she has been in that particular room for fifteen years. She practically said that Rosita didn't exist. I dreamed her up, or something."

"I think you ought to mind your own business, Kate," said Miss Squires severely. "I know nothing about Rosita. I never did. But if a foreigner chooses to do a midnight flit, it isn't any business of yours, is it?"

"It's not a midnight flit," Kate persisted. "It's a sort of Rip Van Winkle thing, as if it were fifteen years since I called on her. Even the room had aged!"

Miss Squires looked at her uneasily.

"Are you sure you're all right?"

"Of course I'm all right."

"You were pretty done in yesterday. I just wondered—oh, well, you'd better see Mrs. Dix when you come back. You can't yet. She's still resting. She had a bad night. And in the meantime there's this urgent errand to do in the city. One of our clients, an elderly lady, Mrs. Mossop, confined to her bed with arthritis, wants some gifts for her twin granddaughters' birthdays. They'll be twenty-one and she thought perhaps wristwatches or simple gold bangles. Something tasteful, not too expensive. The jeweler she'd like you to go to is an old friend of hers. Nicolas Grundy in Hatton Garden. She said he'd help you select something."

"Must I go this morning?" Kate asked.

"I'm afraid so. Why? Don't you feel up to it?"

"Yes, I'm perfectly fit, but I had one or two things to do."

She didn't add that one of them was to put that telephone call through to the number in Rome—urgently. She was indeed learning to be circumspect, not even trusting kind, pedestrian Miss Squires.

"Can't they wait? You'll be back by mid-day. Mrs. Mossop wants you to take the things along to her when you've chosen them. I'll give you her address." Miss Squires smiled placatingly. "We're sending you because you have the best taste of anyone on our staff."

"Very well," said Kate reluctantly. "I'll go."

"Good girl. Oh, and by the way, Mrs. Dix asked me to see if you had Francesca's doll with you in your bag."

"Yes, I have. Why? Do you want to see it?"

"I couldn't care less about it. But the child treasures it, doesn't she? Mrs. Dix thinks it ought to be sent off at once. She told me to see about it."

Kate kept her bag firmly shut.

"Sorry, Miss Squires. This happens to be my pigeon. Francesca does treasure the doll, so I don't intend to risk her not getting it. I have to be quite sure where she is."

Miss Squires frowned in bewilderment. "But didn't Mrs. Dix explain to you that the child was with her father?"

"Oh, she explained to me, yes. She may even believe it herself. But I don't. At least, not yet. I'm waiting to be sure. And in the meantime I'm keeping the doll. Didn't you ever have something you treasured when you were a child?"

Miss Squires blinked. "Well, yes, of course. With me it was usually cats."

"And it would have mattered enormously if you lost one, and it would be up to any responsible adult to see that you got it back. Well, I feel like this about Francesca and her doll." Kate smiled. "It's not silly, it's just being decent. Now where is this place I have to go? Is Mrs. Mossop one of the talkative ones, because if so I'd better cancel my lunch date?"

"Oh, there'll be no need to do that. You'll be back in plenty of time." Miss Squires suddenly squeezed Kate's hand. "You're a nice person, Kate. Good luck."

10

Kate did not care either for Mr. Nicolas Grundy or his shop. The latter was small, dark and very old-fashioned, and, one would imagine, barely a step away from bankruptcy. Mr. Grundy himself had beady, black eyes that gave Kate a prolonged, intent stare, a mouth suggesting craftiness, and slick, dark hair flattened over his forehead.

It was a strange place to be selected by a wealthy and no doubt fastidious old woman, but perhaps it had had past glories, and a family connection for Mrs. Mossop. Perhaps Mr. Grundy had much better wares to offer than the slightly tarnished period silver in the wall cases, or the old-fashioned rings and pendants beneath the glass counter.

However, it was still a fine, sunny morning and Kate's feeling of optimism, despite her strange experience in the house in Egerton Gardens, had returned. So she smiled pleasantly at the beady-eyed gentleman and made known her wishes.

Mr. Grundy immediately nodded with deference and understanding.

"I'll be delighted to help you. If I may say so, I know Mrs. Mossop's tastes rather well. She's a very old customer of mine. Her taste lends itself to the austere. Something simple but good."

"These are gifts for young girls," Kate pointed out. "And I'm not to spend more than twenty pounds."

"Quite, quite. We can select something very nice for that price. What about two identical strings of culture pearls? Or gold pendants? I have a very charming one set with topazes. That's a very fashionable stone these days."

It was true that he had better things than one would have imagined. From hidden drawers he produced turquoise brooches and rings set with amethysts or opals, and a variety of pendants. Kate spent an engrossing fifteen minutes making a choice. Finally, at Mr. Grundy's suggestion, she had several articles wrapped to take to Bloomsbury where Mrs. Mossop lived, so that the old lady might make the final selection.

Mr. Grundy directed her as to which bus to catch. For all his rather crafty and calculating appearance he had been very courteous and helpful. Kate planned to tell Mrs. Mossop so, and congratulate her on her obscure but competent jeweler.

There was nothing mysterious about the house of this client. Ten minutes walk from the bus stop, it was large, well-kept and obviously highly respectable. A very youthful maid answered the door and asked Kate to come in. She was taken into a large, well-furnished room overlooking the street, and asked to wait there while the maid took the package of jewelry upstairs. Mrs. Mossop couldn't come down, she explained, but Kate was to rest and take a glass of sherry.

Rather reluctantly Kate surrendered the package. She didn't know Mrs. Mossop or the two granddaughters, but it had been fun selecting pieces of jewelry, and she hoped her choice would be approved.

She refused the sherry, because she loathed drinking in the morning, but her refusal seemed to upset the maid, who was very young and nervous.

"It's poured," she said anxiously. "And biscuits."

"Very well, thank you," Kate said.

The tray with the single glass on it was brought, then the maid and the package of jewelry vanished upstairs.

Kate looked distastefully at the sherry. Good manners had made her accept it, but why should she have to drink something she didn't want, and which was probably nasty and sweet. She took a sip and her suspicion was confirmed. Sweet and syrupy. The place for that was in the bowl of chrysanthemums on the table.

No time was wasted on that small action. Then Kate sat down and relaxed, thinking with pleasure of the long, cold beer she would have when she met William.

This was a quiet street, with few people about, and only an occasional car passing. A car was parked just opposite. Its driver sat reading a newspaper, as if he were waiting for someone. Kate looked at him, thinking he might have appreciated that glass of sherry more than she had. She was a little drowsy. The strain of the last few days had not quite left her, and Mrs. Mossop was being rather a long time. The quiet of the house and the dilatoriness of her unknown employer lent itself to a five-minute nap. Almost unconsciously Kate closed her eyes.

She opened them a few minutes later and saw the face looking round the door.

A curious, disembodied face, pale and hairless, ancient and evil. It seemed to float in the air for that one horrifying moment, then, as she started up, disappeared.

There was nothing there then but the empty space beyond the partly opened door.

She could have imagined that momentary vision, except that the fear and panic that had swept over her when the lights went out in the Paris night-club now filled her again, the same urgent desire to escape. Still hardly knowing why, she was running for the door.

The jewelry, the pieces to be bought and the pieces to be returned to Mr. Grundy, were still upstairs. But that no longer mattered. There was something evil here. She must get away.

Clutching her bag, telling herself she was a hopeless coward, she hurried across the empty hall and out of the front door.

She hadn't imagined that face. Almost, out in the sunlight, she thought she had. But its uncanniness, its air of gloating, its strange sexlessness, were too vivid in her mind for imagination.

Had it been the assumed bedridden Mrs. Mossop, spying? And how was she to explain to Mrs. Dix that she had run away in such foolish panic? How could she describe her intense sense of danger?

At the moment, none of that mattered. All that mattered was that she was in the clean, normal air again. She shivered violently as she hurried down the steps.

Then she suppressed a cry as suddenly above her a high, querulous voice called, "Wait! Wait!" She looked up swiftly, but only a shadow moved at an upstairs window, a faint, pale blur that might or might not have been that nightmare face.

Too frightened to feel shame at her panic, Kate hurried on down the street. She was vaguely aware of the small black car which had been parked opposite moving slowly forward and turning. Was someone coming out to pursue her?

Even that little maid, young and rather stupid, had been frightened. She realized that now. Why? What had been going to happen? And why was she so sure it had been going to happen to her?

There was a ten minute walk to the bus stop, a turn to the right, a crossing, and then another turn. These were quiet streets, and perhaps in her haste she was careless. She thought she had looked to her right before crossing, but, still obsessed with her strange, unrea-

sonable panic, she hadn't noticed any traffic dangerously close, neither the car that drew up with a screech of brakes nor the small black
one that swerved suddenly, catching her and sending her flying.

It was too absurd. She wasn't knocked unconscious. At least, she
didn't think she had been, but when she sat up slowly, a middle-aged
man was gathering up the scattered contents of her handbag, and a
woman, with a little flowery hat, too youthful for her flushed, middle-
aged face, was saying indignantly, "Are you all right, dear? My, that
was a lucky escape. That road hog! Don't try to get up yet. My husband's got your things. Oh, and your poor nylons! Ruined! Try and
see if any bones are broken."

The voice came from the other side of the Atlantic, and it was
kind. Kate wanted to smile, but was aware only of an excruciating
pain in her left wrist. She hugged it feebly, and fought a growing diz-
ziness.

This really was too absurd, a bump on the head the other night,
and now this, sitting in the gutter nursing an injured wrist!

"What happened?" she asked weakly.

"Why, we were innocently driving across this intersection when
that little car literally shot in front of us. It had to swerve to avoid us,
and hit you, poor dear."

"And didn't stop?"

"No, the bastard," came the deep, indignant voice of the man.

"Actually, Elmer, he did. He slowed right down and put his head
out. But when he saw us he just hurried on."

If the driver was who she thought it was, Kate reflected, of course
he wouldn't stop. For she had caught just a phantom glimpse of the
Oriental face. Or had that been imagination, too?

"You poor dear, you are hurt. Elmer, we're going to take her to
the nearest hospital."

"We certainly will. And here's all your belongings, honey." The
American's kind face was floating in a mist. Kate wanted to protest
violently at being taken to a hospital, she couldn't spare the time, she
had urgent things to do, but suddenly her mouth was stiff and she
couldn't speak. She was only dimly aware of the man grinning as he
held up a vague object.

"We've even rescued your kid's doll."

She wasn't badly hurt, the nurse told her. Her wrist had been
sprained and was now strapped up, and she had suffered from shock.
But she'd be fine by morning. Just rest and not to worry.

Kate didn't know how much later this was. To her horror she had awoken to find herself undressed and in bed. She was in a hospital ward, and outside, beyond the long windows, it was dark.

She sat up in panic. "I can't stay here. I have to go home. Why have you let me sleep like this?"

The nurse's face was young, like the little maid's in that Bloomsbury house had been, but this face did not hide fear. It was round and pleasant and carefree.

"The doctor gave you a shot of something. You needed it. Now what would you like for your supper?"

"Supper!" Kate exclaimed. "It can't be that late."

"It's six o'clock."

"But, good heavens, I had a lunch date."

"It's a little late for that, dear. If you want to send any messages that can be arranged. Now just lie down and relax."

Kate pushed back the bedclothes. "I will not relax. I'm going home."

"Oh, no, dear! You can't do that. Lie down, please. The doctor said—"

"I don't care what the doctor said. This is me, isn't it? This is my body. And all that's wrong with it is a sprained wrist. I can look after that quite well myself. So please tell the sister and bring my clothes."

She was not as strong as she had thought. And her head was full of images, faces, Francesca's, lost and forlorn, the fair and ghostly ones of two Mossop granddaughters who perhaps did not even exist, who were another hallucination, the old woman in Rosita's room, with her straggly witch-locks, Mr. Grundy's sharp, beady eyes watching her, and last of all that indescribably evil thing from which she had fled. . . .

"My dear child, you aren't fit to go home!" That was the firm but kind voice of the ward sister. "Have you anyone to look after you when you get there?"

"Yes," Kate lied. But it wasn't a lie, for Mrs. Peebles would flutter over her, and William, when he heard of her cowardliness, would look at her with cool, assessing eyes.

Those two people, however, would come afterwards. First she had to call on Mrs. Dix, and ask her who and what this strange new client Mrs. Mossop was, and why a man with an Oriental face seemed to be shadowing her.

These events were tied up with Francesca's disappearance. Her conclusions as to this might be illogical, but they were deeply instinctive. Just as her consciousness of danger in that house had been instinctive and unfaceable.

She *was* a coward, but she would overcome her cowardice.

She promised she would go home by taxi, and go straight to bed. The nurse who came to the door with her gave the taxi-driver her address, but as soon as they were out of sight of the hospital Kate tapped on the glass.

"Please go to Chelsea first," she instructed. "I have to make a short call."

Mrs. Dix could no longer go on stalling behind an atmosphere of cosy intimacy and generous brandies and chocolates. This time she had to make some explanations or Kate would threaten to go to the police. The police liked cut-and-dried facts, not this airy-fairy sequence of strange things that were not so much events as anticipated events. Actually, Kate could not make a charge against any single person, except the car driver for dangerous driving and he had disappeared. It would be useless to tell London police about an Italian child lost on a Continental train. She really had no story to take to the police.

But if Mrs. Dix were nervous or had a guilty conscience, the threat would alarm her.

She *had* to know about the strange transformation of Rosita's room, and that disembodied face this morning, white and hairless and indescribably menacing.

Outside Mrs. Dix's office in the narrow, dark street, off the King's Road, Kate asked the taxi-driver to wait.

She would be too late to see Miss Squires, who must surely be wondering why she hadn't reported back that afternoon, but a light showed behind the drawn curtains in Mrs. Dix's upstairs room. Knowing she, at least, was in, Kate pressed the bell and waited.

No one came. She listened for the slow footsteps that would herald Mrs. Dix's approach down the narrow staircase. There was no sound from within.

Kate pushed the bell again, and felt the door move slightly. It hadn't been latched properly. Goodness, Mrs. Dix was no doubt comfortably upstairs having her fourth or fifth brandy, unaware that her offices downstairs could be entered and robbed.

In some nervousness, which was not helped by her aching wrist or her annoying feeling of weakness, Kate pushed the door completely open and stepped over the dark threshold.

She couldn't find the light switch. She groped across the small, outer office, feeling for it, but instead came to the door leading to Miss Squires' office and the stairway. There would be a light at the foot of the stairs, if she could find it.

She could see something white glimmering on the floor. It looked like the plaster head of a child that had used to stand on the stairpost, a rather haunting piece of sculpture with wild locks and an empty lost stare.

Someone must have knocked it down. She stepped aside to avoid it and her foot encountered something else, a large, soft obstacle, a sack of clothes, surely.

She groped with her uninjured hand. Her fingers encountered something cool, pallid.

Her heart stopped, then jerked into a sickening beat. She tried to get to her feet, but could do nothing but sit there calling in a high, unrecognizable voice, "Help! Help!"

Afterwards she could only remember the taxi-driver saying, "Gawd!" She didn't notice him go to the telephone and ring for the police.

He had found the light switch and she wished he hadn't. For now she could see Mrs. Dix's forlorn, upturned face, her body round and bloated in the brown velvet dress.

She sat on the edge of the stairs shivering, until two policemen came, brisk and seemingly unperturbed.

One of them rang for a doctor and an ambulance. The other asked her some brief questions.

Looked as if the lady had fallen down the stairs, he said. Regular death-trap they looked, too, for a woman of her build. Did she suffer from heart trouble? If so, the explanation was simple. Someone had rung the bell and she had hurried down to answer it, but had unfortunately not reached the door alive.

"The door wasn't quite latched," Kate said tonelessly. "If there were someone there, he didn't know how easy it was to get in."

"That was careless," said the constable. "I'd have discovered it on my rounds later, of course. But too late."

Too late indeed, Kate thought, looking with her shocked, exhausted eyes at the chocolate meringue figure lying so still on the floor, the cosy, evasive little person who had never quite told her the truth. And now never would.

As she stumbled into her room at long last, brought home in the police car, and equipped with a sedative given her by the police doctor, a long figure detached itself from the armchair.

"What are you doing here?" she asked crossly.

"Waiting. Waiting since lunchtime for a message or an apology which I was optimistic enough to accept."

"Oh, William, I hadn't a chance. I'm sorry. Too much—just too much—happens."

Her voice was slurring curiously. William crossed the room. "Kate, have you been drinking?"

Brandy. That was what the police had said. They had gone upstairs and found, in Mrs. Dix's warm, brightly-lit room, an empty brandy bottle, a half-filled glass, and an overturned box of chocolates, which indicated that she had sprung up hastily to answer the doorbell. She had not only been tipsy, she had also suffered from a weak heart. A bad fall would be fatal to her, and the dark, steep stairs, and her own unsteady condition, had provided that. There were no marks of violence on her body, and no immediate evidence that anyone else had been in the room, though that would be checked more thoroughly. Kate had been told to go home and get a good rest and not to worry. But also to stay in London as she would probably be required to give evidence at the inquest.

That was all. She had wanted a cut-and-dried fact to present to the police, and now there was one. But it was going to answer exactly nothing.

"Yes, I've just had some brandy," she answered William. "That nice constable gave it to me." She began to shudder. "Ugh! I loathe brandy."

William had switched on another light, and was looking at her properly. "What have you done to yourself? You look as if you've been in a fight."

Kate nursed her wrist. "I survived. Mrs. Dix—Mrs. Dix—" The words wouldn't come out. She looked at William piteously.

"Kate, darling! Tell me. Has something happened to Mrs. Dix?"

She nodded. "The stairs. A death-trap, the police said. And she drinks too much. I didn't know—about the drinking, I mean—until last night. I suppose, with a husband one perpetually grieves over, one gets driven to it. There was this plaster cast of a child's head knocked down beside her. It seemed symbolic, somehow—lost-looking, like Francesca. And those two Mossop granddaughters who probably don't exist. And that diabolic face—they're all hallucinations, every one of them! Excuse me, William. I think I'm going to be sick."

When she came back from the bathroom she was quite calm again.

"Sorry about that," she said matter-of-factly. "I suppose I should have stayed in the hospital. But I'll be all right now."

William was methodically putting the kettle on. He looked up sharply. "The hospital?" His face was a mixture of disbelief and concern, almost comical. "Well, never mind. Tell me later. I'm making some tea. Go and get straight into bed."

"Yes, in a moment—"

"Now."

"I want to make a telephone call first. I'll have to go and see Mrs. Peebles."

"Kate, you can do your telephoning in the morning."

"This I can't. I have to know."

Mrs. Peebles gasped and looked nervous when Kate said she wanted to put a call through to Rome.

"Goodness, will this instrument be good enough?"

"Of course it will. It works, doesn't it?" She didn't need to check the number she had scribbled down in Mrs. Dix's flat last night. It was graven on her mind. The operator said the call would take a little while to come through. In the interval Kate sat in the hall, unable now to move away from the telephone that was presently either going to answer her question or baffle her further.

Mrs. Peebles had noticed her appearance and was staring inquisitively.

"You had an accident, Miss Tempest?"

William had come up the stairs, so Kate, supporting her injured wrist, told them briefly about the speeding car. She didn't add her quite unprovable belief that the driver had been the man with the slant eyes and yellowish face.

"It wasn't serious," she said flatly, "and the Americans were awfully kind. I'd be perfectly all right now if—"

She stopped. She hadn't told Mrs. Peebles about Mrs. Dix. At this moment she couldn't stand the woman's sharp-faced curiosity. She remained silent, and presently felt William's hand on her head. The gesture was meant to be sympathetic and reassuring, but William had a large, heavy hand. It was almost insupportable. She felt like Atlas, with the world on her head, and moved crossly away.

"Don't do that."

"All right, angel. You've got a lot more to tell us. What were you doing in Bloomsbury, for instance."

"Oh, a job. Have you noticed that—that person today, Mrs. Peebles?"

"Who do you mean? The prowler? The scrabbler? No, I haven't seen him, thank goodness. Anyway, you said it was a cat."

"It was, too." Prowler. . . . Scrabbler. . . . Both words came out of the nightmare. Kate felt sick again, and when the telephone suddenly rang she jumped convulsively.

A perfectly unintelligible voice answered hers. She realized someone was speaking in the rapid Italian which sounded so excited and inflammatory. Probably he was merely saying, "Who is it, please?" but the sentence went on for a very long time. At last Kate was able to say slowly, "Is there anyone there who speaks English? *Parla Inglese?*"

There came another long, excitable statement. Kate gave a little despairing sound. William came over and took the receiver from her.

"What is it you want to say?" he inquired laconically.

"Ask him who is speaking and what that number belongs to."

William, in what appeared to be fluent Italian, spoke for a few moments.

Then he turned to Kate, his eyebrows raised.

"Do you want to speak to the night watchman at a cardboard box factory?"

"Is that who it is?"

"That's what he says."

"Oh, my God, I suspected she was making up that call last night. Now I know, and it's too late. I can't ask her why she did it. I can't ask her anything—" The bleak knowledge swept over her. She pressed her hands to her eyes. "Now we'll never know," she said hopelessly.

11

William stayed the night. He carried Kate down the basement stairs and put her to bed.

Helping her to undress he hurt her injured wrist, and she exclaimed with tears in her eyes, "Oh, you're so clumsy! I hate you."

"Get into bed and stop talking." He jerked the bed-clothes straight and grinned down at her significantly. "It will be a different story when you're well."

"It will be no story at all. And I'm not ill."

But the tears continued to run down her face, and even they did not shut out the constant picture of Mrs. Dix's upturned face, and the plump, twisted body in its brown velvet dress. Like a fat chocolate slightly squashed out of its healthy rotundity.

The simile was as grotesque and made Kate begin to sob audibly.

"Your sedative," said William professionally, bringing her two tablets and a glass of water.

"Will I have to go to the inquest?"

"I expect so. But that won't be for a day or two."

"I can't face it. I'm such a coward. I ran away from that face this morning. I just ran away. I couldn't stop myself. This sensation of awful fear comes over me. It did at the night-club in Paris, too." She looked up bleakly. "I despise myself."

William sat on the side of the bed and looked at her reflectively. Her pale face had shrunken by shock and illness to childish proportions, her dark hair was mussed, her eyes tragic. She was impetuous and reckless and tenderhearted, and sometimes deliberately obtuse and maddening, and just now quite plain to look at, but still completely irresistible.

He told her so, in a detached way, and added, "I don't care how cowardly you are. Looking after you is my job. You just have to do the loving."

"Who?" she asked suspiciously.

"You could start with me. After that we'll think of lost children, and poor, foolish old women who stuff themselves with too much sugar and liquor and trip on stairs."

"Do you think that's what happened?"

"I don't know the setup, but would anyone want to murder her and commit no theft?"

"It might have been so that she couldn't tell the truth about Francesca."

William looked at her and gave a short laugh. "Darling Kate, your one-track mind astonishes me. Of all the incredible things you've told me tonight, that is the most fantastic. Now forget it. Take your pills and go to sleep. I'll be in the next room."

Kate sat up. "You will not. What will Mrs. Peebles say?"

"Mrs. Peebles has given me her blessing. She said something about not letting a cat in if it scrabbled. I won't let anything in. Now lie down and go to sleep."

"Oh, go away."

But half an hour later, in a shamed voice, trying in vain to shake off her drugged, haunted half-sleep, she called to him.

"William!"

"Yes. What's the matter?"

He was at the doorway, filling it with his bulk.

"You haven't got any pajamas," she said irrelevantly.

"I don't usually bring an overnight bag. What's the matter? Can't you sleep?"

He stood beside her. She was hot and restless, and her head felt as if it were bursting. There had been so many confusing, terrifying things. She couldn't rest. She couldn't sleep. Nothing was real any more and she wanted to die.

"What's the matter, Kate? Shall I leave the light on?"

She nodded. "I'm such a coward. I should have stayed this morning. I might have found out something."

"Something that wouldn't have been your business."

"Oh, don't be so good-mannered!" she said wildly. "The time is past for behaving politely. I should have gone up the stairs and demanded to see that old woman with her nonexistent granddaughters. I should have found out about that nightmare face. I should have frightened Mrs. Thompson until she confessed about Rosita, who *did* live in that room, I know. I should have insisted on Mrs. Dix"—she closed her eyes miserably—"or is Mrs. Dix meant to be a horrible example to me."

"Just stop talking," said William. "I'll hold your hand. There. Now go to sleep."

Strangely enough, she did. And woke in the morning, in a mood of cool, exhausted sanity, to see William sprawled awkwardly against her bed, his hand slipped from her grasp, his head buried in the blankets.

Dear William, she thought. But he shouldn't have spent the night here. Mrs. Peebles, for all her flap last night, was not going to approve, and Mrs. Peebles, in a disapproving mood, was tiresome. She sulked, and got secretive about telephone messages. Besides, one hadn't been as ill as that. Or had one?

It seemed one had, for when, after drinking the coffee which William had made with surprising efficiency, she tried to get up, her legs collapsed like a stuffed doll's. She was furious with herself and then more furious with William when he announced he was going.

"And leaving me to die!" she cried indignantly.

"I have to shave," he said mildly. "And go to the office and do one or two other things. Besides, I've got an infernal crick in my neck. You might give a thought to that."

"I didn't ask you to sit by my bed all night."

"I didn't intend to. I fell asleep." He rubbed his neck ruefully. Then he swooped over her with his overpowering virility. "You're not too fragile to be kissed, are you?"

His unshaven face scratched her. His hands beneath her shoulders lifted her, and jarred her sore wrist. She wanted to be angry, then, all at once, couldn't be. For, for the first time, Mrs. Dix's dead face vanished from before her eyes. In a curious and irresistible way life

flowed back into her. She couldn't think of anything else but the wonderful exhilarating fact that she was alive, alive. . . .

"Well," said William gruffly, "that was better."

He came back some time later. He hadn't yet been to the office, he
said. As far as that was concerned, his secretary had been told he was
suffering from acute fibrositis. But he had taken it on himself to call
at the house in Bloomsbury, on the pretext that Kate had been
worried about the jewelry she had not returned to Mr. Grundy. There
he had seen not only the small, gauche maid, but the old lady herself.

"Because you're a man!" Kate cried in disgust. "These horrid,
conceited old women!"

"She was in an invalid's chair," William said. "She was very old,
but quite harmless, as far as I could see. She said she'd chosen the
pearl necklaces, and sent the rest of the stuff back to Mr. Grundy
herself. She wanted to know if you'd been taken ill yesterday."

"I was," Kate said bleakly. "I told you. With cowardice."

William ignored that. He went on, "There didn't seem to be anyone else living in the house, but of course I couldn't pry into every
room. I had a glass of sherry—"

"Was it all right?"

"Sweet and nasty. Did you think it was drugged?"

"It could have been," Kate muttered, the shadow of her strange
fear touching her again.

"Well, it wasn't. For me, anyway. But old ladies like me. I heard a
lot of very dull family history, and finally came away. Then I called
on Mr. Nicolas Grundy, and asked if he had any French clocks,
Louis XIV, which was the only period I was interested in. But he
hadn't, which didn't surprise me, in that rather scruffy shop."

Kate began to giggle. "What an absurd detective you would make!
What conclusions did you come to?"

"If anything, that Mr. Grundy knew his stuff too well to run such
an obscure business. But then he may have a mind above money."

"Not with those beady eyes!"

"That sounds like your famous intuition again," William said sceptically. And you know what that gets you."

"What did you do then?"

"I went to see Miss Squires. But she wasn't there. The office was
closed."

"Then she's down at her cottage. And all alone, poor thing. I must
go and see her."

"She'll be up for the funeral. You can see her then."

Kate winced. "Must I go—to the funeral?"

William took her hand in his. "I think so, darling. I want to come with you."

"Oh, I understand. To see who's there?"

"Ostensibly to support you." He patted her hand briskly. "I also saw the police."

"Oh—"

"The inquest is tomorrow. They're not proposing to call you unless the coroner insists. They don't think he will. It's a straightforward case of death by misadventure. There were no fingerprints, nothing."

"The door was unlatched."

"Apparently Miss Squires said Mrs. Dix was sometimes a little careless about that. She would go out late to shop, and not always pull it properly shut behind her. The inference is, of course, her uncertain condition. She hit the brandy bottle rather heavily."

Kate leaned back on her pillows. "So there's nothing. Absolutely nothing."

"Nothing at all."

She gazed bleakly at the ceiling. Then she picked up her sketching pad from the bed and flung it angrily on the floor.

"I've sketched Nicolas Grundy and the woman in Rosita's room from memory, but I can't do that face I saw at Mrs. Mossop's. There's nothing in my memory. Just a feeling. As if it had been projected into my mind. Can you understand?"

"An hallucination," said William calmly, picking up the pad and looking at the sketches she had done. A little later he added, "But the Mossop granddaughters weren't an hallucination. I saw their photographs. Smug creatures who'll grow into stout matrons. Not like you."

"No," said Kate, nursing her wrist. "If I keep on like this I won't have a chance to."

It seemed a very long time, that morning two days later, since she had walked blithely into the small, poor-looking house in the outer suburbs of Rome to collect a little girl dressed in a white party frock. Who would have guessed the anticipated party would be a funeral? At least, this was one thing Francesca was spared. One hoped that somewhere she was innocently and happily pursuing childhood pleasures.

To shut out the forlorn scene in the churchyard, Kate conjured up a picture of Francesca, plump and stolid, splashing happily on the fringe of some blue Italian lake, or eating her way through a large plateful of ravioli in a good restaurant, or even being taken on a shopping expedition to buy a replacement for poor, shabby, lost Pepita.

Coming to the funeral was a gesture of respect for her late employer, but as far as solving any of the problems was concerned, it was a waste of time. For, strangely enough, not even Miss Squires was there. Nor anyone else whom Kate would have recognized. She looked in vain for Rosita, the gray-haired woman who now lived in Rosita's room, even Johnnie Lambert, who might conceivably have been back in London.

Among the seven or eight people, all of whom looked like elderly relatives, either of Mrs. Dix or the late major, there was no familiar face.

Death by misadventure. The coroner had not hesitated to give his verdict. For what semblance of suspicion was there that Mrs. Dix might have met a more violent death?

If, by any long chance, the mystery surrounding Francesca had put Mrs. Dix in danger, Miss Squires would have mentioned it. But Miss Squires, surprisingly, was absent.

Kate listened, stony-faced, to the completion of the service, then slipped her hand into William's arm and whispered, "Let's go."

William helped her into the car. It was her first day out and she was still a little shaky.

"Well," he said. "End of the story."

"End of the chapter only."

"Then I don't know where the next installment is coming from. Nothing could have been more conventional or innocent than that little gathering."

"One doesn't expect intrigue at a funeral."

"No, but one does rather expect one's fellow intriguers to pay their last respects. Even a gangster achieves that recognition."

"I think we expected too much," said Kate sensibly. "I had hoped Rosita, at least, might have been there. But she wasn't. What do you have to do now?"

"Take you home and go to the office."

"You couldn't take the afternoon off, could you?"

William beamed at her. "Darling, that's perfectly sweet of you, but—"

"I'm only using you," Kate said, with her usual honesty. "I want to go down to Sussex to see Miss Squires."

"In that case I'm much too busy. I've got an editorial hanging over me, and Saunders is away with 'flu. I really shouldn't have taken time off to come out here."

"Then I'll have to go by train."

William stopped the car and turned to her. His face was serious.

"Kate, you've got to drop this thing. As far as you're concerned, it's over, and I don't want you ever to go near that office again. You've finished with your old women's shopping and your poodle-minding. If you need a job I'll find you one. Or you could marry me. But you're not going back to that place any more."

Kate's chin went up.

"Or I could take a green line bus," she reflected. "That would actually drop me nearer to the cottage."

"Kate, look here! You've already had two peculiar accidents through inquisitiveness, and I don't like it. If there's anything wrong it's nothing to do with us. So let's drop it and carry on as we were."

Kate's forced calmness deserted her.

"How can anything ever be the same again?" she flared. "Every time I see a little girl in a white dress I'll think of Francesca and how I let her down. All my life this will go on, and it's no use your saying 'Nonsense, you'll forget!' because I won't. I've got to find her, William. She may be ill. She may be dead. At the very least she may be unhappy and bewildered and frightened. If ever I'm to have peace of mind again I've got to find her."

William looked at her for a long time.

"And so you propose looking for her in the depths of Sussex."

"Not for her. For a clue."

William shrugged fatalistically, and started the engine.

"All right, which road do we take?"

"The Kingston bypass. Darling, you are sweet."

"Save your honeyed words for Miss Squires."

Kate snuggled against him. "What's your editorial on?"

"The state of the roads."

"How perfectly splendid. You can get some local color this afternoon. So it needn't be entirely wasted for you, after all."

"My dearest angel," said William, with detached vehemence, "in a very short time I am going to take to beating you."

Beneath her facetiousness, Kate was very glad that William had come. This was her first day out since her accident, and she was ridiculously nervous. She didn't think she could have gone anywhere alone, without all the time looking over her shoulder to see whether the Chinese-faced man had suddenly appeared, like a rabbit out of a magician's hat. If she had travelled on a bus she would have seen him two seats behind her, or he would have been the ticket collector, and as for a train, it was inevitable that he would have been strolling up and down the corridor, never looking at her directly, but always conscious of her.

But he would not be likely to follow William, who was a fast driver, into the heart of Sussex. She relaxed, almost contentedly, and thought of the long talk she would have with Miss Squires in the privacy of her country cottage. With no eavesdropper, Miss Squires would tell her all she knew. For what point now was there in concealing anything?

At first it didn't seem as if anyone were home. The cottage stood behind a high yew hedge which, when Kate had passed through the gate, concealed the car. She had refused to allow William to come with her, fearing that in front of him Miss Squires might refuse to talk. But now, as she stood on the doorstep, she was tempted to call to him. It was growing dark, and the trees and bushes rustled with the country wind. Also, it was strange that although no lights showed Kate had the uncanny, prickly feeling that someone was peeping at her through the blank windows.

She rang the bell again, then rapped.

At last a sound, oddly cautious, came from within. It was almost as if Miss Squires were tiptoeing to the door. Goodness, if she were as nervous as that she shouldn't live alone in the country.

The door opened a little, then wider, as Miss Squires realized who her caller was.

"Kate!" she exclaimed.

"Hullo, can I come in? I want to talk to you."

Miss Squires backed a step away down the dark hall. Oddly, even now, she had not put a light on. Kate realized that she was hugging her black-and-white cat, Tom, who struggled in her arms.

"Yes, come in," she said nervously. "I wasn't expecting anyone. Tom and I were sitting here alone. I thought you were ill."

"I had a slight mishap. I'm better now."

"Mishap?" Miss Squires' eyes, seeming doubly large in the gloom, stared at her. Really, it was as if one had trapped a wild shy owl in this little, dark cottage.

"Oh, just a fall. I sprained my wrist."

"Shut the door, please," begged Miss Squires.

"I'm sorry. It is cold, isn't it?"

"It's not the cold. I don't want Tom to go out. He might—" she hesitated almost imperceptibly, "stray."

Kate followed her square, shortish figure into the little living-room that looked over the back garden. The last time Kate had visited here, this room had been a cheerful place, full of sunlight, gay with chintzes, and Miss Squires' favorite flower reprints. But in the chilly autumn gloom all the color had drained out of it. It was shadowy, box-like, claustrophobic.

"Do you like sitting in the dark?" Kate tried to speak lightly. Miss Squires hadn't gone to Mrs. Dix's funeral, yet all the gloom of the funeral was here. And something else, a feeling of fear, as if, now that she was indoors, the watching eyes were outside, trying to look in.

"I was sitting thinking. I'll put the light on. No, let me draw the curtains first."

She did this rapidly, as if she, too, were conscious of the eyes and the rustle in the syringa bushes.

"There," she said, as she switched the light on. She was still hugging the cat. Her face was quite colorless, Kate noticed, her eyes enormous. "Sit down, Kate. How nice to see you."

"You weren't at the office and you weren't at the funeral. I wanted to talk to you."

"Yes?" The flat monosyllable was not encouraging, and utterly unlike Miss Squires.

"This has been a dreadful shock to you."

"It was you who found her."

"I know. But she wasn't my friend, as she must have been yours. You must have known her very well—I mean, whether this sort of thing was likely to happen."

"It was very likely to happen. I'd begged her for years to have a companion, or a maid. I knew her heart was bad, and she'd got—careless."

Miss Squires didn't look at Kate as she said this. She sounded as if she were reciting a set piece. It was what she had told the police, of course, and no doubt repeated over and over to banish her own self-reproach. She sat squarely in her chair, nursing the heavy cat, hugging him as if she were afraid someone were going to snatch him from her. He was not a particularly attractive cat, being too fat and with a permanently angry expression. He hardly looked a worthy recipient for the possessive love he received. The whole thing was extremely pathetic, the dark, quiet little house, and this lonely woman clinging to her cat.

There was a short silence. Miss Squires made an obvious effort.

"You didn't come all this way alone?"

"No, William drove me. He's outside."

"Oh! Won't he come in—"

"No, please. I wanted to see you alone."

"Alone?" There was no mistaking now the dark alarm in the woman's eyes.

Kate began to speak rapidly. "I know you will think I'm crazy, as William said everyone else does, but what do you know about Francesca? You do know something, don't you? Please tell me."

"That wretched child!" Miss Squires exclaimed. "You haven't come all the way down here about her?"

"Yes, I have. Because I can't get rid of the feeling that Mrs. Dix's death is something to do with her."

"Stuff and nonsense!" But there was a faint shine of perspiration on Miss Squires' brow. And it was cold in this room. Very cold.

"You know where she is, don't you? She isn't at that place in Rome, because I checked the telephone number. Mrs. Dix made it up, for some extraordinary reason. So where is she, and why is she hidden?"

"I know nothing," said Miss Squires loudly. "I can't think why you imagine I should."

"But why has Rosita disappeared, and why does that man follow me? You *must* know something."

"Nothing! Nothing, nothing!"

The cat, alarmed, struggled afresh in Miss Squires' arms. She held on to it and licked her lips, trying to smile, her eyes ashamed.

"I'm sorry, Kate. I'm upset. I still can't believe Mrs. Dix is—dead. And then—"

"Then what?"

"Oh, nothing."

"What?" Kate persisted impatiently.

"Oh, just one of those coincidences. Bad news never comes singly. One of my neighbors is a bird watcher and he can't stand Tom. He wrote me a letter saying he was putting out poison. So now I can't let Tom out of my sight."

"Oh, Miss Squires, how awful! You poor thing, you can't stay here alone."

"I can stay here. No one will make me move. No one will drive me away."

And sit hour after hour holding that great cat, afraid to let it out of her grasp, afraid that the warm life would go out of it, too. . . .

"Then couldn't you get someone to stay with you?"

"Why?"

"Because it really is rather lonely." Kate's voice faltered as she encountered the suddenly inimical stare.

"I like it like this. It was perfect until lately."

"Everything is going wrong for everybody," Kate burst out. "As if there's a blight. Perhaps I am crazy, thinking it started with Francesca. But everything—Rosita disappearing, me being knocked down, Mrs. Dix dying—even Johnnie Lambert being sent away so quickly. He'd only just got home. You must know about that."

"I've never heard of Johnnie Lambert."

"But you must have!"

Miss Squires didn't look up this time. Her eyelids remained over her disturbing eyes. She said in a low voice, "I can tell you nothing, Kate. You've wasted your time. I'm sorry. But it's no use your asking me."

"I think you do know," said Kate slowly. "You won't tell."

"Nothing!" repeated Miss Squires on a rising note. She must have squeezed the cat, for he gave a bad-tempered grumble. "I'm just staying here quietly alone to get over the shock. So please—don't bother me."

Kate stood up miserably. Then, impulsively, she crossed the room and kissed Miss Squires on the cheek. "I wish you could help me."

Miss Squires shook her head. There were tears in her eyes. Her mouth trembled violently. "I'm sorry. I'm sorry."

In the cool darkness Kate climbed into the car beside William.

"Will you stop at the next house, please. I just want a word with Mrs. Wallace. She's a nice little thing. Miss Squires likes her. Or used to."

It was only to ask Mrs. Wallace to keep an eye on Miss Squires, about whom Kate was now acutely worried.

"She thinks someone is going to poison her cat," she explained.

Mrs. Wallace was astonished.

"But who would poison Tom. We're all silly about him. Even Colonel Maitland, who adores his birds. But he wouldn't lift a finger to hurt Tom."

"I think she's a little unbalanced," Kate said. "Her employer died suddenly. It's been an awful shock to her."

"Don't you worry, dear. We'll keep an eye on her," the woman promised.

That was all Kate could do. The trip had been useless as far as getting any information was concerned. Indeed, it had added to her heavy sense of worry, for the memory of Miss Squires sitting hugging her cat was going to haunt her.

She told William all there was to tell, then laid her head against his arm and closed her eyes. Without speaking again, they followed the long road back to London.

12

"You didn't tell me that gentleman was coming to look at the furniture," Mrs. Peebles complained, as Kate came in.

Kate stopped dead. "What gentleman? What furniture?"

"It was the bow-fronted tallboy he was particularly interested in. And you'd told him I'd let him in."

"Did you?" Kate breathed.

Mrs. Peebles nodded. "I didn't know what to do, frankly. But I thought if I stood over him it would be all right. So I did. Breathed down his neck." She gave her harsh dry chuckle.

"And he looked at the tallboy?"

"Oh, yes. Opened every drawer. Mussed among your things a bit, but said he had to see if the mahogany was genuine, or something. Then he seemed disappointed, and said he was afraid it wouldn't interest him. He wondered if you had any other pieces you wanted to sell."

"That tallboy belonged to my great-grandmother," said Kate dispassionately. "I haven't the slightest intention of selling it."

Mrs. Peebles' mouth took on its familiar expression that was comically like a fish gasping for air.

"You mean you didn't ask him to come?"

"I asked no one to come, and I thought you'd have more sense than to let a complete stranger in."

"But he said—I mean he looked so respectable—"

"Not Chinese?"

"You mean the prowler? Oh, no! I wouldn't have been daft enough to let someone like that in. No, this gentleman came from the city, I should think. A bowler hat, and an umbrella. He was short and dark. Had very sharp little eyes."

"Beady eyes?" Kate asked breathlessly.

"You could call them that."

Mr. Grundy. Nicolas Grundy. The jeweler from Hatton Garden. Could it have been him? And if so, why?

Kate was deeply perturbed. She began to walk away.

"I'm sorry, Miss Tempest, if I did the wrong thing."

"I don't suppose any harm has been done." It might have prevented a forced entry during the night, which would have frightened her out of her wits, and perhaps ended with her following Mrs. Dix. . . . Kate fought her fear. "Just don't do it again," she said.

But now one fact, at least, had become clear, and she must have been moronic not to have thought of it before. She had something which somebody badly wanted. That would account for the Oriental shadow, for her room being searched in Paris, for the accident with the swerving car, even for that horrid face that had hung momentarily in the air at Mrs. Mossop's. For if the caller today had been Nicolas Grundy, then he, too, was in the plot, and also the unseen Mrs. Mossop.

That glass of sherry must have been drugged, and someone had been waiting for her to fall asleep. Therefore, whatever it was they wanted must be something she would probably be carrying on her person, or in her handbag.

But also something that at times she might leave behind, so that, given any possible opportunity, her room would be searched. . . .

A jeweler suggested jewels.

She had no jewels of any great value. And she had never been shadowed like this before. It had begun only with her trip to Rome and getting Francesca. . . . Francesca! The extra thing she carried about was Francesca's doll. And that had seemed to interest both Mrs. Dix and Miss Squires. Mrs. Dix had begged to have possession of it. Rosita, at the very beginning, had specially mentioned it. In Rome, Gianetta had reminded them to take it.

Kate flew to her bed where she had not very originally, hidden the doll under the mattress. Usually she had carried it with her in her large handbag, but this morning she had remembered the American waving it at her in the road the other day, and she had decided it was foolish to carry it about with her. Besides, she had taken a smaller handbag. Someone must have been watching, and seen her leave the house with the smaller bag.

But Mrs. Peebles, with her threatening, battle-axe manner, had blocked their rather bungling attempt to search her room.

All this went through Kate's head as she held up the smallish, battered doll and studied it. It was very light. It must be hollow. But if it were stuffed with anything, it would not be particularly light.

Was she imagining the whole thing? She twisted the doll's head and arms, but all were firmly attached. Then she tore the dress off, exposing its rotund stomach. Ah! There was sticking plaster around the middle, stuck on clumsily.

With trembling fingers Kate stripped it, and there was the crack around the doll's middle, faint but unmistakable. It screwed in half.

It took only a few seconds to take it apart.

But there was no miniature Jonah hiding inside its interior, only a folded and much-creased piece of paper.

Kate unfolded it and found it was half of a letter, and it was written obviously to Francesca. It began,

"Hullo, little one,

Get Gianetta to turn this into your own language for you. I am coming to Rome at the beginning of next week and want to see you. Wear your party dress and I'll take you out to tea. Tony and Caroline send their love, and long to see you. Soon perhaps they will. Remember what I told you. Not a word—

And that was all. The last half, no doubt through much creasing, had been torn off, so there was no signature, no clue as to what it was the writer wished Francesca to remember. Nor who the writer was.

The date was two months earlier, and the address a street in St. John's Wood, London.

Kate tried to keep calm and make deductions. The letter was something Francesca had treasured, as proof its careful hiding place. It had been written by someone English, living in London, of whom Francesca was extremely fond. The casual address sounded as if the writer were a man. The vigorous handwriting had a masculine look. There was no doubt the writer was sharing a secret with Francesca. The unfinished sentence "Not a word" was obviously an instruction not to tell anyone either of the letter or of the unknown's imminent arrival.

It might have been done because it was a prank that appealed to Francesca's sober little heart, but it might have had much deeper implications. Even then, it might have been a plot to kidnap the child. . . .

Did this explain Francesca's stubborn determination to wear her party frock when she set out on the journey with Kate? Had she expected then to meet this unknown person? Kate was suddenly remembering her excitement in the train when she had tried to tell Kate of her brief mysterious conversation with a man.

Now she was realizing Mrs. Dix's shrewdness in selecting a courier for Francesca who could not speak Italian. Francesca might have had too many secrets to give away.

Did Mrs. Dix know of this mysterious person who wrote affectionate letters to the Italian child? Or was it to find some evidence, such as this letter, that Kate herself had been followed, and her room broken into?

There was no doubt now that it was possession of the doll that had been desired.

Who knew she had had it? Lucian Cray, Johnnie Lambert, Mrs. Dix, Miss Squires. . . . No one else, except people who might have been informed by one of these. Nicolas Grundy, for instance, and Mrs. Mossop. The Chinese-faced man. The old woman in Rosita's room.

Everything was still a mystery, but there was one practical thing that could be done at once. She could pay a surprise visit to the house in St. John's Wood and see who lived there.

At the thought of doing this, a cold, heavy stone of fear settled in Kate's heart. She tried to think of many valid reasons for not going. She had promised William not to go out again tonight—the matter of Francesca, whether it be a bitter quarrel between the divorced parents, or something more dangerous, was none of her affair—if the child were in trouble, she could not be of any help if she were lured into a strange house and knocked on the head.

But there was no use in arguing with herself. She knew she was going. With all the aplomb she could muster she was once more going to thrust herself uninvited into l'affaire Francesca. And this time, she told herself firmly, no happening, however frightening or grotesque, would induce her to run away.

After she had pressed the bell of the strange house in vain, and then rapped the heavy knocker against the door, Kate stepped back, almost in tears from disappointment. Because now that the house in St. John's Wood seemed to be empty, she had forgotten possible danger, and was conscious only of frustration.

Was this hopeful clue only proving to be another blind alley?

One of the tall windows on the second floor shot up. A vague, stout form leaned out.

"It's no use your knocking down there, young lady. There's no one home."

Kate looked up eagerly. "Do you know when they'll be back?"

"Afraid I don't. She took the children down into the country after her husband died. To her mother's, I suppose. She didn't talk much to anybody. Just passed the time of day if we met on the stairs. And that wasn't often, because I mostly use the side entrance." Belatedly, the old woman, for Kate could discern her halo of white hair now, asked, "Are you a friend of hers?"

"No. It was another matter."

The cool night wind blew the unswept leaves on the steps with a melancholy rustling. Kate looked at the long, blank windows, and had a sensation, not of fear, but of intense sadness. Where were the mysterious woman and children who had lived here, and who was the husband who had died?

"Would you like to come up, dear, and have a glass of sherry?"

The garrulous voice above her may have been purely kind. But Kate was thinking illogically of another old woman, unseen but queerly menacing. Mrs. Mossop.

"That's very kind of you, but I won't. I'll call again."

"Well, I can't say when they'll be home, dear. Before long, I expect, as there's the children's schooling. Caroline was going to a school near here, and the boy—"

"Tony?" Kate broke in.

"Yes, Tony. His mother was taking him to a kindergarten each afternoon. A bright little scamp, the dead spit of his father. Gracious, when that news came—"

"Did the father die unexpectedly?"

"Very suddenly," replied the old woman with macabre relish. "Drowned."

Kate drew in her breath. "How?"

"No one seems to know, dear. They say it was an accident. But those foreigners will say anything."

"Foreigners?"

"Oh, yes, it was in a nasty foreign river. The Tiber."

Kate grasped the iron railings. She thought that her voice, considering the difficulty with which she spoke, was very cunning.

"What did you say his name was?"

"Lor' bless me, didn't you know who you were calling on? It's the Crays. Poor souls!"

Kate took two sleeping tablets that night, and as a consequence seemed to be struggling all night with the cold muddy waters of the Tiber. She awoke feeling limp and with a sensation of horror still hanging over her. It was at that psychological moment that the letter came.

It had been addressed to her care of Mrs. Dix's office, and had been re-addressed. The postmark was "Roma." The letter inside was written in stilted English.

"Dear Miss Tempest,
    You were so kind to the little bambino Francesca. It will be of sorrow to you to hear she is in trouble. She needs a friend. There is only you of whom I know to write. Can you give help?
                                                            Gianetta."

The voice of Kate's stepmother at the other end of the wire was full of surprise and pleasure.

"Kate darling! Are you coming down?"

"Yes, tomorrow, if I may. But only if you can do something for me, Stella."

"Anything, my dear. Anything. And I've masses of vegetables and flowers and fresh eggs for you to take back to town. I'd been going to write to you. Did you know I won the prize with the largest pumpkin? And that new chrysanthemum is a great success. Everyone wants cuttings. What a pity you can't grow a slip in a pot. What is it you want, dear? A piece of furniture? Come and take your pick. It's really yours, just as much as it is mine."

"It's not furniture, Stella. It's money. I have to take an unexpected trip to Rome."

"How exciting! Is it a holiday, or for that odd woman you work for?"

Her stepmother was the most incurious of people. She accepted everything, except a heavy frost that blackened her garden, with equanimity. Nevertheless, one couldn't remotely tell her the truth—that the trip to Rome was to look for a lost child and to find out the reason for a man being drowned in the Tiber. The horror of that last was too recent to be able to talk of it at all.

"A little of each, Stella. I have twenty pounds, but I'll need perhaps another thirty. I'll travel second-class, and I'll pay you back as soon as I possibly can."

"Nonsense, darling! Don't talk of paying back. Haven't I always told you that everything your father left me is yours, too. Come down early tomorrow and we'll have a long day in the garden. I want your opinion of my new rose bed."

She had promised William to do nothing without telling him first. But already the promise was broken. For he would never have allowed her to do this. He would have said she was mad. Perhaps she was mad. Certainly she couldn't reason intelligently. But now she knew, as her intuition had told her all along, that Francesca was in trouble. And in addition there was the tragedy of Lucian Cray. Why should he, who had merely given her friendly assistance on the train, be dragged dead from the Tiber?

She hadn't really fallen in love with him, she told herself passionately. It had only been that his face, somber, dark and exciting, with more than a hint of ruthlessness, had stayed persistently in her mind. She hadn't visualized him with a wife and children. Neither had she believed he was merely putting on a very clever act when he had helped her look for Francesca.

For if he had written that letter to the child, then he was very deeply implicated. So deeply, that the dirty turgid water of the Tiber had claimed him. . . .

She was growing as cunning as everyone else. She packed her bag, and told Mrs. Peebles she was going to stay with her stepmother in Dorset for a few days. Then, because her memory played her a trick and she was suddenly remembering that kiss of William's the other morning, when, sore and aching and exhausted, she had had that moment of strange ecstasy, she rang William.

And found it one of the hardest things she had ever done to lie to him.

But he wouldn't have let her go if he knew the truth. He would even lock her in her room, if necessary. She remembered his overpowering strength which was not always curbed by gentleness, and shuddered with that strange, wry pleasure.

"How are the roads of England?" she asked lightly.

"In a lamentable state. Hullo, darling, I was just going to call you. Aren't you up early?" His deep, lazy voice hid his concern. "Has anything happened?"

"No. I've just decided to go down and see Stella for a day or two." When she heard the relief in his voice she was full of shame.

"Jolly good idea. I'd have suggested it myself if I'd thought you'd listen to my suggestions."

"William, I always do."

"Yes, and then kick them out the door. Well, never mind. Have a nice horticultural time. I'll come down in a day or so, if I may."

"Not until the weekend. Stella and I will be busy, and so will you, for that matter. I guess the magazine likes to see its editor once in a while."

There was a brief silence. She knew he was biting on his pipe. She could see his shaggy eyebrows, and the reflective look in his eyes. She

visualized his big body slumped comfortably in the leather armchair
in which he always worked, his untidy hair, his square, strong hand
gripping the telephone. She had a sudden, lost, dismayed feeling that
all of that, too, was vulnerable, as had been Lucian's finer, slighter
body and dedicated face.

She was a low, contriving, dishonorable person, and it would be
only what she deserved if she never saw William again.

But the thought made her catch her breath.

"Kate—are you all right?" With his uncanny and exasperating intuition he had caught her mood.

"Yes, I'm all right. I'm in rude health, considering everything."

"Your wrist better?"

"I've taken the bandage off. It's almost normal."

"Get Stella to massage it for you. And don't go trying to pull up
hefty weeds, such as thistles. Or mandrake roots."

"They're supposed to cry out."

"Then I promise you I'll hear them and come to the rescue."

Now she had three clear days. Stella, at the weekend, would tell
William where she was. But by then she hoped she would be cabling
that Francesca was found and that all her alarms had signified
nothing.

13

Mrs. Peebles was distrustful by nature. Until she was proved definitely wrong, she regarded all strangers with suspicion. One had to,
living in London, and having all and sundry coming to one's door. Besides, strange things had been happening lately. More than once she
had had the feeling that the house was being watched, though not
again by that slinky little foreigner with the yellow face. It was just a
feeling, one might say, with nothing to substantiate it but the rather
odd way Miss Tempest had been behaving, the dreadful accident that
had happened to her employer, not to mention cats scrabbling at the
window in the night, and yesterday that smug little man who had
said, as cool as could be, that he had been instructed to come and
value Miss Tempest's furniture. Her suspicious nature had served her
well then, for if she had left him alone in the flat what would have
been missing one couldn't guess. As it was, there had been an un-

canny moment when he had glared at her with his little, hard, black eyes.

The queer thing about that was that Miss Tempest didn't have valuables. She was a nice girl, obviously well brought up, but she was as poor as a church mouse. So what she could have that would interest a burglar, goodness only knew.

With these events behind her, it was natural that Mrs. Peebles should look with even greater suspicion at the little square woman with the large round glasses who rang her doorbell soon after Miss Tempest had left for the country.

Glasses. A disguise, of course. Though this was no bold person inveigling her way in, but a strangely timid and frightened-looking woman who got out of a taxi and who carried a wicker cat basket.

Mrs. Peebles had no fear of being unable to cope with this caller. "What do you want?" she asked uncompromisingly.

"Is Miss Tempest in? She does live here, doesn't she?"

"She does, but she's away. Left yesterday." (And no doubt you know it already, my good woman!)

"Oh dear! What shall I do now? Where has she gone, do you mind telling me?"

Mrs. Peebles was beginning to change her mind about this visitor. She seemed to be genuinely upset about something, and she also looked dead beat, standing there holding that basket that contained a now vociferous animal. No one with felonious intent would be fool enough to hamper herself with a cat while on the way to do the dark deed.

So she saw no reason for concealing Miss Tempest's whereabouts. "She's gone down to her stepmother in Dorset for a few days. She needed a rest, poor dear. Looking downright peaky, she was."

The person on the doorstep came closer, thrusting her spectacled face up at Mrs. Peebles appealingly.

"Are you sure? Are you really sure that's where she's gone?"

"I didn't follow her to the train," Mrs. Peebles said tartly. "But I don't see why she should make it up? why should she?"

"That's another thing," the woman muttered. "Oh dear. It's terribly important that I should see her. And it would take me so long to get to Dorset. Besides, Tom hates travelling."

Mrs. Peebles didn't quite know what to do. She said the first thing that came into her head.

"Why don't you go and see Mr. Howard. That's Miss Tempest's boyfriend. He'll know more than me, most likely. And anyway, he's a man." Mrs. Peebles looked wistful as she paid this tribute to the opposite sex. If her husband had been alive he would have known how to deal with these strange callers. It pleased her to forget that in his lifetime he had let most decisions rest on her own tough little shoulders.

"His office is in Fleet Street," she said. "Wait and I'll get the number for you."

So that was how Miss Squires came to be sitting in William's office, occupying the big, low, leather armchair, while Tom squawked grumblingly in the cat basket at her feet, and William, unable for once to relax, walked up and down, frowning thoughtfully.

"What makes you think Kate isn't at her stepmother's at all?"

"Because I'm afraid they'll get her away. Probably back to Rome."

"Rome!"

"That's the most likely place. That's where she thinks the child is."

"But *why*, Miss Squires?"

"I tell you, I don't know. I don't really know anything except that I know too much, if you understand what I mean."

William nodded. The incomprehensible sentence made sense to him. He understood that much. Miss Squires was the inadvertent possessor of a little dangerous knowledge. Hence the threat she had received by telephone that if she should divulge anything at all, or make any suspicious moves, she would receive due punishment. The first thing that would happen would be that her cat would have a mysterious accident, or disappear.

And all that had happened was that Miss Squires had discovered that Mrs. Dix's husband, the long-lost major, had come home. She had left the office one evening but, on her way to Victoria station, had found she had forgotten Tom's fish, so had gone back. The street door, in Mrs. Dix's careless way, had not been quite latched and she had gone in quietly. But there had been a light on the stairs, and from above she had heard voices raised.

"You're telling me you won't do it? But of course you will. You will be my obedient wife, as always. . . ."

Then there had been silence, and Miss Squires, overcome by some strange revulsion, had fled.

The voice, she said, had been pleasant enough, but the words had opened up a vista of possibilities that had filled her with alarm and apprehension. She had finally persuaded herself she must have imagined the conversation, but had plucked up courage to mention the matter lightly to Mrs. Dix the next day.

"I must have been having hallucinations last night. I forgot Tom's fish and came back for it, and I thought I heard someone upstairs saying he was your husband."

Mrs. Dix's eyes, she said, had been so stricken that she had been ashamed she had raised the subject. For Mrs. Dix swore she had been completely alone, as she always was, and what Miss Squires had heard had been merely a play on the radio. Mrs. Dix had it turned on loudly, because after she had had two or three drinks she didn't seem to hear so well. . . .

But in spite of being ashamed of her foolish imagination, Miss Squires had been extremely perturbed when Kate kept on worrying about that lost child, and then when Mrs. Dix had died she had been quite terrified. For, before the police had come down to her cottage to question her as to her employer's habits, the telephone call had come, the low, menacing voice telling her what would happen to Tom, her precious and only living possession, if she should tell anything at all that she may have discovered, or think she had discovered.

So she had been too cowardly to talk to Kate the other night. And now she was terribly sorry.

William stopped pacing up and down, and put his pipe aside.

"You've had quite a time, haven't you," he said kindly. "Would you like some tea? I'll get my secretary to make it. While she's doing that I'll ring Kate in Dorset. That will settle that matter."

It was Kate's stepmother who answered the telephone.

"You want Kate. Oh, is that you, William? But Kate's not here. She left to catch the ferry last night."

"Where to?" William asked sharply.

"She was on her way to Rome. Didn't she tell you? What's the matter with her, William? She was in the strangest mood. Couldn't settle to anything. Didn't even notice my new chrysanthemum that I'm particularly proud of. It won the prize—what's that, dear?"

"Did she tell you where she was planning to stay in Rome?"

"Oh, no, not a clue. She was completely vague. Said she was looking for a face to sketch. What *was* she talking about?"

"She's doing a rogue's gallery," said William. "Look, I must go now."

"William, Kate isn't running away from you, is she?"

"My God, no! She'd better not be."

"So it is true," said Miss Squires, looking up at William with her sad, owlish gaze.

"I'm afraid so."

"What will you do?"

"Follow her. What hotel did she stay at when she was last there?"

"The Romano."

"That's the first clue. She will probably go back there. Now listen, here's what you have to do. Don't attempt to go back to your cottage at present. Go to my flat. I'll give you the keys. No, I'll take you myself. It's not luxurious, but you'll be all right there for a day or two. My housekeeper will look after you. I'll tell her you're doing a research job for me. And she adores cats." William knelt to put his fingers playfully in Tom's basket. He withdrew it hurriedly and sucked it.

For the first time a glimmer of a smile appeared on Miss Squires' worried face.

"He's very naughty. He hates that basket. Mr. Howard, you're being awfully kind. I can't thank you enough."

"Not at all," he said absently. "It's you who ought to be thanked. We'll do that later. Kate and I," he added.

14

At the hotel they remembered her. This was the first pleasant thing that had happened since the commencement of her long journey.

"Miss Tempest! How nice to see you back so soon," the dark-eyed clerk said in impeccable English, and a little of Kate's tiredness and frowstiness melted away.

"I'm afraid I haven't booked."

"No matter. It is the off season. The tourists go home. You would like your old room?"

"Yes, please. If I may."

"But certainly. You will be staying a long time?" The dark, liquid eyes rested on her with genuine pleasure.

"No, not a long time. Probably just a day or two. It depends on some business I have to do."

"Ah, signorina! There are better things to do in Rome than business."

"I absolutely agree. But it can't be helped."

The high-ceilinged room on the third floor, the circle of red carpet making a brilliant pool in the middle of the bare floor, the brass knobs on the bed, the wardrobe big enough to hide in. And if one stuck one's head far enough out of the window, the view of the via Vittoria Veneto, with its sidewalk cafés, gay umbrellas and acacia trees.

Kate had the momentary illusion that nothing of the last fortnight had happened. She had arrived in Rome to get Francesca, and nothing would go wrong. They would reach London safely; Mrs. Dix would welcome them, smiling her cosy smile and offering them chocolates; Rosita would be waiting eagerly to receive her daughter; there would be no tragic body of the young man, who had cast his exciting shadow momentarily over her life, fished out of the Tiber. . . .

If only this were so. If only she could be gay and carefree. But instead of bathing and resting, and then strolling down the via Veneto enjoying the late afternoon sunshine, still warm and golden, she must now set her mind at rest by going at once to the house off the Appian Way to see Gianetta.

Once again, like a repeat scene in a badly edited film, she took a taxi and asked the driver to wait. The house, in the narrow, poor street, seemed even more squalid than she remembered it. Again she was conscious of eyes behind the dark windows of the houses on both sides. A taxi would not often come down this street. It would be a matter of great interest and suspicion, perhaps, when it did.

She had to wait a few moments after knocking on the door. It flashed through her mind that she seemed to have been spending a lot of time over the last few days knocking on doors and wondering, with this sick beat to her heart, who would appear. Supposing, as in Rosita's room, a completely strange person opened this door?

But, no. It was Gianetta. She remembered the thin, dark woman in her faded cotton dress very well. She was overjoyed that for once the right person stood before her.

"Gianetta!" she cried, holding out her hand.

But the woman moved back a step, her dark eyes flickering from Kate to the taxi, and then back to Kate again. There was no recognition on her face.

"You remember me! Kate Tempest from London. I came to get Francesca."

The woman shook her head slowly. Her face was tight with suspicion.

"*Mi perdoni,* signorina." Then she added in her careful English, "I do not remember ever seeing you before. Why have you come here?"

"But I came to get Francesca!" Kate cried. "Less than two weeks ago. You must remember me. Or if you don't you certainly know Francesca."

"Francesca? Who is she?"

Kate had a moment of complete unreality. Was she really standing here before the door of a shabby Italian house, while its tenant backed farther into the darkness of the small rooms behind the open door. Rather frantically she searched in her bag.

"Look, Gianetta, you're simply telling lies. Here's your letter saying you were worried about Francesca. Now what about that?"

The woman took a quick, suspicious glance at the sheet of paper, then she peered closer.

Her head came up, and this time there was no doubting her sincerity.

"It's written in *Inglese*. I cannot write *Inglese*. What does it say?"

"Gianetta, you're not telling the truth. You speak English, you must write it."

"No, no. I only learn to speak, not to write. My husband taught me when he lived. He was a bookseller."

"But here's your name at the bottom. Signed Gianetta."

The woman's eyes flicked down at the sheet of paper, then up again. She had her thin, brown hands clasped tightly against her breast. There was fear in her face, distinct fear.

"I did not write it, signorina. I tell you truthfully."

It almost seemed that she was speaking the truth. But the fear in her eyes made Kate's heart turn cold.

"Then if you didn't write this letter, Gianetta, you still must know something about Francesca. You're her nurse, after all. Is she really with her father, and is she all right?"

"You keep saying this name, Francesca. I tell you I do not know who you talk about. You must have come to the wrong house, signorina. Letters I do not write, women I do not know."

Her voice was growing bolder now, and rather angry. But the fear had been there. Kate hadn't imagined the fear.

"Francesca isn't a woman, she's a child. She wore a white dress and a blue bow in her hair. She had her doll, Pepita." It seemed she had made this description hundreds of times, and no one had really listened to her or believed her. "Of course you know who Francesca is."

The woman shook her head stubbornly.

"And you I have never seen in my life before. You say I lie. It is you who lie, signorina. I ask you to go."

"But I waited in that room!" Kate protested. "I can tell you exactly what you have in it, a table, three chairs, some rush matting on the floor, a plaster statuette of the Virgin above the door—"

The woman gave a faint smile. "You are saying what is in every house on this street. Knock at all the doors and ask for this Francesca. Someone may know what you want. But for me. *Scusi,* signorina, I am busy, I must go."

She was shutting the door. "Gianetta!" Kate cried in despair. "I'm trying to help Francesca. This letter says she needs help. And it has your name on it."

"There is more than one Gianetta in Rome, signorina. Go and find another one who can help you. It is not me. I know nothing that you talk about."

The door slammed in her face.

The taxi-driver was grinning at her sympathetically. He did not speak English so could not have understood what was said, but he knew she had been snubbed. How much worse than snubbed, fortunately, he could not know. For apart from the fact that Gianetta had been most deliberately and outrageously lying when she denied any knowledge of Francesca, it really seemed that she may not have written the letter. And if she had not written it, who had? Was Francesca really in trouble, or had the letter been a trick to get her, Kate, to Rome?

Because Rome was an easier place than London in which to do strange things to English citizens. It would matter, but not too greatly, if the body of a foreigner were found in the Tiber. . . .

She got back into the taxi and told the driver to take her back to her hotel. He backed to the corner and turned with a flourish, in a fast circle that threw Kate against the upholstery and even caused the blasé Italian pedestrian, used to the fast and furious driving of motorized vehicles, to look around.

It was then that Kate caught a glimpse of the yellow watchful face beneath the pulled-down hat brim.

Well, there was her shadow back again. She almost waved him a friendly greeting. She hoped he was a good traveller, or he may have cursed this inconvenient and unexpected journey to Rome. But of course it would not have been unexpected. He had probably known about it before she had known herself.

The letter must have been a trick. Gianetta must have been lying to a certain extent—it *couldn't* have been an hallucination that she had gone there to get Francesca, the rather stout, solemn child in the party frock—but she had not been lying about the letter. Kate was almost certain of that.

So someone else had written it. Who? And why?

She sat in her hotel room pondering the next step. There was an obvious one. To look up the Torlinis in the telephone book and ring them all, one by one.

Or go to see them.

But the thought of more inhospitable doorsteps leading into strange and hostile houses made her flinch. Suddenly she wished she had told William of this impetuous journey. She could have telephoned him from Dover just before the boat sailed. He could not have stopped her at that stage, and if he didn't in thorough exasperation wash his hands of her altogether he might conceivably have caught a plane to Rome. She would not have been afraid to stand on hostile doorsteps if he were beside her. Belatedly, she was realizing that.

The light was dying. The sky was primrose, and the evening mild. If it were not for the Torlinis and their mysterious child she could have gone on a leisurely tour of the fountains, or sat in a café on the via Vittoria Veneto sketching the faces of the passers-by, the priests in their brown habits and Biblical sandals, the street urchins, large-eyed, barefoot and cheerful, the old women in their narrow, economical, black dresses, the laughing young girls with their boy friends. . . .

Reluctantly, because of the mild, lemon-colored evening, not because of her apprehension, she picked up the telephone book.

At the same moment footsteps came down the corridor. They stopped outside her door. There was a brisk knock.

"Come in," Kate said, startled.

The door opened. And Johnnie Lambert was saying in his hearty voice, "Surprise, surprise!"

"Johnnie!"

"So we meet again. How are you, darling! Did you get my flowers the other day?"

"Yes, I did. It was sweet of you."

"Mrs. Dix, the slave driver, didn't give me a chance to be home for five minutes. You were partly responsible for that."

"Me?"

"Yes, with that kid you lost. But let's talk about that later. I say, it's grand to see you again. After you walking out on me in Paris and canceling your air ticket. When I saw your name in the register downstairs I couldn't believe my eyes. They said you got in this afternoon. I've just arrived back from Florence. Couldn't have a nicer welcome than finding you. Let's go and have a drink."

He was looking ridiculously pleased to see her. His round, highly colored face beamed with pleasure. In his tweed jacket, with his ruddy cheeks, pale blue eyes and carefully cut hair he looked very English and familiar. Kate realized she was almost as pleased to see him as he was her.

"I'd love to," she said. "And if you're here about Francesca you're going to save me a lot of trouble. But why didn't Mrs. Dix tell me she had sent you here?"

"And the moment I'd got back to London, confound her! She didn't want to worry you. She said you were in enough of a flap already and the kidnapping, or whatever it was, hadn't been your fault."

Kate hesitated. "You knew Mrs. Dix was dead?"

Johnnie's face sobered. "Yes, poor old girl. They cabled me. Jolly bad show. I'd have come straight home, but I thought the wisest thing was to settle this child business first, if possible. After all, those had been her last instructions to me."

"And you have settled it?" Kate asked, with intense interest.

"Not a bit of it. Quite frankly, I'm no further ahead than when I arrived. I got a clue that the kid might be in Florence, so I hared off there yesterday, but no luck."

"And I went to see Gianetta, the nurse, this afternoon. She absolutely denied ever having heard of Francesca."

Johnnie nodded perplexedly.

"I know. That's what I've met with all the time. Blank faces. Who's Francesca Torlini? Dash it all, I can't even trace her father. I've called on every Torlini in Rome. The whole thing seems to be one enormous myth. Is there anything at all to prove the kid really does exist?"

"Yes, her doll."

"Did you bring it with you?"

"It's here."

Kate took the much-travelled, shabby doll out of her bag and handed it to Johnnie. He studied it casually.

"Nothing particularly ravishing about this. It feels light. Is it hollow?"

"It comes in half. I discovered that quite accidentally. Francesca had used it to keep her love letters in."

"Love letters!"

"Oh, just a rather incomprehensible note from someone in London. Someone was apparently expecting to see her quite soon."

"Who?" Johnnie asked.

"There was no name. It had been torn off. I did call at the address, but there was no one home. Only the woman who lived in the flat above, and she said the house belonged to Lucian Cray. You remember, the man in Paris."

"Ah! Indeed! So he wasn't so innocent after all, by jove."

"Apparently not," Kate said miserably. "Because the woman said he was dead."

"Dead!"

Kate nodded. "Drowned in the Tiber."

"Here! Just recently!" Johnnie was horrified. "The plot thickens."

"He must have come straight back to look for Francesca. He'd pretended on the train not to know her, but he must have, if he wrote that letter. And there was the man she was trying to tell me about who had talked to her on the train. She seemed very excited and pleased. It must have been him."

"But, Kate, this is terrible!"

Kate nodded again and began to weep a little, remembering Lucian's dark, somber face with which, for a while, she had imagined herself falling in love. Johnnie put his arm around her in a comforting way.

"Poor Kate, you have taken this to heart, haven't you? You shouldn't have come back here, you know. I'd no idea the thing was as serious as this. I wonder what the racket is. One thing, I'll bet that wily old fox, Mrs. Dix knew."

"Do you think her death might not have been accidental?"

"Well, that's another thing." He gave her a quick hug, and said, "Look here, let's skip it for a while and have a little relaxation."

"How can we skip it?"

Johnnie had picked up the doll, and lifting its clothing discovered the way its body pulled in half. Thoughtfully he peered into the empty interior.

"Well, there we are. A doll with an empty stomach and Francesca disappeared into thin air. I know what it is, the deuced doll has eaten her, eh? Dash it, I've worked hard this week, and it's wonderful to see you again. Of course, we can take an evening off."

"And go to another doubtful night-club?"

Johnnie grinned apologetically.

"That was a bad show. Something queer going on that night. I'm terribly sorry about it. No, I wasn't planning to go night-clubbing. I thought I'd take you to see some people I know, after dinner. They live a little way out in the Alban Hills. We could drive out and be back by midnight."

"Oh, no, Johnnie. Thank you very much. But I've come here to find Francesca and I can't waste time. Did you say you had called on all the Torlinis?"

"Well, actually," Johnnie admitted, "I wasn't entirely skipping business tonight. These people I want to take you to are Torlinis. They say they don't know anything, but I had a feeling they were hedging a bit. I think you might get them to talk, or you might put two and two together. Women's intuition and what not. Frankly, I haven't a clue what else to do. We're up a blind alley."

"Why didn't you tell me who these people were?"

Johnnie looked wistful. "I'd have been more flattered if you'd just wanted to come with me. Not with this confounded kid's ghost between us."

"Oh, Johnnie! You are silly."

His eyes swept over her, rather lingeringly. "And you're—well, never mind. How long will it take you to get ready?"

"Ten minutes. I'll meet you downstairs."

"Right. I'll have martinis laid on."

Now she was happier and her immediate fear had gone. Good old Johnnie, not the world's most perspicacious private detective, with his open face and his hearty voice, but at least a well-meaning one. Although the plot seemed to thicken ominously it no longer seemed so sinister. It would be difficult for anything to seem sinister in Johnnie's cheerful presence. With his support they might even make a vital discovery this evening.

Alert with anticipation, Kate washed and changed her dress. She was just about to leave her room when the telephone rang.

Impatiently she answered it. Then her fingers tightened around the receiver and she was rigid.

"Kate, is that you? This is Lucian Cray."

"Lucian!" she exclaimed disbelievingly.

"I've just got a moment. Will you listen quickly?" His voice was rapid and breathless. The connection, also, was bad, and the sounds distorted. It seemed like Lucian, but he was dead, drowned. How could she be sure this was Lucian speaking?

"Francesca is in England. She's with—" A whirring and clicking obscured what he said. Then his voice came clear again. "—and Caroline and Tony. You must go home at once. You should never have come here. Will you go home?"

Kate found her voice sufficiently to protest. "She can't be in England. I had a letter saying she needed help here. Who sent me that letter?"

The connection was very bad. There was a roaring and clicking. The voice was more distorted and almost unintelligible.

"—Somerset, just outside Taunton." Then the words, "Letter was a hoax," came clearly, and, "Go home, you interfering little fool! It's not safe here for you."

That was all. The telephone clicked and the speaker, whoever he had been, was gone.

Kate sped down the stairs.

"Hey, have you seen a ghost?" Johnnie asked, getting up from the table in the lounge.

Breathlessly she told him what had happened.

"He said he was Lucian. But the old woman told me he was drowned. Is this a hoax, too?"

"Did it sound like his voice?"

"I couldn't be sure. At first it did, but the connection was so bad. What reason would that woman in the flat have for telling me a lie, saying he was drowned if he wasn't?" Kate pressed her hands to her hot face. "Does everyone in this thing tell lies? What am I to believe? If that was Lucian speaking and not someone impersonating him, he says Francesca is in Somerset, near Taunton. But supposing I get there and find it's not true, that it's just another method of getting me out of the way."

"Poor Kate," said Johnnie, with rather helpless inconsequence. "As if anyone would want to get you out of the way."

"He said I was an interfering little fool. I don't think Lucian would have talked like that."

"Then it was a hoax, darling," Johnnie said soothingly. His eyes were both bewildered and admiring. "You're certainly a girl things happen to, aren't you? I've been here for days and everyone's mouth has been shut as tight as a clam's. You're here for five minutes and you get threatening phone calls."

"It's not funny!"

"No, darling, no. It's just that you're decorative enough to be conspicuous. When you arrive lights shine and bells ring. Look, drink your martini, and we'll do as we planned this evening. Have some dinner, and then drive out to see these people. If nothing comes of it, then we can mull over the situation. Anyway, who does this know-all think he is? You can't catch a plane at a minute's notice. You must sleep on it, at least, before you decide."

15

They must have been some twenty miles out of Rome when the modest little Renault that Johnnie had hired broke down. It simply came to a quiet spot by the roadside, and Johnnie, after striking matches and vainly tinkering with the engine, had to admit that he knew almost nothing about cars mechanically, and that it looked as if they were stranded.

The situation was too old and hackneyed to be either amusing or particularly alarming.

Kate stood on the roadside, shivering a little in the cool wind that rustled the olive trees, and said coldly, "So what?"

"I say, dammit, I'm most awfully sorry. This will teach me to be more careful. I'm afraid the only thing to do is walk until we come to some kind of house or village. This is a little off the beaten track, unfortunately. We must be a good five miles still from the Torlinis. But I'm almost sure I remember a small *albergo* along this road somewhere. We can make for that. Or would you rather wait in the car?"

Kate looked around the empty countryside. The Italian moon, high and bright, showed the olive trees pitting the low slopes, the road a dusty white scar wandering into the darkness. There was no sound except the lonely rustling of the wind. It was an eerie and somber landscape, like the mountains of the moon.

"I'm certainly not waiting in the car," she said tartly. "But you might have told me this was going to happen and I'd have worn walking shoes."

"You don't think I planned it!"

Johnnie's tone of outrage was so emphatic that it may have been assumed. But looking at the bulk of his figure, standing a little way off, perplexed and helpless, she couldn't even indulge in the stimulation of indignation.

"No, I don't suppose you did. It's too ridiculous a place to be stranded. Do you think we'll really find this *albergo?*"

"If we don't we'll come to the Torlinis. After five footsore miles. Dammit, what a bore this is. Come along, darling, I'll take your arm. It's terribly sweet of you not to be mad."

"I am mad," Kate said wearily. "But where does it get me?"

"Nowhere, my pet, I'm sorry to say. You're absolutely dead right."

Johnnie walked away with a swinging stride, surprisingly brisk for his slightly portly figure. At least the effort of keeping up with him had the advantage of shutting other things out of her mind. She stopped thinking of Gianetta's strange behavior, and of the unexplainable telephone call she had had from someone who was presumably dead. Was Lucian really alive, she wondered, his fine austere features not smudged out of recognition by water and mud? She did not dare to dwell on the fact. There was nothing in her mind but the painful hardness and roughness of the dusty road beneath her high-heeled shoes, and the absurdity of being stranded in the Alban Hills, twenty miles from Rome. At least Johnnie was a cheerful person with whom to be stranded. William would have cursed and stormed and she would have had to calm him down. Then he would have burst out laughing and kissed her, and for a moment the infuriating situation would not exist. Suddenly she wanted very much to be at home in her basement flat, with William sprawling in the easy chair, scattering matches and tobacco about him, filling the air with pipe-smoke, and the deep lazy sound of his voice. It was the first time, she thought, that she had had this aching pull towards him. Almost as if, at this moment he also needed her. Curious. . . . Suddenly it was Johnnie tramping along, breathing noisily, beside her, Gianetta's lies, and the unidentifiable, distorted voice on the telephone that were myths. Francesca, too, was a myth. And this Italian moon lighting up the arid countryside. Scenes out of a film. Reality was back in her flat in London.

If only instead of being persuaded to pursue the mysterious Torlinis, she had stayed in the hotel to see if Lucian—or his impersonator —rang again. That, in the end, might have achieved better results. But she could no longer bear the static waiting. So here she was, ridiculously stumbling down the lonely road, stranded out of reach of telephones or news for goodness knew how long.

After a long interval, and a distance of perhaps two miles covered, there were suddenly lights around the bend in the road, an isolated twinkling of two windows and a swinging sign over a petrol pump.

"I was right!" Johnnie exclaimed in triumph. "It is the *albergo.* Jolly good show. You could do with a drink, I expect."

"And how," said Kate thankfully. "Can you speak Italian?"

"Enough to make myself understood."

It was a shabby building, with a shutter flapping on an upstairs window, and the paint peeling beneath the lighted sign, *Albergo Gari-baldi.* The half-open door led straight into a bar where a couple of men with flashing dark eyes and leathery skin leaned across the counter and an enormously fat barman refilled beer glasses.

Kate felt the three pairs of eyes fastened on her as Johnnie explained their predicament. It was as if they were summing her up, deciding whether she were a worthy cause for such a predicament. They would not for a moment think the breakdown of the car was genuine.

But it was genuine enough. Johnnie hadn't enjoyed the walk any more than she had. He was out of condition, and for the last half-mile had wheezed and made grunted exclamations of annoyance. He needed a drink more than she did.

He had a long and rather excited conversation with the barman, then brought two glasses of beer to the table where Kate sat and slumped down angrily.

"There's absolutely no one here who knows anything about cars. The best they can do is for Cesare—that scoundrel there"—he pointed to one of the lolling men—"to drive me into the next village and either find a mechanic or arrange for a tow."

"How long will that take?" Kate asked in dismay.

"Heaven knows. All night, probably. It's past eleven now, and these fellows have no idea of urgency. Tomorrow, next week, the next blasted year, will suit them. Frankly, darling, I think you'd better go to bed."

"To bed!"

"Our fat friend behind the bar, who is, incidentally, the proprietor of this dump, says he has four bedrooms, all empty, all equally desirable. We may have two if we wish, though why we wish two—" Johnnie's eyes popped with a gleam of his old hearty humor. "Well, that's just another idiosyncrasy of the English. Actually, I don't expect I'll see much of mine, by the time I've collected that damn car."

There was no use in being angry. It was a quirk of fate that something, not tragic but farcical, happened each time she went out with Johnnie. The lights going out in the Paris night-club, and now this being stranded in a seedy-looking *albergo* with three frankly-puzzled inhabitants obviously discussing at length and with deep interest why two bedrooms should be required.

Kate shrugged fatalistically.

"Well, I can't sit here half the night being stared at. So I'd better have one of the rooms. But if you get back in reasonable time at all, we'll go back to Rome."

"Splendid," said Johnnie in a relieved voice. "I must say you're being a sport about this. No recriminations?"

"It could happen to anyone." Kate made the expected rejoinder mechanically. She already hated this place, with its dreary brown walls, its dirty floor, the curled and shabby posters of impossibly blue lakes pinned on the walls. But perhaps the bedrooms would be better. Once again her mind was clouded with a mist of tiredness. She had suddenly to prop up her heavy eyelids with her fingers and remember who she was and why she was there.

Sitting in a dubious *albergo* in the Alban Hills was not going to find Francesca.

But did Francesca really exist at all?

A girl of seventeen or so, with a round, lively face, and wearing a rather grubby, peasant blouse that was cut much too low for the leering eyes in the bar, took her up an uncarpeted staircase to her room.

She unlocked the door with a flourish, displaying, with misplaced pride, what would have been better left undisplayed. Kate looked unenthusiastically at the iron bedstead, its brass knobs dull and fly-specked, the sunk-in-the-middle bed covered with a cotton spread, the cheap chest of drawers and mirror, also fly-specked, the unashamedly bare floor. There was dust on the windowsill and the chest of drawers. A mosquito whined in a thin, ghostly sound, and periodically the hanging shutter outside flapped and creaked.

If Johnnie had really planned that breakdown he had done it with singularly little foresight. For even if he had meant, later, to burst through that thin door, who could imagine romance in a room like this?

Again the situation was farcical. But she was too tired to be amused.

The girl had a towel of doubtful whiteness over her arm. This she laid ceremoniously on the bed, and going to the open door pointed down the corridor. Kate realized she was politely indicating the toilet —there could not possibly be a bathroom in a place like this—and thanked her. The girl went out, closing the door.

Alone, Kate looked distastefully at the bed. She sat gingerly on its edge, feeling its unyielding hardness. Nothing, she thought, would induce her to get into it, or to undress. In any case, she had no night things. She would curl up on the cotton counterpane with her coat over her. If she were forced to spend the night here she must get a little sleep, for last night had been spent on the train, and once again, as so often in this turbulent fortnight, weariness was her enemy.

The mosquito continued to whine about the room. One could close the shutters, of course, but that would be unendurable. The cool wind that creaked the hanging shutter, and rustled in the olive trees, made the room chilly, though that was infinitely preferable to its inevitable stuffiness were the shutters closed. The only thing to do was to put out the light and lie down in the darkness and try to sleep a little.

She found her way to the distasteful toilet and had a sketchy wash. There did not seem to be anyone else on this floor. The four or five doors along the corridor remained closed, and no sounds came from within the rooms. Later, she supposed, Johnnie would come banging up to bed, but she hoped by then to be sound asleep.

When she put the light out the moonlight came in and softened the squalor of the room to the austerity of a cell in a monastery. Kate lay down and began to relax. The sounds outside were country sounds, a goat, tethered somewhere near, giving soft bleats, as if to its kid, the rustling of the olive trees, and someone's footsteps dying away down the road. The shutter creaked intermittently, and once there was a small outburst of voices from below, a woman's, shrill and rapid, and a deep, domineering man's voice, probably that of the stout proprietor. Then they ceased, but no footsteps came up the wooden stairs to bed. Obviously this, the guest floor, was untenanted except for herself, and later, Johnnie, if he did not wisely choose to doze in the car.

Creak, bang of the shutter, a cat on the prowl, lifting its thin lugubrious voice, the muttered baa-a of the nanny goat, the rustle of the olives, like a stiff, silk dress she had once had in which she had felt very sophisticated and gay and important. Her first dance dress. But the boy she had gone dancing with had not even particularly noticed it. He had been a youthful Johnnie, lapsing into silence, banishing the smooth romance that a moonlit night in the idyllic English countryside should have held. She had not, she thought, had the romance one dreamed of, the dark, exciting lover who spoke caressingly in her ear, and lifted her on to floating clouds. Lucian Cray might have done that, she thought drowsily.

But she had been stuck with the youthful Johnnie types, who talked about the Budget, and horses and the latest hunt, and then William, who was appallingly honest and left her no vanity, but who sometimes, unexpectedly, produced those floating clouds.

In spite of the hard bed, the whining mosquito, and the unfamiliar country sounds, she must have fallen asleep, for it seemed much later that she heard the fumbling at her door. Someone was opening it.

Not Johnnie! Oh, not Johnnie, she thought unbelievingly. That would be too ludicrous.

She sat up sharply and fumbled for the light. But the switch was at the door, of course. One could not expect a bedside switch in the *Albergo Garibaldi.*

"Who's that?" she demanded, as the opening door showed a deeper darkness beyond than the moonlit darkness of the room.

There was no answer, but the door closed, and a figure stood clearly within the room. A man's figure.

Kate pressed her hand to her mouth.

"Johnnie—if that's you—"

"It's not Johnnie," came a low, grating voice. "I've come to find out where you've hidden the diamonds. You'd better tell me quick."

The man was coming nearer. The moonlight caught his face for a moment, and Kate thought—surely she imagined—she recognized the Oriental cast of the features.

Oh, for a light! But the switch was beyond this menacing intruder, out of reach.

"Get out of here!" she whispered. "If you don't I'll scream."

"Where are the diamonds? That's all I want to know."

"I don't know what you're talking about," Kate gasped. She began to struggle off the bed, but suddenly her wrists were seized. The man's breath was on her cheeks. His face, dark, featureless, with only the faint, terrifying gleam of his eyes, was close to hers.

"If you don't want to end with Cray in the Tiber, tell me where you've hidden them."

"I don't know! I've never seen any diamonds! I don't know!"

Kate's voice rose. As she screamed the fingers tightened on her wrists. She struggled violently. The grip on her wrists was iron. For a moment she was held immobile.

"So you won't tell. We'll see about that. You wait."

Abruptly she was flung back on the bed and as quickly as a cat the figure moved across the floor, opened the door and was gone.

The door shut with a careful click. There was no need now for silence, for her scream must have aroused the whole house. In a moment someone—the round-cheeked girl, the fat proprietor—would come pounding up the stairs.

Kate lay breathing quickly, limp with shock.

Strangely enough, no one came. All at once the house was completely silent. As if there were no one in it at all except herself, and the violent intruder . . . who had melted away as quickly as a form in a nightmare. . . .

Kate struggled up and felt her way to the door to switch on the light. But the switch did not work. At least, nothing happened. She clicked it up and down uselessly and the light did not come on.

There must be a fuse, she told herself feebly. It couldn't be possible that her light was deliberately not functioning. Because it would not be advisable for her to look fully at her midnight visitor.

This was too much! She was leaving this room at once, and going downstairs to find someone. Where was Johnnie? Hadn't he come back? Why hadn't he heard her scream?

Angrily Kate fumbled for and found her shoes, and thrust her feet into them. She snatched up her bag and made for the door.

But the handle refused to turn. It was locked. From the outside.

For one minute, then, she gave way to panic.

She was locked in here to starve, to die. Unless she confessed the whereabouts of some completely mythical diamonds.

Was that why the Chinese-looking man had been stalking her—because he thought she was a jewel thief, or a diamond smuggler? But how had he crept into this hotel, and cared so little about her screams? Why was she locked in?

Kate flew to the window to look out hopefully. But the sill represented a sheer drop to the ground a long way beneath. She could not escape this way without a broken neck or, at best, a broken limb.

The mournful countryside, beneath the high, bright moon, showed no sign of life. There was only the ceaseless sound of the wind, and the creak of the banging shutter, a monotonous sound, as useless as her scream.

Kate looked at her watch and in the moonlight managed to see the time. It was half-past two.

Then where was Johnnie? He must be back by now. Had she slept so soundly she had not heard his return, and was he now sunk so deep in slumber that he did not hear her scream? She couldn't know. She could only sit rigidly on the side of the bed and think that in four hours or a little more it would be dawn, and then there must be someone walking by below whose attention she could attract.

But supposing the man with his cat's walk and his flat, yellow face came back, unlocking her door from the outside. . . .

It seemed to Kate that she could not turn her eyes from the dim shape of the door. But she had nodded and half-dozed before the careful turning of the key made her leap upright.

This time, as the door carefully opened, a sliver of light ran across the floor, then vanished as the door closed, and the intruder stood within.

"I warn you I'll scream the place down," Kate got out before, in her fright and the blurred darkness, she made out that this time her visitor was a woman.

"Oh, no, you won't, Kate, dear," came a friendly voice with the faintest Italian accent. A familiar voice. She had heard it before. Where?

"For one thing there's no one here to hear you. I mean, no one who will pay any attention."

"There's Johnnie!"

"Oh, him. He's not back yet. Cesare is seeing to him. But surely you remember me?"

An indolent voice from a couch, a pair of languorous dark eyes watching her, a petulant complaint that she was not strong enough to travel. . . .

"*Rosita!*" Kate exclaimed.

"None other." The woman crossed the room and sat on the bed beside Kate. She smelled of some expensive scent, her shape was curved and enticing. She was no longer an alien, deserted and peevish, in a foreign country. She was completely Italian, warm and low-voiced and conscious of her femininity.

"But how did you get here?" Kate demanded. "I've been looking for you. I wanted to tell you about Francesca. How on earth did you find me here, and where *is* Francesca?"

"I haven't a clue," Rosita answered languorously. "We really couldn't worry about her. Troublesome little creature."

"You mean you don't care about her!"

"Why should I? She's really no concern of mine."

"No concern! But she's your daughter!"

Rosita gave a light laugh. "That's what you think."

"She's not your daughter! That's a lie, too?" Kate peered exasperatedly into the darkness. "Why can't we have some light? What's wrong with this place? Why has someone locked the door? Why did that man creep in and ask me where the diamonds are? I know nothing about diamonds."

"Actually," said Rosita, in her soft, lazy voice, "that's what I want to know, too. Tell me what you did with them. You must have saved them when Francesca was kidnapped. Otherwise, why did you let her go? Come now, don't play the little innocent any longer. You're in this right up to your neck, and you know it. There'll be light, and the door will be unlocked when you've told us where you've hidden them."

Kate got up warily. She was measuring the distance from the bed to the door. But the other woman had suspected what she was doing, and quickly moved in front of her.

"Don't try that, Kate, dear. There's someone out there with a gun.

We're quite serious, you know. We want those diamonds. They're valuable."

"For the last time," Kate declared angrily, "I know nothing about diamonds. If Francesca was carrying them—" She stopped as suddenly the thing began to come clear, the whole clever gamble that had so nearly come off. The doll, Pepita. The shabby doll with the hollow stomach. Pepita's diet was diamonds, cut or uncut, one didn't know which. But she was fed with them, and disgorged only for the little jet-eyed jeweler in Hatton Garden, Nicolas Grundy.

No wonder this succession of accidents and strange adventures had happened. There had been a continuous attempt to gain possession of the doll, and through her innocent, haphazard behavior, sometimes carrying it with her, sometimes hiding it, she had unwittingly evaded the thieves.

But the thing had been a farce, anyway, for this time Pepita had not been carrying her hidden fortune, as no doubt she had done several times previously. Francesca must have discovered the hitherto unknown opening in her stomach, and thought it a clever place to hide a treasured but secret letter.

So she had started her journey with a valuable hoard, somewhere on the way she had lost it. And only Francesca knew where.

But this last information she must somehow keep from this woman who obviously cared nothing for a child's life. Because if she discovered, and Francesca's whereabouts were known . . .

Who in all the world was going to bother about a stray Italian child, lost and unclaimed. Who was going to report her disappearance to the police and stir up trouble?

"Yes?" said Rosita impatiently, "if Francesca were carrying the diamonds, what would she have done with them? Nothing, because she knew nothing about them. It was you who cleverly kept the doll. So come. You've given us enough trouble. We do not keep our patience forever."

"I have a loud voice," Kate told her. "In a moment I'm going to use it to call for help."

"Call away, call away," Rosita's voice was contemptuous. "I've told you no one will listen. Your precious Johnnie won't be back until morning if I know the sort of drinks he's been having. He's the party type, you know. He'll never make a successful detective."

With a sinking heart, Kate knew she spoke the truth. But this crafty Italian woman was not going to see her giving in.

"Bring in your bodyguard. Let him stand over me with a gun, if he likes. But you can't make me tell something I don't know. And I don't know anything about your filthy diamonds. Nothing. The doll had nothing but a letter written to a child inside it. And I, at least, don't lie. Now get out of here, and leave that door unlocked. If you have got away with one body in the Tiber, you're not going to easily get away with two. I'm here to find that poor, mistreated child, and I'm not going home until I find her. If you think you can frighten me, you're wrong."

"We'll see," murmured Rosita thoughtfully, "we'll see." Still keeping between Kate and the door, she suddenly made a swift movement and hastened out. The key was turned in the lock before Kate could spring after her.

The position was as it had been earlier, and there would be no help until Johnnie, stupid, greedy Johnnie, with a bad hangover, arrived in the morning.

Unless the man with the gun came in.

It was interesting, of course, to have so much explained. Now she knew why she had been constantly shadowed, why she had had those clumsy accidents. It had been supposed that either she was carrying the doll with its dangerous hidden hoard innocently, or else that she had carefully disposed of the contents of Pepita's stomach in a safe place. It had also been supposed that she may have been in league with Francesca's kidnapper.

For now it was certain the child had been kidnapped by someone perhaps even more unscrupulous than Rosita and her confederates. The awful thing now, if they believed her when she said she knew nothing about the diamonds, was that they would track Francesca down, like bloodhounds.

Somehow she had to find the child first.

Kate walked up and down the room, her footsteps echoing on the bare boards. The moon was sinking, its rays growing more golden and the room becoming darker. Now it was even too dark to see the time. Surely it must be morning soon and Johnnie would come back. Why didn't he come? How could he behave like this when he had known he was leaving her in a dubious-looking place.

But a knock-out drink would be nothing to the wicked Cesare. He would administer it with the greatest glee, and Johnnie, the gullible fool, would swallow it.

This organization must be powerful, for even in Paris, at that night-club, there had been the search made of her bag. And in London its octopus tentacles stretched.

She felt as if she hadn't slept for years. Her legs were crumpling beneath her. She was compelled to sit once more on the side of the bed, but she had a rigid determination not to fall asleep. Soon it would be morning. Nothing would seem quite so sinister by daylight. . . .

In spite of her efforts, she did doze, her head falling sideways against the hard iron bed-end. So that she didn't hear the door open the third time. It must have opened very softly, and her visitor entered like a ghost. For Kate's eyes flew open to see, in the gloom, a round, squat figure, with a very faint halo of white hair.

"Have a chocolate, Kate, dear," a cosy voice said.

Kate clapped her hands to her mouth. Now she could not speak at all. Mrs. Dix's voice! The little, round, too-plump figure with the white hair, the busy fingers fumbling in the chocolate box, the noisy sucking of a sweet.

But if the dead walked they did not eat!

"You won't have a chocolate? You young things, you worry too much about your figures. Now, Kate, dear, that little mission. You brought back the diamonds, didn't you? You mislaid the child, but that didn't matter because you had the diamonds. So where are they? Tell us and we promise you'll not be harmed."

"I—don't—know—"

"Come, dear, try to remember. The Tiber is very cold at this time of year, and muddy. Kittens are drowned in it. Not nice to swallow that water. So try to remember."

It was then that Kate's control broke. Anything real she could stand, but this ghost, this caricature, whatever it was, as uncanny as the face that had peered around the door in Mrs. Mossop's London house, was too much.

She began to scream, "You're not Mrs. Dix! Mrs. Dix is dead! You're only trying to frighten me! Go away! Go away, or I'll call the police!"

"The diamonds, dear? Remember?"

"I don't know anything about your horrible diamonds," Kate sobbed. "I wouldn't touch them if I were starving. I know nothing, I tell you. Nothing!"

Dimly she heard the cluck-clucking sound of remorse, then the cosy chuckle. She didn't realize she had her eyes tight shut, and only opened them at the sound of the door closing and finding herself once more alone.

Now she was trembling and dizzy. She lay back on the uninviting pillow and the room swam in a sick swirl of stars and darkness. Then it faded away.

She must have become unconscious from fright and sheer exhaustion, for her half-faint melted into sleep, and when she opened her eyes with a dreadful start of nightmare awareness it was bright morning, and there was another tapping on her door.

"Tea, signorina," called a cheerful young voice, adding, "Please to enter, may I?"

But whoever it was couldn't enter, because the door was locked. Kate tried to speak, then didn't need to, for the door opened as if it were not even latched and the plump girl from the previous evening walked in with a tray and a beaming smile.

"*Buon giorno,* signorina." And then, obviously proud of her English, "Did you sleep well?"

"Sleep!" Kate echoed.

The girl's eyes flickered in surprise over Kate's rumpled but full-dressed appearance.

"You were too tired to take off your clothes, signorina?"

Kate sat up and looked at the breakfast tray. The china looked clean, the rolls were brown and appetizing, and the tea, though probably undrinkable, was a charming thought. They did these thoughtful things in Italy, she remembered—at least the Italy she had previously known. Faint energy and even reassurance stirred in her. If she were going to be murdered, at least it was going to be with the condemned criminal's due, a good breakfast.

"Thank you," she said, with automatic politeness. "Now there is something I want you to do, please. You understand me?"

"A little, signorina."

"Then tell the woman called Rosita I must see her at once."

"Rosita?" The girl frowned perplexedly. "I do not know anyone of that name."

"Now don't you go dumb on me, too. Rosita is here, staying in this God-forsaken *albergo,* and I want to see her at once."

"But I do not know. Honest! There is no woman here but me." The girl smiled ingenuously, thrusting out her plump bosom.

"Then a little fat woman," Kate cried desperately. "Not Mrs. Dix, because Mrs. Dix is dead. I know she's dead. But someone who might have impersonated her."

"Please, signorina?"

"Someone who eats chocolates. *Cioccolata.*"

"You want *cioccolata,* signorina?"

Kate sighed and gave up.

"Is the signor back?" she asked wearily. "The signor with the car."

"*Si,* signorina. You did not hear? He made a great noise. But he has the headache. Oh, bad!" She giggled with naughty glee.

"One last thing," said Kate. "Switch on the light."

"The light? But it is day."

"I know it's day, but last night it wouldn't work. Or so I thought."

The girl gave a flip to the switch and the light sprang on, vying with the early morning sunshine. Her puzzled glance went back to Kate, whom by now she must have supposed to be quite crazy.

Perhaps she was crazy. Purely crazy, and not even simply the victim of a nightmare. Perhaps no one at all had come into her room during the night. There was nothing whatever to prove that they had. Only Johnnie's headache. But Johnnie may not have needed Cesare's potion to encourage him to linger in some bar where there was talk and laughter and liquor. Johnnie was unreliable. It seemed that it would be scarcely worth while even relating her nightmare, or whatever it had been, to him.

16

Johnnie was waiting in the bar which, by morning light, looked even more frowsty.

No one had watched Kate walk down the stairs. She had boldly opened the doors and looked into all the rooms on the top floor, and seen that they were indeed empty. This fact did not reassure her. Rather, it strengthened her unpleasant suspicion that the night may, after all, have been a long-continuing nightmare, and that if she were becoming a victim of such hallucinations she must be neurotic and it was time she went away for a long rest.

The yellow-faced man could well have been there, since he was her self-appointed shadow. But Rosita and especially Mrs. Dix—who lay in her narrow cold bed in a London suburban cemetery—must surely have been imaginary visitors. Even her screams, which so mysteriously went unheard, must have been the soundless ones of nightmare.

The plump maid was sweeping the passage that led into the kitchen. She smiled at Kate and waved her hand.

"*Arrivederci,* signorina," she called cheerfully.

Kate opened her bag and took out some of the squalid-looking lire notes. The girl thanked her profusely. She sang to herself as she returned to her sweeping. In a few years she would be fat and slatternly. But at present she was young and fresh and normal. There were no secrets in her merry, brown face. Kate was grateful for that, at least.

But Johnnie was another story. He was unshaven, bleary-eyed and full of apologies.

"I say, Kate, old girl, I really got into trouble last night. That Cesare! He's quite a lad. Did I get led up the garden path!"

"Is the car all right?" Kate asked briefly.

"Yes, good as gold. It was a faulty plug, the fellow said. Cesare suggested a drink while we waited, and there it was. Fire water!" Johnnie shuddered. "God, I feel loathsome."

"Let's pay the bill and go," Kate suggested.

The stout proprietor behind the bar was watching them, a half smile on his face, his black eyes ironic. But he had looked like that last night. His face was no more secret or knowledgeable than it had been then.

Johnnie got to his feet.

"Quanto debbo?" he asked, and as the fat man laconically gave a figure he exclaimed, "My God, that for a night in this dump! By the way, Kate, you don't look any too brisk yourself. Did you get any sleep?"

"A little. When people weren't walking about. Ask him how many people live here."

Johnnie, occupied in sorting out crumpled lire notes, translated the question uninterestedly.

"He says only himself and his wife. The girl goes home at night."

The fat man went on talking, gesticulating and grinning.

"Oh, and a nanny goat and a kid and two or three cats. Business is bad at this time of the year. If you heard people walking about, angel, you must have been listening to ghosts."

"Yes," Kate murmured involuntarily. For one of them, at least, had been dead.

Voices and darkness . . . darkness and voices. . . . But the strange thing was that they had all had the recurring theme of diamonds. Whether it were intuition or reality, she was sure she had hit on the crux of the matter. Diamonds being smuggled into England by a child with a shabby, much-loved doll. That solution explained so much. And if it were so and it was found that the diamonds were no longer in the doll it really did mean Francesca was in danger.

But one would no longer confide in this sorry caricature of the spruce and self-confident Johnnie Lambert. He was not reliable and he couldn't see beyond his own nose.

"Let's go," she said urgently.

"Do we go straight back to Rome and forget the Torlinis?"

"Yes."

"Right. Wish I had an Alka-Seltzer. Confounded fool I've made of myself. Sorry and all that."

Kate was not concerned with his apologies. But she was alertly interested when, a little later, sunk in his remorse, Johnnie said defensively, "Actually I did make one discovery last night. That fat fellow at the *Albergo Garibaldi* knows the Torlinis. He said he'd never heard of them having a child. So it must be the wrong branch of the family. There are branches all over the place. He thought it would be the Florence one, but I checked that yesterday. The thing's a labyrinth. That's if there is a blasted kid. With all due respect to your evidence as an eye-witness, I strongly believe there isn't."

Later, as they became immersed in the stream of traffic pouring into the city, Johnnie turned to her. "What are you going to do now?"

"Have a hot bath when I get to the hotel."

"I mean after that."

"I haven't decided yet." She was going to see if there were any messages for her, any follow-up to the mysterious telephone call last night. She felt a strange certainty that there would be. But she no longer wanted to confide in Johnnie. It was extraordinary that Mrs. Dix should have employed him for a task needing diplomacy and finesse—unless she had deliberately chosen a bungler. . . .

"Well, I'm throwing in my hand and going back to England. I've had this sort of thing. Needle in a haystack. If there is a needle at all. You'd better come with me."

"I don't think so."

She had to decide whether she would begin looking for that elusive needle in Somerset, as the voice on the telephone yesterday had told her to. But first there was the possibility of something having happened during her enforced night away. Her incurable optimism was showing itself again. She was not going to be defeated.

"I'll drop you at the hotel and go around to the airways office," Johnnie said. "You'd better let me get a ticket for you."

"No, don't do that yet. I haven't made up my mind."

"Then make it up in that hot bath. I'll call you in an hour or so."

"That's very kind of you, Johnnie, but our excursions seem to be ill-fated. I think this is where we part."

"Honestly, Kate, I don't think you should stay here alone. You're too attractive, for one thing."

Kate laughed, avoiding his slightly bleary but anxious and sincere look.

"Johnnie, darling, if I fly with you we'll come limping into London Airport on one engine."

He scowled, not amused. "That's ridiculous nonsense. I'll still ring you later and see if you've changed your mind."

The clerk behind the desk at the Hotel Romano gave her his welcoming smile, his dark eyes suggesting, with approval, that she was making the most of her time by staying out all night.

"You are enjoying Rome, signorina? You have had a wish at the Trevi fountain?"

"No, not yet."

"But you must throw a coin in the fountain, signorina."

And what would she wish for, Kate reflected. Francesca's safety, of course. Suddenly she felt helpless and frightened at the task ahead of her. With only Johnnie, stupid and drink-fuddled, to lean on.

"Tell me," she said casually, "are people often drowned in the Tiber?"

The young man, with his smooth, smiling face, looked startled.

"Sometimes, signorina. Regrettably. Too much *vino,* perhaps, or a wish not to live." He shrugged, abruptly changing from smiling welcome to melancholy.

"Has there been an Englishman drowned recently?"

"You mean yesterday, last week? No, not since the mystery of several weeks ago."

"Several weeks?"

"While the weather was still hot. It was said he had perhaps gone swimming in the moonlight, after a party, you know. It was all very suspicious, but the police could find out nothing more. He was dead, after all. Whatever the reason, he could not be brought back to life."

"What was his name?" Kate asked tensely. "Do you remember?"

"I do, because it was one of your strange English names." The young man gave his charming smile and enunciated carefully, "Gerald Dalrymple."

He looked at Kate anxiously and said, "That means nothing to you? He was not your friend?"

Kate was enormously relieved. "No, he was not my friend. That is the only drowning of an Englishman?"

"That is the only one I know of, signorina." The young man added with his impeccable manners, "I am sorry."

Kate picked up her room key. "Have there been any messages for me?"

"No. Nothing at all."

Now she didn't know what to think, but excitement was rising in her because, after all, that telephone call last night must have been from Lucian. He must be alive, thank heaven, and that also meant it must be true that Francesca was safely in Somerset. Now what should she do?

Nothing, she told herself, until she had had a long luxurious bath, and some food. After that she would be human again, and inspiration would come to her.

The inspiration did come to her while she was in her bath. She leapt out and only half-dry went to the telephone and asked for William's number in London. It was Saturday morning and he would not be at the office. She waited with an eagerness that caused her faint surprise, for the sound of his voice.

But when the call came through it was a woman's voice, vaguely familiar, that answered.

"Mr. Howard isn't here, I'm sorry."

"You mean he isn't in London?"

"No." The voice was cagey, and had that vague familiarity.

"Who is that speaking?" Kate demanded.

"Oh, Kate! That's Kate!" The far-off voice was raised in pleasure. "This is Miss Squires here. I'm staying in William's flat. But hasn't he told you?"

"How could he?" Kate returned, with some asperity. "I'm in Rome."

"But so is he, dear. He left by the early morning flight."

"Oh, the clot! Why can't he keep his nose out of my business? Then he should be here any time?"

"I believe they were held up by fog, but he should be on his way by now. I told him to go to the Hotel Romano. Is that right?"

"So you're in this plot, too," Kate said disgustedly. "Well, I haven't time to talk about it now, but since William isn't there you'll have to do something for me. It's very urgent, and it may be a little difficult." She suddenly remembered Miss Squires sitting hunched and fearful in her cottage hugging her cat, and added doubtfully, "Will you try?"

"Of course," came the answer steadily. "I'm staying in William's flat. His housekeeper will look after Tom. What is it you want me to do?"

"There's a village somewhere near Taunton. I don't know its

name, but I'm guessing it will be quite a small place. I think Francesca is there. She will be staying with a family called either Cray or Dalrymple. That's all I can tell you, except that they have two children called Tony and Caroline. If you can possibly find this family, will you tell them they *must* ask for police protection immediately. It's terribly important. I think they'll know what you're getting at."

Miss Squires' voice was not quite so steady now. "Are you sure Francesca isn't in Rome, then?"

"Not entirely. I want to stay a little longer to be sure. But this other thing is urgent. Do you think you can manage it?"

"I can have a jolly good try," Miss Squires' voice came back, with determined courage. "I know there's a lot more in this than I knew at first. But William will tell you. Goodbye, dear, and I'll ring you the moment I've got anything to report."

"Good girl," said Kate affectionately. "This all may be a hoax, so do be careful. Bless you."

So William was arriving at any moment. After a little while Kate's annoyance left her and she began to feel rather happy about it. Now she needn't feel even the faintest regret that Johnnie was deserting her. William was a much stronger leaning post. And a familiar one. If his car broke down, he would know how to fix it, at least. And also he possessed the incalculable asset of speaking Italian. He could do a little inquiring into the drowning of the mysterious Englishman, Gerald Dalrymple, which, Kate was now convinced, had been the beginning of the whole mysterious affair.

Now she was too excited to sit calmly waiting for William's arrival. On an impulse she scribbled a note:

"Do I have no life of my own? Can't you leave me alone and attend to the roads of England, which are in much more immediate trouble than I am. I'm just dashing out to have another shot at getting Gianetta to talk. If you come while I am away don't move from this room!"

This she stuck in an envelope, addressed it to Mr. William Howard, and propped it on the dressing-table. She would ask the desk clerk to give William her key. He would not quibble at that. He would smile approvingly, and ask her again if she were enjoying Rome, and had she thrown a coin in the Trevi fountain. And there would be no shadow of drowned men or little girls in deadly danger in his bright, friendly eyes.

Just before she left, the telephone rang again. She snatched it up eagerly, hoping that it would be Lucian Cray, with a better connection this time so that she could hear what he said.

But it was Johnnie. She felt rather flat. Poor Johnnie. And he meant so well.

"Hi, Kate. Changed your mind about coming with me?"

"No. William's arriving."

"Who's William?" His voice sounded suddenly peevish and suspicious.

"Oh, just an old friend of mine. He has rather a thing about keeping an eye on me." She knew she was being smug, but the memory of Johnnie's bleary-eyed ineffectiveness rankled.

Johnnie gave a sudden snort of laughter. "So you look for the lost brat and your boy-friend looks for you, and who looks for him? This is becoming a farce."

"Yes, isn't it," said Kate pleasantly. "William knows about cars, too. So you can leave me quite safely."

There was a short silence. "Suppose I deserved that." His voice was lugubrious, and Kate was suddenly ashamed of herself. "But I still think you should come with me. I'll take a wager you don't get any further ahead than I did with your search, William or no William. Or have you had any more mysterious phone calls?"

"No."

"Too bad. You're quite sure you didn't hear the name of that place in Somerset?"

"No, I didn't. I wish I had."

"H-m-m. Well, I've got a booking on the afternoon flight. I rather think I'll take it, you know."

"Don't wait for me," said Kate coolly. "Good luck, Johnnie, and goodbye."

"I think you're being rather reckless, my dear."

"Why? Are you afraid I'll fall in the Tiber, too?"

Johnnie gave his loud, hearty laugh. "Not at all. You're a clever girl. You're too good at taking care of yourself."

Taxis to the street off the via Appia were becoming a luxury. Kate ambitiously took a tram, edging her way into its crowded interior, and clinging hard to a strap as it rocked and clattered down the busy streets. She was alternately flung against garlic-redolent working men who ogled her, and old women in their inevitable black, gnawing at hunks of bread and staring at her with slightly resentful, suspicious eyes. She wanted badly to sketch their brown, withered faces, their hooded eyes that had tantalized Michelangelo and Leonardo da Vinci centuries ago. The sun shone; the chestnuts and acacias reluctantly relinquished their foliage, deliberate leaf by leaf; the tram rattled on, and the city was vibrant with noise and movement.

But the narrow, shabby house in the little street was completely silent. No one came in response to Kate's knock. She waited a little, imagining that Gianetta's dark eyes, like those of a timid captive animal, were peering secretly at her through the window. If they were, Gianetta obviously was not going to open the door.

Kate stepped back, feeling baffled and frustrated, and also conscious of growing apprehension. Those silent, dark rooms of the house could be hiding anything, anything. . . .

She noticed that two or three women in the street had gathered to watch her. She walked towards them, asking optimistically, *"Parla Inglese?"*

Their heads shook regretfully. Then one of them raised her voice and with the shrill Italian intonation called, "Maddale-ee-na!"

A door opened and a young girl of about sixteen came out. The woman who was apparently her mother pointed at her and explained, "She speak *Inglese,* signorina."

The girl gave a shy smile, and Kate said, "I came out here to see Gianetta, but there doesn't seem to be anyone home. Do you know where she is?"

"She has gone to England. Last night late she left."

"To England!" But that couldn't be true. Not shabby little Gianetta, who had obviously never ventured more than a few miles from her home in all her life.

"Si, signorina. To see her daughter who is sick. She had to go quite quickly. And this morning the man came to do the floor but he couldn't get in."

"Did he get in?" Kate asked tensely.

"Through the window." The girl giggled. "Some boards were quite decayed, he said. There is a lot of work to do. Poor Gianetta. She has many troubles."

"Did you know she had a daughter in England?" Kate asked.

"Oh, yes. Francesca. We have always known Francesca." The girl shrugged. "But she has a wealthy grandmother in England—I think Gianetta once worked in her house—and she makes many visits."

"You speak English very well," Kate said automatically.

"Oh, yes. I go to classes."

The circle of watching women, with their avid, baffled eyes, was disturbing, like being watched by a jury of crows who would pronounce some unintelligible verdict. Kate could not take in the information that Francesca was Gianetta's child. No wonder she had looked so aged, so frightened, now that something had gone seriously wrong with those mysterious journeys to England. No wonder she had been so scared and secretive yesterday. How did she know who she could trust?

"The man who came to do the floor," she asked. "What did he look like?"

The girl paused a moment. She said something in rapid Italian to the other women, and they began to nod, their eyes sparkling with amusement.

"We all say," she told Kate, "that he must have come a long way to get to Rome. Or else his mother had." She giggled again, enjoying her cleverness. "We thought he was Chinese."

Kate did not enjoy her journey back by tram. In spite of its rattling bustle, it was much, much too slow. She could not get back quickly enough to see if William had arrived and to tell him of this latest development. For she was so afraid, so dreadfully afraid, that Gianetta had not gone to England, that on the contrary she had not gone at all. But also that it was unlikely she would ever come back. . . .

The clerk greeted her with his unfailing smile, and an air of delight. "Your friend has arrived, signorina."

"Oh, thank heaven! Is he waiting?"

"I gave him your room key as you advised."

"Thank you. I must see him quickly."

She ran up the stairs, not waiting for the lift, and burst into her room. "William, you crazy—" she began, but stopped as the man rose from the chair at the window.

He was not William.

"Sorry to disappoint you, Kate," said Lucian Cray.

17

There was no time to exchange polite greetings. Kate burst out, "They've got Gianetta. What are we to do?"

At least his face did not go blank. He did not say, "Who is Gianetta?" and pretend ignorance, as she had grown accustomed to expect. He said quietly:

"Don't worry. She's halfway to England by now."

"You don't believe that story!"

Although his voice was quiet, his eyes were narrowed and hard. His face still excited her—or perhaps it was the artist in her whom it excited—but now she saw its ruthlessness, and its dedication to some unwavering purpose. He would not be an easy person to live with, or an easy enemy to have.

"Why didn't you go when I told you to?" he repeated.

She flung up her head. "How could I be sure you were telling me the truth?"

"No, I suppose you couldn't be sure, after all that has happened." He regarded her thoughtfully.

"How did you know I was here, even?"

"I have methods as well as Johnnie Lambert."

Kate started a little at that, but the unreality of it all was too much for her.

"I came here thinking you were drowned!"

"Who told you that?"

"Oh, some woman in the upstairs flat of your house in St. John's Wood. It was your house, I suppose?"

"Yes, my house. But not my body in the Tiber." The hard ruthlessness had come back into his face.

"No, the clerk downstairs told me whose that was. Gerald Dalrymple's. But who was he?"

"He was my sister's husband," Lucian said somberly.

"Oh, how dreadful! Tony's and Caroline's father! The person who wrote the letter to Francesca."

"Exactly. You've found out too much, Kate. Even I didn't know about that letter."

"But you knew about the diamonds," Kate said breathlessly.

His eyes pierced her. "How did you find out about them?"

"I had a nightmare last night that people were accusing me of having them. Me! And when I woke up I knew somehow that I had dreamed the truth."

"Didn't I tell you last night to go home, that it wasn't safe."

Kate's eyes widened. "Then it wasn't a nightmare? Were those people really there, in my room in the dark? Even Mrs. Dix—" Her mouth was dry.

"My God, not Mrs. Dix!" he exclaimed. "Whose picturesque flight of imagination was that? Poor Kate! Was it very bad?"

"I screamed my head off. But no one seemed to hear. The wretched place might have been completely empty. That was why it was so fantastic and horrible—so that by daylight I was sure I had been dreaming. I didn't even tell Johnnie. He was too stupid, anyway, and I wasn't sure then that I trusted him."

Lucian gave a tight smile. "Did you tell Johnnie where Francesca was?"

"I told him I'd had your telephone call that she was in Somerset. After all, that was only fair since we were both looking for her. But we thought we'd look up this branch of the Torlini family first. Then the car broke down. . . ." Her voice died away. She said, very slowly, "Shouldn't I have told Johnnie?"

"It's exactly what I hoped you would do. You couldn't have done better—beyond, of course, keeping your inquisitive nose out of the whole business."

Kate felt for a chair and sat down. "What are you trying to tell me?"

"If you hadn't had a kind heart, Kate, I'd have been no further ahead at all, and my poor sister might never have discovered the truth about her husband's death. But thanks to your impulsiveness and your friendliness and your utterly enchanting feminine tendency never to stop and think, we're getting somewhere. Now you say Johnnie has left for Somerset."

Kate nodded miserably. "He was catching the afternoon plane. But he didn't know where in Somerset to go. I couldn't hear what you were saying on the telephone."

"I didn't mean you to. London Airport will be enough. What's wrong, Kate?"

Kate pressed her fingers to her eyes. She couldn't bear that he should see her tears. In his dry, summing-up voice he would make more remarks about her feminine warm-hearted qualities. And she didn't want to be analyzed by Lucian Cray. She wanted William to roar at her, "Kate, you clot, I've a good mind to beat you."

"Shouldn't William be here by now?" she asked tightly.

"That's who you were expecting?"

"Yes. I just heard he'd followed me, to look after me, or something. He does utterly mad and unnecessary things like that."

"I wouldn't say it was unnecessary or particularly mad," Lucian remarked. "If you were my fiancée I'd keep you on a leash."

"I'm not William's fiancée," Kate snapped, with taut nerves.

"No?" Lucian eyed her reflectively. "I still wouldn't trust you out of my sight. One day you'll stick that pretty neck out too far."

"It's nothing to do with you what I do with my neck."

"No, it isn't, after all. What I think you need is some food."

"I'm not hungry." She had controlled her brief weakness, and said more calmly, "Tell me the rest of this fascinating story. Francesca's doll was filled with diamonds, which she discovered, thought they were a lot of dirty stones, threw them away, and put what she valued much more, a letter from your brother-in-law, in their place. He had been coming to Rome and secretly making friends with her, is that right?"

Lucian nodded. "Go on, Kate."

"So now that I was put through the third degree last night, and it was more or less proved that I hadn't got the diamonds, and am up to my neck in this affair only because I'm crazy enough to care what happens to a stray child, someone has been tearing up the floor-boards in Gianetta's house, and someone else is dashing off to find Francesca and frighten her out of her wits until she tells where she put those dirty old stones. Or indeed how she found that her doll split in half. I imagine the opening was pretty well concealed until she did it up clumsily again."

"Kate, your acumen is fairly bright, after all. That's what I assume has happened."

"Were the diamonds cut or uncut?" she asked inconsequentially.

"I'm not sure. There was a jewel robbery in Venice not long ago when a Contessa lost her diamond necklace. It was valued at thirty thousand pounds. I may be wrong, but I think that's what we're looking for. It would be broken up, of course."

"And that's what I've been carrying about in that snake-doll, Pepita!" Kate exclaimed in horror.

"What everyone thought you were carrying about."

Involuntarily Kate began to chuckle with wry amusement.

"Mrs. Dix and Nicolas Grundy and my shadow, the Chinese gentleman, who fortunately is always just one step too many behind, and Mrs. Mossop."

"Mrs. Mossop is Mr. Grundy's sister," said Lucian, "and, incidentally, usually wears a wig. But perhaps deliberately leaves it off at times. I believe you got a fright there one day."

"Then it was she who looked into the room. It was a head like an egg, featureless, utterly horrible." Kate shivered as it all came clear to her. "I was supposed to be asleep from drugged sherry, and naughty Pepita, full of diamonds, was unguarded in my bag. But I ran away!" she said disgustedly.

"It wasn't from courage but from warm-heartedness that you got into this," Lucian reminded her.

"Yes, I suppose so. And what about that old woman in Rosita's room, and the way the room had *aged?*"

"Easy enough to do. An old woman can soon scatter a sort of cobwebbing of her bits and pieces about a room. You were awkward about wanting to see Rosita, so some place had to be arranged for her. I'm not sure, but I think that old woman is another sister of Mr. Grundy."

"Is Mr. Grundy the big noise behind all this?"

"No," said Lucian slowly, "not completely."

"How do you know all these things?"

"Oh—I have my shadows, too. My brother-in-law Gerald was in this game professionally. He'd taught me a few things about private detection."

"Better than my efforts," Kate said regretfully.

"On the contrary. I'm sorry to say that you've been my decoy. It wasn't meant to be this way. It was your own behavior that started it."

But he *had* let her walk into danger, Kate thought. He was brilliant and fascinatingly attractive, but that steel-hardness in him that allowed him to use a child and a woman to achieve his ends left her feeling cold and a little repelled.

"There's a gang of international thieves and smugglers at work," he went on. "Gerald had been employed by one of the big insurance companies to try to get on to their racket. He'd found out something big, but unfortunately didn't live to tell it. Francesca was one of his clues. He'd made friends with her and talked about his own children, Tony and Caroline. When he died Gianetta was too scared to talk. She's a widow and had been a maid in the house of one of these people. She was bribed and terrified into letting Francesca be one of the children to have an occasional trip to England. She hated it, but what could one poor woman with a child to support do against that sort of pressure. When Gerald died the thing became a nightmare to her. She somehow got hold of his diary, and took a big risk in sending it to my sister. There was just enough information in it for me to start on."

"So you kidnapped Francesca!" Kate exclaimed indignantly.

"Merely borrowed her, Kate, dear. I arranged for a friend to meet the train at Basle, and we'd whisk her off. All those schoolchildren were a godsend. They prevented, as you know, your giving the alarm until morning."

He met her outraged gaze.

"I'm sorry, Kate. I didn't know you then. I thought you'd go home and forget about it, especially when I was pretty certain there wouldn't be a public fuss made. But you began to be quite a trouble—"

"You callously kidnap a child—" Kate began.

"Not callously. Francesca was very happy about going to see Tony and Caroline at last. I talked to her for a moment in the train when you were out of the compartment, and she was very excited. You noticed that yourself. She's quite a girl, by the way. She's been kept as much as possible from learning English, in spite of her trips, and she's also been trained not to talk."

"Heading for the secret service, no doubt," Kate said dryly.

Lucian ignored her interruption, and went on, "My friend Peter brought her by car from Basle to Paris, and she even had her ascent of the Eiffel Tower."

"So it *was* her I heard!"

"Kate, believe me, I didn't mean to get you into all this trouble. I thought Francesca would have the diamonds on her, stitched in her clothes, or something. The wretched doll never occurred to me. But she hadn't got them, so there was I, with a stolen child, whom no one was at all interested in because they knew she hadn't got the loot. My bait had completely failed, and I had inadvertently got you into danger. You had the doll, after all, and everyone thought it was full of diamonds. Except you and me. And Francesca, of course."

Kate gave a wan smile.

"Thanks to my stupidity, I never realized I was in real danger. Even in Paris, when the lights went out in that fishy night-club, I thought it was all accidental." That brought her thoughts back to Johnnie Lambert, and she said slowly, "Lucian—which side is Johnnie on? Why are you so glad he's left for England?"

His eyes were enigmatic.

"My bait's been swallowed at last. Extradition orders aren't easy to get without pretty good evidence. They can hold him there on a false passport charge, to begin with."

"But he's so stupid! Surely he's not the big fish."

Lucian looked at her with narrowed, hard eyes.

"The big fish, Kate, dear, is Major Dix."

"Mrs. Dix's dead husband!"

"Mrs. Dix's very-much-alive husband." Lucian didn't give her time to dwell on that startling information. "Now we've got two things to do. Find where Francesca put the diamonds—Gianetta swears she knows nothing—and see when your friend William is due in. I suggest ringing the airport first."

"And then do we go back to England to question Francesca?"

"I've questioned her until I'm blue in the face. She's a child of few

words. She just goes blank and says she doesn't understand. She's the
original Mona Lisa."

Kate smiled reminiscently.

"She's a remarkable child. Is she really safe now?"

"She's never been in danger, as far as she knows. She's having a
whale of a time, refusing to speak English and demanding enormous
platefuls of ravioli. But you'll see for yourself soon enough."

"I can't believe it. What utter heaven! Who cares about the loathsome diamonds?"

18

At first Lucian could get no satisfaction from the airport.

"They say the last flight from London Airport came in two hours
ago."

"But that must be the flight William was on. Miss Squires said he
left ages ago. Why isn't he here?"

"Don't panic," said Lucian. "They're going to check and call me
back. Let's see if we can get some sandwiches and coffee sent up."

"You can eat," Kate said, clenching her hands and beginning to
walk about the room trying to combat her now familiar apprehension.

"And so can you." Lucian's cool eyes surveyed her. "Look at you.
Thin and haggard. Is that any way to greet your fiancé?"

"I told you he isn't my fiancé. We're not even good friends. Or
amicable friends." Kate's voice was curt with nervousness and sus-
pense. "But if that plane came in two hours ago why isn't he here?
He's an editor and a writer. He's not used to this sort of thing. He's
done something foolish—"

"If it comes to that, you're both babes in arms," Lucian said with
his air of detached amusement. "It's a good thing you're an attractive
young woman."

"Why?" Kate asked, with her sharp suspicion.

"Italians—and other nationalities—are rather susceptible to pretty
girls."

Was that why she had been allowed to come back safely after last
night? She remembered Johnnie, with his sudden wistfulness, saying,
"It's a pity you're so attractive."

"William isn't a pretty girl," she said involuntarily. "He hasn't that invisible weapon, or whatever it is."

"He's probably looking at the Pantheon. Relax, Kate. Didn't we say on the train that it will be the same in a thousand years."

Kate made an impatient exclamation. "You can't apply that theory to moments of tension! They last forever."

The telephone rang. Kate jumped nervously.

Lucian spoke into it in Italian. Was it her imagination that his face tightened? He abruptly turned his back to her. The quick, unintelligible words flowed on maddeningly.

Then he put down the receiver and turned.

"What did they say? Where's William? Hasn't he come?"

"Yes, he came by the last flight, a couple of hours ago. But he didn't travel into the terminal by the airways bus. He seemed to meet friends, and they left by car."

"Friends!" Kate exclaimed. "Who would he know? Unless it was someone he travelled with who gave him a lift. But in that case why isn't he here by now?"

"They've stopped for drinks, perhaps. I wonder what's happened to those sandwiches. I'll go down and shake someone up."

"Lucian, don't be absurd! William wouldn't stop two hours for drinks, not when his whole object in coming here was to find me. He is absentminded, I know, but when he's doing a thing, he goes straight to it. He hasn't stopped for drinks. What's happened to him? Oh, God, this awful nightmare again!"

Lucian took her hands and held them a moment, firmly.

"It'll be all right, Kate. Believe me! He's probably forgotten the name of the hotel. Now just wait here while I run down and see a friend of mine. And I'll be back with the sandwiches in a moment."

It was while he was gone that the telephone rang again. Kate stared at it a moment, hypnotized. Then suddenly she snatched it eagerly, expecting William's voice.

"Is that Miss Tempest speaking?" came a clipped, English voice.

"Yes, who is that?" English, she thought, in relief. The people who gave William a lift in from the airport.

"It isn't of importance to you who is speaking, Miss Tempest. But just for the record, it's Major Dix. We have your friend, Howard, with us. Rather against his wishes, I'm afraid. But as soon as we locate what all of us are looking for we'll let him go."

"The diamonds!" Kate gasped.

"Exactly."

"But you know I haven't the slightest clue where they are!"

"Oh, come now, you don't mean to tell me that your friend Cray hasn't got the child to talk. If he hasn't he's a damn fool, and I'm giving you three hours to do so. That's ample time to do a little telephoning to Somerset. I'll call you again at six o'clock. After that it will be dark."

"What do you mean?" Kate whispered.

"More than one foreigner has stumbled drunk into the Tiber." The clipped, cultured voice became contemptuous. "You amateurs shouldn't take on these jobs. They always have fatal results."

"You can't do this!" Anger and fear made Kate raise her voice vehemently. "William is perfectly innocent."

"Then let him stick to his pen."

"We'll call the police—"

"A search would take a long time. Much longer than the time of the moon's rising. Let's be poetic about it, shall we? There's my proposition. The diamonds for your friend's life. Fair enough?"

The telephone clicked just as Lucian came back into the room, followed by a waiter with a tray of coffee and sandwiches.

"Kate! What's happened?"

She had to wait until the waiter had put down the tray and gone out. The disastrous unfairness of this happening to William, who was perfectly innocent, made her forget to be afraid. She was filled with anger and indignation.

She heatedly told Lucian what had happened, and added, "I know where he'll be. At the *Albergo Garibaldi*. I'm sure that's their headquarters. We've got to go at once. Have you got a car?"

Lucian's hand was on her shoulder. "Sit down and tell me again calmly what has happened and exactly what this man said. Here! Have a mouthful of this."

He produced a flask from his pocket and unstoppered it. The neat brandy made Kate gasp, but it steadied her panic.

She related the telephone conversation again, and saw, in a detached way, Lucian's eyes gleam and his mouth tense with excitement.

"The big fish," he said softly, "we've almost hooked him."

"Almost hooked him when you don't even know where he is. And we have this ghastly time limit."

Lucian picked up the telephone and spoke for a moment.

Then he put a sandwich into Kate's hand and poured coffee.

"Giovanni's bringing around the car. He'll be a few minutes. He's a fast driver. Are you nervous?"

"Not any longer of simple things like fast cars," Kate said wryly.

"Yes, it's all a matter of proportion, isn't it? Do you want to tidy up before we leave? I'll wait for you downstairs. I'm not at all sure that this *albergo,* fishy though it sounds, is the place to go. They'll surely know that you remember it all too well. But I'd like to have a look at it."

"Not only the *Albergo Garibaldi,* but the Torlinis' villa farther on. That could be the place."

When Kate was alone she washed her face and combed her hair, and swallowed some more coffee. She couldn't eat. Then she looked around the room with a feeling of surprise that it could seem so ordinary and innocent. One had always heard that drama took place in hotel bedrooms, but one had never expected it to happen to oneself. Not even in Rome, with the forgotten centuries hanging in stone over the noisy, hurrying, effervescent people. Later, she told herself, she and William together would throw coins in the Trevi fountain, and wander in the silence and peace of the Colosseum, where autumn had beheaded the wild flowers growing in the stone cracks, and taken the scent from the vanilla trees.

Let Johnnie Lambert be arrested at London Airport for his false passport. (How had Lucian cleverly discovered that he travelled with a false passport?) Let Gianetta be reunited with her silent, stubborn daughter, and Miss Squires go back safely to her cottage and her cat. Let justice be done over the grave of a drowned Englishman.

But she and William would have their snatched hours of happiness in Rome. How utterly blind and foolish of her never to have realized that William would be the perfect travelling companion. Even if he had two black eyes and a multiplicity of bruises. For he would have been overpowered easily, and he had a violent temper when aroused.

Oh, William, William, please let me be allowed to look after your black eyes. . . .

Giovanni, a slim, smart, flashing-eyed young man, drove extremely well. Although he doubled on his tracks now and again to throw off any pursuer, Lucian explained, he seemed to know the way through the autumn-melancholy countryside to the *Albergo Garibaldi.* When Kate commented on this fact, Lucian said, "Oh, he's been there before." And added cryptically, "We were looking after you as well as possible last night. You are too unpredictable to look after with complete certainty."

Giovanni gave her his flashing smile, the inevitable admiration in his eyes. Kate expected him, too, to ask if she had had a wish at the Trevi fountain, and she wondered absurdly whether he had disguised himself as the goat or the prowling cat last night. Nothing was real to her any more. It was years ago that she had seen a stout little girl in a white starched dress setting out hopefully on a journey.

A deadly little girl who had indirectly robbed Mrs. Dix of her life, Kate of her dearest friend, and Pepita of her stomachful of treasure.

It was siesta time at the *Albergo Garibaldi*. By daylight it looked even more squalid, with the faded paint peeling off the shutters, and a piece of fallen plaster disclosing the bare ribs of the wall within. Giovanni waited in the car. Lucian told Kate to come with him, and together they rang the jangling bell for some time before the stout proprietor, sleepy-eyed and unshaven and reeking of garlic, appeared.

The merest flicker of alarm passed over his face. Then he bowed and leered with repulsive friendliness.

"Ah, so the signorina returns."

"She finds your place irresistible," Lucian said ironically.

Kate's mouth opened in surprise. "You couldn't speak English last night!" she accused.

The man grinned impertinently. "The signorina did not inquire. What can I do for you? I regret we are closed at this time of day."

"We just want to have a look over your place."

"Sorry, signor. We are closed. Later, with pleasure."

"That's too late," Kate cried impetuously. Lucian's fingers tightened warningly on her arm.

"Oh, too bad, too bad," said the man in his oily manner. "But the country is more attractive by moonlight." His black, bold eyes rested significantly on Kate. Their look did not suggest anticipated amours, but the danger that could come by night with the rising of the moon.

Lucian beckoned to Giovanni who slid out of the car and came over.

"We will look over your place now, signor. My friend has a search warrant. Come along, Kate. Show us the room where you had your visitors last night." He turned to say sardonically to the startled proprietor, "You should hire a theatre if you enjoy amateur theatricals."

The leer was replaced by a ferocious frown. The fat man slowly stepped back to let them into the squalid bar.

"Whatever your business," he said, in a voice suddenly shrill, "you will find nothing here."

Nor did they. Swiftly, because of time running out, they went over the shabby, bare-floored bedrooms upstairs, and downstairs the large, dark kitchen in which the round-faced maid stared at them speechlessly, shaking her head violently to all Lucian's brief questions, the backyard, where the goat and kid were tethered and a few scrawny hens picked in the dust, and the two rooms at the back which were obviously the living quarters of the proprietor and his wife.

The woman, as stout as her husband, garbed in black, and scowling with suspicion, sat in the stuffy living-room, and refused to speak. Her plump hands were folded stubbornly in her capacious lap. Her lips were clamped together. She remained immovable while they took a quick look in the bedroom beyond. She was a frowning Buddha scattering unspoken curses on them.

"Nothing here," said Lucian. "Let's go."

But there was. Kate picked up a half-empty box of chocolates from the sideboard and passed it to the woman.

"Have a chocolate, dear," she said in a cooing voice.

The woman's head jerked back. Her eyes widened. Slowly she shook her head. But now it wasn't that she wouldn't speak, she couldn't. Her fear was too obvious.

In the car Lucian slipped his arm along the back of the seat around Kate's shoulders.

"Well done," he said. "First clue. I'll bet that dear, kind soul speaks English without an accent. She looks like a retired variety artist. It's a pity we haven't time at present to check. To the Torlinis', Giovanni, and step on it."

"What's the time?" Kate asked nervously.

"Four-fifteen. We're doing fine."

"Lucian, do you think Mrs. Dix was murdered?"

"I haven't a doubt about it. By her loving husband. But for precisely what reason, I'm not sure. Look, there's the villa. On the hillside among the cypresses. Nice place it looks, as the country residence of a crook."

It looked like the summer residence of a millionaire. There was an orderly row of cypresses leading up to a wide terrace. Slim white ladies, cast in stone, were grouped around the central fountain and made a pale glimmer in the cypress groves. The house itself was of pink marble.

Kate suddenly felt extraordinarily scruffy and jaded. Lucian gave her a sardonic look as she hastily smoothed her hair.

"Don't worry about that. You're not meeting a Prince of the Borghese or even of the Medicis. You're meeting—I hope—a thief and a murderer."

Giovanni said something in his own language to Lucian, and Lucian gave a short, ironic laugh.

"Giovanni says why didn't we discover this place for ourselves, why was it left to you, a girl, to do it."

"We don't even know whose place it is."

"We'll soon find out," Lucian said confidently.

This was not so easy, however. A very old servant opened the door. He looked half blind but he had a wrinkled, crafty face which Kate suspected did not miss much. He talked for a little in a high, quavering voice, shrugging his shoulders and waving his hands. Lucian turned to Kate.

"He says the family are all away. They've gone to spend the winter in Naples. I think we'll take a look, all the same. Keep those sharp eyes of yours open, Kate."

Another inhospitable doorstep, thought Kate. She looked at her watch and her panic grew. Time was running out. Already the daylight was fading. Surely William was not concealed in this large, luxurious house. If he were, he would be making a great noise.

"Make it fast," Lucian said to Giovanni. "We can pick up less important evidence another time."

The old man seemed bewildered, but he understood what Giovanni's badge meant. He hastily stood back, mumbling to himself, as they went in. He did not attempt to follow them, for there seemed nothing to hide. The large reception rooms were dust-sheet shrouded, and upstairs the airy bedrooms, with their fine views of the cypresses and the olive groves, were the same.

At another time Kate would have wanted to linger, looking at the pictures, the statuary and the personal relics of the absent family. As it was, in her despair that the great sleeping house would produce any clues as to William's whereabouts, she noticed only one significant thing. That was a photograph of a young woman with large, dark hooded eyes, and a petulant mouth. She was dressed in the style of ten years earlier. It took a second glance for Kate to realize it was Rosita, the woman who had lain languidly on the couch in London and posed as Francesca's mother.

So Rosita's natural habitat was not the squalid *Albergo Garibaldi*. It was this expensive villa, with its marble floors and the constant sound of fountains playing.

This information seemed to give both Lucian and Giovanni satisfaction. Their quarry, though absent at present, was being run to earth. But would it be unearthed before the rising of the moon?

"Lucian, William isn't here. I know he isn't. The place feels empty. We're wasting our time."

In which of these lofty rooms had Johnnie Lambert sat drinking with Cesare and the half-blind caretaker while keeping out of the way of the amateur theatricals that were taking place at the *Albergo Garibaldi?*

It didn't matter. They had to get another inspiration quickly.

Giovanni said something and Lucian nodded. "There's money in this racket, all right. Giovanni says that group looks like a Bernini."

"Oh, for heaven's sake, we're not on an art appreciation tour!" Kate exclaimed. "I think we've made a mistake. We should have stayed in Rome. Let's go back. After all, the Tiber—"

"Bodies can be transported by car," Lucian said, with unthinking callousness. "Giovanni is going to take a quick look in the cellars. But I think you're right, Kate." Then he patted her shoulder. "Cheer up. This trip hasn't been wasted. We've discovered Mrs. Dix's ghost, and we know Rosita lives here. Probably her family previously owned this place, but it takes illicit wealth to keep it up now. My guess is that she's Major Dix's mistress."

"And Mrs. Dix found out, just the other day!" Kate said intuitively. "That would be it. She adored her husband, you know. She pretended to revere his memory, but really it was his live self. She probably agreed to do anything for him, no matter if it were illegal. And then she must have found out suddenly that he was making love to Rosita. It would shake her badly. Perhaps she threatened to go to the police."

"I think you've got it, Kate. This character has his deserts coming to him. But long overdue. Here's Giovanni. Now, Kate, shut your eyes and pray for an inspiration. I'm foxed, I admit it."

Somewhere near the Tiber, Kate muttered to herself. The daylight was fading inexorably. Although the speedometer needle touched a hundred kilometers, it seemed to be almost dark when they got back into Rome.

The Pantheon, Kate muttered, the Colesseum, Hadrian's Arch, the Baths of Caracalla, the Catacombs, the Appian Way. . . . Where was her inspiration to come from? Where was the name that held a clue?

Not these ancient monuments. Some modern place, some connection with today or yesterday. Connection! The telephone! The mysterious number Mrs. Dix had asked for, seemingly at random, which had proved to be a cardboard box factory. But was it indeed such a place?

Tense with excitement, Kate sat forward, murmuring numbers to herself.

"What is it?" Lucian asked a little disturbed.

"The telephone number. I can't remember it. I wrote it down, though. Where did I write it? Oh, I know. On the telephone pad at the flat. Oh, Lord, I'll have to ring Mrs. Peebles. What's the time? Have we time to get a call through to London?"

"I don't follow one word of what you're talking about, but if you want to call London, Giovanni can get some priority. I don't think I told you. Giovanni is a member of Interpol. But that's not for general consumption. A telephone, Giovanni. *Pronto!*"

Mrs. Peebles' high-pitched and uncomprehending voice at the other end of the wire was maddeningly aggravating. Kate had to repeat slowly and patiently what she wanted, all the time watching the dying light and praying Mrs. Peebles had not torn the top sheet off the telephone pad.

William could look after himself pretty capably, she kept reminding herself.

Even if the moon rose before Mrs. Peebles' dull brain rose equally to the occasion.

"You mean these numbers written here," came back her incredulous voice. "You're phoning me all the way from Rome for these little bits of numbers! Your writing's horrible. I can hardly read it. I'll have to get my glasses."

"Please, Mrs. Peebles! Hurry!"

There was a short interval, then the voice came back, laboriously reading.

"Good," Kate said. "Good. Thank you, Mrs. Peebles."

"When will you be back?"

"I don't know. I'll let you know."

"Things have been quiet since you left. No scrabblers at the window. Oh, a friend of yours called with a cat. I sent her to—"

Regretfully Kate cut her off.

"Here's the number. Find out what place it belongs to. It's only a hunch. They said it was a box factory."

"It may be near the Tiber," Lucian said. He handed the slip of paper to Giovanni who began to make another telephone call. In a few moments he had the address. It was a factory, he said, and it was in the poorer area. They'd go out and take a look at it. He added doubtfully that the signorina might wait, but the signorina said firmly that she was going, too, and was in the car ahead of both the men.

It was only a hunch, she told herself, but now she was tense with apprehension and hope.

Through a labyrinth of streets and then down a meaner, darker one where the shabby cafés and houses dwindled to a space of waste ground, and beyond that a large building that looked derelict. The moon, flame-colored and enormous, was just beginning to rise. Kate hypnotically watched it appear over the low, uneven rooftops. Then, as Giovanni slid the car to a noiseless stop, she scrambled out after him, and picked her way over the rubble to the deserted hulk of the building.

"Kate—" Lucian whispered.

"Don't say it. I'm coming." She added sensibly, "The place isn't derelict because it still has a telephone connection and someone who answers the telephone. Let's look for the office part."

The main doors were locked and bolted. Lucian tried them carefully, but there was no hope of getting in that way. The windows were boarded over. Another smaller door failed to give access, but around at the back, where suddenly there was a gleam of water in the distance and the smell of its coldness on the rising wind, there was another window, unboarded.

Giovanni's efforts to open it were unsuccessful. Suddenly he smashed a pane of glass with what Kate realized shakily was a gun. The noise was shatteringly loud, but when it had died away the dark building was utterly silent. Giovanni thrust his hand in, opened a catch, and slid up the window. In a second he was inside and Lucian had followed.

"Wait there, Kate," begged Lucian.

"Here! All alone!" she asked incredulously, and clambered after them into the damp, cold darkness.

Giovanni produced a torch and shone it cautiously. They were inside the main part of the factory which was obviously disused. There were boxes manufactured and unsold, piled high, and some pieces of rusty machinery. The place looked as if it had been out of use for a long time, probably since early in the war when the business had been closed down or failed.

But somewhere there was a telephone.

It was Kate who found the door. She leaned against it accidentally in the darkness, as Giovanni, with his torch, and Lucian following him, picked their way across the rotted and uneven floor.

It gave behind her and she fell inward. . . .

A hand circled her throat, and something hard stuck into her ribs.

"Stay right where you are!" came William's voice, harshly.

As quick as a flash she twisted herself free.

"William, you *clot!*"

"Good God, it's you, Kate!" William said in surprise.

"Yes, it's me and you've nearly choked me. Where are some lights, for heaven's sake!"

Lucian was there, and Giovanni with his torch, but William had reached over and turned on a glaring, unshaded light in the room into which Kate had stumbled.

"Don't mind the bodies," he said laconically.

One, the small, slim, light-footed man with the Chinese-yellow skin, lay face upwards, his eyes closed, his chest rising and falling with the heavy breathing of unconsciousness. The other, neatly trussed, like a parcel, was lying half under the desk. William, with the bruised face and rapidly blackening eyes that Kate had expected, was grinning cheerfully.

"These birds made a mistake about my left-hook. I haven't tried it out since Varsity days. Well, what did they expect, giving me a lift into Rome and bringing me to this dump. I admit I had a bit of a time getting free." He grimaced as he rubbed deeply wealed wrists. "I won't go into that now, but I'd just made it when I heard you people breaking in and I thought I had to take on another half dozen. As an editor, I'm a bit rusty."

"You shouldn't have trusted them!" Kate stormed. "I told Lucian you'd do something idiotic like that. If you knew the search we've had."

"Was I up for ransom or something?" William asked, interestedly.

"Well, don't gloat over it," Kate snapped. She moved back a little. "Are those men dead?"

"The Chink's breathing," said William. "The other one was tougher. He nearly had me, that one."

"Major Dix," Kate whispered fearfully, as Lucian and Giovanni knelt over the silent, trussed figure, dragging him out from beneath the desk and turning his face to the light.

"Oh, no, it's not!" she gasped, turning white. "It's Johnnie Lambert!"

Lucian loosened the gag around Johnnie's mouth.

"I think your first guess is right, Kate. Major Dix."

The pale, protuberant eyes blinked up at Kate. There was no heartiness in them now, only an enormous disgust and contempt.

"The next time you fall in love, Kate," he said, in the clipped, cultured voice that made the familiar hearty tones she remembered a burlesque, "do me a favor and choose someone who isn't an ex-heavyweight champion."

"I'm not in love," Kate began automatically.

William's swollen eyes looked at her.

"Aren't you?" he said belligerently. "Then I promise you soon will be. If we can't get a marriage license by tomorrow then we do without it. Do you agree, Kate?"

Quite suddenly and helplessly, Kate began to cry. She gasped through her tears. "I'm only crying because I'm happy. It's absolutely the only time I cry. Yes, yes, I long to do without a marriage license. In the meantime, that is. . . ."

Giovanni was at the telephone, the instrument that so recently had been used for the threats to William's life. The yellow-faced man on the floor stirred and groaned. Major Dix, alias Johnnie Lambert, looked up into Lucian's narrowed, ruthless eyes, and his too-plump and ruddy face seemed to wither. His slack lips worked. He was no longer the casual, good-natured, rather noisy companion of an evening out; nor was he the absent husband for whom Mrs. Dix hungered and was eternally faithful to; nor Rosita's dashing lover, giving her back her family home and the luxuries she demanded. Even less was he the cool, clever brain behind an organization of international jewel thieves. He was a man facing his supreme test of courage and failing dismally.

"Don't call the police," he begged. "I'll pay you. I'll make it up to your sister and her kids. Dalrymple's death was an accident. So was my wife's. She got difficult. She'd been drinking and her heart was bad. I'd have told her about buying the villa for Rosita. Damn Rosita, anyway. Damn all women. Just undo these cords, there's a good fellow. I'll pay you. I'm not a poor man. . . ."

Lucian lifted his head. His profile was austere, unyielding, devoid of emotion.

"The moon's up," he said, in a voice of deadly quiet.

Johnnie began to struggle violently. His eyes flickered from Lucian's avenging face to Kate's. Their fear was replaced by a look of rage. "It was you, you interfering little bitch!" he said thickly.

Then he began to sob.

Kate thrust her fingers in her ears and blindly ran into the dark outer room. William followed her. At the broken window he caught her and helped her out. As she swayed, in the cool moonlight, he took her in his arms and drew her into the shadows of the building.

"Kate!" he whispered. "Kate, Kate, Kate!"

They were still there, in the shadow, when the police car drew up. Presently the footsteps, coming and going, ceased. The car started up and swept away. Lucian called tentatively, "Kate!" There was a laugh that was Giovanni's, then Giovanni's car started and moved away. After that it was quiet. The moon, no longer flame-colored, but a pure, clear yellow, made the distant patch of water gleam. And it was warm and safe forever in William's arms.

19

The sun shone again in the morning. The chestnuts clung to the last remnants of their vanity, and with deliberation relinquished another ill-spared handful of leaves. The trams rumbled by, the street vendors shouted in their shrill, long-drawn-out syllables, and the great city hid its memories beneath an unshadowed exterior.

Lucian found Kate and William still at breakfast.

"Well, you two! Not married yet?"

"We decided we couldn't disappoint my stepmother and Mrs. Peebles by depriving them of a wedding," Kate said serenely. "Besides, William can't take two black eyes into a respectable church, and I don't look so madly beautiful myself. But no one can stop us enjoying Rome. We're going to sit like lizards on old stone walls for hours and hours. And later of course we have to throw coins in the fountain, or that darling receptionist will shed tears of disappointment. Oh, and we've had a telephone call from Miss Squires. She says she can't locate Francesca, but she's met a village constable who is awfully helpful, and oddly enough is even more besotted about cats than she is."

"You're talking too much, Kate," said William. His grin was slightly lopsided because of a swollen cheek. "But all that she says is more or less true. How, by the way, are the casualties?"

"In the right hands," said Lucian briefly. "There are a few accessories to the fact to be rounded up, in Paris and London, but that should be child's play, comparatively. The police have located Rosita, spitting like Miss Squires' cat. The case will be a *cause célèbre,* I fear. I wonder if you two lizards can spare half an hour from your sun-bathing this morning."

"Of course," Kate agreed. She added ingenuously, "I'm going to like you again, Lucian, when you get that avenging look off your face." But her hand crept into William's and was lost in its capacious grip.

"Better come to our wedding, old chap," said William.

"Thanks, I'd like to. Giovanni's outside. Can you be ready in ten

minutes or so? This won't take long. I thought you'd like to be there.
Kate, anyway."

"Where?" Kate asked curiously.

But Lucian had turned away, and even later in the car he made no
explanation.

Giovanni drove in his usual swift, hair-raising way to the outskirts
of the city. Then he took a turn Kate knew. She recognized the beginning of the Appian Way, and the street into which they came was disturbingly familiar. Outside Gianetta's house he stopped.

"We're a little early," said Lucian. Then, "No, we're not. They're
coming now."

Another car had turned into the street and was drawing up behind
them. As the inevitable heads began to peer out of windows, Kate
gave a cry. She reached for the door and throwing it open leapt out
of the car.

"Francesca! Francesca!"

The little girl in the stiffly starched white dress who got com-
posedly out of the other car didn't answer or smile. She came towards
Kate, her large, dark eyes full of accusation.

"Where is Pepita?" she asked in careful English.

"Oh! She's at the hotel! I didn't know I was going to see you this
morning. No one told me." Kate could not restrain herself then. She
threw her arms around the child. She was laughing and crying.
"Francesca, it's just so wonderful to see you again. Everyone tried to
tell me you weren't real. But look at you! Fatter than ever. What
have you been eating in England? Ravioli?"

"So that's the dream child," said William. "Blue bow and all. Incredible!"

"Pepita!" said Francesca stolidly.

The young man who got out of the car after her said in a pleasant
Cockney voice, "She would wear those clothes. Didn't half make a
fuss. Mrs. Dalrymple gave up in the end. If we hadn't been flying I
don't think we'd have persuaded her to come at all. What is it she has
to do?"

Lucian spoke swiftly to Francesca in her own language. She listened, blinking her great eyes. Then with decision she shook her
head. She spoke in a high, definite voice. Lucian tried to reason with
her. Giovanni joined in persuasively. Francesca shook her head stubbornly.

"Pepita!" she said.

Giovanni shrugged. Lucian sighed.

"I'm sorry, Kate. We'll have to dash back to the hotel for that wretched doll. She won't do what we want until she gets it. The rest of you can wait here. Sorry, Sergeant. But you know by now what you're dealing with."

The young police sergeant nodded. "If I'd been you, Miss, darned if I wouldn't have pushed her off the train myself. It's just as well airplane windows don't open."

Francesca, gazing from one to another, gave her faint Mona Lisa smile and folded her plump hands on her plump stomach.

When Lucian and Kate returned to the scene some thirty minutes later, however, they found that Pepita as a bribe was no longer necessary. Francesca glanced at her indifferently and turned away. She was sitting on the side of the gutter talking animatedly to William, her plump face breaking into a series of delightful dimpled smiles.

Never, thought Kate furiously, never once had Francesca smiled like that for her.

"What are you telling her?" she demanded.

William gave his slow, maddening grin.

"That when she's grown up and wears these fascinating bits of glass around her neck I'll marry her."

He opened his large hand and there, winking and glittering fabulously in the sunlight, were the diamonds, undoubtedly the stolen and broken-up necklace of the Venetian Contessa.

"Where—" began Lucian.

Giovanni burst into a roar of laughter.

Francesca chattered animatedly, spreading her skirts and preening herself like a little peacock.

"Just here," William said, poking his fingers into the outlet drain of the long-dry gutter. "Poor kids in Rome always play in the gutter. And Francesca thought rightly that these were just a handful of stones. Why should Pepita be cluttered up with them?" Then he looked rueful. "But now I seem to have sown the seeds of vanity. I've told her they make her look pretty."

"Even with two black eyes you have quite a way with girls, haven't you," Kate said scathingly. "Just for that you can help me look after Francesca until her mother gets back."

"Kate! This is our honeymoon!"

"Or we can take her with us on the train back to England."

"Heaven forbid!" William exclaimed.

Francesca gave her unexpected and enchanting dimpled smile.

"No spik *Inglese*," she said, and waited for the usual looks of frustration that would follow her flat and inexorable statement.

When, this time, they didn't come she looked a little puzzled, then philosophically shrugged her plump shoulders, dismissing the adult world which had never particularly interested her, and turned at last to be reunited with Pepita.